FINDING TO

© 2019 KAHLEN

First Edition
Version: 2019.4.7

Cover Design and Formatting by R.A. Mizer of ShoutLines Design. For more information visit Shoutlinesdesign.com.

Cover photos: iStock-692813214, AdobeStock_80009862 & AdobeStock_810022330

Published by Kahlen Aymes Books, Inc.
ISBN: 978-0-9996713-0-6 (eBook)
ISBN: 978-0-9996713-1-3 (Paperback)

FINDING
Tomorrow

KAHLEN AYMES

This book is lovingly dedicated to my readers.

Thank you for your paticence as I finished this book.
I hope I've done you all proud.

SuperDuper THANK YOU to...
The many members of my
#OfficialStreetTeam, #KahlensAngels, #TheSupergirls &
#TheBabes!
You women are THE BEST! You're all DAMSELS in my eyes!
xo
I love you,
Always.

Special Thanks to...
Justine Tevis & Donna Cooksley Sanderson for your editing
prowess, and Rachel Mizer (Shoutlines Design) for her
amazing covers! Thank you to Tammie Lee for your stellar
skills managing the street team groups!
MUAH! You are all AWESOMESAUCE! MUAH!

I COULDN'T LAST A DAY WITHOUT...
the badass bloggers, amazing readers, many author
friends, and
unsung superheros of the romance publishing world!
The many of you who post, pimp, share, and basically just
talk about my books until you're blue in the face...
I'm humbled by the support you show.
I TRULY COULDN'T DO THIS WITHOUT YOU.
Thank you from the bottom of my heart.
xoxoxo

Every review means the the galaxy to me & beyond.

Love & Peace ~ xoxoxo
~Kahlen

HER *last chance*
BEGINS
in his arms.

Prologue

Missy

My heart was pounding so hard; I felt it would claw its way out of my body.

I frantically shoved as many clothes as I could into one suitcase. We had to travel light, but more importantly, it was imperative that Derrick not be able to detect anything missing. *If he did…* I sighed and shook my head. I couldn't let myself think like that. I had to focus. *We had to get away.* I might not survive another failed attempt.

I'd dumped the drawers from the dresser onto the bed, so I was able to pick items I felt I'd need the most, and as quickly as possible; underwear, bras, socks, a couple of pair of jeans, and t-shirts. I pushed everything in on top of my son's things.

I listened intently for any sound that would indicate that my husband was home, but my breathing was ragged, and my heartbeat was pounding a deluge of blood through my ears, making it difficult to hear. My brain was racing, and I was filled with sheer terror; would I be able to get out without injury to myself, or my young son, who was sleeping in his room down the hall?

The house was idyllic; no one could guess the misery that

went on behind these walls. We appeared like the ideal upper-middle-class American family. Materially, we wanted for nothing. Outwardly, appearances were deceiving; a hardworking provider, a loving wife, with a well-behaved child just starting a private school. It was a beautifully constructed illusion; carefully built to hide the real truth. In reality, I lived in fear for my life, and for that of my child, every single day. I breathed a sigh of relief each time my husband walked out of the door and I heard his huge dually truck pull away. I hated that stupid thing. Somehow, it was an iconic symbol of my husband; dark, brooding, battering, rumbling... as if it's size and obnoxiousness were somehow a symbol of him.

The curtain of my loose blonde hair fell over my face as I continued my hasty packing. I shoved it behind one ear, and then quickly reached for more things, barely even registering what they were.

Derrick would be furious with the mess I'd created, and I inwardly cringed. He seemed to be in a constant rage, so I hoped I'd have time to pick it up and get everything else back in place before he arrived home. I had to keep up the illusion for one more night. I had to survive just one more night.

I couldn't seem to do anything to please him; not since the beginning of our marriage. Researching his behavior, I discovered he was a textbook sociopath, and, I'd considered, maybe even a psychopath. His personality deviated right after the honeymoon; like flipping a light switch.

I remembered in horror how dramatically everything changed. Derrick became demanding, mean, and controlling with no sense of remorse or responsibility for his actions. Afterward, he'd apologize, but twist everything around to make it all my fault.

He would beat me for no reason, then tell me it was because I didn't buy the right kind of jelly, because I got out of

2

bed to close a window and disturbed him, or if he didn't like the dinner I'd made. Anything at all could become a trigger, and it was terrifying. My self-esteem was in the toilet, and as time passed, I realized that was the plan. Beating me down emotionally, as well as physically, became his tools of intimidation and control.

When he wanted to have a child, I'd foolishly hoped a baby would change him; soften him somehow, make him more loving. After all, I was giving him what he wanted, but a happily ever after wasn't in the cards. My changing figure and fatigue only set him off. I'd almost lost the baby twice, and now, I was in a constant state of terror, worrying he'd turn his anger on our four-year-old son, Dylan. There wasn't a day I didn't try to refocus Derrick's anger on me rather than my little boy. Most of the time it worked, but not always. The times when Derrick wanted to take Dylan out alone made me insane with worry. I wasn't much interference, but at least if I was around, I managed to redirect Derrick's anger to me. Well, most of the time.

Dylan was expected to have all his toys in an exact place when he was done playing with them, his clothes had to be perfectly pressed and clean, his hair was to be combed a certain way, and he wasn't to cry, fuss, or speak in a disrespectful way. Ever. He wasn't allowed to run about the house or have any friends over. He wasn't permitted to be a child and that was my greatest sadness.

My heart broke just thinking about it. I'd learned to live with the swollen lips and hiding my bruises with long sleeves, slacks, and sunglasses, but in the last couple of years, Dylan was becoming a target. I couldn't stand when Derrick turned his fury on our son. It was the last straw, and no matter what he did to me, or what we had to sacrifice or go without, I had to protect my little boy.

I sucked in a ragged breath, noting how much my hands

were shaking, as I clumsily flipped the lid to shut the case and fumbled trying to zip it closed. My fingers slipped off of the zipper halfway through, and I had to try again, telling myself I had to hold it together or we'd be found out.

I pulled the suitcase off of the bed and lugged it out of the house to my car, careful to stop and look up and down the street for any sign of vehicles or people. It was dark and cold. I started to shiver because I hadn't taken the time to put on shoes or a coat. I had limited time, and I couldn't take the risk; I had to get out and in, tidy up and leave everything seemingly untouched and unmoved; nothing to tip him off. Every second counted.

I planned to leave in the morning right after Derrick went to work. He had a business trip to Toronto, and I hoped it would be enough time to make it to my mom's house in Tallahassee. I wasn't sure what I was going to do after that, because I knew it was the first place Derrick would look. I decided to call Dylan in sick to pre-school, in the hope of getting a few hours head start, but whether I let the school know or not, the administrator would notify Derrick that Dylan wasn't there.

Oh, God. How was I ever going to get through this?

I left the bag by the trunk, opened the car door and quickly pushed the trunk release. Rushing around, I struggled to lift the large case inside. It was overly burdensome because I'd loaded some of Dylan's toys and some of his framed baby pictures in the bottom of it. I couldn't bear to leave without them, but it was a risk that Derrick might notice they were missing.

I slammed the trunk closed and, trembling, made my way back into the house and into the bedroom to begin quickly picking up the clothes strewn about the room. I carefully placed them all back in their respective drawers, careful to fold everything just so, but it was difficult to do in a rush. Adrenaline was pouring into my veins, but it only made things worse. I was freaking out; scared to death. The shaking of my hands wouldn't stop. He would notice even the smallest thing awry, and I'd pay a painful price. I tried to calm myself; quell the tremors and heavy breathing as I went about the task. It felt like each minute was only a second as they sped past, yet at the same time, everything moved in slow motion as terror seeped through me. I couldn't move fast enough.

I had to clean myself up and get control of my emotions before he got home, or he'd know something was up.

Later, I'd have to lay beneath him as he took me against my will; I'd have to pretend I was enjoying it, and, if I didn't want him to turn violent, I had to convince him that he was the best lover to ever touch a woman. It made me sick. It was no better than prostituting myself, but what else could I do? I wouldn't be able to get away if I was injured, but I vowed this would be the last time he'd ever touch me.

For months, I'd been closeting away a dollar here or there, but it wasn't easy because I was required to account for every dime. Control was like bars around every aspect of my life. He had our mail delivered to a post office box and only he had the key. He monitored every letter and every bill we received. I wasn't allowed to have contact with my mother or have any friends; he analyzed every call on our phone bill; every call, coming in or out-going was scrutinized. He said he owned me, and that's how he treated me; like property. I was expected to follow his rules and obey his every whim. I was used to paying a high price, but not just for mistakes I made but for imagined ones as well. He beat me without needing a reason. He had a hair-trigger temper.

I closed my eyes as two tears slipped from beneath my lids. I'd been young and naïve; marrying Derrick only months after meeting him, despite my mother's warnings. He had been ten years older, a successful businessman and, stupidly, I believed my life would be the fairytale he promised. Instead, it was a living hell.

I carefully pushed the last mahogany drawer shut, now that they were securely ensconced back in their proper place in the dresser, with most of the contents correctly folded and positioned as Derrick expected. I wiped off the fingerprints from the surfaces and then laid out one of his favorite negligees on the bed; my costume for this last sacrifice for freedom.

I used both of my hands to push back my hair as I walked into the bathroom. I stood there staring at myself, scared to death of what was coming, and praying I'd get through the next twelve hours. I was overly thin, my cheekbones stuck out, as did the bones on my shoulders and collarbones. My skin was pale; I looked awful. I slowly pivoted to turn on the bath water, sprinkling some scented bath salts under the water as I contemplated what makeup I'd need to hide the dark circles under my eyes.

During my bath, I relaxed and concentrated on making my breathing even. I made sure every inch of my skin was hair free the way he demanded. I smoothed on scented lotion, combed my hair until it shone and used my flat iron to curl the ends under ever so slightly. I put on a little concealer, blush, mascara, and lipgloss before putting on the beautiful lavender and cream nightgown. It was sexy, without being slutty. The silk gown was long and smooth down my legs, and the bodice and hem were trimmed in Chantilly lace. The neckline was low cut leaving the top swells of my breasts and my shoulders bare, and the bodice was held up with the briefest of straps made from the lavender silk.

I sat on the edge of the bed waiting after I lit three candles and flipped on the gas fireplace in the bedroom. My hands were trembling as I sat there with them in my lap, and I had a nervous stomachache that gnawed at my insides.

The outside door opened, and I flinched when it was

violently slammed shut.

Oh, God. This wouldn't be good. I searched my mind for what I could have done to piss him off, but it wouldn't take long for him to tell me.

"Melissa!" Derrick hollered angrily, the sound of his voice echoing through the house.

My heart fell to the pit of my stomach as I scrambled off the side of the bed and rushed toward his voice. "I'm here, Derrick."

"Where did you go, today? The driver's side door of the Lexus is unlocked, and the car is outside of the fucking garage! I told you to stay home!" he railed. He was a handsome man; tall, tan, and always professional and impeccably dressed. His blond hair was combed back and gelled.

I rushed through the house and down the curved staircase to the foyer, almost stumbling in my haste. He was pulling off his tie and flinging his keys on the round marble table in the center of the entryway. His brow furrowed as he scowled at me. "Where the fuck did you go?" he demanded. His eyes took in my attire, his expression filled with disgust. "Answer me!"

"We were…" my brain worked to come up with a plausible excuse. Panic overtook me, and my breath rushed out of my lungs. How could I have made such a stupid mistake? "um …out of milk. I needed it for lunch. I was making tomato soup for Dylan." Over the years I had learned how to keep my voice calm and my movements measured. Derrick was like a caged animal that was agitated. As I reached the bottom of the stairs, I slowly walked up to him and put a calming hand on his forearm. "You know how you like him to have milk with every meal, and I needed it for the homemade soup, too."

His expression became darker as his eyes narrowed skeptically.

"Are you hungry? I can make you something," I moved my

hand from his arm to rest more intimately on his chest. I offered a tumultuous smile. It felt as if any minute the earth would open up and swallow me whole and if it weren't for my son, I would have wished it so.

"No. I ate on the job site."

Derrick owned a big contraction company he'd inherited from his father, and our over-sized house was a monstrous advertisement. I stood there waiting for whatever came next. "That's fine."

He sneered at me making my already frantic heart begin to pound even harder. It was hard not to show fear, but I'd learned that like any predator, the man looming in front of me fed on fear. "I know it's fine," he spat. "I don't answer to you."

"I understand."

Derrick's eyes narrowed. "You're up to something," he accused harshly, grabbing my arm forcefully and turning me around in a one-eighty to start hauling me up the curved staircase. "What is it?"

"Nuh—nothing," I stammered as I stumbled up the stairs, catching myself with my free hand. My fingers dug into the plush sand colored carpet. "I just took a bath because I thought you might like—"

"Goddamn it, Melissa," he huffed. "How many times do I need to tell you, you don't think. I do. You do what I tell you!" he shouted. "I tell you what I like!"

"I'm sorry," I murmured softly.

"Shut up!" He backhanded me hard across my cheek causing my head to snap around as I stumbled backward through the hall landing at the doorway to our suite of rooms; falling in a heap on the floor. I backed up against the wall, looking up at him as he glared down at me. "Stop saying you're sorry! Stop provoking me!" he yelled, livid; his breathing hard. "Don't I give you everything you want? Look at this goddamn place!" He used his hand to usher around over the railing that was open to the foyer below.

"Yes!" I said, bringing a hand up to my aching cheekbone. "You are a wonderful provider."

"Then why do you disobey me? Are you fucking stupid?" Derrick railed. "Is that it?"

Pain shot through my upper arm where his fingers dug cruelly into my tender flesh. Tomorrow I would surely have a nasty bruise.

"Derrick, please. I'll do anything you want," I tried to soothe him. "You know that." I tried hard not to cry. Tears made him even angrier. "I didn't think getting Dylan milk was disobeying you."

"I told you not. To. Leave!"

By now, he was flinging me through the door to our bedroom so hard that I fell to the floor, the rug burning the skin on my knees. "Ugh!" I grunted as I landed hard, silently praying Dylan was sleeping. I wanted it to be true, but in my heart, I knew he heard it; I knew he was frightened and hiding in his bed with his covers over his head. It was far from the first time something like this happened.

Derrick moved to my side and pulled back his foot, to land a kick squarely in my left ribcage. I pulled my knees up to my chest in reaction as pain exploded through my torso.

"Derrick, please!" I begged, tears starting to roll down my face. "Please," I said more calmly. "I just thought the gown would please you." I cowered in place, putting up a hand to try to ward him off. "I thought I could give you a massage and we could make love. That's all." I was used to saying whatever I needed to say in order to appease him or get him to calm down; anything to stop the current assault. "Please, be gentle. I know you love me, Derrick. Please… show me you love me." Inwardly, it made me sick to say the words. He didn't have a fucking clue what real love was. All he knew was how to inflict physical and emotional pain.

He stood above me; legs apart like a crazed animal, trying to decide what he would do next. His chest was rising and falling, heaving in his effort to hurt me; his eyes were wild.

"You shouldn't have gone out!"

I pushed myself up against the foot of the bed so I could look Derrick in the face. I grimaced as excruciating pain exploded in my side. I knew what it meant because it wasn't the first time he'd cracked a rib. "You're right. I was wrong. It won't happen again. I promise." My voice was calm and as sincere as I could manage as I brushed an errant tear from my cheek. "I promise." My hand was still splayed in front of me, as I tried to reason with him, and fend him off.

Derrick blinked as if suddenly having an epiphany. His expression softened. "You know I only put these rules in place to protect you and Dylan." His voice was softer, but still stern. "You know it, and still you defy me."

I nodded, my eyebrows rising together. "I do know. I'm sorry, Derrick. I'll be better. I promise."

"I'm sorry," he said, bending to lift me in his arms and lay me on the bed. I almost screamed at the pain, but bit my lip instead, afraid that if he were confronted with the damage he'd done, it would only set him off again. Derrick was good at business, good at organizing, but he was the worst at taking responsibility for any failures. He would see any signs of physical or emotional pain from me as a criticism or a sign of blaming him.

He *was* to blame, but I couldn't let him think he'd done anything wrong. I'd learned long ago that making him feel guilty only made him angrier. I laid my head on his shoulder to further the illusion.

His cologne settled around me and I wanted to vomit. The

scent reminded me of numerous episodes of pain and rape, abuse and misery. I had to swallow to keep it down. "I'm sorry; you just make me so angry when you don't do what I tell you." I detested this man with everything inside me. I hated him enough to kill him. If it weren't for Dylan, I would have done that ten times over regardless of the consequences to myself. I'd dreamt of murdering him many times, in many different ways, and while it should have frightened me, all I felt was calm and safe. *Finally, safe.*

"I know. It's my fault," I reassured softly, hoping taking the blame would calm Derrick down.

He cupped my face with his big hand. It was rough from years of working in construction and the hours he spent lifting weights. He was strong, and he would be able to snap my neck like a pencil if he wanted to.

"You know I don't mean to hurt you, Melissa. You just always do things to upset me. You have to stop doing that. Okay?"

It was like a sick switch had gone off inside his head, and he was a different person. All I had to do to make it happen was to validate his behavior. "Okay," I nodded again and smiled softly. My side was throbbing, and my knees were still on fire, but I hid it well. I reached up to wrap a hand around his wrist, but my voice still trembled. "I'll be better; I promise."

He bent to kiss me, and though repulsed, I responded as much as I could manage. "We can be everything, Melissa," he said softly between kisses as his hand slid down from my cheek to cover my breast. His fingers squeezed painfully as he pushed me over and further onto the bed. Every touch or kiss was rough and painful. His lips pulled at mine, and his tongue pushed grotesquely inside my mouth like a battering ram. His fingers tore at my tender flesh. I whimpered from the pain, praying, he'd take it as desire.

Derrick didn't know how to be gentle. He stood and peeled off his clothes, never taking his eyes off of me until he was naked. He was handsome, but my hatred of him made me want to scratch his eyes out. I swallowed hard as he climbed onto the bed and pulled my knees apart, ripping the delicate satin and lace of the negligee.

I closed my eyes. This would be the last time I'd let Derrick humiliate me. The last time he'd touch me. The last time he'd hurt me. I just had to make it through this one last night.

Chapter 1

JENSEN

I was on a damn plane. Again.

Relief settled over me as I sat down in my first-class seat, satisfied because I was finished with yet another sporting event. I was going home from a work assignment with ESPN, but maybe soon I'd get the promotion I'd been working for, and the traveling would lessen. At least I'd only be gone two days per week.

I'd applied for a new producer position with one of the Monday Night studio shows, and I was hoping to hell I'd get it. Although the occasions when I was sent off on a moment's notice for an impromptu fill-in for another sportscaster were getting less now that I had seniority, I was still tired as hell from my travel schedule.

Even if I landed the new job, I'd still have to fly to the Connecticut studio Sunday and stay until late Monday night for the live show, but most of the prep and editing of the various segments could be done from the Atlanta offices if I had a good assistant.

The network program director couldn't officially tell me the position of studio producer was mine for sure , but his raised eyebrows and discrete nod the last time we'd talked, made me sigh in relief. The new gig would mean more stability and allow me to spend more time with my little girl, Remi.

I couldn't deny that being on the field with the football players was fun and the excitement of commentating on live games was a rush, but to say that the constant traveling was a bitch was a colossal understatement. Sleeping in hotels, living out of suitcases, and always rushing for a quick turn-around sucked. Now that I was divorced, all of the household chores fell on me, too. I didn't realize how much Teagan did or how hard it was to keep all of my suits dry cleaned, or what a pain in the ass it was to take them in every week. I hated it, but I wasn't sure if the stress of being overworked or the emptiness I felt coming home to my house in Atlanta, was worse.

I was truly happy for Teagan and Chase, but ours wasn't a usual situation. It was a big adjustment when Teagan and Remi left. At first, I'd been terrified that Chase would move the two of them to London where he was playing soccer with one of the regional teams. That little girl had become the center of my universe over the past six and a half years. Now that they were expecting another baby, they had their perfect little family unit. Even though they'd both made a considerable effort to include me and given me plenty of time with Remi, the empty house was hard to get used to, and I couldn't lie to myself; I felt lonely on occasion.

The minute the flight attendant took my jacket and hung it up in one of those hidden closets near the cockpit door, I pulled the knot of my tie loose and unbuttoned the top three buttons on my white dress shirt, now less than crisp after a full day's wear.

"Would you like a hot towel or a cocktail, sir?" The flight attendant was pretty, as so many of them were. She had high cheekbones and a nice figure; her dark hair was pulled back with a few curling tendrils trailing down both of her cheeks. She smiled warmly as she asked in a strong southern American accent.

I inhaled and ran a hand through my hair. The gel the makeup people had lathered it with was stiff and crackly. I regretted the move, grimacing. "Um, sure." I nodded returning her smile. "Dewar's on the rocks. And, I would like a towel, if it's not too much trouble." I could see appreciation in her eyes as she quickly went to fill my request.

"Here you are, Mr. Jeffers." She handed me the drink and used metal prongs to present me with the steaming hot towel. "Careful, this is really hot."

My mouth twitched at the start of a grin as I could see she recognized me. Sometimes that was cool; other times I wished I could blend in. This was one of those times. "Thank you, Amanda." I addressed her with the name on her nametag. "You must be an NFL fan," I suggested pleasantly. Though I covered other sports in the offseason, the football league was my main focus.

"I follow the Cowboys. I was on the cheer squad for three years."

My eyebrows raised and my lower lip went out as I nodded. "I can see that," I said, appreciatively. I wasn't worried about coming off as offensive. If she didn't want admiration, she wouldn't have referenced cheerleading.

She smiled brightly again. "You interviewed Cooper Rush at Cowboy—" she stopped and rolled her eyes, exasperatedly shaking her head. "I mean, AT&T Stadium last year."

"I see." I took a sip of the amber liquid in the glass, welcoming the burn traveling down my throat as I swallowed. "Don't worry. It will always be Cowboy Stadium to most of us in sports. I mean, come on." I shrugged and grinned at her. The stadium name was changed a few years back in a significant money transaction between the company and Jerry Jones, the team owner.

Amanda offered a big smile that said if she were overnighting in Atlanta, I'd have a willing partner for the evening. I might have found the prospect pleasant and quite tempting... if I weren't so wiped out.

"Miss?" A woman two rows in front of me raised her hand to get Amanda's attention. "May I have a glass of red wine, please?"

The flight attendant flushed, suddenly realizing she had others to attend to and she had allowed me to monopolize her time. "Oh, yes, ma'am." Her gaze locked with mine as her expression twisted regretfully. "Bye."

"I'll see you later. I'll need another in a little while." I held up my glass and rattled the ice against the sides.

The plane was pushing back, and a male flight attendant was going through the motions of the pre-flight protocol while the recording of the safety instruction played over the cabin speakers. What seemed like millions of previous flights made me numb and ambivalent to the airline announcements. I knew the drill very well.

I leaned my head back against the cool leather seat, thankful for the comfort of first class, but really, all I wanted was a hot shower and my bed.

I'd taken my phone from my jacket and had it lying on my leg when I heard the familiar ding of a call coming. It was from the senior ESPN program director; my boss, Bryan Walsh.

"Hey, man," I said into the phone.

"Are you on your way home?" he asked.

I took a deep breath and let it out with the single word. "Yes."

"I need to talk to you Monday morning, in my office." His voice was normal, sober; unaffected.

Finally, I thought. He was finally going to make an offer

after a month of needlessly interviewing candidates.

"Sure thing. I'll be in by 8 AM."

"Sounds good. I'll see you then. Have a safe flight."

"Thanks." I turned off the phone and then silenced it, contemplating whether I should power it down completely, or not. I was used to emergency calls about Remi, and part of me was still worried something might go wrong. She'd been well for months, but old habits were hard to break. Before I could decide, it started to vibrate in my hand with Teagan's name flashing on the screen. I quickly answered, speaking low and turning toward the window. The sun was setting in Cleveland; the same time zone as Atlanta.

"Hello?"

"Hey, Jensen," Teagan's defeated voice came through the phone.

"What's up? Is Remi okay?" It was a programmed response. The poor little thing had gone through so much with her cancer treatment; worrying about her was ingrained. It was still so surreal that the bone marrow transplant she received from Chase had cured her leukemia. It was indeed a miracle.

"Oh, yes, she's fine. But I have a favor to ask. I know you're probably exhausted so you can say no if you want to, okay?"

I smiled. "I know I can, but what do you need, Teagan?"

"Chase and I have tickets to a concert, and we're in a bind. Kat was supposed to come up and watch Remi, but one of her boys has the flu. Can you help out?"

"So, let me get this straight; you're asking me to take Remi so you and Chase can go play around?" I teased. "Hmmm..." I already knew my answer, and so did she. I'd take any time with Remi that I could get.

She sighed heavily, being deliberately overdramatic. I could hear the familiar teasing lilt in her voice. "I know it's not your weekend."

"You're just lucky I'm off this weekend."

"I know." She hesitated just a second. "Do you have plans? It's Friday night, and it's such late notice. I shouldn't take for granted that you're available."

Eighty percent of the divorced men I knew dreaded conversations with their ex-wives, but my situation with Teagan was unique. I could hear Remi and Chase playing and laughing in the background, and my heart swelled. She squealed in delight. Chase was roaring at her in a decisive game of cat and mouse. "I'm gonna get you! You'll never escape my wrath, Princess Remi!"

I couldn't help but smile. I knew I'd miss Remi, but I never expected how much. It was the reason I couldn't stand going home to an empty, lifeless house. I was grateful for every second I was able to spend with her.

"I was going back to the house to call it a night. I'm exhausted."

"Oh, I understand, Jensen," Teagan began. "If you don't want to…"

"Don't be ridiculous," I interrupted abruptly. "I'll come by and pick her up on my way home from the airport. Does that work?"

"Really?"

"Don't play all coy like you didn't know all along I'd take her, Teagan. I'll take her anytime I can. She's my little sweet pea."

"I know, but Chase and I still appreciate it! You're a lifesaver! If it's easier for you, I can drop her off at your place."

"Nah, just have her things ready, so that we can take off. I'd like to keep her for the weekend."

"Well, we promised to take her to the zoo tomorrow. She wants to see the pandas. There is a new baby."

Apparently, Chase had some time off as well. He was a

forward with the US Men's National Soccer Team or USMNT to those of us who followed sports, but there was no team facility in Atlanta, so he had to travel to Kansas City or L.A. part of most weeks for training. It was brutal. "Chase doesn't have practice?"

"No, they have a week off." I could hear the hesitation in her voice. "He goes to K.C. on Monday."

Chase also had to travel for every game, so he was gone a lot, too. With Teagan's pregnancy getting closer to term and Remi in school, he couldn't take the two of them with him. No doubt, he might oppose giving up his daughter for the entire weekend. After everything, Chase went through, and all the time he missed with Remi, I had to offer a compromise if I didn't want to come off as dick-ish.

"Well, let's split it. I'll bring Remi home after the zoo on Saturday. Will Chase be cool with that? It will give you two some time alone."

"I'm sure he will be. You're amazing, Jensen." There was soft gratitude lacing her voice.

"Aw, shucks," I said with a chuckle, amused. My words had the desired effect making Teagan laugh again.

"Excuse me, Mr. Jeffers, you'll have to turn off your cell phone. We're about to take off," Amanda said softly, so she wouldn't intrude on the call.

I nodded to the flight attendant and then finished speaking to Teagan. "I know. Tell Chase he owes me one."

Teagan laughed softly. "I will."

"I gotta go. The flight attendant is making me shut down my phone. See you in about two hours."

"I'll have her ready. She'll be so excited to see you."

"Me, too. See ya."

* * *

"Jensey!" Remi squealed as she came running from the hall, pushing in front of her mother the minute Teagan opened the door to the massive house that Chase had recently purchased in Marietta. The place was big, but not gargantuan, even though my best friend could afford more. It was a sprawling stone two-story, and the property was gated. There was a pool in the backyard that came in handy when his parents and siblings visited with their kids, and they always included me. I knew all of the security codes to the grounds and the house in case of an emergency.

The house was more than double the size of the modest home I'd purchased near the Children's Hospital shortly after Remi got sick.

Our situation might have evolved from a shitty set of events, but I was grateful. By some miracle, our friendship survived the years of lies and betrayal. I wasn't proud of it, but if I had the same choice to make, I'd do it again. Chase and I had been friends for years, and his family had been like a second one to me. I'd been the one to introduce him to Teagan, so it was ironic how things evolved. Ultimately it turned out that I was the one to marry her, though I knew her heart belonged to Chase.

"Hello, Jensen," Teagan murmured as she opened the door. She looked radiant in a summery maternity dress. She was six months along by now, and she had that ethereal glow you hear pregnant women get.

"Hi, Teagan," I said as she opened the door and stepped aside for me to enter.

I leaned in to hug her but had barely made it two steps into the foyer when a small body collided with my legs and tiny arms wrapped around them. I looked down at her exuberant face and slid a hand over her silky hair.

"Jensey!" Remi said happily, hugging my thighs as tightly as she could.

I bent and lifted her easily into my arms where she settled

snuggly onto my hip. "Hey, squirt," I said and then kissed her squarely on her cheek. "How have you been?" I asked.

"Good." My focus was squarely on the cherub face and the long dark hair that was curling around her shoulders and down her back. "I have a new boyfriend!"

My eyes widened, and I pulled my head back, surprised. "You do, do you?"

She nodded hard. "Yep! Daddy said I need to cool my jets, but I don't have any jets, do I?"

"It means to calm down, honey." Remi looked so serious that I couldn't help laughing out loud, joined by Teagan and also Chase from further back into the house. "What's his name? Did you meet him in school?"

"Yeah, his name's Tommy. We played at recess after he saved me from that mean boy who pulled my hair."

I frowned. "Who pulled your hair?"

"Nolan." Remi wrinkled her nose in distaste.

"Nolan, huh?" I asked, letting Remi claim my full attention.

"Uh huh. Then Tommy slugged him so hard he fell down, and Nolan cried."

I wasn't sure if I should tell Remi violence never solved anything, or if I should get Tommy and his parents box seats to the next Braves game.

I couldn't help grinning because I liked the second option better. "Then what happened? Did you tell the teacher?"

Remi scowled at my question. "No! She saw him hurt me, but we *all* got a timeout. I don't like Mrs. Weshey. I didn't do nothing but get my hair yanked, and Tommy didn't either! He was just being my knight in shining armor. Daddy said he did the right thing to help me, cuz I was a dis-tersted."

I looked at Teagan, and she had laughter dancing in her blue eyes.

"Dis-tersed?" I let out a short laugh, as Chase appeared

behind Teagan.

My friend reached out to shake my hand, and I obliged. "Distressed. Our little damsel in distress," he said wryly with a sly wink.

"Yeah!" Remi nodded. "A damsel in dis-terst! Mommy said all of us are damsels sometimes."

"But, just sometimes," Teagan agreed, touching the end of Remi's nose with her finger. She waved me further into the foyer in front of the winding mahogany staircase. "We have to go soon, but you're welcome to stay here if you like, Jensen."

Chase reached into the coat closet just inside the door and pulled out a Braves baseball cap and shoved it on his head, low over his eyes. He nodded as he pulled a set of car keys from his pocket. "Sure! If you want to use the pool, you can use one of my suits and order dinner in, on us." He smiled the same smile I saw so often on Remi's little face, as he slid his arm around his pregnant wife's waist.

Chase and Teagan made a beautiful couple, and they certainly made beautiful babies, I thought, looking back into Remi's anxious face.

"Nah, we should get going."

"Oh, that's right; you're tired." Teagan left Chase's side to go into the room behind him, only to return in a few seconds with a dark purple duffel with a caricature of Dora the Explorer embroidered on the side. She handed it to me at the same moment Chase took Remi from me to hug her goodbye.

"Be good, okay, sweetheart?" Chase smoothed Remi's hair at the back of her head as she returned the affection by wrapping her arms around his neck.

Teagan kissed her cheek and patted her back.

"I'm always good, aren't I? Lessen you talk to Mrs. Weshey!" Her eyes got wide as she made a goofy face.

"Did you talk to that teacher?" I asked, meeting Chase's

green gaze over Remi's head. We were practically like brothers, and we had the same inherent values. I knew he'd be as upset about any other child bullying Remi, as I was. The two of us managed a good system of co-fathering, both of us respecting the other's role.

His lip twitched at the start of a smile. "Yes. And, with the principal and both of the boy's parents. I've considered putting Remi into that more elite school across town if it happens again, but Teagan isn't on board. What do you think?"

"Oh, my gosh!" Teagan admonished, giving us both a gentle shove through the side door off the kitchen that led to the garage. She pushed a button to open the garage door, and it began to whir as the one door behind Chase's black Lexus sedan opened. "They're just kids, and it's so far!"

"Yeah, but I don't want her hurt," Chase and I spoke in unison, then I continued.

"If they can't control a six-year-old bully, there are issues with the administration and teaching staff."

Teagan rolled her eyes and hugged me. "Thanks again, Jensen." She pulled away and nodded for Chase to hand Remi over who readily moved from him to me, settling into my embrace.

"Bye, baby." She cupped Remi's cheek lovingly. I could still see Teagan's hesitation when leaving Remi and it was expected after everything she'd gone through. After three years of illness and not knowing if we'd lose her, we all had trouble trusting that she'd be okay. It would be another year before the medical team could officially declare her leukemia cured. Time with Remi was something to be treasured, and none of us took even one minute for granted.

I turned and walked out the open garage door at the same time as Chase and Teagan got into their car.

"Can we get pizza?" Remi asked enthusiastically, waving at

her parents. "Can we go to Chuck E. Cheese, please?"

I carried my little girl to the car using only one arm and had the bag Teagan had filled with her pajamas and a few of her favorite toys slung over the other shoulder. I probably should have let her walk, but I missed her, and I enjoyed the closeness.

It was a balmy Atlanta night, but it was already mostly dark. Just a hint of pink remained on the western horizon as the sky turned a violet blue. The air was humid and heavy, and though I'd discarded my coat and tie, and managed to roll up the sleeves of my button down, I was still hot. Remi didn't seem to notice. Even in the low light from the streetlamps, I could see the bloom on her cheeks. It was such a welcome difference from a year ago when she was on the verge of death.

It didn't matter that I was tired as hell; I'd drag my ass to the end of the earth for Remi. Dressed in a cute outfit with a large ladybug applique on the front of her white shirt and red shorts with black polka dots; Remi was sweet as hell. "Sure. If they're still open. It's kinda late, kiddo."

"Oh, well, that's okay." She smiled big and then hugged my neck. "What'd ya wanna eat?"

"Not sure. We'll find something good." I offered a wink.

"I missed you, Jensey!"

"I missed you, too, sweet pea."

"Don't tell mommy, but I was happy when Jace got sick, cuz I knew she'd get you to come."

I reached the car at the far end of the driveway and pulled open the rear door and placed Remi in the car seat that was a permanent fixture in the back seat of my SUV. It was the one Teagan used to drive, but she didn't take it with her when we divorced. "Remi." I looked at her sternly and shook my head as I buckled her in. "Wishing someone sick is not very nice."

"Well? I did." The deep dimples in her cheeks disappeared as she pouted with a shrug. She was so adorable that it was difficult to reprimand her. "Jackson was mean to me last time they came over, anyways."

Jackson was Chase's sister's ten-year-old son, and her twins, Jace and Jaylan, were seven. I pulled the straps together in front of Remi, securely positioning them and clicking them together and testing them with a short yank to make sure they were snug. "What'd he do?"

"He cheated! Jace, Jaylan, Jackson, and me were playing Twister, and he shoved my arm, so I fell down and got out! Then he laughed," she said petulantly.

I sighed and shook my head, offering her a sympathetic look. "Well, that's too bad." I touched her velvety cheek with my index finger before closing her door, then sliding into the front seat and buckling my own seatbelt. I glanced at my watch. It was already 8:30, and from experience, I knew they closed at nine. "You haven't had much luck with boys being nice lately, huh?"

I started to back out and drive out of the gated property with Chase and Teagan following close behind. I turned left, while they turned right, down the street. They were headed downtown while I was going somewhere to get food, and then go home.

"No. I don't like very many boys. I hope I get a sister."

"A sister would be nice, but a brother would be cute, too, wouldn't it? You and your dad could play football with him."

"Nope!" Her tone was cheerful but adamant. I glanced in the rearview mirror, and she was shaking her head adamantly. "No brothers!"

HER *last chance*
BEGINS
in his arms.

Chapter 2

JENSEN

"Bryan will see you now, Jensen," My boss's secretary, Tracey, said and then ushered me through the door to the big office. We'd both worked at the network long enough to be on a first-name basis.

Bryan rose and offered his hand as I approached the large desk sitting near the window on the far wall. We were both dressed in dark suits; he was wearing a navy-blue pinstripe and mine was black, with a cream dress shirt and black, gold and cream silk tie. "Good morning, Jensen," he said, sitting back down and motioning me to take one of the leather chairs in front of his desk.

I nodded, unbuttoning my suit jacket so I could sit down. "Morning."

"Can I offer you coffee or something?" Bryan asked.

I shook my head. "No, thanks. I'm just stoked to hear your decision."

My boss leaned back in his big leather chair behind the massive oak desk and rubbed a hand over his lower jaw. This was not a good sign.

"Or... am I?" I asked, my left eyebrow shooting up in question.

"If it were up to me, there would be no question, Jensen. But I know you can't move to Bristol, and we have a candidate who is willing to move."

I wanted to argue that I could do most of the job from the Atlanta offices and only fly to Bristol for one day per week and I wouldn't have to live there, but Bryan continued.

"I haven't interviewed her yet, but they've flown her in from Jackson Hole. I have to talk to her, at least, Jensen."

"Jackson Hole?" My face twisted skeptically. "As in, *Wyoming*?" I wasn't a sexist, and I knew a woman could do the job, no problem, but... *Wyoming*? What kind of situation could she be coming from? Was she a local newscaster? Did towns that small even have a sports anchor? I wondered.

His mouth thinned wryly, and he shook his head. "Yes. Wyoming."

Bryan, though fifteen years older than I, was not only my boss, he was my friend, so I felt comfortable asking him the next question. Apparently, he hadn't looked at her resume very closely, or he'd know the answer.

"Does she have any experience? I mean... it's freakin' Wyoming." I'd never been there, but I imagined lots of mountains and evergreen trees, but hardly any population. "I've been with the ESPN forever, you know that I'm ready to run with it."

"I know how hard you've worked, and you've certainly paid your dues traveling so much during your little girl's illness. I get it, but she's coming from a smaller market, and she'd move to Bristol if needed. Corporate is looking at it from a fiscal point of view, and she does have some experience. Before Jackson Hole, she worked at the local FOX station in Dallas for two years, and she was a Cowboy's cheerleader for a while."

I sighed as reality dawned. Okay, I thought, remembering the flight attendant from my recent flight, so this woman had to be gorgeous; she'd have players clamoring to talk to her, which was a plus for the on-air portion for the new job. I ran a hand through my hair in frustration. "It can't compare with the seven years I have here. Was she in production? What kind of on-air experience does she have?

"You know I can't discuss that, Jensen."

"Yet, you can tell me she was a cheerleader and worked at Fox?"

"The basics are public knowledge. I can't share the details."

I really hadn't considered that I might have any real challenges for this job, and even if I didn't think this woman could possibly compete with my resume, the network would have no travel expenses because she'd locate at corporate headquarters, and probably, they'd be able to pay her less due to my seniority. This was a significant roadblock. "Well... shit," I murmured incredulously. "They are seriously going to make this about money?"

Bryan was leaning on the arm of his chair with his elbow, meeting my gaze. "Isn't it always about money?"

I was embarrassed and felt my face flush with heat. I didn't want to move to Bristol, Connecticut, but I didn't want to quit and work at a local station, either. Cable ratings were much higher these days, and I had no intention of going backward in my career. There were a lot more opportunities with specialized cable stations than one of the big four networks because of their limited sports programming. Sure, they all had versions of sports or regional sports networks on dedicated cable stations, but trying to go to Spectrum, NBC Sports Network, or the NFL Network wasn't something I wanted to even consider. I'd have to move, which defeated the whole reason I needed this new job. ESPN was my home, and it was the biggest sports network in the country; worth seven times its closest competitor. Any other network would be like a demotion.

Fuck! My mind railed. I inhaled again and let my head fall back just enough to look at the ceiling briefly as I considered my options. "Yeah."

"I know you don't want to move away from your daughter."

Bryan knew about my divorce from Teagan and the situation with Remi. He knew about my history with Chase because who in the sports industry didn't know Chase Forrester?

My head snapped forward again, and I shook it, slowly. "Exactly. Chase changed teams so I could still see Remi regularly. He quit Arsenal, Bryan. That was huge."

My best friend had made an enormous sacrifice in his career by leaving behind a team he loved in order to keep Remi close to me, and he still commuted. There was no way in hell I could move away from Atlanta after that sacrifice."

"I know this puts you in a bind, but just let me get through the interview before you start worrying, okay?" He glanced at his watch, signaling he had another appointment. "You're a valuable asset to the network, and that will carry a lot of weight." He tried to reassure me, and I reminded myself this woman was from Timbuktu, and couldn't possibly bring to the table what I knew I could. "You have a big future here, Jensen, no matter what happens with this one particular position."

Whatever, I thought in frustration. *Preach that shit to the choir.* "Okay, sure." I rose abruptly and nodded, preparing to leave his office, barely able to quell my frustration.

"Jensen," he called. "I'll call you after lunch?"

"Sure." I left his office. "See you later, Tracey," I murmured, impatiently, as I passed her desk in his outer office.

"Have a good day, Jensen."

"Thanks." I tried to be calm, but I was pissed. I mean, how could they even consider giving my promotion to some unknown from nowhere?

My thoughts annoyed me in the elevator ride down to the lobby. I needed coffee, and there was a street vendor just outside the building who sold an array of beverages and bagels.

As the silver colored doors slid open and I turned to walk through the lobby toward the outer doors, I couldn't help but notice the production supervisor speaking to someone in the waiting area. I glanced at my watch, as it dawned on me; this was more than likely Bryan's interview appointment. This was *Wyoming girl?*

Curiosity got the better of me, and I walked a few more feet forward, dodging several other network employees and moving through the lobby to get a better look. I stopped dead in my tracks, causing Brandon McMillian, another of the correspondents to crash into me from behind. One of the senior staffers shared the first name Brandon, so when McMillian joined the network, we nicknamed him Mick.

"Ugh!" I grunted, looking over my shoulder.

"What the hell, Jeffers?" he admonished. "Walk much?"

"Sorry," I muttered offhandedly. "Do you know who Cindy is talking to?"

He followed my gaze and let out a low whistle that was hidden in the echo of footsteps on the marble and the din of multiple voices. The dinging of the elevators, and the giant screen streaming the station made it even more difficult to hear. I was relieved he didn't draw attention. "No, but I'd like to!"

"Hold on," I put a hand on his shoulder. "I think she's interviewing with Walsh."

"I thought the only job opening in his department is the one you're up for."

I kept my eyes trained on the two women as they talked. "And, you'd be correct."

"Don't take this wrong, but I'll be helping you clean out your desk if she's moving in," he laughed. He was a friend, and I knew he was kidding, but there was no question that the young woman was gorgeous. Stunning, even.

The slender woman's features were beautiful, her bone structure delicate, and her suit was certainly befitting of an interview, with her blonde hair swept up off her graceful neck. I licked my lips, wishing I could hear the conversation and not caring that I was making the wave of people walk around me. I smiled at my friend, before returning my attention to the two women I'd been watching for the past sixty seconds. The blonde was picking up her briefcase and was beginning the trek to the elevators with Cindy.

"Come on, Mick. I'll buy you a cup of coffee on your way out." I nodded toward the doors and started moving with him in that direction, avoiding a run in with the two women.

The tinted windows of our first floor made for a striking contrast when we went out the revolving door and into the bright sunlight. I reached into my pocket and pulled out my sunglasses, shoving them impatiently on my face.

"Seriously, do you think he'll hire her instead of you? Mick asked.

"Nah," I threw out, walking up to the vendor and concentrating on the menu. I shook my head. It didn't matter how gorgeous she was, or that she was the first woman to make me do a double take in months; there was no way I was letting some woman from some obscure market steal my job.

No. Fucking. Way.

Missy

It was another new beginning. Maybe the third time would be the charm. At least, I hoped so.

My mind had been racing during the entire flight to

Atlanta, turning various interview questions over in my mind as I tried to prepare. This was the first significant job I was applying for since my divorce. After two months in Tallahassee, Derrick's threats and stalker tendencies had frightened my mother, so at her suggestion, I'd taken Dylan and fled to Jackson Hole, Wyoming, where we'd lived with my brother, Ben, ever since.

The wide-open spaces of Wyoming suited my big brother, and he knew everyone in town; including the local law enforcement officials. I felt safe there, and by some miracle, Derrick left us alone. I was even able to get a divorce reasonably quickly after only ninety days in the state due to the divorce laws in Wyoming, and the bevy of pictures I'd taken of the various injuries Derrick had inflicted throughout our marriage had sealed the deal. My ex-husband didn't even show up at court to contest custody of our son; sending his sleazy attorney in his stead.

Jackson Hole was uncomplicated, and Dylan had adjusted well, but recently my mother was having issues with her balance, and neither Ben or I could convince her to move to Wyoming. Atlanta wasn't exactly her backyard, but I hoped that if I could land this job with ESPN, it would persuade her to join me there. I wasn't above leveraging her grandson against her if needed. For the first time, I had hope for a new life on my own.

Atlanta was a lot closer to Dallas but given Derrick's previous acquiescence and the time that had passed, I prayed a new move would be uneventful. There would always be an underlying concern he could cause trouble, but I was more anxious about the interview in front of me. This job was mostly production behind the scenes, and I needed to stay under the radar. It would be perfect.

Even though I was confident in my degree and references, ESPN was a huge step up from the local FOX affiliate in Dallas, and I was sure candidates were applying from all over the U.S. I had to be on top of my game for this interview if I had any chance at all.

The yellow cab I'd taken from the hotel pulled away as I walked through the glass doors of the gleaming ESPN building. I inhaled deeply to calm my nerves and smoothed back the sides of the sleek chignon I'd chosen for the occasion. My charcoal grey suit was new, but modest and inexpensive: paired with new matching pumps and a light coral and grey blouse.

I squared my shoulders and walked up to the receptionist desk on the main floor, carrying my old black briefcase and handbag. I was a bit self-conscious that the bag didn't match my shoes, but I'd spent a good portion of my savings on the outfit, and I couldn't afford a new briefcase. Luckily, ESPN picked up the expense of the hotel and flight. The lobby was bustling, and I walked past two security guards positioned just inside the doors, pasting a bright smile on my face; consciously exuding confidence I didn't feel.

A young girl was sitting behind a round sort of desk in the middle of the polished marble floor, and I determined she was my first stop. She was wearing a small headset with a microphone coming down from the right side to position in front of her mouth. Her smile was pleasant as I approached. "Hello. May I help you?"

"Good morning. My name is Melissa Ellington. I have a 9 AM appointment with Mr. Walsh."

She quickly looked at her computer screen, and then glanced up. "Yes, here you are. Just one moment please." She held up a finger and pushed a button on the phone. "Good morning, Mr. Walsh. Melissa Ellington is here to see you. Yes, sir."

I glanced around at the men and women coming in and out of the building, walking through the lobby and waiting at the silver doors of the four elevators that would take them up to one of the seven floors. Almost all of them were either looking at their phones or already speaking on them.

This was a busy place. Many of the people were in expensive suits with perfectly coiffed hair, while several others were more casually dressed. Some could have been described as scruffy, and I guessed these were production staffers. I remembered from my anchor position for the primetime news in Dallas that many of the camera people had a decidedly less polished appearance than the on-air staff; especially those who had to lug equipment around on location. I recognized some of the ESPN on-air personalities, even though if I was honest, I wasn't much of a sports fan. My brother loved sports, especially football, though, and I'd made it a point to binge watch the network in preparation for this interview.

Several people glanced at me curiously, appraising my appearance in the competitive and curious way many women do. Several men stopped to cast appreciative glances in my direction, and I bristled. I was still uncomfortable and wary, wondering if I'd ever get over the fear. I had to shake it off because one thing was certain; I wouldn't fall for a handsome face, flattery, or smooth talk, ever again. That lesson was well learned.

I swallowed, hardening my resolve to never be prey to someone like Derrick ever again. They could size me up all they wanted, but on my intellect, not my looks. I stood up a bit taller and focused my attention back on the receptionist sitting behind the desk. I was a professional, and my mission was to get this job, not worry about what others were thinking about me.

"Mr. Walsh will be down in a few minutes, Ms. Ellington." She gestured to a small waiting area situated against one of the windows on the far side of the lobby. "Please take a seat. He'll be right with you."

I thanked her and made my way across several yards of the shiny floor to the arrangement of sofas tables and upholstered chairs. It was across from the short hallway that housed the elevator shafts. I sat down, carefully placing my briefcase and bag in the chair next to me, smoothing down the fabric of my pencil skirt.

The walls that weren't exterior windows were covered in larger than life photos of the on-air personalities, anchors and correspondents, in clusters with their show logos above them. NFL, NBA, MLB, golf, hockey; my eyes skittered across them, and then looked around the lobby to see if I recognized any of their faces. A couple of them were vaguely familiar, but no one I could place directly. Briefly, I registered that much of the programming was recorded in Los Angeles or Bristol, Connecticut, and that would explain much. I'd done my research; the traveling correspondents domiciled in Atlanta where most of the features were produced.

I was startled out of my thoughts as an attractive and slender woman with shoulder-length red hair, and bright green eyes walked up. She was in her thirties, maybe, and dressed in a short-sleeved dress in a light lavender color, making me even more acutely aware of the temperature difference between Atlanta and Jackson Hole. My jacket over my long-sleeved blouse was overly warm, and I silently prayed I'd get through my appointment without my makeup melting off my face.

"Ms. Ellington?" She asked warmly, a soft smile crossing her pleasant features.

I nodded and stood as she extended her hand. "Yes." I nodded, accepting her handshake.

"I'm Cindy Wells, the staff supervisor for production. Mr. Walsh asked me to escort you up to his office. How are you enjoying Atlanta so far?" She asked as I gathered my things and began to walk with her toward the elevators.

"Oh." I smiled guiltily. "To be honest, I haven't seen that much of it yet, but I love the weather."

The elevator doors opened, and we stepped inside with five

others. Miss Wells pressed the button for the seventh floor, as well as the third and fourth that other people requested.

A bit of small talk later, I learned that the woman was a native of Atlanta and had worked with ESPN since she'd graduated from Georgia State.

"Here we are," she murmured as the elevator doors opened. The executive offices were opulent, and the marble floors were almost sparkling, reflecting the dark wood and metal fixtures. A secretary was sitting at a desk in front of the imposing floor-to-ceiling door at one end of the floor, and she was busily typing something into her computer, glancing up with a bright smile as we approached. Everyone who worked here seemed to be busy and happy. I felt encouraged.

"Tracey, this is Melissa Ellington. She's Mr. Walsh's nine o'clock." Cindy shook my hand again. "Good luck! I'll see you again when the interview concludes."

"Thank you." She turned and retraced the distance we'd just come from the elevators.

"Follow me," Tracey said, happily, and walked the twenty feet to the large cherry wood door, giving it a knock then quickly pushing it open. I wondered why she didn't use the intercom, but I was grateful to get the interview underway. "Bryan, uh…" she stammered with a coy grin and shrug. "I mean, Mr. Walsh? Melissa Ellington is here for her appointment."

"Yes, yes. Bring her in, Tracey," his deep voice called from within the office.

"Right this way," she ushered me through the heavy door. The room was huge; much bigger than I would have imagined, and the imposing desk several yards inside. I followed Tracey inside. "Here we are."

"Hello. I'm Melissa Ellington," I nodded a greeting to the middle-aged man who was rising and coming around the desk to shake my hand. He was handsome and distinguished, with just a touch of grey starting in his dark hair at the temples and dressed impeccably.

"Nice to meet you. Have a seat. Would you like any water or coffee? Coke?" He indicated a chair in front of his desk.

"Thank you, Mr. Walsh. Water would be nice."

"Fine. Fine. I'll have black coffee, Tracey." The man nodded at his secretary, and she calmly left the office to do his bidding.

I sat my briefcase and purse at my feet, sitting up straight.

After Tracey had brought in the beverages, the interview commenced pretty uneventfully, though I couldn't get a gauge on what he thought of me as I recounted my experience and education. Mr. Walsh asked basic interview questions about my strengths and what I thought I could bring to the network. I gave detail of my background beyond the anchor desk, but also reporting and research.

"Why do you really want this job?" Mr. Walsh asked frankly, sitting back in his chair, waiting for my answer.

"Well," I began. "The obvious reason is that ESPN is a large and respected network and I'm hoping that if I do well and prove my worth, I'll get promoted."

His eyes narrowed. "Sure, that's an answer. But what's the underlying reason? What drives you? Yes, ESPN is big and reputable, but I run my team as a separate entity. I like to get to know my staff personally. I find that it makes for a more cohesive working arrangement," he continued.

The hairs on my arms stood up as goose bumps raced across my skin; a programmed response my body took whenever I felt threatened. What did Mr. Walsh mean; get to know his staff personally? How personally? I realized that I didn't have to disclose anything personal if I didn't want to.

"In what way?" I asked cautiously. I wanted this job, but not if he was implying something improper.

He cleared his throat. "In that, if someone is sick or can't do their shift for some reason, the staff know each other well enough to reach out if needed and should be willing to cover for each other in return. I find that I can avoid attrition if I cultivate an atmosphere of friendship and teamwork. We're a close-knit group and on a first name basis. The network regularly hosts training camps and team-building activities."

"Oh." I took a slow, deep breath of relief. "Well," I hesitated.

"Look, Melissa. You're well qualified, no question, but this is a team, and we all need to work well together. I want to know what makes you tick so I can tell whether you'll fit in."

"Yes, sir." It appeared his interest was sincere, and I could see that it wasn't about me; it was about the workings of his staff. "I understand."

"What is your personality like?"

"I'm willing to work with anyone and do more than my share, but I tend to keep to myself." I saw him stiffen. This was not a good sign, but I wasn't going to lie. "I'll be professional and focused." Several photos lined the bookcase behind his desk, which I hoped would help my case. Clearly, he would understand being motivated by family obligations. "But to answer your earlier question; my son is my motivation. I'm a single mother, and I need a position that has the potential to grow over time; with hard work. To put it bluntly; my ex-husband does not take an active or financial role in raising him. It's all on me."

"I see." His eyes narrowed as if he was thinking something over. "How old is he, Melissa?"

"Just six and a half." I swallowed at the emotions trying to overtake me. Talking about Dylan made me emotional. "He starts first grade in the fall, and I'm hoping to get him settled in a school district for good."

He studied me before responding. "Will you have any help

at all? This job will require relocating to Bristol, Connecticut. There will be some late nights, weekends, and a bit of traveling. Or, we have considered allowing the person to commute from Atlanta once a week, on Sunday, to Monday."

"That would work out better for me, Mr. Walsh. If I'm lucky enough to get an offer, I'm hoping to persuade my mother to move to Atlanta from Tallahassee. I'm almost certain she will agree because he is her only grandchild, but if not, I'll figure it out." I had no choice. I needed this job. "I promise, if you give me this chance, I won't let you down. I'm looking to provide Dylan with a better future." The best way to negotiate was from a position of strength, but I was feeling more desperate than I wanted to let on. "A long-term relationship with ESPN is my goal."

His thumb and index finger were plucking at his eyebrow as he contemplated my words. "I see. I admire your dedication to your son and your commitment to a good work ethic. I also appreciate your honesty. In that vein, I feel I have to be honest, as well. I have a strong internal candidate who has a lot of experience at ESPN. While your qualifications are impressive, he has been with us for several years. In fact, he is the reason I even considered letting the position commute because he has strong ties in Atlanta."

My heart fell. There was no chance I'd land this job over someone like that. "I see." I sat in my chair unmoving, uncertain what I should do next. Would he fly me here just to waste my time?

"His job will be open if he's offered this position. It's not entry level, and it will give you some good experience with the network. Would you be open at all?"

"In Atlanta?" I asked.

He nodded. "With some traveling."

"Depending what it is, yes."

"Segment and on-site sportscaster; mainly for the NFL at the moment, but it could eventually work up to anchor for Sports Center prime-time."

It was a great opportunity, and under normal circumstances, I'd jump at it, but a position so visible wasn't ideal. Sports Center was "the" show to aspire to at ESPN, but why wasn't this mystery man after it?

I wanted to groan aloud. "I'd love to take it, but if at all possible, I'd prefer something behind the scenes."

"But why? It would suit your experience perfectly and allow me to make an immediate offer."

"It's personal," I blurted, feeling flustered. There was no way Mr. Walsh would be open to hiring me if I spilled my past troubles with Derrick, or how a visible position might stir up his stalker tendencies. It wasn't a risk I wanted to take; Derrick finding out my new location or sharing too much of my personal problems with a potential new boss. I'd never get the job if he knew about Derrick's psychotic tendencies. "What about an assistant to the producer position?" I asked hopefully.

He shook his head. "You're overqualified for that, I'm afraid, and it's possible that eventually you'd become unhappy and want to leave and that isn't prudent for the network."

My hands had been resting in my lap, and I threaded them together to keep from wringing them. "I understand, sir. I want to come to work here, but I'm not sure about being in front of the camera." Until I could be sure what the job involved, how could I make a decision?

Mr. Walsh took a drink from his coffee cup, his stern brow furrowed. Clearly, he was mistaking my hesitation for stage fright. "Why don't we do this? I'll have Cindy give you a tour of the talent department and introduce you around. If you feel like you can seriously consider it, we'll put you up for a couple of days, and you can get a feel for the job, okay?"

It sounded reasonable, though it would mean calling Ben and making sure he was willing to watch Dylan for a few more days. Whatever position I landed, working at this network was a dream job.

"That sounds amazing. Thank you, Mr. Walsh."

"Good." He smiled and nodded his head, reaching for his phone, pushing a single button on it. "Tracey? Can you get Cindy back in here, please?"

Chapter 3

JENSEN

I bought a black coffee for both of us, and a whole-wheat bagel with cream cheese for myself. I handed Mick a cup and then paid the vendor as he took off to join his camera crew, who were already waiting with the van. "See ya! Have a good flight," I called after him."

"Thanks! Let me know what happens with the hottie!" he returned, climbing inside the waiting vehicle.

I took a big bite of my breakfast, walking briskly back into the office building and up the elevator into my office. Hopefully, nothing would happen with this new applicant. I hadn't dated anyone seriously since Teagan and I split. A casual date or one-night stand here or there didn't count. In any other circumstances I'd be chomping at the bit to meet a woman that beautiful, but now, I just wanted her to go away so I could get on with my promotion. She was the competition, no matter how beautiful.

I walked back into my office, sat the coffee down on my desk, and continued to eat the bagel as I logged on to my computer, intent on shuffling through my company email. Until Bryan gave me the go ahead, I still had my current job to do. I needed to look at the schedules and see what my assignment would be for the coming week or weekend.

A sharp rap on the doorframe made me look up to see Jerry Stanley, one of the staff writers walk in. He worked on segment pieces and additional online content for the network website. He was sort of an awkward dork, but a really nice guy who'd do anything for anyone.

"Hey, who's that gorgeous woman Cindy is showing around?" He was barely leaning into my office, his shoulder still on the doorframe and his hand pointing over his shoulder. He had a shit-eating grin plastered squarely on his acne-ridden face. His skin was angry and red, with sores all over. Poor kid. That shit had to hurt like a motherfucker.

I picked up my coffee and took a sip of the steaming liquid. "I don't know her name, but supposedly she's interviewing with Walsh."

Jerry was sort of nerdy and reminded me of that Jimmy kid from Superman. He wasn't even cool enough to be Clark Kent. His eyes got wide at my words, clearly understanding the implication. "In production or on-air?"

Ugh. I groaned internally but wanted to do so aloud. "Production," I admitted flatly. It would be great if my friends would stop bringing it up so I could just believe the job was mine without challenge.

"But we only have that Monday night producer position, open, right? I would have gone for it, but I didn't think I'd be able to beat you out. Why bother, right?" He was rambling.

I motioned him into the office with my free hand as my email opened up. The last thing I wanted was to make it known that I was the least bit threatened by another candidate and he wasn't exactly discreet.

"Good call," I nodded with a casual, confident grin. "Your day will come, buddy. I was a writer for three years before I got the chance to be in front of the camera. You're just getting started."

"But you're good-looking, and I'm..." he motioned to his face by drawing a circle around it in the air. "Hideous," he finished. "I'll never get a chance to be on camera or have a chance with a woman as fine as that, either."

"Fine, huh?" I asked, still focused on my computer screen. I already knew she was pretty because I'd seen her in the lobby, but I put on an air of nonchalance. I'd learned that there were fine women everywhere, but genuine, sweet, loving... those qualities were hard to find. I'd had my share of dates; many of them were beautiful and fun to be with, but none motivated me to make a commitment. Besides, my focus was on my job and Remi right now.

I had a long list of emails waiting for me. One from the travel department with my flight details for the coming week, one from Tyler, one of the cameramen I worked with trying to make plans to get a beer after work, and another from Chase, asking if I would be able to join the family on a cruise vacation the following summer. I smiled to myself. He was a very good friend. It was amazing how we'd moved on from all of the misunderstandings and the huge cluster-fuck we'd made of our friendship. I couldn't think of another man who would not only forgive me but also invite me on trips so that I could be with Remi as much as possible. We'd all grown up a lot and were putting Remi first.

"Yes." He pushed his glasses up on his nose and leaned in so he could half-whisper. "She's super-hot."

"She might be a shrew or an idiot, Jerry. You can't judge by a pretty face or tight skirt."

"Ah ha!" Jerry's eyes widened, and he quickly sat down across the desk from me. "You know she's hot! You've already seen her," he accused.

I started typing out a response to affirm the travel plans

but glanced up and grimaced at his raging hormones. "So, what? I don't want her to get the job, obviously."

"I guess," he said, his tone clearly disappointed. He looked over his shoulder again, straining out of his chair a bit to check the woman out again.

"Dude." I shook my head. "First of all, you don't know if she's hired or is even a contender, second, if she is, you can't act all goofy around her, or you'll never have a shot. On top of that, you have to be professional. You can't approach her at work. Haven't you learned anything from the news lately?"

Five network employees had already lost their jobs due to sexual harassment allegations over the past three months. While sexual harassment couldn't be tolerated, even a compliment could be misinterpreted, and so my co-worker needed to chill. Of all the men I worked with, Jerry might offend someone just because he had no clue how to approach a woman.

He craned to look over his shoulder, ignoring my words. "But, she's soooo pretty."

Jesus, I thought. "Pretty or not, I have network experience. Your admiration is moot because that job belongs to me."

I wondered why, if she was so attractive, Bryan wasn't trying to get her to anchor one of the shows instead of producing, or maybe take my place as correspondent. It was a good idea, and if it came down to it, it was a win-win-win. I'd still get my well-deserved promotion, she'd get hired, and Jerry could drool over her from afar. I almost laughed out loud at the thought.

I glanced up at Jerry as I opened another email. "You're not hideous," I admonished reassuringly. "You have character, and you're smart. Women care more about intelligence and a good sense of humor than a pretty mug, anyway. Trust me."

Jerry shoved his hands in his pockets as he hovered over my desk. "Easy for you to say," he mumbled. "You can get any woman you want. Mary Jane asked me to introduce her, and I heard Janice talking to Ellen about you at the water cooler."

I rolled my eyes in exaggerated mocking. Janice was pretty but too fake and conceited for my taste, and Mary Jane was just some starry-eyed kid who tripped over herself for any of us who were on-air because that's what she aspired to someday. "I guess they haven't been paying attention to national news either, then."

"Guess not." He chuckled.

"I'm scheduled for the L.A. Rams-Broncos game." I was talking more to myself than to him. I didn't like going to L.A. I hated LAX; I hated the traffic and the long hours on the plane. "I'd give anything if this game were in Denver, instead." I looked up, and he was still sitting there, and it didn't seem like he had any intention of getting on with his day. "Hey, sorry, Jerry. I'm going to do a little research and make some calls to line up some interviews. Why don't you go get Cindy to introduce you to that woman and fill me in on the details later?"

"Oh, sure," he said happily, rising from the chair and backing out of my office awkwardly. "Catch 'ya later, then, man."

I stopped typing and held his gaze, still waiting for him to split. "Okay. Later."

I was curious as hell about the woman, too; wanting to size up the competition more than anything else, and I cared more about her brain than her looks. Either way, I'd be damned if I was going to act like I was one bit worried. Nope. I was going to sit my ass at my desk and carry on as usual, though I couldn't help glancing through the glass walls of my office a few times.

The offices were lined up around the perimeter of the floor with dozens of cubicles in the middle. I could see Cindy walking toward the opposite end of the big room, and the slender woman with upswept blonde hair was following her. Jerry was now lopping up behind them. I felt sorry for him. He had zero finesse and was in desperate need of a good dermatologist. I shook my head and watched for a minute.

She wore a dark grey suit jacket and seemed tall in her tasteful high heels. Cindy was introducing her around which told me Bryan was seriously considering hiring her. *Fuck.*

I threw the pen I was holding down on my desk and reached for the phone. It wasn't after lunch yet, but I was going to get to the bottom of whatever the hell was going on.

"Mr. Walsh's office," Tracey answered the phone.

"Tracey, it's Jensen. Put me through to Walsh."

"He stepped out for a few minutes, Jensen, but I'll tell him you called."

In the middle of the call, Cindy and the mystery woman suddenly appeared in the open doorway of my office.

"Okay, well, have him call me, please."

"Sure thing, Jensen."

"Thanks." I hung up the phone and sat back in my chair, glancing between Cindy's face and that of the other woman. She was exquisite, no question, but she seemed a tad stiff. Her face was classically beautiful, and her eyes an amazing shade of dark aquamarine and were fringed with long dark lashes that made them pop. Her expression was somber and reserved; emotionless. If her demeanor was her true nature and not just nervousness, we were all in for a real treat. She was slender, but her figure swelled gently in all the right places. Many of the women in this business were bone thin, but at least she had breasts, I couldn't help but note. I swallowed and brushed my hand over my lower face. I admonished myself for having the same thoughts I'd just warned Jerry Stanley about. "Um... hi?"

"Jensen," Cindy began. "This is Melissa Ellington. Mr. Walsh asked me to show her around and introduce her."

My lips thinned, and I nodded. "I see," I acknowledged before standing and politely offering my hand to her across the desk. "Jensen Jeffers."

"Nice to meet you," she said and took my hand in the briefest of contact. Her voice had a professional quality about it that would suit well to this gig, but she was not what I'd call an extrovert. "I've seen you on NFL Sunday and Monday Night Football."

"Thanks," I said, shoving my hands into the pockets of my dress slacks. I wasn't sure if it was a compliment or not. I looked her over, and she was doing the same. We were obviously sizing each other up. I wondered if she knew we were trying to snag the same job. I wanted to ask Cindy but doubted she'd know more than I would. Surely, Bryan would tell me his decision before spreading it around.

Cindy could sense the tension and shifted in place. "Well, Melissa is interviewing with Mr. Walsh, and she is going to be staying with us for a couple of days. She'll be shadowing some of you to see if ESPN would be a good fit for her."

I couldn't help the way my jaw shot out and my eyes locked with hers. I was in an awkward position. I found her extremely attractive but didn't know this woman. I didn't know what she was after. Every instinct told me to put up my guard and keep it up.

I glanced at Cindy. "I see. Production or on-air?" I asked pointedly. There was more than one way to find out what I needed to know.

"Both, actually," Melissa Ellington answered before Cindy could do so.

Okay, so maybe she wasn't as shy as I initially thought. "I gather I'm up first?" I directed the question at Cindy.

"Yes, please, Jensen," she replied.

"I was supposed to hear from Bryan after lunch," I hedged. "Alone."

"He said to tell you he'd be in touch." She smiled brightly and then looked from me to the new girl. "Will you be okay?

Melissa, just ask if you need anything. Jensen knows my extension."

"Please, call me Missy." She smiled warmly showing dimples that only made her more attractive. "Thank you so much for showing me around. I love it, already."

I stood there, with my hands in my pockets, watching the exchange and wondering what in the hell was going on. As soon as Cindy left, I gestured to one of the chairs in front of the desk and suggested Missy sit down, taking a seat myself as soon as she settled into hers.

"Listen, Missy—" I began, but she put up her hand to stop me.

"Melissa," she said.

What the hell? I huffed in irritation, my eyes narrowed, snapping up to meet her gaze without flinching. So, this was starting off with a bang. "Excuse me? You just told Cindy to call you Missy."

"Yes, but professionally, I go by Melissa. I prefer to maintain a certain professional decorum between myself and my direct co-workers."

I sensed she wanted to say more, but I spoke instead. "I see, well, we don't know if we'll be working together yet, now do we?"

"I could sense your..." she searched for the right word, "hesitation, the minute Cindy brought me in here. Let's just be honest, shall we? I know you're up for the same position, Jensen."

"Mr. Jeffers," I said shortly, causing both of her eyebrows to rise. "Decorum, right?"

Melissa paused and had the grace to flush, and the corner of her pink lips twitched slightly. I wasn't sure if she was amused or pissed. "Touché. My apologies. It won't happen again."

"I will respect your boundaries, Melissa, but personally, I

think it's cutting off your nose to spite your face." I resumed scrolling through my emails and deleting any that I felt were worthless.

"You don't know my history, so you can't adequately judge."

I paused shortly, glancing. "And, apparently, I won't in the future, given the igloo around you. That's fine if that's the way you want it."

She seemed taken aback by my bluntness and maybe I'd made her think. "As I said, this job—"

"You're right. The production promotion is mine to lose, and I have no intentions of doing so, however, I will tell you that if you're gonna be so off-putting, you won't do well in this office. I can't speak for the Bristol office, but this one is smaller and close-knit. Didn't Bryan tell you we're like a family here?"

She crossed one shapely leg over the other; her back straight as a rail as she sat on the edge of the chair. "Even in the closest families, there's always someone waiting for an opportunity to stab you in the back. I've learned to be cautious, that's all. I didn't mean to offend you."

"Being cautious is fine," I typed out a response to one of the new assignments and sent it off. "Being unprofessional or shrewish isn't," I warned sternly. Melissa's mouth opened in a soft gasp, but I continued. "You seem awfully shocked by my bluntness, in light of your own."

Her eyes widened slightly, and her chin jutted out. "No, it's just that you seem so much more charming on-air."

Wow. A zinger. I huffed out a surprised and somewhat pissed off laugh, meeting her defiant gaze unflinchingly. So, she was spunky, and I liked that about her. Being a bit of ice queen might help her hold her own with some of the more obnoxious players. Professional football was a male sport, and some of the players could get rough and suggestive with the female correspondents. I'd seen it a hundred times before. It took a certain amount of guts and a very thick skin to deal with it. I wasn't sure she had it.

"Look, I'm not sure what your previous jobs were like, or what type of environment you're used to, but we cover events globally, and there are times when we need to be able to depend on each other to pick up the slack or get us out of difficult situations." I shook my head, disgusted. "I'm not sure what Bryan's plans are for you, but whatever it is, there will be times when you'll need help, or others will rely on you to step up. It's better to get along and save the attitude for the locker rooms."

"But production doesn't deal with the players directly, do —?"

Thankfully, I was offered a reprieve when my phone started ringing. I grabbed the receiver. "Excuse me while I take this."

"Do I need to step out?" she asked quietly, pointing toward the door.

I shook my head and held up my hand indicating that I wanted her to stay put. "Hello?" I said into the phone. The caller ID told me it was Bryan.

"Have you had lunch?" Bryan asked.

"Not yet." I knew my tone was still irritated. "Have you made a decision?" I countered.

"Yes. I'm hoping Ms. Ellington will accept your current position, but I haven't offered it to her officially yet."

I breathed a sigh of relief and smiled softly. "I see." It wasn't my place to tell the woman sitting across the desk the details, but I couldn't help looking at her while I was sitting there on the phone with my program director. I could see Melissa felt uncomfortable after our slightly heated exchange. If she took this job, I'd be her boss, and I wasn't sure that was something I wanted. "Do I have anything to say about it?"

He cleared his throat. "Of course. She'd report to you, so it needs to be a good fit. I have to tell you, she's got looks and *brains*, but more importantly, she wants it pretty badly, so she'll work hard."

So, this was why Cindy brought Melissa into my office. She wasn't going to shadow a few of us. Just me. Fuck.

"So, what do you think?" he asked through the phone.

"I got the new assignment from production today, and also spoke to Cindy." I was hedging, unsure if I should have this conversation in front of this woman, but she would find out soon enough. "The two things don't mesh very well, because there is traveling involved in the main one." Was he suggesting that I take her with me to L.A.?

"Yeah, they do. You always have a crew, so adding one more shouldn't throw you off that much."

I groaned internally; certain displeasure was painted all over my face. I swiveled my chair around, so it was half facing the window to hide it from Melissa. "Did you clear this with her?"

"Not yet. You can do that."

"Gee, thanks." My response was a mixture of resignation and wry displeasure.

"That doesn't sound good. Don't you like her?"

I leaned an elbow on the arm of my chair, bending my head into the phone to hold it against my shoulder; then lowered my voice. "The jury is still out."

"Well, spend the day with her and then decide. I'm leaving this in your hands but try to be objective."

"Always," I said flatly. "You know me."

Bryan laughed heartily on the other end of the line. "That, I do. Congratulations."

"Yeah, thanks. I appreciate it."

"Keep me posted," he said and then hung up the phone.

I swiveled my chair and then placed the phone back in its cradle, my eyes skittering over Melissa again. She was eyeing a picture of me with Remi that Chase had taken in Disney World, and there were a couple of others of the four of us, and one of Chase and me from college. My office was smallish and didn't have space for a big bookcase or sideboard, so most of them were displayed on the "L" of my desk.

Melissa pointed at the one of Chase and me. "Is that Chase Forrester?" She glanced at me as her words fell off, her mouth hanging open with Chase's name hanging off of her lips.

I pressed my lips together and nodded. So, she had a grasp of soccer and football. *Yay.* "Yeah. It is. It's a long story that we don't have time for."

"Okay." she accepted my reluctance without more questions and looked at me with clear expectation on her face.

I sighed and closed my laptop and confirmed her suspicions. "So, that was Bryan Walsh. I got the producer position."

"Oh, I see. I thought he was going to wait until I'd had a chance to be here a few days, but... oh, well." It was clear she was disappointed as she bent to retrieve her briefcase and handbag from the floor next to her chair. "Sorry to have wasted your time, Mr. Jeffers."

It just felt goofy for her to call me Mr. Jeffers despite her weird boundary logic.

"Jensen," I blurted and waved my hand in front of myself. "I'm no Mr. Jeffers."

By now Melissa was on her feet and had pivoted to begin her trek out of my office. She paused and nodded. "Okay, then. Thank you, Jensen."

"Wait."

She turned more fully back toward the desk when I stopped her, her expression curious.

"Sit down. We aren't done."

"But I thought..." she began cautiously.

"Please, sit down," I said again. When Melissa complied, holding her bags protectively in her lap, I continued. "This is still a trial run if you want it, but for my current job as field correspondent." I pointed at my desk and waited for her to reply.

"Um..."

I could see her visibly swallow and then she bit her lip, clearly considering the opportunity. Personally, I thought it would be a no-brainer, requiring no thought at all. "Is something wrong? This is a great opportunity, and it will get you on a solid career path with the network. It's a better break than I had. It took me years to get this job, and you have the chance to start at this level. Providing, that is, that we mesh, and I feel you're a good fit. So, why the hesitation?"

"I guess... I wasn't planning for an on-camera position." She started fidgeting, suddenly nervous.

"But you have experience with the Dallas station, right?" I didn't have a copy of her resume, but I'd ask Bryan to forward it via email later. I had plenty of time over the next couple of days to look it over while we were on assignment.

"I do, but it's been a few years since."

The reticence she was displaying seemed unnecessary. I'd never seen someone so apprehensive about a job offer before; especially a position this advanced. I offered a wry expression and a short shrug. "It's like riding a bike, but if you don't want it, I'll let Bryan know you aren't interested so we won't waste each other's time." I flipped open my laptop again.

"No," she answered quickly. "I don't want to make a decision before I have an opportunity to check it out."

I looked up at her. "Fair enough. I have an assignment to cover a Rams game in L.A. this weekend, and Bryan would like you to accompany the crew. It will give you the chance to see what would be expected of you in this position and give me a chance to see how you'll do and if you'll fit in with the rest of the staff."

There was a brief look of shock on her face before she shook it off. "How long will it take? I have to make arrangements for my little boy. I wasn't planning on being gone beyond today. I was flying home tonight."

Ah, so that was it. If anyone understood the responsibility and heart-hold a child had on a parent, it was me.

"I see. How old is he?"

"He's six. He's with my brother, now, but I have to make sure Ben can keep him for the weekend. I don't think it will be a problem."

I wanted her to feel a level of camaraderie between us so that she would relax, which would make the next few days easier on both of us. Plus, I wanted her to embrace the job, so I didn't have to spend the first weeks of my new promotion trying to fill my old position. Bryan had already given Melissa the green light, which was good enough for me; provided she did well on location and the team liked her. "I have a daughter about that age. I get it."

"The little girl in these pictures?"

I nodded, smiling brightly. "Yes. She's a little spitfire."

"She's beautiful."

"Thank you. What's your son's name?"

"Dylan. I have to make a call to my brother to see if he can watch my son." She reached for her purse and pulled out her phone.

"Fine. I'll step out for a minute while you do that. I have to speak to the travel department to get arrangements made for you."

I didn't really need to walk to the department personally; I could have called or emailed, but I wanted to give her privacy to make her call. I got up and walked around my desk and past her speaking as I left the office. "Take your time."

I pulled the door shut behind me and made my way to the operations floor. I hardly ever walked through the offices, and never on the sixth floor. It was a lot more sterile than the levels inhabited by the news, writing, research, and on-air staffs. There were only a few offices on this level, and I didn't know where I was going. There was a dark-haired young man, probably a college intern judging by his T-shirt, sitting in the closest cubicle about ten feet from the elevators. He was concentrating hard on his computer screen, clearly engrossed. "Hey, man. Can you please tell me where I can find the travel department?"

He glanced up as a look of disbelief spread across his face. "Mr. Jeffers!" He stood up abruptly and pointed toward the southwest corner of the building. "It's right over there, sir!"

I patted his shoulder as I passed. "Thanks. What's your name?"

"Mark Weaver, sir." He seemed almost giddy; his smile was infectious.

"Keep up the good work, Mark."

"Thank you, sir!"

I flashed him one in return and continued to my destination. The travel department was essentially the network's own travel agency and was separated from the rest of the floor by two glass walls with a door in the one facing the cubicles.

When I went in; all ten of the people working inside looked up from what they were doing, even those talking on the phone.

"May I help you?" A thin, older woman walked forward toward me, dressed in business casual, as was everyone who wasn't at executive level or talent.

"Yes, thank you. I'm Jensen Jeffers, and I have an assignment in L.A. with a crew tonight, but I need to add one more person to the roster. She'll need a plane ticket and a hotel room."

She went to her desk and picked up a piece of paper. "Melissa Ellington? Yes, we have it all arranged."

That son of a bitch, Walsh! I thought, incredulously. He was one step ahead of me.

"Alright, then. Thank you…" I glanced at the nameplate on her desk. "Natalie." I grinned at her.

"My pleasure, Jensen. Since you're down here, you're saving me the trouble of sending these up." She handed me a manila envelope with my name printed on the label. I knew from experience that the envelope contained the itinerary, the boarding passes and hotel information for the entire team, as well as car information.

"Thanks." I held it up in a sort of farewell salute as I pushed open the glass door to leave the department; once again weaving through the mass of cubicles on my way to the elevators. Employees glanced up at me and smiled, though continuing their work.

The elevator took me down to the second floor where the room full of company paraphernalia was located. Melissa probably didn't have many clothes with her, and I decided to get her a couple of ESPN shirts, a jacket, and a hat. She probably wouldn't need the coat in L.A., but Wyoming was decidedly colder. I had to pause, wondering why I'd be thinking about her in any way beyond this weekend. It wasn't a good idea, and I needed to stop.

The small room required a key, and I didn't have one, so I went in search of Cindy who would be able to open it for me. In a matter of two minutes, she was unlocking the door and going inside with me. She flipped on the light and pulled a clipboard off of the nail it was hanging on just inside the door.

"That clipboard is a bit archaic, isn't it?" I teased.

"It is, but it's easier than remembering what the staff takes out of here and entering it into inventory at my desk. This way, I just have to do it once a month."

"Ever heard of an iPad? Or, you could bring your laptop with you," I added sardonically. Cindy was a nice woman, and she and I had become friends over the years. She knew my entire story.

"Okay, smartass," she shot back, rolling her eyes. "What do you need?"

"I'm thinking one of the T-shirts, a polo, jacket, and a hat?"

"For Missy?"

I nodded, scanning the labels that were stuck on the shelves to indicate the item and size of the various stacks of clothing above them. Cindy's use of Melissa's nickname made me pause. It suited her. I was hoping that soon she'd feel comfortable enough to allow the crew to use it; myself included.

"Yes. What's her story? She's intelligent and pretty, but she seems... I don't know..." I shrugged. "Closed off."

Cindy had compiled a stack of items, longer than I'd asked.

"Well, you're trying to hire her, not date her." She grabbed a hat from another pile. There were many different styles and with different logos for various shows.

"No, shit? Really?" I asked, wide-eyed and mocking. I bent over to scrutinize the shelves, finally finding what I was looking for and adding it to the stack. Cindy picked it up and looked at the label inside the neck and wrote it on the clipboard. "I'm just not sure an on-air job will be her thing."

"Take this weekend before you make up your mind, Jens. ESPN can be intimidating. She's been on-air before this."

"I know that, but she admitted she didn't want to be in the talent pool. This could all be for nothing."

"Just get through the next few days. I think this should be

enough clothing."

"Agreed." I found an empty box and placed all of the items in it, before picking it up. "What do you know about her?"

"Not much. She and her young son live in Jackson Hole, Wyoming with her brother, and she's worked in a couple of network jobs. That's about it."

She wasn't much more help than Melissa herself. "Thanks for the stuff. See you, next week."

"Have a good weekend," she said.

"You, too."

When I got back to my office, Melissa was no longer on the phone, but Lonnie Baxter, another reporting correspondent, was hanging out talking to her. She looked uncomfortable as he loomed over her in the cramped space.

"No, but thank you, anyway." I could see she was bristling and her demeanor, while professional, was visibly cold.

"Lonnie," I greeted him, as I walked in, back around to my chair and setting the box of clothing on my desk. "Can I help you with something?" My question was pointed and implying that if he didn't have a real reason to talk to me, he needed to get the fuck out.

"No. I just wanted to meet this stunning woman."

I offered a bland look. "Melissa, Lonnie Baxter. Lonnie, Melissa Ellington." I waved a hand between them. "You've met her. Now, can you excuse us?"

His job was on the same level as mine before my promotion, but we didn't work directly together. We were never on the same assignment and had separate crews, so I only knew him casually though he had a reputation, which he was proving more than well-deserved.

He hovered, not wanting to leave. "What's your hurry, Jeffers?" I cringed. Lonnie had been with the network longer than I, and he was always trying to throw his superiority in my face. He was in for a big surprise when he found out I would soon be his boss."

"We're working."

"What's going on?" Lonnie prodded rudely. Now I knew why I didn't like this guy. "Are we hiring her?"

"Bye," was all I said, nodding hard at the open door. "Adios."

He figured out he wasn't getting anywhere and so changed his tactic. "I just came in here to invite you both," a sly grin spread on his smarmy face, "out to Jake's for drinks after work."

"We're on assignment. The flight is at seven. Sorry."

"I get it," he persisted. "I get you." He pointed at me with his index finger, offering a wink and a smug nod.

God, he was a dick; I scowled at him, hard. He was such a disrespectful fucker. Melissa's expression filled with anger and her back visibly stiffened as she sat up straighter in her chair. I racked my brain as to why he still had a job, something I might be able to correct soon. "That's where you're wrong. You don't *get* anything. Get out of my office."

"Woa…" he put up both hands.

I walked around my desk, prepared to push him out the door, but my forward movement caused him to step back and outside of the office. I shut the door in his face the second he cleared the doorframe.

"Sorry about the village idiot," I offered with a sympathetic smile and a roll of my eyes; then reached inside the box to pull out the smallest item.

"It's okay. He's a bit…" she struggled for the right word.

"Dickish?" I offered, chuckling.

She couldn't help but huff out a surprised laugh, and for the first time, she seemed to relax, even if it was against her will. I was still trying to figure out the reason behind her closed demeanor. Maybe there were too many morons like Lonnie in her past.

"That certainly... fits."

"You have no idea. Here." I pushed the box toward her. "These are for you. Did you bring any jeans to Atlanta?"

"I have one pair with me."

"Good. You'll need them on this trip. Did you clear it with your brother?"

"Yes."

"Good." I held up an ESPN Sports Center Football jersey in a medium youth size. "Will this fit Dylan?"

Her beautiful face split into a bright smile and I could swear there was a catch in her voice when she spoke. For the first time, I found myself hoping for a thaw.

"It's just a little big, but, thank you. He'll love it. He'll *really* love it."

Chapter 4

Missy

Unexpectedly, and somehow unnervingly, I was sitting in coach smashed between Jensen and a two hundred and fifty-pound cameraman on my way to L.A., instead of back to Wyoming. The cameraman was so huge that he needed the aisle seat so he could spill over. It was a problem when the flight attendants were doing the beverage service.

I was still in my business suit while everyone else was in jeans and ESPN gear. I felt a little out of place, but I was saving my one pair of jeans for the game on Sunday, but I'd probably have to wear them both days. I wasn't sure if I was excited or apprehensive… but it felt good just being here, doing this… having a chance to go back to work, even if it wasn't the job I'd planned on.

I was happy there was still an opportunity to work at ESPN after Jensen Jeffers had landed the job that I thought I was interviewing for, but I was frustrated. Why did they even bother talking to me if Bryan Walsh already had his mind made up? Which was surely the case.

Getting back in front of the camera would be a fantastic prospect if it weren't for my need to lay low out of Derrick's purview; more for my son, than me. The last thing I wanted to risk was being on-air and Derrick showing up to cause trouble.

He did come to Jackson Hole once after I'd moved in with Ben. There was a nasty confrontation, and it had been easy to get a restraining order after that. I had no idea why he didn't push to stop the divorce or why he'd left us alone thus far, but it was entirely out of character, despite the restraining order. I had no sense of security moving forward because the document only had jurisdiction in Jackson Hole, and I wouldn't have my brother to protect me in Atlanta.

Derrick was, no doubt, still volatile, and I just wanted to stay off his radar to build a nice life for me, and Dylan. That was all I needed. My heart seized in fear; being on camera would be a monumental risk.

Wyoming was beautiful, but it was too far from my mother, and I missed city life. I'd been looking forward to this job, and now this.

The handsome man to my left, who might become my boss, was reading something on his laptop and working. I'd seen him on television a few times registering briefly how gorgeous he was, but never dreaming that one day we might work together.

He sensed me looking at him and glanced in my direction, pulling one of his white earbuds out of his ears. "Is Eric's snoring keeping you awake?"

Jensen had the small light over his seat turned on, but the one over my head and Eric's were dark. Overall, the lights in the jet's cabin were low. The flight from Atlanta to L.A. was non-stop, at least.

After the trauma I'd suffered at Derrick's hands, I'd vowed never to let another man hurt me, or my son, ever again. In response, my heart had hardened, and I'd protected myself by not allowing anyone close to me. Admittedly, I had a hard time trusting most people, but there was something gentle about

Jensen that caught me off guard. I realized I'd have to be extra careful around him. I'd learned that I couldn't take people at face value, and it was the hardest lesson of my life. Even though he seemed honest, I couldn't blindly trust him. It wasn't personal; I didn't do that with anyone anymore.

"No. Yes." I couldn't help but smile, putting a hand up to cup my mouth so that the sleeping man wouldn't hear my criticism of him. "He *is* really loud."

Jensen chuckled. "Yeah. The travel department always books his room on a different floor from the rest of us. He can be like a freight train if he's sleeping hard. This is not even close," he joked.

"Does this crew always travel together, then?" I asked quietly.

"Yes." He nodded, answering softly, and then pulled his other earbud free. "Except when one of us has vacation or becomes ill. Depending on the situation, the rest of us take up the slack when one of us is M.I.A."

I had to admit that a bunch of people having each other's back did sound nice. I stuck out my lower lip and nodded. "The family thing."

His eyebrows shot up, and he flashed a brilliant grin that made him even more disarming. Even in the half-light throwing part of his face into shadow, he was striking.

"See? You *were* listening."

"I'm good at it," I shot back.

"Noted. Check off one job requirement."

"What are you working on?"

"Researching a couple of the newer players' stats."

It made sense. Jensen had been reporting on the NFL for years, so he'd know most every player by heart. In Dallas, I was one of the prime-time news anchors, and much of my commentary had been written for me. I only wrote the outside segments, that I investigated and reported on, myself. I never did sports of any kind, and that was the part of working at ESPN that seemed a bit daunting.

"I see. How do you keep them all straight? The teams and players, I mean."

"Over time, you'll learn the teams, the players' names, and their positions. Some are more memorable because they stick around the game longer, while some are flash-in-the-pan, but even then, there's usually a college career so begin your research there. Until you get it down, someone will be feeding it to you through an earpiece." He grinned and closed his laptop. I couldn't help noticing how his smile went all the way up into his deep cobalt eyes. "Namely, me." He was studying me. "At least, at first."

"What do you mean, at first?"

"During your interview with Walsh didn't he tell you what the production job covered? What shows, segments, etcetera?"

"He just said it was a producer position. No specifics."

"Well, it's over the Monday Night football show. At least; during the season, but I'll also be working with my current crew on a few things here or there. One weekly show won't keep me busy because some segments are produced through local affiliates."

"Oh, I see. The remote segments are produced by someone else?"

"Yes. We have regional producers that do that. You'd be working mostly with them."

"That's if you hire me." I found myself wanting to work with Jensen and was a bit disappointed that it wouldn't be all the time.

"Yes. Are you worried?"

"Outside of the fact that I know so little about football, not at all. I know I can do the job."

"I'm not worried, either."

I felt good about his vote of confidence but was curious about something. "If you won't be my boss most of the time, why is Mr. Walsh making it your decision?"

"Probably because he does want to hire you and feels my job would be a good fit. Who better to judge if you can do it?"

"Is this position a direct report to him, then?"

His eyes were back on his computer screen. "Yes and no. As I said, it's assignment by assignment. Overall, yes."

It made sense to a point, but if there were several of these teams, maybe they would move me around from crew to crew. I shook myself from my thoughts. I wasn't even sure if I wanted an on-air position, so I shouldn't be getting ahead of myself.

"Are you planning on putting me on the air this weekend?" I asked.

"No. But you'll have a headset to listen to everything, and you'll see how it all goes down."

I sighed in silent relief until he said his next words.

"And, you'll be following me around on the field and in the locker room."

"Locker room?" Obviously, I'd heard that women went into male locker rooms all the time, but I never really thought I'd be one of them. "Really?" I grimaced.

"Yes. Don't worry, though. Men aren't as bashful as women." Jensen's tone was amused.

"Oh, I'm not bashful," I quickly assured him, though I was inwardly quaking. I'd only ever been with one man, and I wasn't sure how I'd handle a bunch of burly football players walking around with their junk hanging out on display.

"You'll get used to it." He chuckled, flipping over one of the pages and glancing down at it. "There's also the option of moving to Bristol and anchoring a daily show. The hours are better, and there's almost zero traveling."

I wondered why he wasn't doing that, himself. He was obviously attractive enough; the deep blue eyes and dark hair made for a striking combination. He was also very knowledgeable, and from what I'd seen of him on television, he had a quiet confidence that didn't come off as arrogance. "Why don't you do that? Take a studio job, I mean."

He lifted one shoulder in a half shrug. "Simple. I don't want to move to Connecticut."

"I see." I glanced down at his left hand. No ring, but some men didn't wear rings. "Your family is here, huh?"

He nodded, and his whole face lit up. "My daughter, Remi."

So, he wasn't married, and his ex-wife must have custody of their child. I could see the love radiate out of him whenever he mentioned her, and I found myself thankful that I wouldn't be working with Jensen Jeffers, after all. I wasn't sure if it was because he was way too charming, or because part of me didn't want him to be my boss.

"Remi. That's unusual."

"It's short for Remilia."

I was about to comment on how beautiful and unique the name was when we hit a patch of turbulence. The plane jolted dramatically, feeling like one of those amusement park rides where you have a sharp, sudden drop. My stomach lurched, and the soft drink I had sitting on my tray table tipped over, spilling the contents. I scrambled to mop it up with the napkin and put the ice back in the glass, but the small bit of paper hardly did the job.

"Snugsshuggggh!" Eric jolted awake with a huge snort. "What the hell?" The huge man turned slightly in his chair, grumbling as his elbow knocked roughly into my shoulder.

"Ugh," I complained in pain.

"It was only an air pocket," Jensen explained, unperturbed

by the whole incident, his attention once again on his computer screen.

I looked at him with skeptical amusement, and the other man just grunted and closed his eyes, intent on resuming his nap and snore-fest.

"Air pocket?" I was skeptical of the term.

He laughed gently, his eyes softening again. "That's what Remi calls turbulence."

"I've never taken Dylan on a plane."

"Really?"

I shook my head. "We don't take many trips." The past couple of years had been tough, and I was still paying off my divorce attorney, but that wasn't the explanation I wanted to share with a potential co-worker-slash-boss. "Dylan adores his Uncle Ben; they go fishing and camping a lot. We don't travel outside of the region that much."

"I've never been to Wyoming, but I hear it's just gorgeous."

"Yes, but no professional sports teams." My eyes widened for emphasis, and I shrugged sympathetically.

"Right. Camping isn't something I've ever done with Remi, but I bet she'd love it."

A male flight attendant went around gathering up everyone's trash as an announcement flooded the cabin. "Ladies, and gentleman, we'll be landing soon. Please put away all electronic devices, and make sure they are securely stowed at this time. Also, please return your seats and tray tables to their upright and original positions." A female flight attendant spoke over the speaker system.

Jensen leaned forward to speak to Eric, who amazingly had fallen back into a deep sleep in just a minute or two. "Dude. Wake up. We're landing."

His eyes opened, and he yawned, forgetting to cover his mouth. "Schhuggg," he snorted again loudly, startling awake.

"Oh."

I turned away and toward Jensen, who rolled his eyes. "Manners aren't required behind the camera. *Eric's* camera, at least. Sorry."

"It's okay. I'm tired, too." I was looking forward to getting to the hotel and taking a hot bath. Jensen closed his laptop again, shoving the stack of papers he was looking at inside and on top of the keyboard between it and the lid. Reaching down, he pulled his black computer case from underneath the seat in front of him and was soon returned to its former place with the laptop inside.

"I hate these fucking planes," he murmured, and then looked at me with a grin, two dimples showing up in both cheeks. "Oops. I guess I don't have manners, either."

I couldn't help the happy laugh that burst from me. I was in serious, serious trouble with this man. "It's okay."

He was tall, and I could see how the cramped seating on a long flight was bothersome. While the cameraman overflowed his seat, Jensen's legs were clearly bent in the one position for the entire time on board. He ran a hand through his hair and then over his face. I couldn't help noticing the strength in his forearms or the way the shirt tightened over his biceps and shoulders when he'd moved to stow his computer beneath the seat in front of him. "These long flights are a bitch."

Something about this man made me relax, but on the other hand, I was on pins and needles. He had my career, literally in his hands, and it wasn't the least concerning. My experiences with Derrick weren't something I wanted to repeat and had colored my entire view of men, so I'd adopted a cool demeanor to keep them at bay. After what happened to me, I had to be cautious... but this man was different, and that made him dangerous. I barely knew him, but he made me feel safe and at the same time, excited. While it was a fantastic feeling, it was also terrifying. The last time I trusted a man had ended with a lot of physical and emotional pain.

No. I had to keep my wits about me with this one.

JENSEN

The network had hired a van service that would be on call for us throughout the weekend, and the drivers picked us up at the airport and took us to the Lux hotel. We always stayed there when we were in L.A.

Before we even arrived at the hotel, a few crewmembers were already talking about meeting for drinks at the hotel bar. There was a three-hour time difference between the east and west coasts, which meant we could stay up a few hours and still be well-rested for the next day. The game wasn't until Sunday and tomorrow would be spent watching practice on the field and doing pre-taped interviews with the coaches and some of the players. A few of them would be shot live on Sunday, but others were done in advance so they could be edited for length and the producers could use them as needed for filler.

I was riding in front with the driver, and Melissa, the potential new hire, had chosen to get into the very back of the van with Liz Anderson, the director's assistant, and Michelle Broadmore, the digital editor.

There were enough of us to fill two of the large vans which caravanned to the hotel. I was in awe how many people were involved in the process of producing segments to run during the games; director, lighting director, video editor, graphics, producer, talent, camera and production crews.

Each of the big black vans had four rows of seats, and in this one, the single guys all but fell over each other to help Melissa with her luggage or help her into the van. From the moment we left the offices in Atlanta, their eagerness was barely disguised. She was hot and getting to know her made her even more intriguing; I couldn't lie. However, as a potential co-worker, it wasn't a good idea to let myself think of her as a woman; especially a beautiful, delicately feminine one.

I tried to be discrete as I observed and listened to the various crew make exchanges with her as we loaded bags and got into the vehicle. I couldn't help noticing she was polite, but her tone was measured and cool to the men, but warmer to the women. When we were talking on the plane, she didn't seem standoffish to me, but maybe it was because I would be making a recommendation to Bryan Walsh. The thought was brief, but I was disappointed by the possibility.

This was her normal time zone and no doubt, she was up early in Atlanta so she might need to go to sleep earlier than the rest of us. Maybe she was just tired, but instinctively, I felt that there was more to the story behind her aloofness. I hoped so, and I was curious. Unprofessionally so.

I mentally shook myself and let out a resigned sigh as we all piled out of the vans in front of the hotel, waiting for the drivers to open undercarriage compartments and get out the bags. As they sat them on the pavement one by one, the owners of each one picked them up and headed into the hotel amongst more conversation about the bar.

Missy collected her black roller bag and waited by the entrance for me.

"Jens! Are you coming to the bar?? Jeremy Nielson, one of the audio techs paused by the electronic doors as several of the others walked on through. "Eric said you're buying the first round."

My eyes widened and rolled. "Of course, he did," I scoffed wryly. "Yeah, maybe. I don't know. I'm going to dump off my bags in the room, and maybe I'll come down. If I see you, I see you."

He walked up to me so that he could speak softly. "Will

you bring her?"

I swallowed and hoisted my duffel over my shoulder. "Um, her name is Melissa, and I'm sure she knows she's welcome to join. Socializing isn't a requirement for her job trial."

I wanted to remind him that he needed to chill. I understood his enthusiasm, but I also knew that even though, for now, she hadn't been hired, it was still essential to maintain a professional atmosphere. She was an unknown, and while we knew how Liz and Michelle handled basic male teasing, we had to be careful. The last thing we needed was a misunderstanding of someone's intentions. I cast a cautious glance over at Melissa while she was speaking to the other women.

"But you seemed pretty cozy on the plane. Can you ask her?" He waggled his eyes at me suggestively and punched me lightly on the bicep.

"Down boy. We weren't cozy. We were making fun of Eric's snoring." I couldn't help the slow smile that slid across my face.

"Come on. That's cozy," Jeremy insisted eagerly.

I shook my head. "She might be a colleague soon, so stop ogling, would you? You can't flirt with her." I looked him straight in the eye. *None of us could*; I reminded myself.

"Maybe she won't get hired, though," he offered his own misguided reasoning. "Then she's fair game."

Could his dick really be clouding his judgment that much? If she didn't get hired, he'd never see her again. What a freaking loser.

"Hmmmph!" I huffed aloud and shook my head. "Doesn't matter, man. She's here on trial, so technically, it's the same thing." He was one of those people that was smart as hell about technology, or other things they learned from books, yet didn't have one shred of common sense. Walsh wouldn't send Missy on this trip if he weren't seriously considering hiring her, so I had to keep this kid in check.

"Just bring her." He winked and went to gather up a blue duffel that the driver had placed on the pavement near the back of the van.

"Should I knock her over the head with my caveman club and drag her there by the hair?" I mocked dryly.

"Whatever works."

Jesus Christ. I glared at him in annoyance, which did little to quell his moronic agenda. He still wore that stupid expression that said he was going to hit on her hard and heavy despite my warning. *Ignorant asshole*, I thought in disgust.

Once inside, the staff began to check us into our rooms. There were only two desk clerks on duty, so we all hovered as we waited our turn. The hotel bar, off to one end of the lobby, was pretty busy, but then, it was Friday night. There were several televisions around that usually had sports on them, but tonight it was karaoke. Some poor sap who sounded like a wounded moose was singing, and his awful voice echoed loudly through the lobby.

"Oh, my God," Liz mumbled. "I don't know about drinks if we have to suffer that all night."

I had ushered Missy, and the other two women, in front of me into the check-in line.

"It is pretty bad," Michelle added.

"My brother, Ben, loves karaoke," Missy added. "But that guy sounds like a wounded animal." The crew around her laughed, but I tried to seem disinterested, concentrating on scrolling through the messages on my phone. I smiled softly to myself, noting that Missy had thoughts similar to mine about the pathetic fool wailing in the other room.

"Oh, do you sing?" Liz piped up, her brown eyes getting wide.

Before Missy could answer, Jeremy was embedding himself into the conversation. "I bet you're awesome. I'd love to hear you sing. Can I carry your bag for you?"

"No. I mean, I don't actually sing much. And, thank you," Missy answered stiffly, scooting the suitcase closer to her feet. The easy-going demeanor evaporated instantly, and everyone noticed. Jeremy's face showed his shock at the rebuff and the women's surprise registered on both of their faces. Missy bristled. "I've got it."

Jeremy's eyes met mine over their heads, and I could see he was pissed. I licked my lips and shook my head almost imperceptibly, hoping he'd back off, but he wouldn't let it go. "Don't," I mouthed adamantly, though the word didn't escape my lips.

"I was only trying to help," he sulked.

"I don't need your help." Missy's tone was abrupt and a bit sharper than needed, and she folded her arms over her chest and looked at the floor. "Thank you, though," she added, more softly.

"You like to carry your own shit. Got it," Jeremy retorted, indignantly.

"Jeremy," I admonished, holding out a hand that told him to lay-off, even though I felt the arctic freeze coming off of Missy during their exchange. Even if I thought she was overreacting, he needed to back the hell off.

I realized that since we landed and after our onboard conversation, I was thinking of her as Missy and not Melissa, but her tone with Jeremy was definitely more formal. She had the grace to flush and turned away from him quickly. Nothing more was spoken until we'd all checked in. I could see by the shocked expressions on their faces that Liz and Michelle were uncomfortable with the exchange.

The other's made plans to stow their gear and then meet downstairs for food and drinks. I walked to the elevator with Missy and pressed the up button.

"Listen, Jeremy didn't mean anything before. He's just an

eager young kid." My tone was gentle, but she was still cautious.

"I know," she began, glancing up and over at me as we stood next to each other, waiting. The elevator's arrival announced with a ding, and then the steel doors slid open, and we walked inside. Due to her earlier reaction, I hadn't offered to help her with her bag, so she pulled it behind her. I had a suit bag and my duffel, carrying both easily over one shoulder. "It's just…" she stammered a bit, and her eyes flitted to mine and then away again. "I prefer to keep things professional. I have to set boundaries early on."

"It's not a problem, but if you do get this job, remember what I said. You'll have to work with these people. Just consider that it will make things a lot more enjoyable if you can make a few friends."

She looked indignant, which was confirmed a second later when her chin shot out. "I understand, and I meant no offense. I'm sorry if I was short with him, but I've seen that look before, and I have no intention of encouraging it."

"Noted." I rubbed the back of my neck in resignation. My own attraction for her was making me uncomfortable given her current attitude. Beyond the co-worker thing, she just seemed closed off to men. All men. It wasn't my business, either way, but it didn't sit well for some reason that I didn't even try to reconcile. "I'm sure he'll keep his distance now that you've been clear with him, but if you want to break the ice with the others, we'll be in the bar. Otherwise, I'll email you a copy of the itinerary, and you can meet us in the lobby at 8:30 in the morning."

The elevator doors opened on my floor, and I started to walk out. "Jensen," she called, so I put a hand out to stop the doors from closing behind me as I turned back toward her.

"Yes?"

"It's not personal. The professional thing."

I shrugged. "Okay."

"It's just that… even though this isn't the position I wanted originally, being independent is important to me. For me, and my son, and that's my focus. I don't want anything to mess up my chances."

"Socializing with the crew isn't part of the requirements for getting the job but trust me when I tell you that doing the job long-term will be more enjoyable if you like your crew and they like you because it will help your working relationship. That said; it's not okay for you to be made to feel uncomfortable or for some jerk-off to get pushy."

"I understand. Thank you." The woman I spoke to on the plane had disappeared and in her place was one who seemed scared to death. "Will the other girls be in the bar, later?"

The elevator groaned and tried to close, but I held it open. "They usually do join."

"Okay. I'll be down, then."

"You'll be fine. See you later then, *Missy*."

She smiled softly at my use of the nickname and seemed to relax. She nodded as I let the door to the elevator go and made my way down the hall, searching for my room number on the doors. I had been inclined to shower and order room service, but now, I felt I needed to meet the others in the bar.

"Fuck," I mumbled aloud as I found my room and opened the door, dumping my bags and computer on the bed nearest to me. I didn't want to go to the bar, but I wasn't as confident as my words implied. I wasn't sure the other guys would leave her be and even if their interest wasn't overbearing, I had no idea how she'd take it. Plus, I'd basically pushed her to join the others, so I'd be an asshole if I didn't participate as well and be there to run interference if needed.

I flipped on the television and then checked my phone for messages.

There was a video message from Teagan, which I knew would be the goodnight call from Remi. I smiled as I opened it and her precious little face lit up the screen. I looked forward to this call every night.

She was waving happily. "Jensey!" She used both of her hands to blow me several kisses in swift succession. "Mwuh! Mwuh! Mwuh! I asked God to make sure you came back safe so we can play at the zoo again!" She waved again, and I couldn't help the tightening that compressed my throat or the burning in the back of my eyes. Such a short time ago her little life hung in a precarious balance. "Mwuh! Mwuh! Mwuh!" She resumed blowing kisses into the screen.

"Come on, Remi. Time for bed, baby" Teagan said in the background. "Tell Jensey goodnight."

"Oh, okay," Remi grumbled and climbed into her bed, scrambling under the covers while her mother filmed it all. "Night night, Jensey! I love you! Come see me when you get home!"

Teagan said goodnight as she tucked Remi in and then the video ended leaving me sad that I'd missed talking to my little girl. I closed my phone quickly, then cleaned up. I washed my face, splashed on some cologne, put on a fresh button-down, and I was out the door. I didn't shave, because it was the end of a long day, and even if I was attracted to this woman, I couldn't, or shouldn't, do a damn thing about it.

Most of the others were already in the noisy bar and gathered around a few tables in one corner when I entered the dark space. My eyes found Liz and Michelle, conspicuously without Missy, at the end of one of the tables. There were two chairs free there, and I walked over to take one of them.

The group burst out into a chorus of guffaws and shouts as they saw me enter.

"Jensen!"

"It's about time, man!"

"Now the party can start!"

"Get out your wallet, Jeffers!"

I put my hands up to quiet them down with a wry twist to my expression. "Yeah, yeah."

"Ladies," I nodded to them as I pulled up one of the chairs and sat down. Within seconds, the waiter was asking what I wanted to drink, and before I'd ordered a draft beer, Jeremy was hovering.

"Is Missy coming?" he asked eagerly.

"She said she prefers Melissa," I glanced up at him. He'd certainly forgotten the rebuff she'd given him in the parking lot. "I think she will but chill out. If you don't, she's liable to kick you in the balls." I smiled and reached forward to grab a nacho from the plate at the center of the table. "Wasn't that message delivered in the lobby?"

Liz and Michelle laughed. "Yeah, back off, Jeremy," Liz admonished. "You're just a kid. She's sophisticated. Even if your balls *had* dropped, there's no way she'd be interested in you. Give it ten years."

I shook my head, and my mouth twisted wryly. "Not even then."

"Thanks a lot," he muttered, moving away, clearly embarrassed.

Those within hearing range burst out laughing, myself included. Leave it to Liz. She didn't pull any punches. Jeremy's face turned a bright red, and he left to rejoin a group of the crew around his own age at the other end of the table.

Liz rolled her eyes. "Give the kid a break, you guys. He's cute."

"He's jailbait," I added.

Michelle's head cocked to one side, as she looked him over, clearly sizing him up. "Oh, I don't know. He's over eighteen."

"The next thing I know, he'll be reporting *you* for sexual harassment, Michelle." The waiter came and sat a glass of beer in front of me, and I handed him my credit card. "One round for everyone, please." The DJ was calling a middle-aged couple up to the microphone to do their rendition of *New York, New York* at the same time that Missy walked into the dark bar; scanning the scene for us. She wore jeans and the blouse from her suit but had discarded the jacket and took her hair down. She was even more stunning with her blonde waves flowing around her shoulders and the men in the bar, including those in my crew, all noticed her entrance.

"Yes, sir," the waiter said.

"See that young woman walking in?" I nodded in her direction. "Add her drink to the order, as well, please."

He nodded and left, and I stood and indicated the empty chair between me, and Liz.

It only took a few seconds for her to reach our side of the bar. The guys all stood as she approached. "Would you look at that?" Michelle murmured. "They're all acting like she's a brand-new toy at Christmas."

"Blame their dicks. They can't help it," Liz stated dryly. "Pathetic display of testosterone."

A dimple on one side of my face deepened as I fought to laugh out loud at Liz's sarcastic retort. She had a dry sense of humor that I found intensely amusing. Michelle giggled softly.

"What will you have?" I asked as Missy sat down next to me.

"Just a glass of white wine," she said softly and then repeated it more loudly for the waiter to hear over the sad wailing of the couple on the podium.

I couldn't help but notice the contrast between her and the other two women. The other two were pretty, but Missy was softer, finer... more beautiful, and I wasn't the only one to notice. There was an air of vulnerability about her which called out to my masculinity, despite her attempts to hide it. It was incredibly attractive. I sucked in my breath and reached for my drink.

Over the next couple of hours, various members of the crew came over to meet Missy and had short conversations with her, while Liz or Michelle were up singing or ordering more drinks at the bar.

I didn't move from her side all night, instinctively sensing her apprehension when some of the larger, more boisterous men sat down beside her. Even though outwardly, she appeared confident and secure, if aloof, the way her eyes glanced off of mine told me she was nervous. Suddenly, I found myself wanting to know why and I felt unnaturally protective. I had to remind myself that I barely knew her and if I knew what was good for me, I'd mind my own damn business.

It was getting late, and I glanced at my watch and met Missy's eyes. "Are you doing okay?"

Her striking eyes flashed up to mine. "I'm fine. Why?"

I half shrugged, reaching for the glass containing the last couple of swallows of my third beer. "Not sure. I sense you're a bit guarded."

She lifted her wine glass to her mouth and took a sip, and at the same time, she stiffened. "I'm fine."

It didn't escape my notice that everyone else had two or three drinks while she was still nursing her first glass of Chardonnay. Apparently, she wasn't ready to talk about it.

"Okay," I answered. "I'm going to head up. I still have some stuff to go over for tomorrow, and I'm sure you're beat. You had a three-hour head start on your normal day today, right?"

"Yes," Missy nodded gratefully. "I am really tired." She started to get up, but then sat down again, her expression indicating she was considering the implications of leaving with me.

"Liz and Michelle will be going up soon. I'll mention that I want them to walk you out."

Missy smiled; relief flooding her expression. "Thank you."

"My pleasure. See you at breakfast." I stood and threw a twenty on the table to tip the waiter and then said goodnight to the others. I walked up to where Liz was ordering drinks for herself and two other people. "Hey," I said, leaning on the bar next to her. "Can you walk Missy out of here? She's tired and wants to go to her room."

Liz looked at me pointedly. "She's a big girl with two perfectly good legs."

My eyes met hers, silently imploring that she do as I ask. I cocked my head to one side. "Can you just do it, please?"

"Why can't she go with you?" The alcohol was making Liz a bit indignant.

"I don't want people getting the wrong idea."

"Bullshit." She paid the bartender for her drinks and then I closed out my bill. "You don't want the other guys making a move. You've got your own eyes on her."

I shook my head with a bland look planted firmly on my face. "Wrong. I just want to fill my job so I can take the promotion, and I don't want these over-eager idiots scaring her off."

"Uh, huh," Liz said knowingly. "That's why you stayed so close to her all night."

"Right; to keep the idiots away. So, will you do it?" I gave her my best pleading look. "Please?"

"Okay, I'll do it." She picked up the drinks she'd ordered and turned away from the bar. "But you don't fool me with your weak-ass excuses, Jeffers. You're into her just as much as any other guy here. It's written all over you."

I met her eyes and cocked my head. My mouth flattened wryly as if to say, *please.* Liz's brows arched, and her eyes widened knowingly.

Yep, I was busted.

HER *last chance*
BEGINS
in his arms.

Chapter 5

Missy

It was hard to not like Jensen Jeffers; the past two days had proven that.

He was kind and considerate. He was handsome, funny, and smart. And, to top it all off; he was hot. I mean, really hot; the total package kind of hot. He was tall and built with broad shoulders, dimples, and dark blue eyes that seemed to look right through me and make my stomach flutter. He had an easy camaraderie with everyone, and it was clear that he was well respected. He led this group, even though there were producers and the director who were technically supervisors. I found myself wondering what kind of crazy his ex-wife was to let him go.

I was making a concerted effort to keep my cool demeanor around him, just as I did with all of the other men, but it wasn't as easy. Jensen picked up on her distant persona last night at the bar, and it unsettled me, only serving to reinforce that I had to be careful. He could read me, despite my efforts to keep everything inside.

His easy-going demeanor was comforting like my brother Ben's; just his presence alone set me at ease. The problem was, I was afraid to be at ease because then my guard would drop, and I might do or say something I shouldn't. I couldn't let myself get too comfortable with him, too soon.

As I watched him work, both in front of the camera and behind it, with men and women, my respect for him grew. He treated everyone the same, and I admired that greatly. I'd been around my share of arrogant assholes, who thought their looks, their contacts, or their money, gave them some sort of right to treat people as if they were insignificant or somehow beneath them. Jensen didn't have Derrick's money, but he did have all the rest of it in spades, and I couldn't imagine him ever acting so arrogant, uncaring... or violent.

I cleared my throat as I stood beside Eric, the cameraman I'd sat next to on the flight. He was filming Jensen during an interview of one of the Ram's defensive backs just before we finished up for the day.

At first, I blushed when we were in the locker room earlier in the day. Big, burly men were half dressed or completely nude milling around, but thankfully, during this interview, the players was dressed in their uniforms.

Michelle was in the booth getting ready for the live show, and Liz was chasing around making sure the teleprompters were working properly. They all had everything they needed all lined up before the game began. The technicians had the lights and the rest of the equipment wired and hooked up with power sources before we'd even arrived that morning.

I'd been with Jensen all day Saturday listening to the calming tone in his voice and the respectful way he talked, being surrounded by the incredible scent of his cologne, graced with the easy smile that was ever present on his handsome face. I wondered if I was overly sensitive because I hadn't been this close to a man, other than Ben, in such a long time, or he really was that amazing? Whatever it was, he was hitting me like a ton of bricks. Even my horrible experiences with Derrick couldn't make me put up my usual wall.

Even though my heart and instincts told me that every man wasn't as hateful as Derrick had been; in this man I had proof. The pain, bruises, and fear that I lived with day-in-and-day-out for years had me on guard with every man I'd met since my divorce, but something about Jensen Jeffers screamed safety… and that made my heart swell. I wanted to drown in my thoughts and let myself feel for him.

It was stupid. I hardly knew him, and yet, I wanted to trust him. I wanted to know him. I wanted to feel his arms around me. I found myself imagining what it would be like to kiss him. I'd never felt like this before, even in the early days with Derrick.

After we finished at the stadium, the entire crew ended up back at the hotel bandying around various evening plans. Some wanted to get dinner and crash, a few others wanted to go to a restaurant in Hollywood, but about half of the crew decided to go to Disneyland for the evening, including Liz, Michelle, Jeremy, and Eric.

"Hey, little lady," Eric said. "You gonna come along? Disney isn't just for kids, you know."

"Well," I glanced at Jensen and then back at Eric. "I'd love to, but my son would be heartbroken if I went to Disney without him." My shoulders lifted in a shrug and I offered an apologetic grimace. "He's always wanted to go there."

"Ah, no worries," he nodded. "I understand."

"Are you sure?" Liz asked with a smile. "It's a lot of fun."

I nodded. "I'm sure."

As the crew split off in groups only George Nelson, another of the career cameramen, Jensen, and I were left standing in the hotel lobby.

"Do you want to get dinner?" Jensen asked, of both George and I, using his thumb to point behind him at the door to the hotel. "Somewhere else besides the hotel? The food here is almost as bad as the karaoke singers."

An easy smile slid over my mouth. I was inclined to agree. "Sure."

"George?" Jensen asked again.

George's dark gray eyes glanced between us, a thoughtful, but wise expression settling on his kind features. "Nah. I'm gonna get a shower and room service. Gotta call the wife, or she'll divorce me for sure." He patted Jensen's upper arm and nodded at me. "You two kids have a nice time." With that, he walked off toward the elevators and left the two of us standing in the lobby.

"Do you want a shower first or should we just go?" Jensen looked at me expectantly, but I had no idea how early we had to be back at the stadium the following day. The one thing I did know was that I needed to call Dylan before he went to sleep.

"I'm not sure?"

"If it's okay, I'd rather just go and then come back and crash."

I wanted to tease him about getting his beauty sleep before going live on-air the following day but thought better of it. "Sounds good. I wanted to call my son, later."

Jensen nodded with a twitch of the corner of his mouth. "Honestly, that's why I want to get back early, too. I was too late to speak to Remi last night."

"Wow, we're pathetic." There was another thing about Jensen that put him head and shoulders above Derrick. He actually cared about his child.

Thud. My heart slammed into my ribcage. He was miraculous.

"Hmmph!" Jensen snorted and ushered me outside. "Honestly, I can't imagine being any other way."

It was a lovely fall evening. The southern California climate made the air warm, but the season kept the humidity down. Jensen hailed a cab, and we both got inside. "Better than those forensic vans," Jensen murmured as we settled inside. "L.A. is teaming with black SUVs, limos, and vans."

"Where to?" The cabby looked over his shoulder and smiled brightly at me, showing some badly decayed teeth. My eyes widened involuntarily, but then I looked away.

"Uh… um?" I shrugged and looked at Jensen.

He looked down at his jeans and his white polo emblazoned with the orange ESPN logo and grimaced. "Shit, I guess I should have figured this out." He used both hands to point to his shirt. "Well, considering our fetching attire, I'd say somewhere casual. Tacos and beer?"

I loved Mexican food, so his choice suited me fine. "Sounds good."

"Revolutionario, please," Jensen told the driver, and in seconds we were pulling out of the hotel driveway. "If you like Mediterranean cuisine, you'll love this place. It's a hidden gem. Casual, but the food rocks."

"I love!" the cab driver added enthusiastically. Many of the cabbies in the bigger cities were from other countries, but I couldn't place his accent. "Very, very good!"

"Mediterranean?" I asked. "Tacos?"

"Yes. It's northern African. It's sort of a cross between traditional tacos and Indian or Middle Eastern cuisine."

"Sounds interesting."

"Trust me. It's really good."

His happy enthusiasm was contagious, and my stomach rumbled. The restaurant was less than a mile from the hotel, and I got out and waited while Jensen paid the driver. I was looking forward to this time alone with him. It was the first and only time during the weekend that we could talk without others listening in.

He held the door to the restaurant open for me as I entered, and an incredible aroma hit my nostrils. I couldn't quite place it, but it smelled delicious. We walked up to the counter and ten minutes later had the meal ordered. There were all kinds of exotic teas and drinks, and I chose a loose leaf brewed iced tea before Jensen ordered some strange-sounding beer I'd never heard of.

"Do you want to eat inside or out?" He paused and waited for my answer, carrying the tray full of food. The restaurant was cozy and had small pictures on the walls of what I could only assume were regulars and also scenery from the parts of the world the cuisine originated. "There's a small patio on the west side. It's nice at sundown."

"Sounds perfect." I followed him to the door, but he held it open with one hand so I could precede him through it, while still balancing the tray on the other.

It was early Saturday evening and there were several people sitting outside on the patio, but the inside of the restaurant was pretty packed, too. We choose a small table on the edge of the patio by the short iron fence that went around it.

He was a perfect gentleman, setting the tray on the table and then coming around to pull out my chair and scoot it in again once I was seated. As I watched him, I couldn't help but note all of the contrasts between him and Derrick. Besides the obvious physical differences of his more polished exterior, dark hair, and slimmer build, or the classic handsomeness of his features, it went deeper. Jensen was always smiling, and it went all the way to his eyes. He was kind to people and undemanding.

I smoothed the napkin across my lap, wishing I was dressed in anything other than jeans and my ESPN T-shirt complete with press pass hanging from the lanyard around my neck.

Jensen placed my chicken tacos and tea in front of me, and

then his barbacoa beef burrito and beer on the table near him. He was obviously waiting for me to pick up one of my tacos before he would begin eating. He nodded at my food and smiled. "Scared?"

"No. It smells great." I picked up one of them and took a bite. My eyes opened wider as the flavor of tandoori chicken, yogurt sauce and cilantro burst on my tongue. "Oh, my God! It's so good!" I said, covering my mouth with the back of my hand, embarrassed that I'd spoken with my mouth full. If I'd done that in front of Derrick, I would have gotten a beating. Instead, Jensen was grinning at me.

"I know, right?" Jensen gathered up the huge burrito to take a bite. He studied me carefully while we both chewed, clearly considering his words until he swallowed. "Listen, you did a good job this weekend."

The corners of my lips curved upward. Praise from Jensen mattered. When Derrick complimented me on something I'd done, I felt more like he was patting me on the head like a dog who had obeyed. With Jensen, it meant he sincerely thought I'd done well. I could see it in the admiration and respect behind his eyes. "Does that mean I get the job?" I asked boldly, reaching for my glass of tea to take a sip from the straw. The whole time, I couldn't take my eyes off of him.

Jensen put down his half-eaten burrito and grabbed his beer, leaning back in the chair. "If it were up to me, you would, but Bryan will probably want to do a screen test, too. Are you ready for that?"

A shiver ran through me at the intensity of his gaze. "I think so."

"I know so. You'll be fine." He raised his right eyebrow, and he nodded in affirmation.

My heart started hammering against my ribcage and actually skipped a beat. "If I pass, it will be this team, right?"

"Yes." He took another swig from the longneck beer. "Can I ask you something?"

My breath hitched and stopped before I inhaled deeply. "Of course."

"Why the hesitation about being in front of the camera?"

Here it was. Should I tell him? My instincts told me to spill everything but letting someone know all of my darkest fears, made me feel very vulnerable. It would bring him into my world, if only at the margins, and even if we did work together, he couldn't be in my life like that. I couldn't *let him* be; even if my mind and body were screaming for me to let down my walls. And if I did, would that look of admiration in his eyes change to disgust?

My brother pointed out that if I didn't want to spend my life alone, I had to trust another man eventually. Ben saw some of the bruises, but he didn't know about the concussions or the broken bones, or how many times Derrick had raped me. He didn't have the full picture of what had happened, so he didn't understand how deep the scars went. I didn't want anyone to know the whole truth because I was concerned that it would make them look at me or treat me differently.

Jensen didn't miss my hesitation. "Sorry, if it's too personal. I'm just trying to understand your hesitation."

I swallowed so hard, my throat hurt. "It's okay. Without getting into too much detail, it's because of my ex-husband. We didn't have a great divorce."

Understanding dawned on Jensen's face and then his brows dropped over his eyes in a frown. "Does he see your son?"

I shook my head. Suddenly, I'd lost my appetite. "No. He hasn't for two years."

I could see Jensen's chest rise as he took a deep breath and then carefully set his beer back on the table by the basket containing the remnants of his food.

I might have just blown this job. Technically, ESPN couldn't discriminate based on my marital status or personal life, but Jensen was a model father, and he might think I was keeping Dylan from his dad. "Um," I stammered. "I mean…"

"He doesn't know where you are?"

"No, he does," I answered quickly. "In Jackson Hole."

Jensen was quickly putting the puzzle together in his mind. I could see it unfurl.

"So, he doesn't want to be a father to your son?"

Relief flooded me when he didn't automatically blame me.

"Well," I started wringing my hands that were now lying in my lap. "He does, but Derrick is not the kind of father I want for my son," I blurted awkwardly.

"I see." Anger flashed darkly across his face. "Clearly, it's an uncomfortable topic. I'm sorry; I didn't mean to pry." I was certain he was wondering what happened or in what way I thought my ex was not suitable for my son. "I just don't get men who don't step up for their kids."

"After my divorce, I moved in with my brother in Wyoming. We've always been close, and he and Dylan adore each other. He's a solid role model, and it was the best I could do for my son at the time." I sat up a little straighter in my chair, feeling a little defensive. "I'm sorry if that changes your opinion of me, but it doesn't inhibit my ability to do this job."

He huffed out a disgusted laugh. "I know that, and no, it doesn't change my opinion. I have a lot of respect for you. I can't imagine any man not doing everything he can to be with his child."

I was going to lay it out with as little words as possible, so as not to expose too much. I didn't want him to hold my past against me, nor did I want it to be the reason he hired me. "Derrick is a self-absorbed bastard and saw his wife and child as an extension of himself. He took us out like trophies when it suited him and otherwise, we were to fade into the background. He was overly strict, and he frightened Dylan. As a mother, I had to take him out of that situation. I'd do it again. I'd do it a hundred times."

A knowing look settled onto the face of the gorgeous man across from me. "So, you don't want to be on camera because then your ex-husband will know you've moved away from your brother."

"Yes. Ben is well connected in Jackson Hole. Derrick hasn't tried anything there." I didn't think I needed to get into the details of the confrontation that led to my restraining order.

"There wasn't a visitation order written into the divorce decree?"

I shook my head. "No. I had a restraining order against him."

"Was he… abusive?" His voice was concerned so it encouraged me to answer honestly.

"Yes. To both of us."

"Holy hell," Jensen huffed. "I'm sorry. I shouldn't have asked." Concern returned to his eyes. "I can try to get Bryan to put you on the production staff instead, but the salary isn't as good. It would be an hourly wage."

"No. The sportscaster position is fine. It's a new start for Dylan and me, and I can't continue to run from Derrick forever."

"As you see, there's a lot of traveling. Who will watch your son?"

"You know, technically, you can't ask me this kind of thing."

He shrugged and picked up his beer. "Yeah, I know, but I have a kid, and I can relate. Remi is the reason I'm changing jobs. I didn't want to be out of town so much. I'm not asking because your answer will affect my recommendation to Bryan, but I know how difficult it can be to leave a child behind week after week, and I'd understand if you want to reconsider. You need a safe place for Dylan, or you'll be miserable."

"I'm hoping my mother will move to Atlanta. She lives alone in Tallahassee, so hopefully, it will benefit everyone."

"Sounds like you've got it worked out." He picked up his burrito and took another bite while I did the same with my taco.

"Yep." I wanted to ask him about his situation with his daughter. He wasn't wearing a wedding ring, and so he must be divorced, too. I remembered my conversation with Bryan Walsh about him commuting to and from Bristol once a week, so did he share custody of his daughter? I found myself wanting the answers but decided it was none of my business.

The first order of business was getting hired, and the only thing that sucked about it was that the man across from me was probably going to be my boss. For the first time since my divorce, I felt like I wanted to get to know a man; one who had all the qualities I thought I'd found in Derrick, and who made me feel that I could trust him; but I worked with him, so he was off limits; at least, he should be. I wasn't sure I was ready for a man in my life or Dylan's, but if I was, I could only pray for one as good as Jensen Jeffers.

***

The next day pre-game, I couldn't stop thinking about dinner the previous evening or the dream I'd had afterward.

Oh, my God, *the dream.*

The rest of the meal was spent without stress and filled with conversation about ESPN, Jensen's history with the company, his experiences in the job I would have if hired, and the basic rules of football. He said he'd put together a cheat sheet with all of the game rules and the stats of the leading players in the NFL. I'd half-assed suggested that I would need a new cheat sheet weekly, to which he'd quickly agreed. He was a complete gentleman, with only gentle flirting, so what in the hell made me have a dream like that?

I'd gotten back to my room just in time to call Dylan and tell him a story over the phone, but the rest of the evening was spent packing and then lying in the dark thinking about my dinner companion, and hopefully my future boss. Sure, he was a genuine, and an all-around nice man, but he was sexy as hell; the kind of hot that went way beyond physical beauty, and all the way to the soul.

I imagined an intense connection was possible with Jensen and so sex with him would be intense. I wasn't sure how I knew, I just knew. As much as my subconscious tried to lump him in with the typical stereotype that kept men at arm's length, I couldn't manage it. I was thinking about him in ways I hadn't thought about a man in a long while, but I wasn't prepared to dream about him. Especially, not *that* kind of dream.

I hadn't had a sexual thought about a man in what seemed like forever, so I wasn't ready for the level of arousal I felt when I was around him, or when I just thought about him. After Derrick, just the thought of sex with anyone had been abhorrent. Jensen's gentle, unobtrusive teasing had me thinking things I'd been afraid to consider, and there was an invisible, yet tangible, pull between us. It didn't hurt that he was gorgeous, but I'd come across many attractive men in the two years since my divorce, and none of them had this effect on me. My heart desperately wanted to trust him, to believe a man could actually be as good as he seemed, and to let him close to me.

Admittedly, I wanted him, or I wouldn't be all twisted up in knots. The dream had been incredible, the kind of super-hot sex hardly any man can live up to; the kind of sex that bonds hearts and forges intimate, unbreakable connections. Even now, recalling how I felt when I woke made my whole body ignite with heat and my stomach get all fluttery.

It started out so soft and subtle.

Jensen's fingers traced gently over my body; down my arms, up my legs and slowly kneaded the muscles of my butt and back; coaxing out a response, relaxing me, and making me trust him.

"I've wanted to touch you like this, to make slow, sweet love to you since the very moment I laid eyes on you, Missy." His sexy voice dripped over me like warm honey, making my body surge under his fingers and my head lift toward his, begging for his mouth to take mine. "You're so incredibly beautiful. Say it's okay."

I closed my eyes, letting my thoughts wash over me, and swallowed at the emotion welling in my throat. Just thinking about it had my body reacting.

The touch of his hands was electric; sending shivers and goosebumps rushing over every inch of my skin. His hot breath washed over my cheek and down the cord of my neck as I arched it to one side giving him the access he wanted. Jensen nuzzled and kissed his way down to my shoulder and then my breasts lavishing slow attention designed to titillate. I was awash in sensations, scents, and sounds. My body was vibrating in anticipation of what was coming; of having his body thrusting into mine.

"It's okay," I breathed out. I wasn't sure how we got there, but we were already in my bed, and I longed to touch him; to run my fingers over the curves of his muscles and the hardness of his broad shoulders, to cradle his head and let him know how badly I wanted him to kiss me. I was starving, but as he continued to explore my body, ghosting over the curve of my breasts, barely touching my nipples through my silk chemise. Barely a touch, but it had the desired effect. I was dying for more. "Uhhhhh," I sighed out. "Jensen, please. I want to touch you."

He shook his head. "Not yet." His low whisper was like a current that ran through me and ended at my clit.

The tips of his fingers traced the soft swell of my breasts, moving along my collarbone and over my shoulder, then down my arm as his mouth opened against my neck in a soft, sucking kiss. Long, languid movements joined deep, slow kisses; more intimate than any I'd ever experienced.

"Please," I begged again, turning my head so when he lifted his head his mouth was hovering over mine. "Please."

He moved slowly, taking my mouth in a deep, passionate kiss. His tongue played with mine, teasing it to join its intimate dance at the same time as his hand ran down the side of my body, over the side of my breast and rib cage, over my hip.

I wanted to get closer, to feel him over me, dominating me in his amazing gentle way. I could feel my body spreading; opening as the kisses got deeper. Jensen used his knee to gently nudge my legs apart, pulling his mouth from mine to concentrate his kisses on my breasts, his tongue making slow circles around first one nipple, then the other. My back arched, and I was acutely aware that Jensen was between my legs, yet, hovering above me. The distance between our bodies screamed as one hand pushed up the pink silk of my nightgown until he exposed the matching string bikini panties and my stomach above the waistband.

"Jesus," he breathed against my skin, kissing and laving this tongue along the top of my panties. He was driving me crazy, and my hands fell into the silky strands of his hair. His hot breath rushed over the skin below my bellybutton, and he rested his forehead on my ribcage. He was holding back, and I could feel it. My body arched of its own volition, wanting... seeking anything to assuage the throbbing ache deep inside me.

Finally, he moved above me, his eyes full of glittering intensity in the darkness. I slid my hands up his arms as he braced himself over me, reveling in the feel of him. He was so strong, but, somehow, he was as vulnerable as I was.

"I want you, Melissa." His use of my full name in that guttural tone was perfect. This was serious, and we both knew it. The gravity of it hung in the air between us like a thundering calm before a violent storm. Our eyes locked as I kneaded his flesh with my willing fingers and I hooked one heel behind his thigh, exerting enough pressure to let Jensen know what I wanted. I felt wanton, wanting to give pleasure to him, knowing he'd give more than he took. I felt safe in giving myself. I licked my lips and nodded. "Yes."

His brow dropped. "Are you sure?"

"Yes." Admitting it was as if I'd set myself free. I was flying in this man's arms. I moved the sole of my foot up and down his muscled thigh, as my fingers fluttered down his back and pressed harder into his naked ass. "I want you, too."

He bent to begin an onslaught of kisses, each one deeper than the last. His mouth played, teased and sucked on mine for what felt like forever. When he finally pushed his tongue deep inside the recess of my mouth, I sucked it in further loving the taste of him. He was as delicious as I knew he would be. Jensen groaned and brought his body down on mine, fitting perfectly into the cradle of my body. The feel of his hardness pushing against my soft, moist folds was exhilarating. I wanted him in a way that I'd never wanted a man in my entire life. My body craved his, yet he took his time teasing my body with his erection, nudging and hinting at the pleasure to come. Our kisses became more passionate, and my fingers pulled at his arms and shoulders to bring him closer. We continued to move together; the friction building, and the tension growing until I was gasping. Both of us knew where it had to lead.

It was like we were two kids making out in our parent's basement, so anxious for our first time together. I didn't know where we were, and I didn't care. My world was filled up by this beautiful man whose fingers, mouth and body brought me to the brink of orgasm and had me begging him to take me. "Jensen..." His name was like a prayer on my lips.

"Uh uh. I want to make it good for you." His words rolled over me like a warm wave. His fingers slid down my torso and into my panties.

My legs fell further open as he parted my slick flesh. I was ready for him, but his fingers moved in small circles until I was panting and arching upward. "Mmmmm," I moaned. The building was slow and purposeful, and I knew the orgasm at the end of it would be the hardest I'd ever had. I was going to come; my heart ready to burst at his unselfishness and utter tenderness. Never had a man touched me with such reverence.

I woke up to the ringing of my phone. I was disoriented as I sat up in bed, with my body throbbing. I huffed in frustration and fell back on the pillows back into my sex-craved stupor. I cursed the phone until I realized it might be Dylan. It wasn't. It was my mom, and I punched the pillows, angry that she disregarded the three-hour time difference and interrupted the delicious conclusion I was craving.

For so long, I'd been terrified to be with a man, and I'd deliberately sabotaged any possible relationship. Several of Ben's friends had asked me out over the past two years, but I wasn't ready, and now I was finally completely attracted to someone, and it couldn't happen. Except in my dreams. It was cruel irony, and it was not lost on me.

Just like the day before, I was following Jensen around, listening to every word he said, but today, my body was buzzing the entire time. It was to the point of getting uncomfortable, and I was sure lust was written all over my face. *Damn dream*, I cursed.

At the moment, he was speaking with the Rams quarterback, Jared Goff, asking him how he was getting along with the new offensive coach that the Rams had recently hired. It was clear that the two men knew each other and might even be friends, but the minute the camera started to record, Jensen was all business. Goff was an all American kid; clean cut, tall and blond, but my eyes were glued on Jensen; polished perfection in his suit and tie, his hair perfectly in place and the make-up for the camera giving his complexion a bit more color under the lights.

I watched him interview some of the other players the day before, but today it was only the one-on-ones with the quarterbacks and coaches from both teams that needed completion before the game. The rough film would be rushed over to Michelle who would then edit it and get it ready for airing. At the same time, the rest of us went up to the booth to get situated for the live game. Michelle spliced everything together at the speed of light, adding graphics, player stats, and lead-ins where necessary. That girl was amazing at her job, and I was in complete awe of her.

The previous night at dinner, Jensen told me that ESPN had a booth at every major sporting venue in the country, but the cameras were operated across the field, and all edited live from the board in the booth. It was a lot to take in, but these people all worked together like a well-oiled machine. It was clear that whoever took Jensen's place would have big shoes to fill.

Sitting next to Michelle and Liz in the booth, I watched the game on the monitor. It was no different than watching the ESPN feed live on the network. Listening to Jensen and his partner, Jarvis Mills, commentate throughout the game, it was clear they had a distinctive rhythm and in-depth knowledge of the players and the rules; surely more than just the cheat sheet version. I'd have to learn fast if I landed this job. I didn't want to get fired soon after for lacking the skills. My heart sank. I was sure that I was smart enough to learn everything but wondered if I'd be able to get up to speed quickly enough, or whether I'd have as much passion for the sport that these two did. It showed in every syllable of every word they uttered.

It was just another reason I should be working behind the camera, not in front of it and I found myself wishing, again, that I could be part of this crew. Jensen said he would speak to Mr. Walsh about another job, but I realized I'd never have a chance like this again. Besides, another position might not pay enough to support Dylan, my mother, and me.

After the game, I'd be taking a plane from L. A. to Jackson Hole and Jensen would take a separate flight back to Atlanta to give his report to his boss, who would then decide if he was going to offer me a position. And what if he didn't hire me? Would I ever speak to Jensen again? My heart fell into the pit of my stomach, and I couldn't attribute it to excitement at being in the booth.

My head said I shouldn't care about the job offer, one way or the other. There would be other opportunities and maybe some without the worry of falling for my boss. *Sometime boss,* I reminded myself gratefully. I sucked in a deep breath as I watched the monitors where Jensen and Jarvis were discussing first downs, old injuries, punts, fumbles, recoveries, and mad-dashes to the end zone. I had my laptop out and was taking down notes as fast as my fingers could type.

"You know, the games are all recorded." Liz leaned over to mention. "You don't have to get it all down the minute it happens."

"I know, but I'm also taking notes on what's going on in the booth. There is so much to learn." Also, I hoped to keep focus and not let my thoughts wander to a more personal track about the man in front of the camera.

"If you get this job, all you'll need to remember is what goes on behind that desk and in the interviews. Keep your eyes on Jensen."

I gave an involuntary eye roll. As if I could help it. He was absolutely magnetic.

"Liz," I asked hesitantly wanting confirmation of Jensen's marital status. "He speaks of his little girl, Remi, a lot. Do you think his wife would be up for a play date for Remi and Dylan? I mean, if I get the job? He won't have any friends if we move."

Liz smiled. "Oh, I'm sure she would. Teagan's a peach, but they're not married, hon. Now, there's a long story, for ya!"

So, I was right. He wasn't married. I remembered the photo in his office of the little girl with Jensen, Chase Forrester, and a beautiful dark-haired woman, and realized she must be Remi's mother. A loud roar from the crowd in the stadium beyond the glass startled me and followed by a boisterous statement from Jensen.

"The Broncos fumble! Martinez snags it! The Rams

tailback recovers the ball and Martinez is off! He's at the forty, the thirty!" Jensen shouted. His enthusiasm made me smile. "Oh, my God! He's a rocket! This could be the game!"

"The Bronco's linemen can't catch him! Twenty, ten!" Jarvis Mills yelled. "That's it! Touchdown! The Rams come from behind to win it!"

The crowd in the stadium went wild for their home team, and I wanted to jump up and down and scream right along with them. I couldn't get into football from the living room sofa, but this was altogether different. Adrenaline was pumping through the veins of everyone in this booth. "This is fantastic!" I gushed to Liz.

"The Rams win 45 to 42 for another regular season win! This amazing play by Martinez coupled with some incredible passing earlier by Goff squeaked out the difference," Jensen said. "This is what I call a game!"

"Yes! We'll see how the Ram's management's investment in Goff's growth pays off for the rest of the season," Jarvis added.

The pair of them seemed like a Fred and Ginger in a sort of vocal dance, passing the verbal baton back and forth. I sat star-struck by the whole experience, as they wound up the end of the broadcast. As soon as it was over, Jensen stood and began yanking off his tie at the same time as he and Jarvis approached me at the back of the booth.

"So? What'd you think?" Jensen asked with a brilliant smile. His cheeks were flushed with excitement and his deep blue eyes sparkled. "Awesome, right?"

"Yes! I loved it!" I couldn't keep the elation from my own voice, or the shudder that ran through me at his nearness. He smelled so good; his heady cologne mixed with the clean scent of shampoo. "Though, I'm not sure I can do as well as you two!"

"This is Jarvis Mills," Jensen introduced. "You'll be working with him. Jarvis, may I present, Melissa Ellington?"

The big ex-football player extended a hand. He was easily six-foot-six, and two hundred fifty pounds, maybe more, with massively wide shoulders. He was the kind of guy you imagined would have a mass of hair growing on his back from his ass to his head, but like Jensen, his face was clean-shaven, and the hair on his head was well groomed. He was respectful, courteous, and athletic; though Jensen was leaner. Other than that, there was a night and day difference between them. I paused, letting his words sink in. Did he mean he was going to recommend me for the position?

"Nice to meet you, Melissa," Jarvis stated warmly. "I hope you get the job."

"Thank you, Mr. Mills. I have a lot to learn."

"Not to worry!" he said jovially. "We'll get you up to speed in no time, but call me Jarvis, Little Bit."

I smiled at the nickname. Jarvis was at least ten years older than Jensen and me, but his eyes were just as kind. Hope unfurled inside me. Maybe I'd be able to take this job and have the guidance necessary to succeed, and possibly Dylan and I would be safe surrounded by all of these people. There was still a part of me that said I had to proceed with caution and not be too trusting too fast, but I wanted this job; I wanted this life. I was excited at the possibilities opening up to me.

The rest of the afternoon flew by as we all packed up equipment and loaded everything into the vans that would take us all to the airport. The rest of the crew was all flying out on the same airline and leaving before my flight, so they were dropped off at United Airline's, first.

The driver got out as well as the new friends I'd made over the weekend, and I said my goodbyes to them amid their wishes of good luck. Many commented that they hoped they'd be working with me soon. Liz hugged me unexpectedly in a sincere expression of friendship. Jensen had said they were like a big family, and it felt good to be a part of it. I hugged her back; hopeful I'd see her again, soon.

When everyone was out and heading in, Jensen poked his head back into the sliding side door of the van. "Have a safe flight." His eyes met mine; it was as if he'd physically touched me.

I felt a sudden sadness come over me. "I will. You, too. Thanks for everything, Jensen. You've been great."

"If you have any questions; give me a call." We already had each other's phone numbers because we texted each other to coordinate throughout the past couple of days. He paused awkwardly.

"I will." Only the driver and I remained inside the van. My heart was heavy. My mind was already processing that if I didn't land this job, this could be the last time I'd see this incredible man.

"Call me," he said again.

"Sure. Let me know what Mr. Walsh says." I was trying to find an excuse for him to call me, too.

"Will do." Jensen winked, and reached into his duffel bag and pulled out a football, leaned in and handed it to me. "I had Jared Goff sign this." His eyes flashed up to mine. "I thought you might like to give it to your little boy. Kids always like presents when their parents go on trips. At least, Remi does."

My mouth fell open in surprise. Never, had Derrick done something so kind for my son. "That's…." My eyes burned with tears and my vision blurred as I took the ball from him. "Amazing. Thank you. I'm sure he'll love it."

"My pleasure. See ya, later." He flashed a brilliant smile and wink before sliding the heavy door closed. When it locked into place, Jensen hit the side of the vehicle with the flat of his hand and then walked into the terminal. I couldn't tear my eyes off of him as he disappeared into the building and the van pulled away from the curb.

Would I see him later? Oh, my God. My heart hoped so.

Chapter 6

JENSEN

I was sure of one thing; I didn't want to be Melissa Ellington's boss.

I didn't want her reporting to me because I was completely attracted to her and I didn't know if that was good, or if it put me in deep shit. I counted at least fifteen times I had a raging boner in the past two days.

I mulled it over as I made boxed macaroni and cheese for my dinner. My thoughts had been filled with Missy ever since I'd left her at the curb at the airport with her eyes glistening with tears. She was so fucking gorgeous. I surprised her with the ball for her son, and that pleased me very much. It meant that I'd be on her mind, just like she'd be on mine.

I wanted to make sure that Bryan offered her a job, but which one? I wanted to offer her my old correspondent position, but I wasn't sure if Bryan was going to put me in charge of that team on occasion or not. I couldn't supervise her if I wanted to date her. And, I did want to date her. I also had this protective vibe going on with her... I sensed there was more to her story; something that put her on guard with men and something that made her wary of the camera. I had to find out what it was that held her back.

Anger welled up inside without even knowing the extent of it. She admitted her husband had been abusive, but how badly had she been hurt? How badly had he hurt her son? As a parent, I couldn't think of anything worse. Hatred for the faceless bastard surged up inside me.

I'd offered Missy my number hoping she'd call me about the job and then I could delve deeper into getting to know her.

I dumped the absurdly bright orange noodles into a cereal bowl and left the wooden spoon inside the pan, setting it back on the stove. I took a beer from the fridge, a fork from the drawer, and made my way into the living room before forking up a bite of my mac and cheese.

I set the bowl on the coffee table and picked up the remote and flipped on the TV. This was a far fucking cry from my dinner the other night at Revolutionario with Missy. I'd gotten used to boxed dinners and frozen entrées the past few years when Remi was sick. Teagan and I spent most of our free time at the hospital, and other than laundry, we didn't have much time for the household chores. As much as I missed Remi, I couldn't say I was sorry that I was divorced, or that Teagan was now married to my best friend, Chase. Without Chase coming back to Atlanta and into all of our lives, Remi wouldn't be with us. He saved her life, and I was thankful for that. There was no way I could begrudge him anything then, or now. After everything, he was still the best friend I ever had.

Flipping through the channels, I was careful to avoid ESPN. I preferred to get away from the network, and sports in general, on my off hours. I continued to look for a movie to watch and finally landed on a classic; *Indiana Jones*.

Finishing my dinner, I took a swig of beer and leaned back on the sofa. I'd changed into old grey sweats and a white V-neck T-shirt the second I'd come home and settled in just as the movie began. I was tired, and laid down on the sofa, flinging an arm over my head. Indiana Jones had barely made it out of the cave with the giant rolling ball and was being chased by the Bushmen when my phone buzzed from its resting place on the oak coffee table. As I watched it move across the wood due to the vibration, I was tempted to let it go, but habit made me reach out and pick it up. Glancing down, I saw that it was Bryan. I should have expected him to be impatient and not wait until the morning to talk. He'd want to ask me about the weekend.

"Hello?"

"Are you back in Atlanta, yet?" There was a lot of noise in the background of the call, like people milling around and glasses clinking. He didn't give me a chance to answer his question before he was firing off the real reason he called. "How'd it go with Melissa? Do you think she'll be a good addition to the team?"

"Um…" I hesitated and swung my legs over the edge of the sofa to sit up, leaning over my knees. "She seems capable, and she fit in well with Liz and Michelle."

"But not the men?" He huffed in agitation. "That figures. Jesus Christ."

"She was fine. Just a little cool when a couple of them got a little over-zealous." I ran a hand through my hair, not wanting him to rush to judgment, though I had to be honest. "Jeremy came on a bit strong, and she was a little put-off. Her guard came up."

"Fuck! If she can't handle that skinny kid, then the big boys of the NFL will eat her for lunch, not to mention the sports agents. Those bastards are like vipers."

"It's not that she couldn't handle him." I searched for words to tell him exactly what I meant. "The girls on this crew are used to the crassness of the comments from some of the guys and take it all in stride. I can't tell yet how Missy will react to them. She didn't go crazy or freak out; she just shut him off."

"Missy is it?" he asked slyly.

"It suits her much better than Melissa."

"She seemed professional enough, but if she can't deal with the field assignments, then—"

"She'll deal with it," I shot back. I found myself defensive of this woman who I barely knew. "You should hire her, but I don't want her under me."

There was a significant pause from my boss, and I cringed when I realized what I'd just said and how he was inferring it.

"Or, maybe you do want her *under you*, in another way. You're no different than Nielson, eh?"

Bryan was my friend as much as he was my boss, so I felt I could speak my mind despite the sensitivity of the subject matter. "I'd have to be blind not to be attracted to her, but I'm patently aware that it's inappropriate to date someone who works for me. Besides, if you think that about me, maybe I should find another job." I was irritated; irritated by assholes, who through their behavior, made life hell for normal guys, and irritated that Bryan would put me in the same bowl of bad apples. "You know me better than that."

"I get it. So, you don't want her to be a direct report," Bryan said, astutely.

"No." I was torn. I wanted to be around to fend off other male attention if needed, but I wanted to get to know her on a more personal level than the work environment allowed. "I don't."

"Well, I guess you won't have to produce for your old team, though I thought you might like to. I can't promise I won't assign you two together on occasion, here or there, if I need you. It depends on the workload and circumstances, but J, even if you work at the same network, you could be putting yourself in a precarious position. While most of these harassment reports are legit, a few could be a spiteful accusation with nothing to back them up. You can't be too careful, and you don't know her yet."

"I understand, but I don't think Missy would report something that wasn't true. I sense a certain..." I searched for the words, "reticence in her."

"I see. So, you think she experienced some sort of harassment in the past?" His tone took on a cautious tone. "If that's true, maybe she's more likely to take an innocent comment out of context."

Bryan's generation may have taken a more relaxed opinion of what constituted harassment and what didn't, but either way, I'd make sure that I maintained a professional distance between Missy, and myself, until I could gauge her reaction to my asking her out on a date. Technically, we shouldn't even be having this conversation. I didn't even know how we got on this subject other than I didn't want to be her direct report. I had to tell him the real reason, or he'd think I considered her challenging to work with and then he might not offer her the job. Either way; I was screwed. If I kept my mouth shut and sang her praises, Bryan would have assigned her to work with me more often, and I didn't want that. While I'd welcome the chance to work with her occasionally, I didn't want to be her boss.

"I think Missy can tell the difference between a casual remark made out of sincere admiration and a lecherous dick making a move. Basically, the guys need to treat all of the women with respect—end of story. Most of them do. Lonnie was the only one who came off as obnoxious, and I handled him. Jeremy was just over-eager, and she handled him."

"Lonnie has been a problem for some of the other women, too."

"He's a fucking moron."

"It's not like the old days when a guy could tell a woman she looked nice, and that was that. Now, I'm afraid to compliment any woman I work with."

I nodded, even though Bryan couldn't see me. "Yes, well, it's a bit more than that, in his case. I could almost see the drool dripping from his mouth as he loomed over her trying to look down her blouse in my office. Why don't you do us all a favor and fire him?"

"I will; when I have someone to take his place."

"What about Jerry Stanley? He'd like to move up."

"He's not exactly on-air material, kid," he said dryly, confirming what I expected of his opinion.

I could see his point. "Okay. Just keep an eye out for Lonnie's replacement. I don't want him leering at the new hire."

"You keep your wits about you, too, Jensen," he warned.

"I will. Missy seems like she needs a few allies and then her confidence will come along, and she'll be a great addition to the network." I wanted to know what he knew about Missy from his interview with her. Maybe she confided more of why she moved to Jackson Hole. "By the way, what's her story?"

"She's divorced and has a kid," he said, sounding distracted. "Lives with her brother, and other than that; you saw her resume. Her references check out."

I rolled my eyes at his hesitation and took a pull from my beer. I knew that much from talking to her, myself. "And?" I probed.

"And?" He retorted incredulously. "You're kidding me, right? I spent an hour with her in my office; you were with her for two days. Surely you know more than I do. You should be filling me in!"

He was right. "Yeah, okay. Are you planning on offering her the job, then?"

"Yes. I'll make the call as soon as I can, but it won't be tonight."

"Good. Thanks."

"Okay, I gotta go. My wife is about to put my balls in a

vice. She's shooting daggers at me with her eyes. I'm at dinner with my in-laws, and she's pissed that I'm doing business at the dinner table, but God knows, anything to distract me from her father's snoring. Alice's mother expects everyone to fawn all over her constantly."

I laughed, finding it hard to picture Bryan fawning all over anyone. "I'll see you in the morning."

When I ended the call, I figured he'd call her early the next morning. I could look forward to going in to work the next day, cleaning out my office and moving to a new one on a different floor. Now came the part I hated: waiting. Would Missy accept the position?

Missy

"Mom!" My boisterous son and two of his friends came running like a herd of buffalo down the stairs of my brother's two-story home.

"What'd ya bring me, huh?" he asked as he barreled into my legs, hugging them briefly and almost knocking me over. His two friends followed closely behind him, only to stop short and hover in the living room. I smiled as Jensen's words echoed in my mind; *"Kid's always like presents when their parents go on trips."*

"Easy, cowboy!" I was excited by his exuberance! "Hello, Marcus! Hello, Joey!" I greeted his friends and then bent to wrap my little son in my arms. His blond hair was bushy as if he'd slept on it wet, but then I realized that was precisely what happened. I tried to smooth it down, and it popped right back into its previous position. How could I have forgotten that his Uncle Ben was in charge and would let him wait to take his shower until the last minute before his bedtime? It didn't appear to have been combed all day either, which was standard practice when he stayed alone with my brother. I ruffled the silky, overly long strands with my hand.

The bitter cold of Jackson Hole contrasted horribly with the moderate temperature I'd just come from in Georgia, and the wind whipped the screen door around with a series of wild bangs.

"Hey, sis!" Ben came out of the kitchen, wiping his hands on a white dishtowel and went outside on the porch to get my suitcases. "How'd it go?" His face lit up when he saw me lifting Dylan off the floor as I stood to hold him close and kiss his cheek. He was a healthy, growing boy, and I adored him.

I turned my attention to my brother who was standing opposite us in the entryway, as I held on tight to my son. "It went well, I think."

"Aw, Mom!" He wiggled in my arms, which only made me tighten them around him even more. "No mushy stuff in front of the guys," he whispered.

"Hold up, buster! I missed you!" I exclaimed, thrilled to see him. Dylan and I had never been separated overnight before I'd gone on this trip.

"Not in front of my pals," he implored, wiping at his face with the back of his hand, I assumed to wipe off any evidence that I'd kissed him. "Please?"

"Oh, okay," I said, kissing him soundly on the cheek several times again before setting his squirming form onto his feet again. "But you might not get your present if you keep that up!" I smiled down at him as he threw his arms around my legs.

"Did ya get me somethin' good?" His head fell back, and he beamed up at me, his cornflower blue eyes wide.

"Would I get you something bad? Let me get my bags up to my room, and maybe I'll get your presents after dinner."

"Presents?" Dylan was excited as he ran back into the living room where his friends were waiting. "Hey, guys! Did you hear? I got presents!"

"Something smells amazing!" I said after Ben had returned from taking my bags up to my room. I followed him into the kitchen and sat down at the small table there. The house was a small three bedroom, but perfect for a bachelor. He'd graciously offered for Dylan and me to move in when I'd needed him, and I feared it kept him from delving into an intimate relationship. He was my only sibling, and we were close, but I knew it was time to move out and give him his space.

"Oh, that's teriyaki chicken and rice," Ben said, winking. "I promised the boys Chinese."

"Mmm." I got up and went to the skillet and looked inside. His idea of Chinese and mine were two different things. Ben had rice boiling in another pan. "It looks like chicken and soy sauce," I said, with a wry arch of one brow; my skepticism clear. I wondered how it could smell that good with so few ingredients. I doubted he'd added any ginger or garlic. I opened the drawer with the silverware inside and took out a fork, intent on tasting a piece of the meat.

"Hush," he whispered with a grin and a shrug. "They won't know the difference. They're six."

I couldn't help but chuckle, realizing how much I'd miss my brother if I moved to Atlanta. Still, he had his dream of being a fireman, and I had mine. I wasn't content with living with my brother, and now that Dylan would be going to school full-time, it was time to get my life back on track.

"Not a drop of seasoning, Ben?" I asked as my suspicions were confirmed.

"Sure, it does. Soy sauce!" He grinned. "I figured you'd be home to take over." He unwrapped the towel he had tied around his waist and handed it to me. "So? Tell me all about it. Judging by your attire," he glanced at the ESPN logo on the left side of my shirt. "I'd say you've got the job."

His eyes were darker blue, and his hair a deeper shade of

blond than mine; more like Dylan's. I was thankful that when I looked at my son, I saw my brother and not my awful ex-husband. "Well…" I began as I tied the makeshift apron around my waist and opened the refrigerator to gather the small jars of chopped ginger and garlic I kept on the top shelf in the door. "If they offer me a position, it will be on-air."

My brother's jovial expression sobered. "On-air? I thought you applied for a production job?"

I nodded, adding small amounts of each spice to the pot. "It was, but an internal applicant landed it."

"Then, why did you have to go to L.A.?" He looked pissed. "Were they just jerking your chain? Stupid of them to pay for a plane ticket."

I gave a half shrug, adding garlic to the pan. "I don't think they had decided yet. This job is a traveling sportscaster position. They wanted to see how I fit in with the team and if the job would suit me." I stirred in the garlic and ginger and then gave it a taste. It was pretty much a hopeless cause at this point in the cooking. I shut off the heat and pushed the pot to one of the cool burners. Turning to my brother; I leaned one hip against the counter. "It was exciting, but I'd have to make sure Mom could come to Atlanta with me to watch Dylan when I'm out of town on assignments."

"Oh, boy," he said with a sigh, running a hand through his short hair and then leaning elbows on the table. "She might agree, but what about being out in the open? Derrick might find you, and I don't trust that cocksucker."

My eyes widened at his colorful description, but I resigned myself to my brother's hatred of my ex-husband. "I can't hide forever, Ben. I mean, I'm grateful for being here, but it's time for us to go. You deserve to have your house back."

"You could move out, but do you have to leave Wyoming? You can get a job at the Gazette."

"Doing what?"

"I don't know. Research? Writing?"

"Maybe, but it couldn't compare to the growth opportunities at a national network. ESPN offers a much larger future and Dylan deserves that."

"I don't know. Jackson Hole has a lot to offer. You might not start at the same level, but you never know where it could lead."

I groaned inwardly. "The senior staffers aren't going anywhere until they die, and you know it." My tone was droll, but the reality was, I was right. "No. If I want to advance, I can't stay local."

"He'll miss me," he said simply, but I knew Ben would miss my son just as much.

I put my hands up in front of me. "We're getting ahead of ourselves. I haven't gotten the offer yet."

"You will." Ben had unwavering faith in me and always had. He'd been the person I could always count on since we were kids.

I went to the cabinet and pulled down the plates. "Only two other boys?" I asked.

"Yup. Been here all weekend."

"Wow, Uncle Ben. You're ambitious!" I knew how exuberant three young boys could be. Marcus, Joey, and Dylan were practically joined at the hip and had been since they met on the first day of kindergarten. I'd offered to watch the other two boys for half days because their mothers worked, and it gave me some cash. I'd planned on getting a part-time job when Dylan started school, but couldn't find anything for just the mornings, and the situation worked out well. It allowed me enough money to contribute, at least a little, to my brother's bills and groceries.

"You're just lucky I had time off."

I nodded, smiling, as I set the table for five. "I know I am.

I'm sure you'll be glad to have some privacy. You'll be able to have women over."

"Hey" Ben protested. "Don't think I've thought of you and Dylan as a burden or a cramp in my social life. You know I'd do anything for you two."

I gave a short nod as I arranged the silverware around the plates. "I know, but it's time for you to have a family of your own. You're not getting any younger."

"Hey, now," Ben winked at me, filling five glasses with ice and then water from the filtered pitcher in the refrigerator. "I'm happy with things the way they are. I date."

"Uh-huh, right," I admonished. "A date here or there isn't what I mean. It's time you stopped using taking care of your little sister as an excuse to keep women at arm's length." He was a confirmed bachelor and liked the life he had, though I did wonder if he secretly longed for a committed relationship with a woman.

"Let's just get your life figured out before we start working on mine, okay? Boys! Dinner!"

"Yeah!"

"Whoo Hoo!" The hoots came as the three boys scrambled into the kitchen and pulled out chairs.

"Nothing motivates little boys like their stomachs! But, wait!" I stopped them as they came into the kitchen. "Have you washed your hands?"

Groans replaced their enthusiasm, and their expressions turned imploring; especially Dylan's.

"Okay," I motioned for them all to get up. "Into the bathroom with the lot of you!"

"Aww, Mom!"

I cocked an eyebrow and pursed my lips sternly. "No arguments." I shook my head, pointing both index fingers in a swooshing motion in the direction of the bathroom. "No dinner until you wash up. Germs are not on the menu! Go."

The other two were already on their way away from the table. I moved to my son and put both hands on his shoulders, bending down to whisper in his ear. "The sooner you have dinner, the sooner you get presents."

That did the trick. In a flash, he was running after his friends.

"What'd you bring him?" Ben wanted to know. He had the food on the table family style, putting a potholder underneath the hot pot so as not to scorch the wood of the oak table.

"An ESPN football jersey and a signed football. Jared Goff."

Ben looked incredulous and motioned like I'd shot him in the heart. "Ugh! You're killing me, Smalls! What'd ya bring your old brother?" he mocked. "A big goose egg, huh?"

My heart fell as I rushed to explain in a lowered voice. "Well, it wasn't really me who arranged the gifts."

"What?" Ben was curious as he pulled out a chair and sat down. I joined him as we waited for the boys.

"The commentator who I was trailing, Jensen Jeffers, got them for me."

"Yeah, I know who he is. He works with Jarvis Mills. They do a great job."

"Yes. Anyway, he said that kids always want presents when parents come home from trips."

"He's right. So do big brothers. Especially when they're signed balls."

"You have enough balls," I teased, tongue-in-cheek.

Ben shook his head, a wide grin splitting his handsome face. "Wrong, sis. A real man can never have enough balls."

* * *

Dylan had a bath and I got him ready for bed while he chattered on about his time with Ben. Dressed in his favorite Spiderman pajamas, and his formerly unruly hair freshly washed and combed into place, Dylan waited impatiently. I sat on the edge of his bed and pulled him onto my lap. My luggage, in my room next door, waited to be unpacked, but while Dylan had been brushing his teeth, I'd gathered the shirt and football out of the biggest one and wrapped them in a towel. The makeshift package waited on the bed next to us.

"Can I have my present now, Mom?"

He'd stopped calling me "Mommy" when he started school, and I felt very sad that he was growing up so fast, however, being around other boys and Ben had been good for him.

"Oh, okay," I said, smiling and pulled the towel-covered mound onto his lap. "Sorry, I didn't have time to wrap it."

"It's okay!" He pushed aside the towel to reveal the blue, white, and orange football jersey and signed ball. "Wow! Thanks! "Where'd ya get it?" Dylan could barely contain his excitement.

"A nice man named Jensen got them for me to give to you. Wasn't that nice?"

"Yeah, it sure was! I can't wait to show Uncle Ben and my friends! We can play like a real team!" His little face lit up, and his cheeks were still rosy from his bath.

My arms tightened around him, and I kissed his temple. "You might not want to play with that ball. Look." I carefully turned it over to show him the signature near the laces. "Jared Goff, the Rams quarterback, signed it for you. It's a collector's item."

"Oh, man!" he exclaimed. "Jared Goff! This is awesome, Mom!" He turned in my lap, still holding his ball. I didn't even know he knew who the quarterback was. "Can I collect a bunch of them?"

I laughed out loud. Leave it to Dylan's mind to race ten steps ahead. I touched the tip of his nose with my index finger. "We'll see. It depends if I get this job. You know it will mean moving away from Uncle Ben, right?"

He sobered for a minute, and I quickly went on to the positives.

"But, we'll be closer to Grandma, and we can visit Uncle Ben and your friends, and you'll make new friends, sweetheart."

His eyes filled with tears and he looked down at his lap. "I don't want to leave Uncle Ben. Who will play with me?"

Two fat drops tumbled down his cheeks, and I wiped them away lovingly. "Hey, let's not get ahead of ourselves. Mommy doesn't have the job yet."

"But you will," he cried, harder now. My heart broke for him. I wanted to provide a better life for him, but I never considered what moving away from Jackson Hole would mean for my son. After Derrick, he'd come to depend on Ben's kindness, unconditional love, and when needed, discipline.

"Well, if I do, you can still keep in touch with Uncle Ben and your friends. Maybe we can have them visit next summer, or you can come back here for a few weeks if we can arrange it. Uncle Ben will Skype with you all the time, and it will almost feel like he's with you."

"It's not the same."

"Well, let's cross that bridge when we get to it. If we do move, let's think of it as a new adventure!" I'd told him we were going on a big adventure as an explanation when we moved to Wyoming, too. "It's a lot warmer in Atlanta and *much* closer to Disney World. With a new job, I'll be able to take you there for vacation. Maybe Uncle Ben and Grandma can come, too."

He sniffed and wiped his nose on the back of his hand, all the while holding tight to his new football. "Okay," he agreed tearfully.

"And, if I work at ESPN, you have a much better chance of adding to your new ball collection because I'll be meeting many more players and teams." I touched the ball. "We don't have to decide any of this tonight. Now, into bed with you; you have school in the morning."

The room was furnished with an old bedroom set that Ben and I found at a flea market not long after I'd moved up here. We had to leave all of our belongings behind when we ran away from Derrick. It was old, but Ben and I had sanded and stained it to look like new.

Dylan slid off of my lap and walked over to his toy box and, as if it was made of glass, gently set the football on the top. I folded the shirt and moved across the small room to put it in the middle drawer of the dresser with the rest of his shirts. "Would you like to wear this to school tomorrow?"

"Sure." He nodded and his thick blond hair, now dry, moved with the motion.

"Up you go," I lifted him into bed and pulled the covers up, tucking them in around him. I leaned in to kiss his head, my hand cupping his cheek. "It's going to be alright. You'll see. Goodnight, honey."

I turned off the bedside lamp but left the light on in the hall and left his door cracked before going into to unpack my suitcase. I needed a bath, but I was exhausted. I turned on the lamp and sat down on the bed at the same time as a text came in on my phone. My heart flipped inside my chest. Somehow, I knew it was Jensen.

How'd Dylan like the football?

I smiled when I read it, and then didn't hesitate to type out a response.

Loved it, of course! Thanks, again.

I tried to begin pulling items from my roller bag, separating the dirty clothes from the few clean ones, but kept glancing at the screen, waiting for Jensen's response. I literally jumped at the next bling from my phone.

> **You're welcome. Have you heard from Bryan Walsh?**

The corners of my mouth lifted at the start of a soft smile as I typed.

> *Not yet. Is he going to call?*

> **If I told you that, you'd know you got the job. ;-)**
> **If you want it.**

A small laugh burst out as happiness filled me.

> *I do!!!*

> **Good. Start packing.**

I sucked in a deep breath of relief. Somehow, I'd ended up sitting back down on the bed as I wrote the next words.

> *Will you be my boss?*

Fear gripped me as I waited for his next text. It didn't take long.

> **Well... about that...**

Oh, my God. What did that mean? Didn't he want me on his crew? Was I going to work with that God-awful Lonnie person?

What about it?

Can I call you?

By now, my heart was pounding a hundred beats a minute. This didn't feel like a business conversation, and I wasn't sure if I was ready for it to be personal.

Yes. Just give me a few minutes to unpack.

NP. I'll hop in the shower and call you after. Will that give you enough time?

I closed my eyes. Just what I needed: to imagine Jensen Jeffers naked in the shower with water running down all that perfect flesh. The way his muscles flexed under his shirt on the plane was enough to cause a physical response in my body. I'd been watching him all weekend, and everything about him was attractive. He wasn't even near me, but after the dream, I had the night before, I was already flushing with heat. I pressed the back of my hand against one of my cheeks, and it was warm to the touch. I was in deep trouble.

Sure.

I sat there, excitement flowing through me; wondering if it was this man or just the fact that I hadn't had sex in years that made me go all gooey on the inside. I avoided sexy movies or books for what seemed like forever; I couldn't stand thinking about Derrick like that. But now, my face felt flushed with heat, and my body was opening at just the thought of him. I licked my lips. If this was how I was reacting to just a couple of texts, maybe not working with him was a good thing. I'd be hard-pressed not to picture Jensen all tan and bare-chested; wearing only a towel slung low on his hips when he called.

"Get a grip, Missy," I chastised myself aloud. "You're fine. You'll be fine." I got up and emptied the rest of my suitcase on the bed, folded the clean clothes and put the rest of the dirty ones in the hamper in the corner. "He just wants to talk to discuss work details."

But no matter what I told myself, I knew it wasn't true. I wouldn't be fine. Maybe I'd be better than fine. When the phone rang, I wasn't ready for it.

"Hello?"

"Hey," his smooth voice came over the phone, showing no hint of the nervousness I was experiencing. Even though we'd only spent the weekend together, his voice was familiar and soothing. "Whatcha' doin?"

"Um... I'm just putting my suitcase away."

"Don't put it too far away. You'll need it soon," he said. "Don't tell Bryan I spilled the beans."

I laughed softly. "Okay. So, you spoke with him, then?"

"Yes, and I gave a glowing report, but I wanted to talk to you before you get back to Atlanta."

I sank to the floor in the low light of the room. "I see. No screen test, then?"

"Nope."

"Will I be on your team?" I'd already asked on text, and felt sure he was about to tell me, but I couldn't help probing.

"Yes, you'll be on that team, but I won't produce for it regularly."

"Oh," I said, unable to hide my disappointment. "I guess I did know that the production job I applied for didn't travel much."

"Yes. Beyond that," Jensen stopped. "Look, I've never been good at beating around the bush, Missy."

"Then, don't." I pulled my knees up until I could wrap an arm around them. "You sound like you have misgivings about having me at ESPN."

"No, but I sense... Jesus, this is tough." His frustration permeated his tone.

"Sense... what?" I asked.

"A certain hesitance to immerse yourself in the team."

My back stiffened as my defenses came up like the clash of two steel swords in front of me. "You mean because I won't cozy up to the men?" I couldn't help my harder tone. After years of play-acting with Derrick, I pretty much let my feelings rip now. "I didn't think it was a job requirement."

"Whoa. It isn't. I'm asking, not for the team, but for me. I wanted to get to know you, but I don't want you to take it the wrong way. I want you to know there are zero strings attached, and I thought it might be easier to talk candidly if we weren't face-to-face."

"I see." I was hoping he was feeling the same attraction between us that I was, but instead, it appeared he wanted to give me a lecture on my attitude.

"I'm not sure you do, but I'm not going to lie. I find you extremely attractive myself, but from what I saw, you don't want... Oh, fuck!" Jensen exclaimed in frustration. "I won't do anything about how I feel if you aren't open to it. I'd really like to see you outside of work, and maybe introduce the kids. Dylan won't have any friends, and so I wondered how you'd feel about it?"

My heart suddenly resumed its thunderous hammering, and I felt ashamed that I'd doubted his intent. I'd completely jumped to the wrong conclusion. I sucked in a deep breath. "Well, you're right, my experience with my ex-husband may have made me a little sensitive, and I'm extremely cautious about who I introduce to Dylan. I'm sorry if I came off as a bitch."

"No. I mean, you weren't a bitch, but I sensed you had a red line, and that you didn't want it crossed. I figured it was because of him when you told me he was abusive."

"Yes, he was."

His voice was low, sexy, and intense, though I doubted he was even aware. "If you don't want to tell me about it, yet, I understand, but we've all got a backstory that makes us who we are. I hoped that maybe if I told you more about the situation surrounding my divorce, you'd feel more at ease sharing yours. That's if you want to hear about it."

I leaned back against the bed. "I would. I mean, I'd love to."

"Well, remember when you saw the picture in my office, then asked about Chase Forrester? I told you it was a long story?"

"Yes?"

Jensen cleared his throat. His voice was so close; as if he was sitting right next to me. "Well, we've been best friends for a long time. We both went to college at Clemson, and we both played on the soccer team. He was the star forward, and I was one of the goalies."

"Really? Were you any good?"

"Yeah. Not as good as Chase, clearly."

I laughed softly. "Obviously," I teased, trying to relax. This was good. Finding out about this man was right.

"We both met Teagan the same night; at a college party. The three of us were solid after that. Teagan called us 'The Three Musketeers', but Chase and Teagan fell in love."

"But I thought—"

"Yeah, that's the *long story* part of this whole thing. Chase got an offer from Arsenal in the middle of our senior year, and he left to go to London."

"How'd you end up married to her, then?"

"I'm getting to that, but Chase is Remi's real father."

Wow. What? "He is?"

"Yes. Teagan found out she was pregnant right after he left, and she had some dumbass idea that she'd ruin his chances for a professional soccer career if she told him about the baby."

"So, you married her? Like a knight in shining armor?"

"I'm not sure how shiny it was."

"Wasn't he coming back?" I asked incredulously. "Later, I mean?"

"Yes, but Teagan's father is an asshole politician, and he was more concerned about his career than he was his daughter's happiness. He never approved of Chase, and he knew what buttons to push to get Teagan to walk away from him. He knew she'd put Chase first, so he threatened to ruin his career before it even got started. The sun rose and set in Chase for Teagan, and professional soccer had been his dream since he was a kid. I tried to convince her to tell him, but she wouldn't. She knew if she told him the truth, he'd give up Arsenal."

"Why didn't you tell him? If you were his best friend?"

He sighed heavily. "You make it sound so simple. Chase's family lived in the area, and his dad and brother have a business that could have been impacted. Teagan didn't want a scandal."

"Scandal? A lot of people have babies without being married."

"This is the South, and her father is a U.S. Senator. Even so, I wasn't thinking straight. I cared about Teagan, and I was pissed at Chase; for leaving her to play fucking soccer. Soccer was all he wanted to do, but I thought she should have meant more; he should have waited for another opportunity after graduation so he could have taken Teagan with him."

My heart hurt for Teagan even though I'd never met her. "I agree, but you were all young. We all make stupid choices when we're young." *Look at me?* I thought. *I married the wrong person without taking the time to know him.*

"I guess," Jensen answered. "She cried and cried that she had to protect him, whatever the cost to herself. She wouldn't listen to me, so I went to her dad and told him the baby was mine and I'd do what was right by her. I thought I was saving Teagan's reputation and, at the same time, doing what I had to do to secure Chase's career."

"Wow," I murmured softly, stunned by the story I was hearing. "What did that do to your friendship?"

"It completely destroyed it. We couldn't tell him, or we would have had the result that Teagan didn't want; he'd quit Arsenal and hightail it back to the States. Later, I wanted to tell him, but he wouldn't listen to me, or even Teagan, when we tried to explain. I guess I didn't do such a good job of trying. But..." he paused to shrug. "I was wrong to marry Teagan behind his back."

Selfishly, I wanted to ask if he ever really loved Teagan, but his actions told me all I needed to know.

"So, he was gone when Remi was born, and you've been her father ever since," I stated.

"Yes, and I love her like she was mine."

The love in his tone and the catch in his voice brought a tear to my eye. I dabbed at the corner of my eye with my pinkie finger. "She is yours, Jensen. You raised her."

"Yeah. She went through a lot. Teagan and I were going to get a divorce when Remi was barely three, but then the poor little shit was diagnosed with leukemia. We decided to stay married to keep the insurance current during treatment. We wanted to keep her life as normal as possible. Teagan quit nursing to be with Remi twenty-four/seven, and I worked my way up the ladder at

ESPN, seeing Remi whenever I could. I missed her, and I was terrified she'd die while I was gone on assignment, but we needed the insurance and the money."

My breath caught as another tear fell. "Oh, my God. That must have been horrible. You're a good man, Jensen."

"I don't know how good I was. Over the next three years, Remi went through treatment twice and went into remission, but then the leukemia returned, again. Each time a patient falls out of remission, it gets harder to fight the disease. It was horrible to watch. She called the chemo 'mean medicine,' and we couldn't put her through it again. Her only hope was a bone marrow transplant, and Teagan wasn't a complete match. Even her bastard father tested, and he failed as well. We were running out of time waiting for a match through the donor registry."

"Oh, I see. So... you had to bring Chase back into her life. To see if he could save her?"

"Part of me was selfish. I didn't want to lose Remi, but Chase deserved to know about her anyway. As you can imagine, he was furious with both of us and hurt that we'd waited so long to tell him."

"Was he a match, though?"

"Yes, thankfully. She's completely cancer-free now, and he and Teagan are back together."

I held my breath waiting to hear the rest of the story. "How did Remi take it?"

"Remarkably well. Teagan told her that she had two dads from the time she could talk. Even showed her pictures, so she loves us both. To his credit, Chase has made changes in his life that kept Remi near me. He even left Arsenal and plays with the U. S. National Team. We're still friends, and we co-parent really well."

"Wow." I was blown away. Talk about a happy ending. "That's... an incredible story."

"I was worried she wouldn't love me anymore. Remi, not Teagan," he clarified with a huffed laugh.

I smiled that he'd made the distinction for my benefit. "How could she not love you? You're an incredible father."

"That's nice of you to say."

"Not at all. I can hear it in your voice when you talk about her, Jensen. I wish Derrick had been half the father to Dylan that you are to Remi."

"I want to hear all about it, but not tonight. Mull this over and when you're ready you can tell me your story, okay? No pressure."

"You're amazing, Jensen." I wanted to pinch myself. How remarkable he was, couldn't be real.

"But, you're afraid to trust me..." he responded, knowingly.

I wanted to tell him everything, but I was thankful for his understanding that I needed to take things slow. "I've been afraid to trust any man, except Ben."

"I sensed that, but don't worry; I'll convince you if you give me a chance. All I'm asking for, right now, is a play date. If you behave, we'll go from there." There was a teasing lilt to his voice that set me at ease.

I couldn't help but laugh out loud, and Jensen chuckled in return. This was the most carefree and light-hearted I'd felt in a long time. "Behave, huh? Sounds good."

"Good. Tomorrow when Walsh calls, act surprised."

I found myself reluctant to end the call. It was as if he'd lassoed me through the phone line and was pulling me through it. "I will."

"Goodnight, Missy."

"Night, Jensen. And, thank you."

As I put my phone on my bedside table, I felt anxious for the sun to rise and for Bryan Walsh's call so I could start making plans. My heart was full. After hearing Jensen's story, I realized good men did exist. I had real hope; for me, for Dylan; hope for a real future and a real life.

Chapter 7

JENSEN

It was Thursday night, and Missy was starting at the station on Monday. I was anxious. *Very* anxious.

In the two weeks that had passed since Bryan offered her the job, we'd spoken on the phone twice. I guess you could say we'd become friends because she confided in me by sharing a bit of her past with her ex-husband, Derrick. He had a general contracting company in Dallas, and she'd met and married him when she was very young. He isolated her by forcing her to quit her job at FOX and stay home, even before they had Dylan.

I already had a solid hatred brewing within me for that prick, though she hadn't told me the whole story yet. I sensed, by her hesitation, that the part she hadn't told me was terrible. I didn't press her and figured she'd tell me if, and when, she was ready. I could guess he was the typical abusive asshole; intimidate the woman, trash her self-esteem, make sure she has no friends, control everything, and make her think it's because she is at fault. Just thinking about it made me want to fucking kill something.

I wouldn't be there to welcome her on Monday because I wouldn't fly back to Atlanta until late Monday night after my show taped in Bristol.

"What's on your mind, man?" Chase asked. He noticed my preoccupation. We were having a beer in his backyard as steaks sizzled on the grill. They smelled amazing when he opened the lid to check on them. "Is it about your new gig?"

I glanced up from where I was sitting in one of the Adirondack chairs around the pool. It always amazed me how a simple wooden chair could be so comfortable. It wasn't the first time Chase and I hung out drinking beer and cooking steaks, but this time Remi was paddling around the shallow end with her inflatable arm floaties and having a marvelous time. Her laughter tinkled in the warm air, as the sky turned a brilliant lilac leading down to bright orange as the sun set in the west. Teagan was sitting close by, hip deep in water, on the steps leading into the pool.

"Nah. That's going well," I said, though I had only been at it a week. "It's a big change. I like not being in front of the camera, but there's a lot more to producing a show than just showing up and reading the teleprompter." I sat back, grinning, and lifted my beer to my lips.

"Look at me! Daddy! Jensey!" Remi called from the pool, dog paddling around in a circle. "I'm swimming!"

"Watch what you're doing, baby," Teagan admonished. Her swollen stomach was the only tell that she was pregnant. "Jensen, do you remember Norine?"

I nodded. "Yes. She was one of the nurses at the oncologist's office, right?"

"Yep. She asked about you today when I took Remi in for her six-month check-up." Teagan's expression turned teasing, and she nodded suggestively.

I grimaced; glad to have an opportunity to bypass the subject of Norine. "How'd it go?"

"All clear. She was so brave."

"We sang *Happy* while they poked me," Remi piped up

from the water. There were lights under the water in the sides of the pool to illuminate it after dark. "Even nurse Norine, except'n she sounded kinda funny."

"Maybe someday you won't have to have any more needle pokes, sweet pea." She always hated needles, and she'd had more than her share in her short life.

"What do you think about Norine?" Teagan persisted. "Would you want to take her to dinner next weekend? Or, maybe we can invite you both over here one night."

"Teagan, there's something extremely warped about my ex trying to set me up."

Chase chuckled and joined in with Teagan's teasing, flipping over the burger he was making for Remi. "It's not any more wrong than me cooking my wife's ex a steak, is it?"

We all laughed together. "I guess not, but I like you, and I don't like Norine."

To outsiders, my relationship with Teagan and Chase might seem strange, but we'd been through a lot together, and we were all focused on one thing; raising Remi and what was best for her. There might have been some bad feelings between us at one point, but we'd cleared the air and gotten on the same page.

"I'd just like to see you settled and happy, Jens," Teagan murmured, then redirected her attention at the little girl in the pool. "Come over this way, Remi. Stay away from the deep end."

"She's fine, babe. Jensen can jump in if something happens to her floaties." Chase's dry sense of humor was not lost on me, and I huffed out a laugh. "Seriously, J. You need to get out there." He loaded the cooked steaks and burgers onto a platter and brought them to the table, then went back to get the corn and potatoes roasting on the side burners.

"I'm interested in the woman who is taking over my old job at the network, so cool your jets."

"Yeah! Cool your jets," Remi echoed, continuing to circle

the shallow end of the pool. I laughed out loud as I went toward the pool and motioned for Remi to come to the edge so I could lift her out. "Time to eat, squirt."

"Goodie! I want a cheeseburger, please!"

"One cheeseburger, coming up!" Chase answered enthusiastically, grabbing a hamburger bun from the open package and using a spatula to load it with the freshly grilled meat dripping with cheese.

I could tell Teagan's interest was piqued when she stood and got out of the pool, grabbing the towel that was sitting beside her poolside, before wrapping it around her body and coming to join us at the table. "Really?" She poured iced tea into two glasses and added ice from the cooler sitting beside the table, reaching back in to lift out two more beers for Chase and me. "Has she already come to work there?"

I picked up my dripping child by her arms, holding her away from me until I could set her down by a chaise lounge where another towel was waiting. I removed the floaties and wound the towel around her little body. "She starts on Monday. I met her a couple of weeks ago when I had to take her on a test run. That trip to L.A."

"Tell us about her," Teagan urged, making Remi a plate while I sat her down in a chair between Chase's and mine. He came around with a hoodie and held it out for me. Without a word, I took it and held it while Remi slid her arms into the sleeves. "Chase, there's another towel over there. Put it over her legs. It might get chilly now that the sun has set." When it came to Remi, we were like a well-oiled machine.

"Jensen?" Teagan asked again. "Where's this mystery woman from?"

I proceeded to relay what I knew about Missy to my friends, telling them about her roots at the FOX affiliate in Dallas and then her move to Wyoming to live with her brother following her divorce. Purposely, I left out what I knew of Missy and Dylan's suffering at the hands of her ex-husband. It wasn't my place to share.

"She has a little boy about Remi's age. I thought it would be nice if they could play together."

"Maybe Teagan can help them get settled," Chase suggested, cutting off a piece of steak and forking it into his mouth.

"Missy asked my advice on a temporary place to stay until she found something, but I don't think she has much money because she hasn't really worked in the past couple of years; outside of babysitting some of her son's friends in the afternoons after their morning kindergarten. I think she plans on leaving Dylan in Wyoming for at least a few weeks until she's settled."

"Why don't they just stay here until they find a place? We've got plenty of room," Chase suggested. "That's if you trust her."

"I do, but…"

Teagan's face lit up at her husband's suggestion. "That's a wonderful idea, babe! Then she can bring her little boy with her! I'm home all day, and he can go to school and playgroups with Remi."

"Is he mean like Nolan?" Remi piped up, picking out an extra browned piece of potato and moving it to the edge of her plate. She wrinkled her nose and pursed her lips in a pout.

"Remi, I'm sure this little boy is very nice," Teagan said. "He doesn't have any friends yet, so wouldn't it be nice to make him and his mommy feel welcome?"

She nodded and took a bite from her burger. "Okay," she said with her mouth full. It was clear that her time in the pool had worked up her appetite.

Once again, Chase and Teagan amazed me. "That's

extremely generous, but I'm not sure she'd accept." I scooped a pile of potatoes onto my plate next to the ribeye Chase had grilled to a perfect medium rare.

"Why not?" Chase asked.

"She's proud. She didn't share that she was low on funds, I'm just assuming. I'm not sure how to bring it up without seeming presumptuous."

"Well, you don't have to mention anything about money!" Teagan insisted. Her long brown hair twisted into a topknot, and she didn't have any makeup on. "You never know until you ask. If she's new to the area, I can help her look for a place."

"She might get piss—" I stopped at Teagan's stern look. "Uh, she might get upset if I start making decisions for her, but she probably does need help."

"She's a damsel!" Remi said simply, with a little shrug, before diving into her burger again.

My eyes locked with Chase's and then flashed to Teagan. We all grinned at the wisdom of our daughter, trying hard not to laugh out loud while continuing with our meal.

My little Remi was right on the mark. Missy was a damsel, all right.

* * *

Later that night and back at my house, I decided to call Missy to tell her about Teagan's offer.

I took out my phone as soon as I threw my keys on the coffee table and kicked off my shoes. Would Missy think it was weird that my ex was offering to have her stay at her home? It wasn't as if we were already dating, so hopefully she'd see it in simple terms; as help from the friend of a friend.

As the phone rang, I was still pondering if it was even a good idea. I'd thought about little else the entire drive home.

Missy seemed very proud, and the last thing I wanted was to insult her by assuming she didn't have the money to work things out on her own. I was basing my opinion entirely on what she had told me, but I had no idea what her divorce settlement was. For all I knew, she could be loaded. It was a slippery slope.

We hadn't spoken about anything personal since our conversation about my marriage to Teagan. Though I had hoped she'd bring it up sometime in the interim before her start date at ESPN, but she hadn't. I was more than a little disappointed. I'd been thinking about her non-stop since we'd said goodbye at LAX, and I'd had to rely on what few details I could dig out of Bryan and Cindy.

I wasn't usually nervous when approaching women; even being decidedly out of practice since the divorce. I'd discovered it was like riding a bike and I just had to get back in the saddle. I felt differently with Missy, and my heart was pounding wildly in anticipation of a simple phone call.

I wasn't sure if it was because we could be working together sometimes, or that I didn't want her to conflate her undoubtedly colored opinion of men, onto me. She hadn't said what kind of abuse she'd suffered at the hands of her evil ex-husband, but it gnawed at me. I imagined all sorts of horrible things that bastard had done to her and her son. My imagination was probably worse than the truth, but I felt uptight and worried, and I didn't like it. Maybe I'd be able to relax once she moved to Atlanta and I could keep a closer eye on her. I shook my head at myself as the phone rang. What the fuck was I doing? I barely knew this woman. I shouldn't be going all caveman about her.

"Hello?" she answered; her voice already familiar to me.

"Hi, stranger," I murmured. "Are you ready to start your new job?"

"Hey." I couldn't tell if the tone in Missy's voice was one of surprise or pleasure. "I'm all packed, if that's what you mean?" I could hear the sadness in her answer, even though she tried to sound positive.

I rubbed a hand over the back of my neck as I plopped down on the sofa getting ready to drop the bomb. "I realize Atlanta and ESPN will be a big change from Jackson Hole, but I think you'll do great."

"How's the production thing working out?"

Her redirection of the conversation told me she was feeling sad. I didn't know how I knew, but I did. "It's going well. It's only been a week."

"Is Jarvis working alone for now?"

"Yeah, but you'll be there to save him soon enough." I was trying to lift her spirits. "I've got your promos all figured out; *Missy and Mills.*"

She huffed out a laugh, but melancholy still laced her tone. "That's cute."

"Missy, if you're having second thoughts, I'm sure Walsh would understand."

"It's not that," she murmured softly.

"Is Dylan upset about the move?" It was the logical place for my mind to land. That, and her worry over being in front of the camera.

"Yes. He doesn't want to leave Ben and his friends, but I think I'm just anxious about leaving him here. I'll need to spend every minute of my free time looking for a place that I can afford."

"There are a lot of nice neighborhoods in Atlanta. Not all of them are over-the-top on cost of living," I reassured her. "I certainly don't live in the most affluent area."

She sighed into the phone. "I've been researching the school districts and looking at the bus lines. Mr. Walsh said after I get settled, I can take some time off to fly home and drive back with Dylan. Until then, I won't have a car, and I'm staying in the motel that Nicole arranged near the station."

Shit, I thought. I'd completely underestimated how difficult it was to move all the way across the country. I'd grown up around this area and gone to college not far away in Clemson, South Carolina. That was nothing compared to the long-distance trek Missy and Dylan were making.

I was lost in my thoughts until she continued. "I'll have to leave Dylan here with Ben for a month or two, and that's what's killing me. Coming down for my interview was the longest I've been away from him since he was born."

I smiled to myself, softly, knowing I was about to solve that problem. She was setting this up for me. "Yeah, that'll be tough, but what if you didn't have to leave him?"

"What?" Missy asked hesitantly. "I've tried to figure out a way to have him with me, but I can't work it out. My mother is trying to sell her house, but until she does, she can't move. I can't pull him out of school until I know where I'm going to live. I don't want to bounce him around."

I was happy to hear that her plans to have her mother join her were going to materialize because it would help her feel better about traveling out of town for assignments. "I understand all that, but I've figured it out. Or, at least, Teagan has."

"You're ex-wife? You were discussing me with her?" Her tone hardened slightly.

I seemed to be putting my foot into my mouth. "Don't be upset about it. I told you, Teagan and Chase are my friends. So are you," I said gently; waiting for her to answer.

"Yeah?"

"Yeah," I said firmly. "But only if you think you can trust me." I truly wanted more from her than friendship, but if that was all she was comfortable with, I still wanted to help her. "Remi is the same age as Dylan, and Teagan is home all day. She offered to have you and Dylan stay with them until you found a place of your own. They've got a huge house and Chase is gone half the time. She'd welcome the company and Dylan would have a new friend, too."

"Jensen." She seemed at a loss for words. "I don't know what to say. No one has ever done anything like this for me before."

"It's up to you, but just so you know, there is no catch. I just thought it would be easier. So, did Chase and Teagan."

"Um… What about enrolling him into school? I'll worry about him if I'm not settled permanently. What about my car? How will I get it down there? I can't afford to have it shipped." There was an embarrassed silence that followed. Obviously, pride dictated that she kept the state of her personal finances to herself. She might be low on money now, but that was about to change in a few weeks when she received her first paycheck or two.

My mind was racing for a way to make it work. "Is Ben working this weekend? Can he drive you down? I can call travel and get them to switch out your plane ticket for him to use flying back."

"That would be great, but he works the overnight shift on Saturday, and I don't know if he can get anyone to take his shift."

"Shit," I murmured, my mind searching for a way around it. I knew how important it was to have Dylan with her.

"It's very kind of you to think of me, but I don't know how I can work it out.

"Hold on." I got up and went into the dining room where my laptop was sitting on one end of the table, along with a stack of bills and the notebook I used to keep my research notes in. I flipped open the computer and quickly called up MapQuest, looking at the driving directions between Jackson Hole and Atlanta. I quickly looked at the route. It was interstate the entire way. "It's about a twenty-six-hour drive. There is plenty of time to get you here between Friday and Sunday."

"Twenty-six hours," she said defeated. "I guess I can drive myself," she said, more excited now. "I can stay in a motel half-way down."

Something inside me felt protective of both her and her son. I resisted her solution. "It will be too hard to deal with a small child on such a long trip. I know. Remi is a handful during road trips. It's either excitement or boredom overload." I chuckled.

"He'd have to adjust, that's all."

My eyes traced the route on the map. "You'll be exhausted, too," I said absently. "Halfway will be Omaha. You take I-90 East until you hit Sioux Falls and then I-29 South into Omaha."

"I have to pack up the rest of his things. He won't be happy leaving his friends so abruptly."

"Kids are resilient. Can Ben drive with you until Omaha? You can be there by late tomorrow night, and I can meet you there on Saturday morning. Ben can fly out with plenty of time to spare for his shift, and I'll drive with you the rest of the way."

"That's sweet of you, but you don't need to do that," Missy protested quietly. "How will it look? What will Bryan say?"

"He won't even know, but he wouldn't give a damn either way. All he cares about is that I'm in Connecticut on Sunday night and you're in the office on Monday. Trust me on this."

She was silent for a beat. "I really appreciate all you're trying to do, but— it's too much, Jensen. You'll be so tired Sunday when you have to go to work. I can't expect this from a man I barely know."

"I understand your hesitation, but I'm telling you, I want to do this for you, Missy." Her insecurities were rearing, and I guessed that she was hesitant about being alone with me, even if her son was with her. "I'll bring Remi with me so she and Dylan can get acquainted, and we'll drive back Saturday. No overnights." I tried to waylay all of her objections. "It will give us a chance to talk, and the kids will get to know each other better. Will your brother agree?"

"He's pretty protective. I'm not sure he'll trust someone he hasn't met."

"You can trust me, Missy. If you do, he will, too. Do you?"

"Yes. I'm not sure why, but I do." Her voice held the slightest tremor as she became more emotional.

I wanted her to trust me more than I'd ever wanted anything; other than Remi to be cured of leukemia. "It will get easier."

"Promise?"

"I promise." In reality, I had no fucking clue if being around me would get any easier because I didn't know what she'd gone through to make her fear men. She had real fear, and the cold bravado she projected at first impression was the result. That son of a bitch must have really hurt her, and I was more determined than ever to find out what happened; when she was ready to tell me.

"You go a long way for a play date," she said with a tearful laugh.

My heart filled with happiness. Missy was letting me help her, and it was a baby step toward the trust I wanted to build between us. A playful chuckle burst from me. "You ain't seen nothin' yet."

Missy

Jensen had arranged everything, and Ben had reluctantly agreed, though it took a lot of talking to convince him to trust that Dylan and I would be safe with Jensen.

Nicole, the manager of the ESPN travel department, had

been happy to efficiently and quickly exchange my ticket to
Atlanta for one from Omaha to Jackson Hole for Ben. She put
us up in the Hilton, near Eppley Airfield in Omaha, on Friday
night, as well. She explained that it was only a short distance
from the terminal and very nice. The airport in Omaha was one
of the easiest to navigate that I'd ever seen.

It was a warm late September day with a bright blue,
cloudless sky. I couldn't believe that we were waiting for Jensen
and Remi to walk up the ramp from the hub at the south end of
the airport. Ben had checked in and had his boarding pass and
would be going through security and would be flying out on the
same airline. It all seemed surreal.

My stomach was full of butterflies, and it must have shown
on my face because my brother noticed. "Are you sure about this,
sis? How well do you know this guy?"

Dylan was sitting on his lap on one of the upholstered
chairs near a Hudson newsstand. There was a coffee Kiosk
directly nearby where we'd gotten breakfast. Dylan happily
munched on half of a glazed donut. Normally, I wouldn't allow
him to have two, but it was Ben's second one, and when he
offered to share it with Dylan, I didn't have the heart to say no.
Ben was about to fly out of our lives and sadness was written all
over my little boy.

"We've discussed this. If I'm worried, it's due to Derrick,
not Jensen. I trust him." I offered a nervous smile. Ben and I had
talked at length about Jensen on the way down to Omaha, and
Jensen had put me in touch with Teagan, who Facetimed with
me last night at the hotel. Teagan was beautiful and welcoming,
and Remi, who she called over for a second to introduce her to
Dylan, was adorable and precocious.

"What makes you so sure?" Ben was skeptical. His
expression was a mixture of wry sarcasm and worry.

I shrugged. "I guess... he's the polar opposite of someone

else."

"He could be a wolf in sheep's clothing."

I shook my head and reached out to squeeze my brother's forearm. "I don't think so."

"Okay, but you keep in touch with me via text once an hour. I mean it, and when you get down there if that bastard, Derrick, shows up, I'll be there as soon as I can fly out."

I put my arm around Ben's broad shoulders and laid my head on the one closest to me. "You're an amazing big brother, Ben."

He held Dylan on his knee with one arm and slid the other around me. "You're my baby sister. If anything happens to you, I'll be down there to beat someone's ass."

I let out a small laugh. "That won't be necessary."

It was only a few minutes until Jensen's plane arrived and he and a beautiful little girl were walking hand-in-hand up the long, curved ramp toward us. Remi was looking up at Jensen and chattering away, and his face was graced with a brilliant and indulgent smile as he nodded and spoke to her. I stood up. "There they are," I murmured, excitement racing through me.

There was an increase in volume as the din of the voices of passengers came up and met their loved ones and friends, but my eyes locked on Jensen, and I couldn't help but grin when his blue gaze finally found mine.

He bent down a bit as they moved forward and pointed at the three of us. "There they are," he said as they approached.

I felt Ben rise to stand close beside me, picking up my son off his lap to set him down.

Remi had on a pretty pink top, jeans and tennis shoes; a similar outfit to what I'd dressed Dylan in this morning, though he insisted on wearing the ESPN football jersey that Jensen had sent home with me.

Jensen was also wearing jeans topped with an un-tucked

white Henley with the sleeves shoved up over his forearms. I couldn't help but notice how the shirt hugged his muscular form underneath, showing the curves of his biceps and the outline of his pecs. I cleared my throat and put my hand on Dylan's back. He was licking the last of the donut glaze off of his fingers, and I wished I'd given him a napkin.

I smiled nervously. "Hey. Did you guys have a good trip?"

Remi nodded and piped up. "We had some air pockets, but those are fun!" Her green eyes sparkled above her rosy cheeks.

I couldn't help but grin, remembering Jensen telling me about Remi's air pockets on our flight from Atlanta to L.A. His eyebrows rose and he mouthed. "Told ya." He was so handsome that he took my breath away, and I was unprepared for it.

"I'm Ben. Missy's brother." Ben held out his hand to Jensen who quickly took it in a firm handshake.

"Glad to meet you." I could see Ben was sizing up Jensen, who knew it and seemed completely unperturbed. They were both about the same height and could look each other in the eye.

"You, too," Ben answered.

"This is Remi." Jensen picked her up and held her with one arm beneath her bottom. "My little munchkin." My heart couldn't help but swell at the sight of the two of them. Remi's arm went easily around his neck. The little girl's hair was in ringlets and pulled off her face with a sparkly pink barrette. He looked down at Dylan with a warm expression. "You must be Dylan. I've heard a lot about you."

Jensen had a duffel slung over one shoulder, and Remi still in his arms, but he reached out to ruffle Dylan's dark blond hair with his free hand.

Dylan stood between my brother and me, looking up at Jensen with curious blue eyes, with one arm around Ben's thigh. He was a little scared, and I hoped Remi's secure exuberance would rub off on him.

Jensen's eyes flashed up to meet mine. "It's good to see you. Remi, this is Missy, Ben, and Dylan. What do you say?"

"Nice to meet you," she said with a grin. To our surprise, she held out her little hand to Ben and me. It was hard to imagine this vibrant little thing sick with leukemia. When she finished her adult introductions, she leaned in to half-whisper in Jensen's ear. "Jensey, you gotta let me down if I'm gonna talk to that boy." She pointed at Dylan.

"Oh, yes, ma'am. What was I thinking?" he answered, setting her on her feet.

She walked the few feet to Dylan. "Hello. My name is Remi. Do you wanna be friends with me?"

"Hi," he said, hesitantly. "I'm Dylan. I've never had a friend who's a girl before."

"We don't got cooties, ya know," she said, annoyed.

Jensen's expression was apologetic. "Be nice, Remi. What time is your flight, Ben?"

"I have to go now. I just heard my boarding call. Take care of these two," Ben said to Jensen.

"No worries. I will."

Ben enveloped me in a tight embrace and then kissed my cheek. "Take care of yourself and remember what I said."

"I will. I love you. Thank you, Ben." My eyes implored him. "I mean it. For everything."

"What's a big brother for?"

When he squatted down to Dylan's level, my son was fighting to hold back his tears. "Hey," Ben said softly, nudging Dylan's chin. My eyes started to sting. I wasn't sure how he was going to get along without his Uncle Ben. The two had become so close. "You're the man of the house now, and I'm counting on you to take good care of your mom."

Dylan sniffed. "Okay, Uncle Ben. I will."

Ben pulled him between his bent knees and rubbed Dylan's

back through the football jersey. "Why don't you tell Jensen all about your friends? I bet he'll play football with you sometimes, too."

His little chin trembled, and two big tears fell from his eyes and rolled down his cheeks. "It won't be the suh-same," he stuttered.

My heart was breaking for my son, and I had to wipe away a few of my own tears. Jensen's hand landed on the middle of my back and moved up to squeeze my shoulder in a show of support. It didn't feel alien to have him touch me, offering comfort, because I was drawn to him. I wished I could fall right into his arms and cry my eyes out.

"Sure, I will! I might even get my friends to join in with their kids," Jensen added. "We'll have a real game and a picnic in the park."

"Doesn't that sound fun? I'll be so jealous; I'll have to visit real soon so I can play, too." Ben's voice was starting to tighten as he held my little son in his arms, and he looked up at me with sad eyes. He cleared his throat. "Listen, buddy, I have to go, or I'll miss my flight. I'll Facetime with you, tonight, okay?"

Dylan sniffed and stood near me after Ben had released him. I reached out and ran a hand over the back of his head as Ben got to his feet. "Okay."

He hugged me again and shook Jensen's hand. "It was very nice to meet you, Little Miss Remi. You two have fun on the trip." Remi curtsied and smiled beguilingly at Ben who was totally won over. "She's a doll," he said to Jensen, then turned to me. "I love you. Be good."

"We love you, too." My throat felt thick, but I did my best to push down my sadness. I offered a tumultuous smile as Ben took three steps backward.

"Call me when you get to Atlanta," he winked at me, and then turned and walked down the same ramp Remi and Jensen had come up, only minutes before. Ben stopped to wait at the security checkpoint that would take him down to the terminal.

I sucked in a big breath. This was it. The start of a new life.

My son turned and buried his face in my stomach and his arms wrapped around my waist. My hands instantly went into his silky hair as he cried. "It's okay, sweetheart."

Remi came over and touched Dylan on the shoulder. "Yeah! We're gonna have fun!" Remi said. "You'll see! We have a pool with a slide and everything!"

"It's too cold to swim in fall." Dylan, who had separated from me, eyed Remi with skepticism.

"Not in Atlanta, silly. Even if it snows, the pool is warm. It steams like a bowl of soup."

Dylan's eyes got wide as saucers. It appeared Remi had succeeded in distracting him from his sadness. "Really?"

"Yeah!"

"Cool! Mom, can we swim when we get there?" He was excited, and he wore an exuberant expression.

I sighed in relief. "If Remi's mom says it's alright."

"She will," Remi assured. "Do you need floaties? I got one pair is all, so we might need to get some for you."

Dylan frowned. "No way. I don't need floaties." He rolled his eyes. "My Uncle Ben taught me how to swim at the YMCA."

"Are you ready to go?" Jensen asked, his duffel still slung over his shoulder. "We still have thirteen hours in front of us."

I nodded but groaned at the thought. Yesterday left me exhausted. "The car is in the garage."

It wasn't long before we'd walked across the road into the short-term parking garage and loaded the bags into the trunk of the car, and we were driving back to the hotel parking lot to pick up the small U-Haul trailer that Ben had disconnected the night before.

The kids were chattering from the backseat, and I got out

to help Jensen, but he didn't need me. I found myself watching his muscles work beneath his shirt as he lifted the fully loaded trailer hitch over the ball on the back of the car. It had to be heavy as hell, and his muscles bulged with the effort, though he didn't seem to struggle. He proceeded to get to work, hooking up the three chains and cranking the handle on the hitch tight. In no time, Jensen had it completely attached to the back of my older model Lexus.

I was embarrassed that I found his show of strength so attractive and looked away even though he was concentrating on the trailer and didn't see my face.

What was I doing? If I weren't careful, I'd be making an utter fool of myself in a matter of minutes. It had been so long since I'd wanted a man, that I didn't know how to handle it.

The back window of the Lexus rolled down, and Dylan was out the window to his waist. "Hey, Mom! We're hungry, and Remi has to go to the bathroom."

"Oh," I looked around. The obvious answer was the bathroom in the lobby of the hotel and lunch at the restaurant there. "Okay."

I walked over and opened the backseat door and motioned for the kids to pile out. "Grab your coats." The air temperature was cool, but Jensen wasn't wearing a coat and was completely unaware of the direction of events. "Jensen, Remi has to use the bathroom, so I'm going to take her inside. Do you want to grab a bite to eat before we get on the road? The hotel has a nice restaurant."

"We ate there last night," Dylan added.

Jensen straightened after completing his task. "Sure." He looked around the parking lot. "There aren't a lot of cars here, so I'll just stop in and tell the front desk we'll be taking this out of the lot soon."

"Jensey, I have to go potty!" Remi reminded urgently.

"I'll take you, Remi," I said, holding out my hand. "Dylan, do you have to go, or do you want to go with Jensen?"

He crossed his arms adamantly, and I was sure that even if he was in danger of peeing his pants, there was no way he would go into a woman's bathroom with Remi and me. I didn't feel safe letting him go into the men's alone and Jensen read the concern on my face.

Jensen's hand came down on Dylan's shoulder. "We men will stick together and meet you in the restaurant. Cool?"

I glanced at Dylan who nodded. "Cool," he repeated.

My eyebrow rose in surprise. He was taking to Jensen much better than I'd believed he would. The man in question smirked and nodded toward the entrance. "Shall we? Ladies first."

In the large lobby, Jensen and Dylan walked in one direction, and I took Remi in another. She was looking up into my face, studying me the entire time until I pushed open the oversized mahogany door to the women's restroom.

"What is it, Remi?"

"Oh, nothing. You're just real pretty. I like your yellow hair. It's just like Cinderella."

My face split into a genuine smile. Yellow must be her word for blonde. "Thank you. I think you're just beautiful, too." I tapped the tip of her upturned nose with my index finger. "Do you need help, honey?"

"Just to get that paper thing down and on the seat."

"Okay." I went into a stall with her and got her all set up, then went out to wait until she was finished.

Remi walked up to the sink with her hands out, but she was too little to reach. I turned on the warm water and lifted her, balancing her on my bent knee so she could get soap on her hands and then rub them together under the warm running water.

"This is just how my mommy does it," she said.

"I think I'm going to like your mommy."

When Remi was done, she nodded, and then went to dry her hands with the air dryer. The force of it blew her dark hair around her head. "I do, too. She's real pretty, too. She's a good mommy."

If Remi was anything to go by, there was no question that Teagan was a great mom.

"Don't you think you'll like staying with us?" she asked, her little voice echoing around the tiled room.

"Yes, of course, we will."

"Then, why are you sad?" Remi asked. I could see the curiosity in her expression, yet she seemed so understanding.

"I'm not sad, exactly, but I'm upset that I need so much help from your dad."

"Don't worry. All girls are damsels sometimes," Remi explained simply in her wise six-year-old voice. "Do you know what a damsel is?" Her green eyes were wide as she asked me, her little pink lips turned up in a bow. I could see why Jensen adored her so.

I smiled. I knew the definition, but I was curious what Remi would say. "No, what is it?"

"Well," she said thoughtfully, "it's a princess who needs help from a prince."

I couldn't stop the helpless smile that lifted my lips. This little girl was so charming that I was beside myself, and already in love with her. "Oh, I see." I bit my lip to keep from out and out laughing.

"My mommy says boys need us to be damsels, cuz it gives them stuff to do, and makes them feel like a prince. I think Jensey needs you to be a damsel, right now." Her expression was serious, and I found her absolutely irresistible.

I couldn't hold back my delighted laughter any longer, and it burst forth breathlessly. "That's a wonderful explanation, Remi. Thank you. I'll keep that in mind." I smiled down at her.

She nodded in satisfaction. "Don't tell Jensey, I told ya. It's a secret between princesses. Kay?"

I hugged her close and then offered my pinkie with a big smile. Remi curled hers around it with a giggle, and we shook one time. "Definitely! Princess pinkie swear!"

Chapter 8

JENSEN

We'd been driving for about two hours and were coming into Kansas City on southbound I-29. The soft rock coming out of the stereo speakers was relaxing as it filled the inside of the vehicle. Missy was driving her Lexus; an older model without the luxury of satellite radio and I'd just found the station.

After I was done fiddling with the radio, we drove in silence for a while; just listening. It gave me a chance to study her classic profile, wondering about the thoughts running through her head. She was so beautiful; more so when her expression was serene like it was now. I tried not to make my observation of her visible but had to remind myself to stop staring; thankful that my mirrored Ray Bans hid my eyes. I offered to drive after lunch, but she had opted to do so.

"Do you need gas?" I asked, glancing behind me to check on the kids. Their chatter had stopped about an hour outside of Omaha. They were both fast asleep on pillows that Missy had brought from Wyoming.

She shook her head. "Nope. Ben filled up when we got into Omaha last night, and he said it should get us just about to St. Louis."

I turned my head toward her and smiled. I wish I would

have had more time to get to know Ben; more time to get him comfortable with me. After all, I would be alone with his sister and nephew for fourteen hours. "He's got your back."

"He does," she agreed happily with a wistful look on her face. "He's a great big brother. I don't know what I'd do without him."

"Is it just the two of you?"

"Yes. My dad left us high and dry when we were little. My mom worked like a dog to support us, and Ben had a job after school bagging groceries to help out. As soon as he was old enough, he joined the Fire Department training program and moved to Wyoming after I was at college. What about you? Tell me about your family."

"We were just the typical middle-class family. My parents both had to work very hard. My dad is a salesman for a restaurant supplier, and my mom worked the morning shift at a local diner. They worked together; my dad took me to school, and my mom picked me up until I was old enough to take the bus. All-in-all, I had a stable childhood, but no frills. I was lucky to get a chance to go to college." My parents had scrimped and saved my entire life so that I could have opportunities that their parents were not able to provide for them. Still, I had to help, but thankfully, I had scholarships for academics and soccer.

"No siblings?"

"Nah. Chase is the closest thing I have to a brother." I eyed her, wondering if she'd asked Remi anything about Chase when they went to the restroom at the hotel. "I've known him for years."

"I'm still processing the story you told me about him, Teagan, and Remi."

"Yeah," I said in understanding. "I suppose if it weren't for Remi's illness, Chase and I might never have reconciled."

"You don't think Teagan and Chase would still have gotten

back together?" She glanced at me and then back to the highway. "I mean, you said you were going to divorce when Remi was three, so maybe you would have anyway?"

"I'm not sure if Teagan would have gone to England and told him everything. He had the life she sacrificed so much to secure, and he wasn't exactly open to hearing from either of us. He hardly ever came home from London."

"Well, I'm glad it worked out. Remi is sure an angel," she said, which of course brought a soft smile to my lips.

"That's for sure. Dylan is a good boy, too. I figured he'd be shy after what you told me about his dad not being around, but he got in there," I made a motion with my hands to mimic hooking up the trailer, "and told me how he helped his Uncle Ben." I chuckled softly. "I was pleasantly surprised. If I'd have known, I would have asked him to help me, too."

Missy glanced in the review mirror to see if the kids were still napping. "I don't think he remembers much about Derrick, which, I'm grateful for."

It was the perfect segue into finding out what I wanted to know since I'd met her. "Forgive me for asking, Missy, but it's been eating away at me since we had dinner in L.A. What did that bastard do to you?"

Her hands tightened on the steering wheel, and she inhaled deeply.

"Look, I'm sorry to ask, but I've imagined all sorts of horrible things. If you're not ready to talk about it, I understand."

I could almost see the fear radiating out of her, and she paused meeting my eyes before training hers back on the highway. "I just don't like to relive it, I guess. I don't see the point."

I sighed heavily. I understood, but something deep inside me was screaming to know everything about her.

"Why do you want to know?"

Boom. There it was. *Everything*, my mind acknowledged.

It was my turn to ponder my words. I looked at Missy for a good ten seconds. I didn't want to scare her, so I chose my words carefully. "I want to know you. I believe we all carry the past forward, like it or not, and I think if you tell me, it might help you trust me." I shrugged. "And I desperately want you to trust me."

Her forehead wrinkled. "But, why? You barely know me."

Here is where the rubber hit the road. To get her to feel secure with me, I had to be completely honest. "But I want to. I really, *really*, want to."

She kept driving, not looking at me. "Doesn't the fact that you're here, alone with my son and me in my car driving through Missouri, tell you that I trust you? At least a little?"

"That's true." I had to admit it. "But I want you to trust me enough to let me get close to you." I could see her stiffen and I put up my hand. "Don't take that wrong. I'm attracted to you, yes. You know that already, and I'm hoping that you'll agree to go on a date with me, but I don't want you to think I'm disingenuous."

Missy sighed, and I made a concerted effort not to watch her breasts rise and fall with her effort.

"I've had men in my face and trying to get up my skirt and in my pants on every job I've ever had, Jensen. I don't want that to be you." She got the little crinkle above her nose again as she frowned.

"I sensed that, but I am different. If I weren't, I wouldn't have told Walsh that I wouldn't take assignments with my old team consistently. I don't want to work with you, though it was fun, and we'd do great together. I asked him to put you with Jarvis because I knew he'd look out for you and not hit on you. Now, I'll get assigned with that asshole, Lonnie. Do you think I'd put up with that idiot if I only wanted to sleep with you?"

Missy looked over at me again, an incredulous expression on her face. I wanted to reach out and touch her so damn badly. Her skin looked like silk, and I could imagine how velvet it would feel underneath the caress of my lips.

"I admit I was a bit disappointed that you wouldn't be producing for my team because of the L.A. trip, but it helps to have an explanation," she acknowledged with a half-smile, then her top teeth came out to bite her lower lip. It was adorable.

"Exactly. I'd like to know about your ex, so I know how to be around you. I understand if it's too soon, but can you tell me if he was physically or mentally abusive?"

"Both."

I cringed at her admission but held back the expletives I wanted to let loose. It was just as I'd thought. What a motherfucker!

"It was bad. Derrick was a tyrant. Dylan wasn't allowed to make any noise or play with his toys; he was scared to death. Having one little thing out of place when his father came home meant he'd be punished. It made me sick. I'm not sure what his reaction would be if he ever saw Derrick again, but I hope I never have to find out."

"And, you?" I prodded gently. I knew that knowing would probably eat at me even more than not knowing, but it was part of her, and the protector in me needed the truth. I had a feeling about this prick, and it wasn't good.

"It was the same for me. I had to have everything just so; the house spotless, dinner on the table by a certain time, but if he was late and the food was cold, somehow it was always my fault. He beat me at the drop of a hat. Anything set him off. I tried so hard to be perfect, and I took it for years." Her left shoulder lifted nonchalantly. "But, when he started directing all of his bottled-up anger at Dylan, I knew that we had to get out of there. I planned it out for months in advance; saving pennies left over from my grocery allowance until I had enough for the gas. Derrick had Dylan's school in his pocket, and they called him for every little thing; if our son had a doctor's appointment, if he was tardy, or if I called him in sick. I only had an hour head start before they would notify Derrick. The week I left was the most terrifying week of my life." Missy seemed lost in thought, her voice soft. "I never want to make a trip like that again."

Her words dropped off, and she shook her head, waiting for my response. Anger rose up inside me like a bomb about to explode. I knew where she was going with the story, and she didn't have to. She didn't have to say he forced her in bed, or that he beat her repeatedly; I could tell by the fear on her face and the shaking in her voice. It was written all over her.

My fingers curled into fists, and my teeth clenched, causing the muscle in my jaw to flex back and forth. "I don't understand what motivates a man to beat a woman or a child. It's seriously fucked up!" I spat out angrily.

"That trip, and how scared I was during it, was the only reason Ben agreed to let you meet us half-way. He knew I'd be terrified alone on the road with Dylan. I hate that Derrick has so much power over my emotions after all of this time. I fucking hate him!" Tears dripped silently from her eyes, and she wiped them away with one hand. "I'm sorry." Her voice broke. "I don't usually cry about it anymore."

"He needs to die," I said, letting my true thoughts slip out of my mouth before I could stop them. Missy let out a surprised gasp. "Bastards like that shouldn't be walking around."

She shook her head, adamantly. "There were many times I wanted to kill him," she admitted. "But what would have happened to my little boy if something happened to me? He would have gone into the system, or worse; if I failed, Derrick would have raised him without me. Nothing is worth that,

Jensen. He's nothing now except an unpleasant memory."

And a few scars, I thought heatedly. "He's scum. Jesus Christ! I don't even know him, and my blood is boiling! I can see you're still afraid of him, Missy." I wished I could comfort her or take those fucking memories away. She remembered it every time a man came close to her; whether she admitted it or not.

"I'll always be afraid, but I can't let him ruin the rest of my life, or Dylan's. I try to make it through one day at a time." She huffed out an embarrassed laugh and ran a hand through her hair, then wiped away the last errant tear from her cheek. "I don't know why I'm telling you all of this. The less I talk about it, the less I have to remember. But moving—" she shrugged. "Atlanta is so much closer to Derrick, and I won't have my brother with me. He was my security blanket. Ben and his firefighter friends would pummel the hell out of Derrick if he tried anything."

Everything inside of me wanted to protect her and make her feel the same sense of security she had with her brother. I reached out an open palm in an invitation for her to put hers into it. I knew every step we took had to be her choice. After everything she'd gone through, if we were ever going to get to a place where I could touch her without her thinking about that bastard, I had to move at a snail's pace.

When she gave me her hand, mine curled around it. "It'll be okay. You've felt secure with Ben, and this is all new. Thank you for trusting me. I won't let anything happen to you or Dylan, I promise." I lifted her hand to my mouth and brushed my lips across her knuckles. "And, just so you know, nothing will happen between us that you don't want to happen. If all you want to be is my friend, that's okay, too."

Her light blue eyes widened in disbelief. "Really? You mean that?"

I sighed and flashed her a big smile. "I do. It would seriously suck, but I mean every word."

Missy laughed through her tears. "Thank you, Jensen. Again, you've left me speechless."

I leaned back in my seat, still holding her hand in mine, and covering it with my other one. "Well, that's a start." I grinned again. "I want you to trust me, and I'm ready to prove to you that you can."

Her fingers tightened around mine, and it was a physical and emotional rush. It meant she trusted me, and she was letting me touch her. I was encouraged.

"What did you and Remi discuss in the bathroom?" I asked, thinking that my little Remi would have a lot to say; she always did.

Missy burst out laughing, and I was glad to have distracted her from thoughts of her prick of an ex-husband.

"Oh, no." My mouth quirked up at one corner in a lopsided smile. "What'd she say?"

"Just something about princes and princesses," she said happily. "She's just precious."

"Ah!" I acknowledged. "Remi is well-versed on the subject. I think Dylan's awesome, too. He asked if I could get ESPN jerseys for his friends, Marcus and Joey, too. Did you tell him it was from me?" The boy's exuberance had been infectious, and he was cuter than hell.

"I told him a nice man named Jensen got them for us."

"Nice?" I grunted in amusement. "Gee, thanks."

"You're a lot more than nice, Jensen. But I didn't know that then."

The corner of my mouth curved in the start of a crooked smile. "Sure, you did, but okay," I said with satisfaction. "I can live with that. For now."

I squeezed her hand as the miles flew by. I was going to be sad when we pulled into Teagan and Chase's driveway this evening. Very sad, indeed.

Missy

It was almost midnight, and we were just getting into Atlanta.

Jensen was driving, and both of the kids were still sleeping. We'd been quiet for the last hour, and though I feigned sleep, I found myself studying my new…

Hmm. How should I classify Jensen? Co-worker? Yes. Friend? Definitely. Potential lover? A shiver ran down my spine and skittered like electricity over my skin.

I rubbed a hand up and down one arm and shifted in my seat, turning to face him. I had my seatbelt on, but I could still change position and pulled my knees up in front of my body, hugging them. I was acutely aware of the move after I'd done it. Maybe it was a subconscious way to shield myself from my feelings, or perhaps, to hide them from the masculine man across from me. My mouth suddenly went dry. I swallowed hard and then licked my lips as my eyes ran over his lean and muscular body. His eyes trained on the road, so when he spoke, I was surprised.

"Are you cold?" Jensen asked, concerned. In the short time I'd known him, he always seemed so in tune with me; noticing my slightest movement though, right now his attention was trained on the road and his expression, only moments earlier, had looked deep in thought.

The bluish-green glow from the dashboard landed on his strong profile, throwing parts of his face into shadow, but highlighting his strong jaw, nose, and firm lips. He made me hungry. I hadn't been hungry for a long time, and maybe never this hungry. I recognized the flutters in my stomach and the involuntary rush of desire.

He reached forward to adjust the cabin temperature. It was warmer in Georgia than it was in Wyoming, but it was still fall, and there was a slight chill to the air. I seized the opportunity to use it as an excuse for my shivering. "A little."

"Do you want my jacket?" Jensen asked, and then reached behind me, into the backseat and the floorboard, lifting the coat over the seat and into my arms. I welcomed the warmth and the delicious scent of his cologne that wafted up from the material and settled around me.

"Mmmm," I closed my eyes letting the essence of him envelop me. "Thank you."

"You look like a cat that just got a warm bowl of cream," he teased gently. "What are you thinking about?"

We zoomed past the I-575 interchange, staying on I-75 South, overhead lights flashing past and businesses blurring outside in the darkness.

A small smile tugged at my lips. Should I tell Jensen how he affected me? It would give him power, and after all I'd been through with Derrick, I'd learned not to give a man any kind of control over me. "I plead the fifth."

He huffed out a soft laugh. "Okay, be that way. Though, I think it would be much more fun if you shared."

I glanced in the backseat, making sure the kids were covered up with the blanket from Dylan's bed. They were sharing, and my heart swelled slightly. It would be good for Dylan to have a friend in Atlanta and make the transition easier for him. I snuggled down into Jensen's coat, sliding my arms into the sleeves backward. "You would." I liked this gentle, unobtrusive teasing between us.

"You would, too, if you'd give it a chance."

"Who said I wasn't going to give it a chance?"

A slow grin spread over his face, and I loved how his dimples deepened. He was so attractive I could barely keep myself from staring.

"Are you?" He looked at me seriously, then, his hand

reached over and took mine in his again.

I wanted him to touch me. I had since he'd let go of my hand hours before. He looked like he was struggling inside, just like I was. "Sure, it's just…"

"I know what it is, but I really want this to happen. I'm not like him, and all I ask is a chance to prove it."

"Why me?" I needed to know the answer. "You can have any woman you want."

"That's just it. I don't want just anyone." His thumb started to move, brushing back and forth over the top of my hand. "I'm not sure what you want me to say. That you're beautiful? You are. That I'm extremely attracted to you? I don't want to scare you. I feel protective, I guess." He shrugged casually. "I'm kind of fumbling around, here."

"Is it because you see me as needy or broken?" I had to ask. Was it my situation that motivated the superhero in him, or the similarity of my plight to that of his ex-wife's? Maybe he just needed to be that guy who saved everyone.

Remi's words echoed in my head. *Jensey needs you to be a damsel, right now.*

"Because if that's what it is, I'd rather not. I'm trying to be independent. For my mental health, I can't depend on anyone, and that's not why I'd want any man to want me." I pulled my hand free, suddenly uncomfortable. Not because I didn't like his touch, but because I didn't want his pity.

He lifted the hand that I'd just released and ran it tiredly through his thick dark hair. "You know, Missy, everyone doesn't always have an ulterior motive." His tone was irritated. "Maybe, I just like you. Maybe, I like your kid. Maybe I want to make sure you do well at the network."

I sat up in my seat, turning toward the front and putting my feet on the floor. "I'm sorry, but it's been my experience that men always want something from women."

He shook his head, his jaw jutting out. I couldn't tell if Jensen was disgusted or just royally pissed. "Yeah? That's nature. Men and women need something from each other. It's the way of things."

I looked down at my hands, my fingers fiddling around with each other in my lap. "I'm sorry. I guess I'm just cautious." I flushed, realizing that after what he'd done for Teagan and Remi, and now, Dylan and me, I should give him the benefit of the doubt. I desperately wanted to, but there was a deep-seated fear inside me.

There was a time that I'd trusted Derrick; I loved him, and then he turned into a monster the minute I married him. It was wrong to project that on Jensen, but part of me was utterly terrified of the same thing happening again. Jensen would be easy to open up to, easy to trust… easy to love, if only I could get over this damned fear. I'd gone to counseling for a year and felt pretty strong, but then again, I'd never met a man I'd wanted to try having a relationship with, until now. Seeing his distress over the turn our conversation was taking, pained me, and it was a clue that I already cared about him. I inhaled a shuttering breath.

He took an exit into a suburb filled with high-end businesses and then a few minutes later, turned right into a subdivision of large, looming houses with even larger lots, some with big trees and others were new construction without any at all, but most of them were gated.

Many of the windows were dark, with only floodlights around the garages for security, but we pulled up to a wrought iron gate, where the house was further back from the street than the others. Jensen pushed the button for the power window, and it whizzed down. He reached out and entered a six-digit security code, and the gates clicked and then opened in front of us. "This is it. We're here."

166

"Wow," was all I could say.

"Chase is away at a game this weekend, so you'll only meet Teagan, tonight."

I reached out and laid a hand on Jensen's forearm as he pulled up to the house and stopped my Lexus, pulling out the keys and holding them out to me. "Jensen, I'm sorry," I said again. "I want this to work, too. I'll try, okay?" I took the keys; my fingers closing around them. "I know you're nothing like my ex-husband."

His deep blue eyes appeared black in the dark interior of the car, and he nodded. He reached out one finger and ran it down the outline of my face, and then he cupped my cheek in his palm. "Okay," he murmured softly. "Remember what I said; nothing happens unless you want it. Trust that."

His touch was electric, and though a similar caress from someone else would be innocent, with Jensen, it felt so, so intimate.

"I do, but I'm scared," I admitted.

"Naw," he smiled and shook his head gently, running his thumb over my lower lip at the same time. "You are Melissa fucking Ellington. Badass sportscaster. No one messes with you. You had Jeremy shitting himself in Los Angeles. I know who you are, and so do you."

The confidence and support he was showing toward me made my heart explode. I wanted nothing more than to throw myself in his arms and feel his mouth crushing mine. At least, that's what my heart desired. My brain warned to proceed with caution. I leaned in and very gently kissed his mouth. Jensen was surprised. He stiffened, as he let me take the lead on the kiss. It felt amazing and right. My hand found the hard wall of his chest and slid upward over his shoulder and into his hair at his nape. I wanted and needed his response, so I nudged and pulled at his lower lip with both of mine. Finally, he responded; his lips as gentle as his hand caressing the side of my face. His hand moved down around my forearm as he pulled back and rested his forehead on mine, inhaling deeply. I wanted more; my chin tilted so my lips could reach for his once more.

He stopped me. "It's late," he ground out. "We should get the kids inside, and I have an early flight tomorrow afternoon."

My hand stroked through his hair as I closed my eyes, not wanting to end the contact. He bent and placed another soft kiss on my lips. "To be continued," he promised, pulling back slowly, touching my cheek with gentle fingertips. "I'll get your suitcases." Jensen reached around to pop the trunk and open his door, his reluctance to end the intimacy echoed my own. I sat there, stunned by my own reaction, trying to get myself together.

The sound of the trunk closing woke up the kids. "Mom, are we there yet?" Dylan asked sleepily.

"Yes, sweetheart. We're here."

"Are we gonna live in this place?" Dylan was only half awake and asked in as much wonder as he could manage, looking out the window; taking in the massive house and yard. "It's a mansion," he said, rubbing his eyes with a closed fist.

"We're going to stay here until we can find a place of our own."

"Cool!"

By now, I'd gotten out of the car, walked around, and opened the door to release the buckle on Dylan's car seat. The kids must be so tired of sitting in one position, I thought. Even though we'd stopped every couple of hours, their little bottoms must be numb.

As I took Dylan out of the car, Jensen went to the door of the large stone house, carrying our two suitcases and Remi's duffel bag, leaving his own on the driveway by the back of the car. The door opened, and he disappeared inside for fifteen seconds but was soon back at the car to lift his sleeping child out of her car seat and into his arms. At the same time, he caught Dylan's eye and winked. "Hey, buddy. How are you doing? Are you ready to go inside?"

"I'm good." Dylan nodded. He was standing beside me holding my hand when Jensen nodded toward the door, and we all started walking toward it.

"Let's go. Sorry, I know it's a bit overwhelming, but they're great people."

I smiled, confident that if Remi and Jensen were anything to go by, I had nothing to worry about.

We walked up the expensive stone steps, and a beautiful pregnant brunette was holding the door open. "Welcome!" she said, smiling warmly. "Come on in!"

"I'm just going to put Remi in her bed," Jensen said softly.

"Okay. I've laid out her pajamas, but if she's zonked, you can just put her in bed with her clothes on."

Jensen nodded, and disappeared up the staircase with a sleeping Remi on his shoulder and carrying her bag and the sneakers she'd removed during the drive. Apparently, he knew his way around this house.

The woman, who must be Teagan, turned to me, reaching out to me above Dylan's head. "You must be Missy and Dylan."

"Hello," I said, offering my hand to shake hers.

"I'm Dylan," my son piped up. "I'm six."

Teagan's face split into an indulgent smile. "You certainly are! You're a handsome young man. Are you hungry or thirsty? I have some warm cookies and milk in the kitchen, and then I can show you to your rooms."

"What kind?" He wanted to know.

"Hmmm, let's see," Teagan teased. "Chocolate chip, of course! Is there any other kind?"

"Those are my favorite!" Dylan looked up at me, expectantly. "Can I, Mom?"

"Just one. It's time for bed." I looked at Teagan apologetically. "I'd love to have a chat, but if it's alright, I'd like to get him settled, first."

"Of course, I understand. Come with me, Dylan. The kitchen is right through here." Teagan pointed behind her past the foyer and held out her hand to my little boy, who took it readily.

My son would do anything for chocolate chip cookies and milk.

The open concept and the vaulted ceilings were spectacular, with high windows. The stone fireplace to my left just through the great room left me breathless. "Your home is amazing," I murmured, following the two of them.

Teagan lifted Dylan onto one of the six mahogany and wrought iron bar stools that lined the dark cream marble island in the center of the kitchen. The cupboards and hardwood floors were also dark mahogany, and the whole effect was stunning. This house had to cost a fortune. "Chase never does anything halfway, though I would have been happy with something smaller."

I could see that about Teagan. Her husband might be a superstar soccer player, but she was very down-to-earth. Judging by the magnificence of the house alone, one might expect her to be one of the Atlanta Housewives, spending a thousand dollars on a salon visit, but she was relaxed, welcoming and unpretentious. Even her style was low key. Her hair was twisted up into a messy topknot, and she was wearing a fleece nightshirt and fuzzy ankle socks.

"Here you go, honey," Teagan said, setting a small glass of milk and a plate with one cookie on it, in front of him. He quickly picked up the delicious looking pastry and plowed into it.

"Dylan, what do you say?"

"This is amazing!" he said with his mouth full.

My eyebrows arched. "Thank you," I instructed.

Teagan waved away the need for the nicety. "You've got to be exhausted, and I've got one of those," she pointed at my son. "I know how it is. Would you like a cookie, too?"

I shook my head. "Thank you for letting us stay with you. I can't tell you what it means to me to have my little man with me."

"Like I said, I know how it is to be a mom. I couldn't imagine being away from Remi. Her overnights with Jensen are about all I can stand."

I stood behind Dylan's chair and rubbed his back at the same time Jensen appeared around the corner after coming back downstairs. "She's all settled. Thanks for letting me take her with me."

"Are you kidding? Remi wouldn't have let me hear the end of it. Besides, it gave me a nice break."

He came to stand next to me and ran a loving caress down my arm. "Will you be okay? I should get going. I still have to pack for my flight tomorrow."

I nodded, enjoying the feel of his hand as it moved over my skin. If Teagan noticed she didn't show it, and instead focused on Dylan, asking him about the trip and if Remi had behaved.

"Yes. This house is amazing. Teagan... is fantastic!" I couldn't help but wonder if his heart was broken by his divorce.

He nodded. "She is." He reached around and grabbed two of the warm cookies from the cookie sheet on the counter and wrapped them in a napkin he'd taken from a stack.

"Walk me out?" His eyes were serious but suggestive. I couldn't help the jolt of electricity that shot through me at just the thought.

"Sure."

"See ya, Teags! Is it okay to leave Missy's car with her trailer hitch where it is? Maybe Chase can move it or unhitch it tomorrow?"

"Sure. Have a great trip!" Teagan called from the kitchen, as Jensen and I walked away and back out toward the front door.

Jensen's hand found mine. "Relax tomorrow. Promise?"

My fingers entwined with his as easily as if I'd known him for years. I nodded. "I promise."

He opened the door and gently tugged me outside, quietly closing the door behind us. He turned me to face him, still holding my hand. "I'm going to kiss you, now," he warned. "I've wanted to do it all day. I have since L.A., to be honest."

A warm flush rushed up under the skin of my cheeks, and I knew I was blushing.

Jensen had the cookies in one hand and my hand in the other. I was sure it was a deliberate attempt to reassure me he wasn't going to touch me in a way I might find intrusive. My eyes flashed up to his and held; my mouth dropped open in wanton anticipation. His head swooped slowly, hovering. My breath hitched. I was about to get a small taste of him; to see if he was everything that my dreams were made of. Literally.

"Okay?" he asked, so close I could feel his warm breath on my face, and his lips were almost touching mine.

My chin tilted up, almost involuntarily, the air between us vibrating.

"Promises, promises," I whispered as my eyelids fell over my eyes.

I could feel his lips curve into a smile as he huffed out a soft laugh. "I always keep my promises."

I was hungry for him, anxious to feel his soft lips; wondering how he would kiss me. Would he be gentle or demanding, or a combination of both?

His lips nudged a response out of mine, the kiss starting slowly, languidly coaxing mine into action. My mouth parted, and his became firmer and more demanding. I could feel the urgency building between us, the tips of our tongues touching tentatively. Jensen groaned as he pulled away, my lips clinging to his, reluctant to end the kiss. I wanted more. Much more.

"That was incredible, but I need to go." He cleared his throat; his face filled with regret. Clearly, he was reluctant to end our closeness.

I nodded and licked my lips. "Yeah. Of course. Have a safe trip."

I was acutely aware of his thumb rubbing over the top of my hand; the only place we were still connected. "I will; if I can call you."

"Yes." I didn't even need to speak the word. After the kiss we'd just shared, there was no question in my mind.

"Okay." He bent and placed another soft kiss on my mouth. It was delicious. "See ya," he said with a sigh. He walked down the steps, and our hands fell reluctantly away from each other.

"Bye." I watched him walk away, pick up his ESPN duffel bag and head over to a Toyota Rav4 parked on the other side of the garage.

He put the bag in the back seat and then rested both arms on the roof. "Are you gonna watch me drive off? It's too late for the sunset thing," he said wryly. The floodlights over the four-car garage illuminated almost the entire driveway, and I could see the adorable grin on his face.

"I have a good imagination," I teased, laughing lightly.

His handsome face took on a wry expression, and his grin turned into a brilliant smile. "Good to know," he said with a wink.

HER *last chance* BEGINS
in his arms.

Chapter 9

Missy

My pulse was pounding after the kiss. That first kiss.

As I watched Jensen get in his car, I ripped myself away and turned back toward the house. I didn't want to seem over eager or foolish by standing on the stoop and watching him drive off. Once the door was closed, however, I turned and looked out one of the long, beveled glass windows on the left side of the door. My hand flattened on the expensive wood, and my forehead dropped to touch the glass. He was wonderful, but there was a tiny voice in my head telling me to put on the brakes, even though my heart and body wanted to plunge in with both feet.

I could hear Dylan chatting away with Teagan in the kitchen, telling her about Ben and his friends, and about his quest to get more signed footballs.

"Would you like a signed soccer ball?" Teagan asked, putting a refilled glass of milk in front of my son. He was sitting on a bar stool happily munching what I knew had to be his second chocolate chip cookie. "I know a pretty famous soccer star," she said, smiling.

Dylan grabbed the glass with both hands and took a drink,

leaving a milk mustache on his face. "I sure would! Who is it?"

I walked into the kitchen and smiled at my hostess, hoping she could see gratitude in my expression.

"Chase Forrester. Ever heard of him?" she asked.

He paused for a second as he considered her question, picking up what was left of his cookie. "I'm not sure, but maybe my Uncle Ben would. Do ya think so, Mom?"

I was sure Ben had because I'd recognized the picture in Jensen's office, and I'd only be able to do that if I'd been present when Ben was watching soccer on TV "I do!"

"Have a seat, Missy," Teagan said, indicating the empty barstool next to Dylan. "Can I get you anything? Since you don't want milk and cookies?" She waggled her eyebrows and rested a hand on her swollen belly. "A glass of wine? Just because I can't imbibe, doesn't mean you can't. It might help you unwind after the drive. I have some merlot and chardonnay."

I shook my head. I was tired, but I had to get Dylan situated before I could relax for the night. "Thank you for the lovely offer, but maybe after he goes to sleep." I nodded at my son who was shoving the last quarter of the cookie into his mouth. "But, I'd love some water."

"Of course!" Teagan turned and took a glass from the cupboard behind her and filled it with ice and filtered water from the refrigerator door, then handed it to me.

The water felt cool on my throat as I took a long drink. "Thank you. I didn't realize how thirsty I was."

"Well, it's a long trip." Teagan was putting the cookies in a soccer shaped cookie jar and then shoving it back against the backsplash. "I'm sure you just want to rest. I've got you in two of the guestrooms upstairs, right next to each other. I should have asked Jensen to carry your bags up when he took Remi to bed."

When Jensen had left, and I'd walked through the entryway

with him, I hadn't noticed any of our bags. "I think he did. At least, they've disappeared from the landing."

"He's kind of awesome like that." Teagan studied me for a second and then sprang into action. "Come on, sweet pea," she held her hand out to Dylan. "I'll show you your room."

As I followed the two of them up the winding staircase to the second floor, I couldn't help but admire the rest of the house. It was lavish but comfortable, and the bedrooms were each filled with heavy furniture and decorated nicely, but it wasn't like something out of *Better Homes & Garden or Interior Design* magazines. You could tell a real person, and not an interior design firm, decorated this house.

She showed us into two bedrooms joined by a bathroom in the middle, and miraculously, our suitcases were sitting inside the door of the first one.

"This is so nice, Teagan. Thank you."

She smiled. "My pleasure. I'll leave you to get settled, and if you'd like to talk after Dylan goes to sleep, the offer of wine is still open."

"Thank you."

Dylan was tugging on the bottom of my shirt. "What, honey?"

"All my books are packed in the trailer. We always read a book." I was about to say that I'd have to tell one from memory when Teagan interjected.

"Oh! I can get you a few of Remi's to read. What do you like? She has a lot of Clifford books, or what about *Goodnight, Moon,* some Sesame Street books, or *Ferdinand the Bull?*"

Dylan's eyes lit up in delight. That was a book I'd read to him since he was a baby. "Ferdinand!"

"Okay! I'll be right back."

Teagan hurried from the room, and I went to gather up Dylan's small roller bag and placed it on the bed, intent on gathering out the pajamas that he'd worn the night before at the hotel in Omaha.

Dylan climbed up on the bed and threw himself back on the plush pillows. "I like this place, Mom," he said matter-of-factly.

"I bet you do," I said, reaching over and pulling his T-shirt up and over his head and pulling the pajama top on instead. "But we have to be respectful and careful not to make a mess or break anything."

"They got a kid, Mom," he said unabashedly as if that explained everything.

I couldn't help but smile. "I know, but let's just be a little careful, okay?"

I pulled off his sneakers and socks, shoving the socks into the shoes and setting them on the floor of the closet. "Hurry up, Mom! I gotta get dressed before Miss Teagan comes back!" Dylan said, shimmying out of his jeans and pulling on his Spidey bottoms. "She can't see my unders!" he whispered tiredly.

I tried to hide my soft chuckle. "Oh, okay," I smiled, agreeing with an answering whisper. I helped my son put on his pants and then pulled down the covers on the queen size bed, patting the mattress. "Hop up, babe."

Teagan came in with the book and handed it to me. "Here you are. I'll be downstairs, Missy. Sleep tight, Dylan."

"Will Remi's dad come over tomorrow? He promised to play some football with me."

"He has to work, sweetheart," I said, tucking the covers around my son and fluffing his pillow, wondering how I'd explain Remi's two fathers to my son.

Teagan's expression filled with pleasure. "Um... maybe we can coax him over for Sunday brunch. My husband, Chase, will also be home in the morning. Maybe you can all kick it around, hmm?"

"Awesome!" Dylan exclaimed, suddenly awake.

"There are extra towels in the tall cupboard in the bathroom but let me know if you need anything else."

She was pregnant, so surely, she needed rest. "We'll be fine, Teagan. Thank you for everything."

"Of course. Come down for a bit, if you want. I'll be up for a while. I'm working on a project."

I settled in and read Dylan the story of *Ferdinand the Bull,* and he fell asleep before I was half finished with the book. I switched off the bedside lamp, leaving the bathroom light on for Dylan, in case he woke up and became disoriented by the new surroundings. I then proceeded to find my way back downstairs in search of Jensen's ex-wife.

I was amazed at the easy friendship between them, and how Jensen knew his way around Teagan and Chase's house. I couldn't imagine having such a cordial and open relationship with Derrick. Obviously, our circumstances were different, and I was curious as hell about more details. It was one thing to hear it from Jensen, and another to get Teagan's side of the story. I didn't want to pry, but I did want to know what it was like from her perspective. After sacrificing so much for her, how could Teagan give Jensen up? What were her real feelings?

She was sitting in a big chair in the great room off the entry to the magnificent house, with her feet perched on the matching ottoman. She had her head down working on what looked like a blanket, though the television was on low in the background.

She looked up as I entered. "Wow, that was fast!" She had an embroidery hoop and was working on what looked like a square for a baby quilt.

I entered tentatively. Nothing about this woman made me feel uneasy, but she was opening up her home to me, and I was extremely attracted to her ex-husband. It could get weird, and I couldn't help my apprehension. "Yes. He went out like a light.

He's had a big couple of days."

"Yes. I checked on Remi before I came downstairs and she didn't even whimper when I took off her clothes and put on a nightgown. Take a seat." Teagan used her hand to indicate I should sit down on the matching olive-green sofa, as she set aside her embroidery and started to rise. "Wine, right? Red or white? I found some chardonnay."

"White, please," I answered, settling down on the couch. It was plush, and I sank into its deep comfortable cushions as she left to pour my wine and was soon back and handing me a large wine glass, filled about a third of the way with the sweet-smelling chardonnay. The glass was lightweight and made of fine crystal, though the style of it was simple. "Thank you." I took a sip of cool wine. It was dry, with a light green apple essence and a buttery aroma. "This is delicious. Thank you."

"So?" Teagan's expression was inquisitive and gracious. "Tell me about the trip? Did Remi behave?"

I curled my legs up underneath me on the couch having removed my shoes and left them in my room. Teagan didn't resume her work but seemed keen on our conversation. I couldn't help but huff out a soft laugh.

"Oh my gosh! Was she too precocious?" Teagan asked

"No, she was great. She's quite a little girl."

Teagan's face shone with pride. "I agree, but I'm her mother, so I have to think so. She's been through so much; I'm afraid we might spoil her just a tad."

"She was perfect," I said, remembering what Remi said during our bathroom visit at the hotel that morning. "She's a princess."

"Oh my God! Everything is *princess* around here. Chase calls her his little princess. Her room is decorated like the inside of a castle tower and looks like her fairy godmother threw up! Her grandmother spoils her with dress-up gowns and tiaras. Chase and I even got married at Disney World for her."

I smiled. "Yes, Remi is certainly all girl and a welcome change from the bevy of boys always surrounding my son."

"How did they get along?"

"Fine, why?"

Teagan rolled her eyes. "She's got a boy in Kindergarten who is mean to her, and a couple of her cousins haven't been the best to her. either."

"Oh, no!" I felt terrible for Remi. She was such a sweet little girl; it was hard to imagine anyone being cruel to her.

"We're all trying to talk her through it. The good news is she tells us she has another boy in her class who stands up for her, though we have talked with the teacher."

"Ah! Her own Prince Charming! How sweet is that?"

"Yes, exactly!" Teagan agreed with a small laugh. "I'm sure she milks it to the max!"

"She told me it's okay to be a damsel in distress," I said, sipping on my wine. "She said Jensen wants to help me."

"I hope that didn't make you feel bad," Teagan said apologetically, her face filling up with concern. "I'm sure she didn't mean anything by it. I hope you don't think that we think you needed help. I just wanted to offer our home so you could bring Dylan right away. I can't imagine being away from Remi for the month it would take to find a home."

"Not at all," I reassured. "I'm extremely grateful. I don't want Jensen to see me as needy. How much of my story did Jensen share?"

"Just that you didn't have family here, and that you'd been in Wyoming with your brother since your divorce two years ago."

"That's it?"

"Yes." Teagan's face took on a concerned expression. "Don't take it as a negative that Jensen wants to help. He's a *real* knight in shining armor. He has a huge heart."

I shifted uncomfortably. The last thing I wanted to hear was that Jensen behaved with every woman, the way he did with me. "Yes. He is amazing to Dylan and me."

Teagan was seated back in the big chair and had her elbow resting on the arm of the chair and her chin resting against her hand. "He is an extraordinary man. He was there for me when I needed him, too."

"Is this weird? Talking about him like this?"

Teagan's eyebrows arched, and she shook her head. "Not for me," she waved away my concern. "Didn't Jensen tell you about us? About Chase and Remi?"

I flushed, knowing I couldn't hide the truth. "He did, but he only touched on it. He said you all met in college, but you were with Chase…" I let my words drop off, unsure how to continue. How could I tell her that, no matter what her situation was, I thought her reasons for marrying Jensen were selfish and stupid?

"Yes, although I'm sure he didn't do the story justice."

I had to confess. "He did enlighten me about Chase and Arsenal, and you and your father."

Teagan nodded, inhaling deeply. "Look, Missy, I'm just going to cut to it. I was young, stupid, and scared to death, and in hindsight, I would have done everything differently. In fact, I was going to tell my father to go to hell, drop out of Clemson and follow Chase to London. Then, I called him to tell him I was coming, and a strange woman answered his phone. She made me believe Chase was unfaithful to me with her."

"Oh, my God!" This was the part that Jensen left out. "That's terrible."

"Pregnancy made me emotional, and I literally lost it. I couldn't face him, and or my father. Despite thinking Chase had cheated, I couldn't let my father ruin his career. I didn't ask Jensen to marry me, but he was my closest friend. I cried on his shoulder many nights. I guess, deep down, he would have talked to Chase if I'd allowed it, but instead, he went to my dad without telling me. I felt backed up against the wall; as if Jensen was the only person I could trust. At least, that's what I thought at the time."

"Wow. He definitely left out the important stuff," I said trying to tamp down the incredulity in my voice.

"Jensen," she said, shaking her head. "He didn't want to make me look bad and, I suppose he'll always be protective of Remi and me."

"What happened with the woman on the phone?" Despite the short time we'd known each other, Teagan's openness seemed to permit me to ask.

"She was Chase's personal trainer, Bronwyn. She swiped his phone when he was in the hot tub or something. He didn't know about the call, and I only found out the circumstances when she came with him to Atlanta last year."

"What a bitch," I said under my breath, and then instantly regretted it. "Oh, I'm sorry. I can't believe she came here."

"No, it's okay. Chase was seeing her when I asked him to help Remi, but I didn't know until later that she was the one I spoke to years ago."

I was horrified. Was Teagan's husband seeing that other woman for six years? I decided to save my questions for another time. "In that case, she's worse than I thought."

"You're right. She was extremely unkind to me on the phone, but I blame myself. Chase was the love of my life. I should have trusted him. I should have asked him, and not blindly believed her lies. It ended up ruining Chase and Jensen's friendship and breaking all of our hearts. They were the best of friends, and we were all close, then everything blew up."

"It seems to have worked out now." I felt bad for Teagan. It must have been horrible to feel betrayed and then to sacrifice her own happiness for someone she believed cheated on her. "Jensen doesn't seem to regret anything. He just adores Remi!"

Teagan nodded. "I'm very thankful she has him. I've made a ton of mistakes where Jensen and Chase are concerned, but she is the one good thing to come out of it."

"She's a beautiful child."

"She's literally a miracle."

"Yes. Jensen told me about her leukemia."

Teagan's face took on a wistful and sad expression. "It was hell, and I cursed it for so many years. I thought it punishment for what I did to Chase, but in the end, it brought him back to us. To all of us. We've been blessed with two miracles."

I was speechless. It was an incredible story, and I was feeling emotional. Teagan was able to find the silver lining of such a horrific situation. "You're all so strong."

"We're all doing well now, and it's time for Jensen to find someone to be happy with. Look, Missy, I'm going to be blunt; he likes you, a lot, and he's concerned about you. He didn't tell me why, but he is, and I want to assure you that you won't meet a better man than Jensen."

Teagan reached out to squeeze my hand, and emotion started to well up inside me. My throat started to get tight, and tears burned the back of my eyes. "I sense that, and I'm trying to trust my instincts with him."

Teagan's express twisted in disbelief, "Why wouldn't you?"

I hesitated only slightly. I felt I could trust this woman who was quickly becoming a friend. "My ex-husband was abusive. Finally, I ran away with Dylan two years ago. We had a restraining order in Wyoming, but it's no good here."

Her mouth fell open in disbelief. Jensen hadn't told her, which made me trust him even more. "Holy crap. I'm so sorry! I didn't know, or I wouldn't have brought it up."

I shook my head. "No, it's okay. You couldn't have known."

It was apparent she was sympathetic. "Well, you have a great new job, and new friends, here in Atlanta. Everything will be okay."

My fingers played with the stem of my wine glass. "I am a bit worried about being on-air. Derrick could find us."

"This place is like a fortress, and you can stay with us as long as you'd like."

I knew that to get on with my life, in a healthy way, I had to get my own place and learn to be self-sufficient. "My mother is moving to town soon, and I need to stand on my own two feet. I have to do this, if I'm ever going to truly get over being terrified."

Teagan got up and moved over to the couch. She hugged me tightly. "I understand, but we'll be here if you need us. I feel like we're good friends, already."

My heart filled up to the point of bursting, gratitude rushing over me. I barely knew these people, and I felt like they were the best friends I had in the world. I hugged her back, fighting the tears that threatened to spill from my eyes. This young woman had been through hell, and she was having a baby in a couple of months, yet she was opening her home and her heart to me, and my son.

When I pulled back, I sniffed and met her sincere brown eyes. "You don't know how much that means to me."

"It's late. Why don't you go on up, take a hot shower and crawl into bed? You'll feel better in the morning." Teagan's voice was comforting. She was so sure everything would work out; I almost believed her.

JENSEN

Teagan says to get your ass over here for brunch before your flight, or she'll fry your bacon.

Chase's text had pinged early in the morning. My flight was just after 1 PM, so I'd rushed around and packed my bag hoping to get over to their house as soon as possible, thankful for the excuse to see Missy, Dylan, and Remi. I couldn't stay long, but it was better than nothing.

My mind was jacked up. I couldn't stop wondering what Teagan and Missy talked about the night before and was aching to ask Teagan the first chance that presented itself. When I walked through the front door, the incredible aromas of coffee, bacon, and cinnamon filled the air inside the house. Remi was watching *The Little Mermaid* in the living room to my left. As soon as she saw me, she came running out, and I bent and lifted her into my embrace. I'd never get sick of looking at this angelic face, all rosy with health; her brown curls were still matted from sleep, and she was wearing the Cinderella nightgown my mom had given her for Christmas.

"Jensey! Wanna come watch Ariel with me? It's getting to the good part." I knew that "the good part" was *Part of Your World*. Remi knew the words by heart, and I had heard her belt it out with the cartoon princess on many occasions.

I kissed her forehead. "I'd love to, squirt, but I have to eat quick and get to the airport."

"Again?" she lamented sadly.

"Yep," I answered. "But I'd love to have breakfast with you. Will you sit by me? It smells amazing. What's Mom cooking?"

"Miss Missy made us a cake for coffee! I think that's good enough, but Daddy said he wants bacon and eggs."

"Bacon and coffeecake sound good to me!" I agreed. I was unprepared for how pleased I'd be hearing that Missy was cooking in the kitchen with Teagan. It was a good indication she was feeling at home.

"Miss Missy said I don't have'ta have coffee, though," Remi

insisted.

Could this scene be any more perfect? Contentment settled down on me like a warm blanket. "What's your dad doing?" I asked as I returned Remi to her own two feet.

"Talking to Dylan. Can I go watch my movie, please? Ariel is gonna rescue Prince Eric right now."

"She is?" I loved her adorable little face.

'Yeah! Eric's her damsel!"

I burst out laughing. She was adorable. "I don't think that's how it works, squirt. It's usually girls that get to be damsels."

"What is he, then?" Remi gazed up at me with a perplexed look in her deep green eyes.

I was amused at the same time as I was uncertain how to explain it to her. "Hmm… well…" I searched for the right word. "Maybe a *bachelor* in distress?" It was a stretch, but I didn't know what else to say without the benefit of Google. Leave it to Remi to stump me.

She considered my answer for a moment and accepted it without a demand for further clarification. "Okay. So, can I go watch now?"

"Sure. But don't forget to sit by me at breakfast!"

"I won't!" she said happily and disappeared into the living room as I walked through the house toward the kitchen. I could hear a lot of happy conversation as I approached.

Dylan was sitting next to Chase at the kitchen bar, clearly mesmerized by my friend. The two women were laughing together as they prepared the meal. Missy was standing next to the counter buttering toast, and Teagan was frying bacon and eggs at the range top.

"Thanks for the invitation," I said, my eyes darting to Missy to catch her reaction on seeing me. "I'm starving."

Her face lit up in a smile, and the sound of her voice caused my heart to leap inside my chest. "You're just in time! Breakfast is almost ready."

"It smells fantastic." I wanted to walk over and greet her properly, maybe even kiss her but considered she might not be ready. I'd told myself that baby steps were needed to build trust between us, and I wasn't sure how she'd take any PDAs in front of the others. I contented myself to concentrate on her son. "How are you, buddy?" I ruffled Dylan's hair; who looked up from his talk with Chase to beam at me. "Did you sleep well?"

"Yep! Chase said we could play ball later. Can you play with us, too?"

The little boy looked at me anxiously, and I found myself wishing I didn't have to fly out today.

"I want to, but I have to work later."

"But, it's Sunday!" he complained, as his face fell.

I rolled my eyes wryly. "Unfortunately, I work a lot on Sundays."

"Awww! No fair!" His disappointment was evident, and I felt elated that the little boy wanted to spend time with me, too. I wanted to make time for him. I was acutely aware that he had no real father and he would miss his Uncle Ben immensely.

"I'll be back on Tuesday. How about we play then? Chase will you be in town so you can join?"

My friend was stealing a piece of bacon from the serving platter that Teagan was putting it on and she slapped his hand away. "Yes. Ow!" he mocked, pretending she'd injured him. "That's what I get after being gone for a week?"

Teagan's hand came up to his face as he stood behind her and he bent to kiss her temple. Chase's hands settled over her swollen belly. "That's what you get for stealing bacon."

The oven timer went off, and Missy grabbed some potholders and took out a delicious looking coffee cake with streusel topping from the oven.

"Chase, please pour the orange juice. Who wants coffee?"

Teagan asked. "Remi! Come eat, honey!"

A few minutes of bustling around the kitchen later we were all seated at the table with our plates loaded and enjoying the tasty food. Remi and Dylan were sitting next to each other and, as promised, I was next to Remi. The position gave me a chance to look at Missy and gaze at her across the table. A soft smile curved her lips every time our eyes met, and my heart surged and thumped harder each time.

Everyone was still wearing their pajamas, and I was pleased that she felt so at ease with Teagan and Chase. She looked all soft and alluring from sleep. Her hair was combed, and she looked like she might have a small amount of make-up on, but she was a natural beauty. She and Teagan were two peas in a pod, and a certain satisfaction came over me that they were becoming friends. The secret looks and smiles between the two piqued my curiosity. They had to be up to something.

I was still dying to know what was said about me after I'd left last night and decided to text Teagan later while I was waiting for my flight. I felt like I was back in college and Teagan was covertly helping me find information about a girl I was interested in; and whether she liked me in return. Looking at the two of them, though, I wondered if Missy had hijacked my partner in crime. I huffed in silent amusement—what a thought.

Missy was adding a little bit of salt to the scrambled eggs on her son's plate from the soccer ball-shaped saltshaker that she'd picked up from the middle of the kitchen table.

"Why is there so many soccer balls here?" Dylan asked, scooping up a forkful and eating it.

"Are, honey," Missy corrected. "Why *are* there so many soccer balls here?"

"You mean footballs, don't cha?" Remi asked, using her fork to pick up a bite of scrambled egg. Her cinnamon coffee cake had already been devoured.

"That's a soccer ball," Dylan argued wryly, pointing at the black and white object, obviously dismissing Remi as clueless.

"Is not!"

"Is, too!"

"Is not!"

Oh, boy. I could see where this was going. Chase and I looked at each other, grinning.

"Uh uh!" Dylan denied. "Footballs aren't round. They're brown and shaped like this." He outlined the more pointed oval shape of a football in the air with one index finger. "Girls don't know nothin' about sports," he scoffed.

"Oh, yeah?" Remi spouted back. "You don't even use your feet with that stupid ball, so why do they call it *foot*ball, then, huh?"

"I just got one from a real famous quarterback, so I know what I'm talking about!"

"Boys are dumb! My dad is a famous footballer, so I oughta know!" she huffed.

Dylan looked at Remi and frowned, his little face filling with rage. "No, he ain't! He works on the TV like my mom!"

"Remi! Be nice!" Teagan exclaimed.

"Dylan, be polite!" Missy cautioned. "We're guests here."

Both mothers jumped in to reprimand their respective children and just in the nick of time.

Things were getting heated between the two kids, and Chase stepped in to calm things down. "I got this," he said calmly. "Relax, you two. You're both right. The game Americans' know as soccer is called football in several other countries, such as the United Kingdom, where I used to play for a team in London. That's why Remi knows soccer as football, Dylan. And Remi, American football uses the ball that Dylan described. I know it's confusing, but they're both different games, sometimes called the same thing."

"Told ya!" Remi's head tilted back abruptly as she huffed.

"Did not! You didn't know it was two different games!"

"Kids!" I interjected. "What'd ya say we all go out back and play Ferris Wheel for a few minutes before I have to leave? How about it, Chase?"

It was a game Chase and I made up so we could both play with Remi together. We'd each hold one of her ankles and wrists and then swing her in a big arc, sometimes all the way up and over our heads. It always made her giggle, and I hoped Dylan would enjoy it as well. Hopefully, they'd have so much fun they'd forget about their disagreement.

"Sure! Ferris Wheel sounds like a great idea right now." He looked at Teagan, who nodded her agreement. "Let's go, kids!"

"Chase, they just ate," Teagan warned, but he waved off her concern giving her a wry look. "Don't make them sick."

"What is Ferris Wheel?" Dylan asked.

"It's super fun! Come on!" Remi said, jumping down off of her chair and running toward the sliding glass doors of the walkout that led to the pool and the big fenced-in backyard.

"Can I, Mom?" He was excited, without even knowing what it entailed. "I saw a play-set out there with swings and a fort, too! Can I play on that?"

Missy nodded, and Dylan took off after Remi, their little spat apparently forgotten. "Yes. Just be careful, and mind Mr. Chase and Mr. Jensen! What's Ferris Wheel?" she turned to me as they scrambled from the kitchen. I got up from the table and laid my napkin next to my plate.

"It's an amazing child pacification method. Works every time." I gave her a wink, and then Chase and I followed the kids outside.

"Oh, God, you guys!" Teagan moaned behind me. "If they puke, you're the ones cleaning it up!"

HER *last chance* BEGINS *in his arms.*

Chapter 10

JENSEN

"I know what I said, Bryan, but I'd just feel better if I could do this myself."

I was sitting in my boss's office trying to justify my case. I'd been thinking about Missy non-stop for days. The entire time I was up in Bristol I was pre-occupied; which wasn't exactly good for my new job. It was only my second week, and all I could think about was helping her feel more comfortable getting into her first assignment. Janice Walker, the producer who was assigned to her crew the first week out of the gate, was a hard-ass. My entire team had dreaded working with her.

"What are you doing, Jeffers," he glared at me, clearly irritated. "Are you going to let yourself be led around by your dick every week? Because, if you are, maybe you'd rather go back to your correspondence gig."

I sat there cockeyed in his chair, slouching over and using my right hand to pluck at my lower lip.

"No," I met his stare unmoved. "I don't want Missy's first assignment to be from hell. It's for the good of the company." The corner of my mouth quirked up in the start of an amused grin, which, if his pissed off expression was any sort of tell, just made him less likely to grant my request. It could be that ESPN would suffer over time if Missy's confidence were undermined due to a poor producer: although that wasn't my primary motivation.

"Janice is the back-up, and Willy was sick. I'm up against a fucking wall."

"Janice is a bitch to everyone who works with her, and you know it," I accused. "Do you think I don't know why she hasn't gotten a permanent assignment, yet? She's a fucking loose cannon, and no one can stand her."

"If I agree, it will mean you forfeit your weekend off. I'm not getting someone to cover for you in Connecticut, next week."

I'd already considered that if I produced the Sunday game with my old team, I'd have to fly straight to Bristol from location. All I could hope was that it wasn't somewhere on the west coast or my ass would be dragging. "I don't expect you to."

Bryan's countenance was pissed off and impatient, but my willingness to do my own job and cover this assignment seemed to cool him off a bit.

"I'm up to my ass in personnel problems already. I don't have time to screw with Janice or play social secretary so you can babysit a new hire." Bryan said, absently shuffling papers around on his desk

"So, I'll ask Cindy to change it," I suggested with a cheeky grin, rising out of the chair, ready to leave his office.

He stopped, perturbed, shaking his head. "Okay, but this is it. No more special schedules; you arrogant prick."

"Leave my arrogant prick out of this." I laughed as I exited his office and then breezed by a surprised Tracey in Bryan's outer office very satisfied with myself.

"Oh, hey, Jensen," she said. She was distracted, barely looking up from her computer as I passed.

"Hey, Trace!" I greeted her happily.

After I'd stopped by Cindy's desk to get the schedule changed, I was smiling from ear-to-ear over her not-so-subtle teasing; teaming with excitement on my way down to my old office to give Missy the news that I'd be producing her team. It had only been two days since I'd seen her, but I couldn't wait to lay my eyes on her. I told myself to calm-the-fuck down because it was probably written all over me and that wouldn't do. I was like a kid at Christmas. When I walked out of the elevator onto my old floor, I slowed my steps and made small talk with various employees who crossed my path while I wandered through the familiar space.

I stopped into the employee lounge to get coffee and pulled out my phone to text Teagan.

Can you watch Dylan tonight? I'd like to take Missy out to dinner to celebrate her new job.

I poured the coffee, withstanding my urge to get two cups, as I waited for Teagan's answer. I took a sip of the steaming black liquid and continued on my way to find Missy.

She was concentrating on her computer with a small crinkle between her eyebrows; focused on what she was reading. The blinds in the office windows were half open, so I had a covert view of her as I approached.

I popped my head around the corner of the doorway, waiting for her to notice me. It was weird coming into this office when it wasn't mine. There was a box of office supplies in one of the spare chairs with a silver picture frame sitting on top. It was a picture of her holding a chubby baby boy up so she could press her cheek to his. She was thinner than she was now, but otherwise immaculate, as was the baby in the picture. I could only assume it was Dylan when he was six or seven months old.

When the printer by the wall began to whiz, she finally saw me as she turned in her chair to get the document.

A surprised smile instantly replaced Missy's frustrated expression, and her aqua eyes lit up as they locked with mine. I knew she didn't want me to see her struggle while she tried to acclimate to her job, and she quickly tried to mask her consternation.

"Hey, you," she said. She was wearing a tailored black suit and a light pink silk blouse that brought out the bloom in her cheeks. Her hair was straight and sleek, and she had a pair of dark glasses on her face that made her look like a hot college professor. She looked professionally stunning.

If all of the men weren't salivating before, they'd be lining up now, I admitted to myself. Knowing how she felt about men panting over her wasn't the only cause for my unease, but happiness spread over my face at her greeting. "Hey, yourself," I murmured softly. "How are you settling in?"

We'd talked briefly the previous afternoon when I called to see how her first day was going, but it was only minutes before I had to go live on my program, so I didn't get a chance to really find out how she was doing.

"Oh!" She jumped up to move the cardboard box so that I could come in and take the chair in front of the desk. "As you can see, I haven't unpacked anything. Can you sit down for a minute?"

I took the box out of her hands and put it on the floor in the corner of the small office. "Sure," I said. "I just wanted to check on you to see if you needed anything." My eyes were drinking in every inch of her, conscious of the pencil skirt that was skimming the top of her knees, her firm calves, and her black high heels.

She threw up her hands as she sat back down behind the desk. "I'm trying to research the teams and players for the game

I have coming up. I have to admit it's a bit daunting."

"Is Lonnie leaving you alone?" I got straight to the point as my eyes narrowed in suspicion.

Her head cocked to one side, and she shot me a wry look. "I can handle him."

"That didn't answer my question," I persisted.

"He hovered for about an hour yesterday morning, but I told him to fuck off."

The dimples in my face deepened as I held back a laugh. "Literally?"

She nodded, back to concentrating on the computer screen. "Literally."

I smiled broadly; happy as hell she'd put him in his place. "Good. It might start rumors if I had to do it."

Her head snapped up and our eyes connected. "You don't," she warned.

I put both hands up, fingers spread. "Okay. I won't interfere."

"Good." She sighed heavily. "Sorry, I just don't want to get off on the wrong foot and if you're always running to my rescue —"

"I get it. Are those team rosters?" I asked, nodding at the stack of papers she was putting into a black binder on her desk.

"Yes. If I'm honest, Jensen, it's the information overload that scares me to death. I don't want to embarrass myself the first time I'm in front of the camera. The only way I can prove I deserve this job is to nail it every time. Failing isn't an option."

I leaned back in the chair to study her, holding my coffee cup in my right hand. "You'll be fine. The commentary for the interviews is mostly on the teleprompter, and Jarvis will handle most of it during the game until you get the hang of things. Don't freak out. What game is it?" I said calmly and took a swallow of the still steaming coffee.

"Buffalo at Baltimore." Her face twisted hopelessly. "I didn't even know Baltimore had a professional football team. I'm feeling a bit frazzled. Some of the agents are calling for interviews and telling me all of this crap about this player or that. I can't keep all of them straight. You were right; they're pushy as hell."

She was different in the work environment; not hard, exactly, but it was clear she wanted to nail her first broadcast and every one going forward. Professionalism and bitchiness were sometimes the only ways for a woman to get respect in the workplace. Notably, the beautiful ones. Even saying it in my head, it sounded ridiculous that it would still be that way, but I'd seen it many times during my professional career. Some men tended to discount a woman's worth, thinking any successes she achieved were attained only by her looks. Even other women would profess the same thing as a sort of excuse why someone excelled over them, rather than accepting that it was skill, and skill alone, that propelled certain people over others.

"They will be, especially at first. It's like the playground bully; they think you're new and they can take advantage of you. Just remember that they're always thinking of their next contract because they don't get paid until their players do. They try to get their guys in front of the camera as much as possible. Push back hard, and they'll learn to respect you. *You*," I pointed at her, "are in control of who gets airtime, not them." *Sweetheart*, my mind added.

I wished I could reach out and cover her hand with mine. She picked up another sheet of paper off of the printer.

"Didn't Jarvis help you? He should be doing the main interviews for a few weeks to give you time to get your feet under you."

"We haven't talked about it, yet. Cindy said he takes Mondays off, and I haven't seen him yet today." She ran a nervous hand through her hair.

"Generally, it's any players in the current news, the quarterbacks, and or the managers. What about the producer?" I asked gingerly, wondering if any of the others had told her about Janice. "Has she come down to introduce herself? I hear its Janice Walker."

Missy's eyes widened, and she sat back a bit in exaggerated skepticism. "Oh, God, no. Liz already warned me about her. She said she'd try to trip me up as much as possible the first time out. Like she *wants* me to fail."

I sat my empty coffee cup on the corner of her desk nearest me and crossed my arms. "Leave it to her to tank a team just to put you in your place. She's just a bitch, in general," I admitted. "Don't take it personally."

"Great," Missy huffed. "I can hardly wait."

I could put her out of her misery by just telling her I was taking the assignment, but I decided it would be more fun to surprise her over dinner.

"You can handle her, Melissa." I used her real name as a way to reinforce her confidence.

"Damn right, I can."

Bam. Just like that, her confidence was solid, and she flashed a bright smile.

I couldn't take my eyes off of her and a good five seconds passed before I spoke. "Good. Now that that's settled, I'll get to the real reason I came down here."

Missy stopped what she was doing and looked up. "Oh? What is it?"

"I'd like to take you out to dinner, tonight. To celebrate all of this."

Her face took on a rosy flush, and she pushed a lock of hair behind her ear. "That's… sweet of you, Jensen."

"Well, don't spread it around," I teased. "So, is that a yes?"

"I'd love to, but what about Dylan?"

"Teagan's got us covered."

Her hand went over her heart. "Really?"

I nodded, memorizing every curve of her face. She was stunning, schoolmarm glasses and all. "So?"

"So, I'd love to. Thank you."

That second, Jarvis showed up in the doorway of her office, his vast frame completely filling it. "Good morning!" His dark gaze roamed over both Missy and I. "Am I interrupting something?"

"Nope," I sat up and then stood, picking up my coffee cup. "I just came in to wish her luck, Jarvis. I'm heading back upstairs, but can I see you in the hall for a minute?" My brows rose, hoping he'd get a clue that I didn't want Missy to listen in.

"Sure. I'll be back in a few minutes, Missy. We can go over the interviews."

"That sounds good, Jarvis. Thank you."

"See you later," I nodded at the gorgeous woman behind the desk and then exited with Jarvis trailing me. A few feet from her office, I stopped to face him. "Missy is unaware that I'm taking over the assignment from Janice. Keep it under your hat, please."

He patted my arm. "No problem, but what about the rest of the crew? They might spill the beans. Eric was almost pissing himself, he was so happy about it," he said, grinning.

A guttural laugh burst forth. That shit was hilarious. "I'll send out an email. If you see any of them, tell them to keep it to themselves. But, be discrete, Jarvis, okay?"

"Surprising her, huh? No problem." His hand came down on my shoulder, and he knowingly gave it a squeeze.

I knew I had to get my ass upstairs to send out that email right away. Information traveled at the speed of technology, which was only slightly slower than the wagging tongues around here. I sure as hell hoped Cindy came up with a plausible reason why she was switching my assignment with Janice Walker's. The last thing Missy needed were rumors about her and me. I didn't want her standing at the station colored by any relationship hanging over her head. I wanted to cement the respect she deserved.

My cheeks hurt from smiling, but I tried to wipe the grin from my face as I headed back upstairs. Keeping my feelings to myself was going to be fucking hard.

Missy

"You look real pretty, Miss Missy," Remi said.

She was sitting on the vanity next to me, while Dylan was watching TV in the bedroom, as I put on the last of my make up in the bathroom. I was excited about the coming evening with Jensen. It was the first real date I'd been on in several years.

I stopped my thoughts as I stared at myself in the mirror. Jensen said to dress casually, so I had on a lightweight burgundy sweater that hugged my figure with cutouts in the shoulders paired with dark dressy jeans and high-heeled black boots.

"Thank you, sweetheart," I glanced down at her little face. "Do you want a little?" I said, holding up the clear lip-gloss I'd just put on my lips only seconds before.

"Yes, please. Does it taste good? Mommy gave me some that tasted like cotton candy." She puckered her lips and stuck them out. I chuckled out loud; she was the sweetest little thing.

"Mmm... I think this is vanilla." I bent over and carefully used the wand to coat her little lips in some of the shiny gloss.

Remi smacked her lips together and then turned to look in the mirror, pursing them as she admired herself. She picked up my hairbrush and began an attempt at brushing her soft curls. The brush barely connected with her hair, but she put it down and patted the silky waves like it was a professional job.

Oh, my God! She was so adorable I could hardly stand it.

"What do girls need all that glop for?" Dylan asked, now standing in the bathroom doorway. He was holding a soccer ball in both hands. Chase worked with him over the past few days, and he took a real interest in the sport. I was concerned Chase would start to become annoyed with how much Dylan wanted to play and learn, but he had a real passion for the game and seemed unperturbed by Dylan's bugging. The two of them became immersed, and Monday night when I'd returned home from the station, Teagan was making dinner in the kitchen, and both of the kids were in the backyard with Chase.

Now, Remi turned to look at Dylan, taking in his disgruntled expression and raising an eyebrow. "Because princes like princesses to look pretty." Her answer was matter-of-fact, and then she scowled at my son. "Don't you know anything?"

I looked between the two children, both of them precocious, with their own personalities.

"Who said you're a princess, anyway?" Dylan asked, annoyed.

"My daddy, that's who," Remi answered.

Dylan grunted and then huffed. "He's your dad. He hasta!"

"Someday you're gonna wanna be a prince for me and I won't let ya!" Remi's brow furrowed in a frown, and her lower lip stuck out in a pout.

I lifted her down from the counter and then got down on my haunches and smoothed her hair. "You look beautiful. Any prince would be happy to dance with you."

"Come on, kids! The pizza is ready!" Teagan called from the foot of the stairs, thankfully heading off a tiff between the kids.

"Pizza!" Remi was excited and took off like a shot, but Dylan hung behind. He looked sad and made no move to follow the little girl out.

Maybe he was sad I was going out, or perhaps he was jealous that I'd just been primping with Remi.

"Hey, sport," I said, sliding an arm around his shoulders and giving him a little squeeze. "Do you want me to comb this for you?"

"Nah." Disappointment laced his voice as he shrugged. He wouldn't meet my eyes and instead was concentrating on the black and white ball.

I put my hands on both of his shoulders and turned him around and gave a gentle nudge until we were both standing in my bedroom. I bent and lifted Dylan into my arms and then sat down on the bed with him on my lap. "Wanna tell me what's bugging you? Don't you want me to go out with Jensen, tonight? Teagan has pizza, and she has a movie night all planned. She said she'd even make kettle corn." I rubbed his back in a slow, steady rhythm. "Chase will be home later, too."

Dylan hung his head and then shook it, sadly. I could hear him snuffling, and my heart hurt for him.

"Honey, what's the matter?" I pushed his hair back off of his face, but it quickly fell right back into place. "I can't fix this if I don't know what's wrong. Don't you like it here?"

He rubbed his nose with the back of his hand, and for the first time, he lifted his head and looked at me with sorrow-filled eyes. "No, I mean, yeah," he said tearfully.

I pulled him close and hugged him close to me, kissing his forehead. "Then, what is it?"

"How come Remi gets to have two daddies, and I can't even have one?"

Two fat crocodile tears tumbled from his eyes and down his cheeks, and he wiped at them with both hands. He was trying not to out-and-out cry, but his chin was trembling. My heart broke for him. Only days before I'd asked myself how I'd deal with this when it came up, never dreaming it would be so soon. "It's not fair!" he cried.

I sighed heavily and tightened my arms around him. Dylan was barely six, and though he acted tough for his age, he had a soft heart and tender feelings. It was no wonder, considering what he'd been through with Derrick, though I wasn't sure how much of it he remembered.

My own eyes flooded. I blinked against my tears and cleared the tightness from my throat. If only I could tell Dylan how lucky he was not to have his dad around anymore. I searched my mind for a way to talk to him about this sensitive subject.

"Well, Remi has a special situation. Chase is her biological dad and Jensen was married to Teagan, and so, I guess he's like a stepdad; kind of like Joey's." I sucked in my breath, hoping he would understand. "You know how his parents got a divorce, and then his mom got married again?"

"Yeah, but Joey hates his stepdad. Jensey is like a real daddy."

My heart flipped inside my chest. He called Teagan and Chase Miss Teagan and Mr. Chase, like I'd taught him to do as a sign of respect for adults who were outside of our family. But Dylan referred to Jensen in the same way that Remi did, and somehow, it felt right. Despite the short time Jensen had been in both of our lives, Dylan could sense that Jensen was doing what he could to take care of us.

I prayed that my son wouldn't ask why Jensen was married to Remi's mother before Chase. It was just like his little mind to figure out that real dads come first.

"You're right," I affirmed. What could I say? Jensen *was* like Remi's real dad. I wanted to say Jensen was special, but I was terrified he'd get attached to him and then what if it didn't work out between Jensen and me? "It's a rare situation when real fathers are friends with stepfathers, but Chase and Jensen are, and that's what makes Remi so lucky."

"But, where's my daddy?" His little voice broke and his face crumpled. "Doesn't he love me?"

My heart, so full a second ago when I was thinking and talking about Jensen, turned stone cold when Derrick came to mind. Someone so selfish and mean should never have children. I shouldn't be in this shitty position. Should I break my son's heart by telling him the truth, or should I offer a white lie to spare him knowing what a bastard his father was? If he couldn't remember the nasty details, I didn't want to make him.

I proceeded with caution. "Do you remember him, baby?"

Dylan shook his head and relief spread through me as I held my son against me stroking his hair over and over and kissing his head.

"Well, he runs a big company, and he wasn't home very much. I guess, he just didn't have time to be a dad, and so I decided to take you to be with Uncle Ben." I took a deep breath to steady my voice. "Do you understand?"

"That's why you got divorced? Cuz he didn't want to be my dad?"

The pain in my chest exploded at Dylan's heartbroken question. The only thing I could be thankful for was that my son didn't seem to remember how mean he was; to both of us. "I think he wanted to be, baby, but he just didn't know how to be the kind of father that little boys need."

"You mean the kind who plays sports and stuff?" Dylan was less tearful now, and more curious.

No, the kind that is always there, and doesn't hurt you, my mind screamed. *The kind that loves their kids.* "Mmmm... yes, and stuff," I agreed, hoping that would end the conversation until he was older.

There was some squealing from Remi downstairs, and I

knew Jensen had arrived to pick me up.

"Let's dry your eyes and go get you some pizza. It's rude to make Miss Teagan wait on us for dinner, okay?"

"Okay." He nodded. "Is that Jensey?" Dylan asked, jumping off my lap. He lifted the hem of his T-shirt and wiped his eyes; the skin around them still splotchy.

"I'm sure it is."

"I hope its pepperoni pizza."

Knowing Teagan, she would have asked in advance what kind of pizza Dylan liked. She'd done everything she could to make us feel at home.

Dylan ran from the room and down the stairs while I stayed where I was, sitting on the bed to compose myself. I didn't want Jensen to see me rattled. I wanted tonight to be special, and that couldn't happen if Derrick were part of the conversation. I'd forgotten how much I hated my ex-husband. He was out of our lives, but he still caused pain. I fucking despised him.

When I walked down the stairs just a minute later, I paused to observe the scene in the landing on the first floor. Jensen was down on his haunches to get down on my son's level and was talking to him; concern clearly etched on his handsome features. My breath caught, and I sank down on the stairs so I could watch their interaction undetected.

"Hey, buddy," Jensen said, brushing my son's unruly mop off his forehead. "Are you okay? What's the matter?"

Dylan was reluctant to admit he'd been crying. "Nothin'," he replied sadly.

Jensen picked up my son with one arm and rubbed Dylan's stomach through his shirt. I watched in awe as my son put both arms around Jensen's neck to hug him tight. After a second's surprise, Jensen returned the embrace in full measure. My heart stopped beating in that second.

"Hey, I know I have a date with your mom tonight, but

how about you, Remi, and I all do something together next week?"

Dylan's head popped up from Jensen's shoulder, and a wide grin spread out on his face. "Like go to a game or somethin' like that?" he asked hopefully.

"I have a lot of work this weekend, but we'll work it out the first chance I get, okay?"

"That's awesome!" Dylan beamed.

"Now, where is everybody?" Jensen asked, giving Dylan one last squeeze.

"In the kitchen eating pizza! Let's go!"

Jensen chuckled and set my son down. "Okay. Lead the way. Did Teagan make pepperoni? It's my favorite."

"Mine, too!" Dylan was looking up at Jensen like he hung the moon and Jensen reached down to cup his face.

"Let's find out." He nodded in the direction of the kitchen and Dylan shot off in that direction.

"Okay! Come on!"

My fingers closed around the rungs, and my forehead pressed against the railing of the banister. I closed my eyes, throat aching and willed myself not to cry as my heart bloomed. A mixture of elation and pain filled every cell in my body and in that moment, I admitted to myself that he had me.

I'd been fighting my feelings for Jensen, worried about Dylan's. I didn't want him to fall in love with him, too, and then for things not to work out between us. The last thing a mother wants is for her child to suffer pain, but after what I'd just seen, my heart splintered into a million pieces. Was there a better man on earth than Jensen Jeffers?

I couldn't help the tears that fell from my eyes as I sat there struggling to compose myself. Was it possible that someone could totally change your entire life after only a few weeks? Was it possible to trust him and more importantly, with my heart?

Even without how incredible he was with Dylan, I'd been falling in love with him from the moment I sat down in front of his desk on the day I interviewed with ESPN.

I sucked in my breath until my lungs felt they would explode, and then hurried back to my room to touch up my makeup, wanting to be beautiful for him.

Tonight, I was going to let whatever happened, happen. I was going to let Jensen touch me and kiss me. I would completely trust my heart.

Chapter 11

JENSEN

I had been staring at Missy all through dinner and glanced across at her now, as I pulled out of the parking lot of the restaurant. Throughout the evening she'd gotten more and more relaxed, and her smiles had come easily, which had me flying. I couldn't help noticing the graceful curve of her neck, the soft swell of her breasts above the neckline of her sweater, or the curve of her shoulders showing through the cutout material. Her flowing blonde hair called for my fingers to run through it; I knew it would feel like liquid silk. I felt like a kid standing on the outside of a candy store salivating over everything inside but allowed only to peer through the window and dream about its contents. She was simply stunning.

Our hands were lightly entwined together, as they had been from almost the minute that I'd picked her up. We talked about work, we talked about our kids, and she asked me what parts of Atlanta I thought she should look in for a home or apartment. Selfishly, I wanted her to find something near me. If her mother wasn't moving in with her, and if I'd known her longer, I probably would have suggested that she and Dylan move-in with me.

I wanted her in a way that drove me crazy. I felt hungry,

but in a profound, more insatiable way than I'd ever been. I felt jealous when any other man even looked at her sideways. It was ludicrous to have these thoughts, but something deep inside my soul said this was it. She was the one.

When I was away from her; she was all I thought about. I couldn't wait to see her, and when we were together, like now, I was giddy with the happiness that filled every fiber of my soul. The small smile that lifted the corners of her mouth as she looked dreamily out of the window was a strong indication that she felt safe with me, and I reveled in it. I wanted to ask what she was feeling, but instincts told me it might be too soon to press. It was going to be harder than hell to be around her, want her so badly, yet still hold back. But... I had to bide my time. Testosterone was teeming, and my instincts were screaming for me to act.

I turned my eyes back to the road, trying to calm down my inner demons. "So, this is the part of the evening where I ask what you want to do next?"

I sensed it when her head turned toward me, and I could feel her eyes studying my face as if it were an actual caress. I swallowed and slid her a quick glance. "Well?" I asked, an eyebrow shooting up.

Her head cocked to one side, and her gaze was still intense and contemplative as she considered my question. "Mmmm...." There was palpable energy between us; not just in where our hands touched, but in the air around us. The thumb on my right hand brushed slowly back and forth over the knuckles of her left. "What are my choices?" she asked softly.

Maybe she didn't mean it to sound so seductive, but the languid way the words slipped out went straight to my dick.

I sucked in a slow, steadying breath, hoping she wouldn't notice. "It's a little chilly for a walk along Riverwalk, but there are a lot of bars; some with music if you'd like to dance or get a drink. It's beautiful down there... so we could do that. We could see a movie, or," I was about to jump off the cliff. I shouldn't even be suggesting it, but I wanted to be alone with her, and whether that resulted in making love or not, I wanted to have her to myself. It would also tell me if she trusted me.

"Or?" She was leaning back in her seat, half turned toward me, with one leg curled beneath her. The serious look on her face told me she knew what I was about to say.

"Or, we could go to my place. I have wine or ice cream." I huffed out a small laugh, a sardonic grin starting on my face as I looked over at her again.

Wine, or fucking ice cream? I scolded myself. I felt like I was in high school, fumbling around in the dark for my dick, for Christ's sake. I was a complete idiot. "I mean we can talk some more, without interruption."

Oh, my God; I thought. She probably thinks I'm like every other horny bastard who tries to get in her pants. Could I have said anything more asinine?

"Over drinks or dessert?" she asked.

I nodded, not wanting to shove my foot further into my mouth. "Yes. Anything you want to do. I'm up for anything."

Shit.

I felt heat creeping up my face as I prayed to God she didn't take that as an erection reference. I'd never been so conscious of every syllable that came out of my mouth, or so worried about its interpretation, in my entire life. I was out of my element.

The sun had set so I couldn't see the color of her eyes, but they were definitely darker and trained right on me. "Wine or ice cream." Missy's voice was soft and sultry, but decisive as she repeated my words. "That's my choice. I'd like to see where you live."

My heart literally leapt as a short, relieved laugh burst from within my chest. "Okay," I turned onto the expressway that would take me toward Decatur on the northeast side of town and squeezed Missy's hand that I still held in mine. "My house isn't anything like Chase and Teagan's. I'm just warning you."

She snorted in amusement. "I didn't expect that. I doubt the governor's mansion compares. I'm sure it's really nice, though," she said, her hand tightening on mine. "Like you."

"We didn't choose it for its aesthetics. It's near a couple of the big hospitals," I explained unnecessarily, then chastising myself because the last thing I fucking wanted was for Missy to think of Teagan and me in that house.

Missy seemed to understand. "Of course, that would have to be your first priority. How long have you lived there?"

"Just under four years. I've been considering a move, but I figured Remi was used to the place, and the promotion became my main goal, I guess."

"Is it a long commute to ESPN?"

I shrugged. "Moderate. That's definitely something to consider when you're looking for a place. Traffic during rush hour is a bear."

I pulled into the older part of the neighborhood further off of the main thoroughfares where my house stood on a quiet street lined with tall trees and dotted with streetlights. The homes were older, but they had character.

"The houses are nice, and the neighborhood is well maintained. Though, I did rip out the orange shag carpet when we moved in. It was gross, especially in the kitchen. The rest of the stuff I could live with." I explained, pulling into the driveway and braked to a stop.

"In the kitchen?" Missy grimaced.

I smiled. "Yes, my thoughts exactly, but in the seventies and eighties it was the thing."

She reached out and covered my hand with hers. "You

don't have to worry about the house. My family isn't well to do. My mother raised us alone, remember?"

I turned off my SUV and paused, looking her in the eyes. I half-shrugged. "Yes. I don't want you to be turned off because of incidentals."

"You'd rather I was turned off by non-incidentals?" she teased. The streetlights were behind us, so her face was thrown into shadow, but her gentle ribbing put me at ease.

I shook my head with a chuckle and flipped my hand over beneath hers to capture her fingers in mine. "I'd rather you not be turned off. Period."

She sucked in a quick breath. "I don't think you're in danger of that."

I brought her hand up to my mouth and gently kissed her palm. "Counting on it."

I leaned toward her, and she met me halfway. When our lips met, there was a sort of bridled tension begging to be unleashed. Our mouths played gently with each other's, ghosting and then in a series of soft, sucking kisses. It was glorious, and my body reacted instantly. My hand came up to slide to the back of her neck, under the curtain of her flowing hair and I deepened the kiss. Missy responded, opening her mouth to mine and lightly sucking on my tongue.

I broke the contact with a groan, utterly miserable that I couldn't keep kissing her, but hoping we'd continue a bit later. I rested my forehead against hers, our reluctant breath mingling in a hot wave. "You wanna come in?"

"Yes." Her white teeth flashed. "I want my wine and ice cream."

I couldn't help the laugh that burst from me. "Well, let's hope I have some wine that goes well with vanilla. It's Remi's favorite and all I have, at present." I pretended to grimace and opened my door, quickly walking around to open the passenger door and helping Missy out.

Her eyes were flirty. "Then, I think white would be best. Do you have any?"

I slid my arm around her back and started to lead her up the few stairs to the door. "I do." I shoved the key into the lock and opened the door, indicating she should precede me in. I reached around the doorframe to flip on the light.

Missy waited for me to come in and shut the door behind us, and I helped her out of the light leather jacket she wore over her sweater and jeans. The dark chocolate color complimented her outfit perfectly. I wanted to keep the lights low, so after I'd hung up her coat, and mine, in the entryway closet, I hooked my pinkie with hers and pulled her further into the house, leaving on only light in the entryway.

My first instinct was to pull her into my eager arms and take up where we left off in the car, but as I watched her look around the place, taking in the modest furnishings, I reminded myself again that she was fragile, and I needed to handle her with kid gloves.

The couch and matching chair were upholstered in a light beige fabric flecked with burgundy, and the oak tables were some that Teagan and I had gotten at a flea market. The furniture was weathered. Even the lamps were second hand. The only redeeming feature of the place was the hardwood floors I'd installed in the kitchen and dining room. I'd also given the kitchen a little overhaul with new paint and blinds.

I led Missy into the kitchen and turned on the light over the stove, wishing to hell I had some candles, but it wasn't like I ever had women over here. The few nights I'd spent with females after my divorce were either in hotel rooms or at their place.

"This is nice," Missy murmured, running her hand over the quartz countertop. "Did you do the remodel?"

"Is it that obvious?" I asked, rolling my eyes and then

taking down two wine glasses from a cupboard and then opening the refrigerator to find the white wine.

She smiled, shaking her head, and then sat down on one of the bar stools around the island. "No, but it's newer than the rest of the house, so I'm putting two and two together."

I popped the cork and filled two of the large wine glasses half full as a slow smile slid across my lips. "Beautiful *and* smart. I like it." I offered a sly wink. "The project was more for my own sanity than anything else. I did it the first time Remi went through chemo and needed to keep busy."

Missy took the glass I offered and leaned on her elbows after taking a small sip, her eyes sympathetic. "I can't imagine how hard that must have been."

I took a swallow of wine from my glass. "I have no words for it. I'm just thankful Dylan is healthy." I'd wanted to ask her all night why Dylan was crying when I arrived to pick her up, but I didn't want to intrude on something personal.

"This is delicious."

"Sorry I don't have any candles," I said, studying her seriously. The tension between us was so palpable that I wanted to be close to her. "It's either the microwave light or the television in the living room for ambiance," I suggested.

A small smile curved her luscious mouth. "It's like we're a couple of college kids drinking wine in a dorm or something. I like this better than the TV," she said indicating the rays coming down over the stove.

I swallowed some more wine, never breaking her gaze. The soft golden light gave her skin a glow and made her hair shine. "I wish I would have known you back then." I set down my glass on the counter. "Wait here." I left her to retrieve two of the large throw pillows from the loveseat. When I returned, I moved the bar stools out of the way and plopped the two pillows side by side on the floor under the bar. "After you," I motioned for her to have a seat on one of the makeshift cushions. I held her glass as she slid off of her stool to the hardwood. I retrieved my own wine, and the bottle before I joined her. We were able to sit very close together and used the bar for a backrest. The island overhang blocked out more of the light, and it felt like we were in a cozy little cave.

We sat, our shoulders touching, and I could almost feel her heartbeat through the connection.

"This is nice," she said. "Who needs chandeliers and ten-foot ceilings?"

"It is," I agreed. I wanted to touch her. In fact, every cell in my body was thrumming out their demand that I do so. I shifted my glass to my right hand and then laced my fingers with hers. "I find that I can't be around you without touching you." It was an admission that I hope she shared. "I feel this connection between us, and I want to make it physical."

Missy's face was turned toward mine as our eyes locked. "Me, too," she almost whispered.

I already had an erection, just sitting next to her, but her words made the blood surge into it more forcefully. I was in agony. "I'm trying like hell not to rush you, but I am fucking dying." I closed my eyes, conscious of the throb in my voice. "Melissa…"

I vowed to take it easy with her, but this slow burn could turn into a flash fire with just one word from her. Only one word and we could combust.

She leaned in so her forehead rested on my cheek and I turned to kiss her temple. Her perfume, a mixture of spring flowers and musk, was a heady combination that had been wafting around me all evening.

"Will you go slow?" Her voice was a mere whisper. "No one has touched me in a long time."

In that second, I made the decision. My needs be damned.

I wanted to focus on Missy's pleasure because that's what she needed.

I turned toward her, careful of our wine glasses. "I told myself this wasn't going to happen, yet." My voice was low and soothing as my fingers traced her cheek and then down to her chin. I ran my thumb over her full lower lip. "I don't want to scare you, but I am incredibly desperate to be close to you."

She took a deep breath, and I watched her gorgeous breasts rise and fall. "You don't scare me like this, but I can't promise how I'll feel when we get into it. The damage is deep."

As aroused as I was, fury exploded inside my heart. She let me touch her, and even kiss her, so if she was afraid of sex, then her husband must have raped her. At that moment, I vowed that if I ever laid eyes on that son of a bitch, I'd beat him within an inch of his life. Internally I was raging, but outwardly, I was calm, stroking softly down her neck and running my knuckles lightly over the top swells of her breasts.

She was far too beautiful and delicate to have suffered at the hands of a madman.

"All I want to do is touch you," I reassured. "Nothing will happen that you don't want, or that doesn't feel amazing." Her aquamarine eyes appeared deeper, like the color of the Mediterranean and glittered in the half-light. "Do you trust me?" I leaned in and kissed her mouth, the kiss like a whisper, as I waited for her response.

"I trust you," she breathed against my lips. "I—" she stopped mid-sentence.

My eyes roamed over the beautiful curves of her face, lingering on her eyes and lips. "What is it? You can tell me anything."

"After our dinner in L.A., that night..."

I brushed her cheekbone with my fingers, my face hovering so close to hers that I could taste the wine on her breath. I loved the scent of her. "Just say it, babe," I commanded softly. "Whatever it is, it's okay."

"I had a dream…"

A sultry smile started on one corner of my mouth and slid across my lips as my eyes widened. "A lovemaking dream?" I asked hopefully.

Missy pulled her eyes from mine and looked down, then nodded.

"Well, don't worry. I've been thinking about you day and night."

"You have?"

"Like it's a secret. Every man at the station has," I admitted out loud. "You're so beautiful, how could they not?"

Her eyes flashed back up to mine. "You're the only one who matters."

I swallowed hard as emotions overwhelmed me. My heart expanded so much it hurt. Physically, I was literally vibrating, and my cock was throbbing and so swollen I thought it would split the zipper of my jeans. It was almost painful, but this wasn't about me, it was about her. My head dropped to meet hers. I wanted to pull her to me and kiss her until she was breathless, but instead, I inhaled to calm my breathing and steady my words. "You're so fucking amazing, do you know that?"

She shook her head. "I think you are."

"Come on," I said, reaching up to set my glass on the surface of the island. I stood and pulled her up. I cupped her face and kissed her slowly, but deeper than I'd ever kissed her. My body was aching, but my heart was singing as she kissed me back; opening her mouth so my tongue could access the deepest recesses. Over and over we kissed, creating a sort of blissful torture. When I pulled away, I couldn't help going back for a series of smaller kisses that still worshiped her lips. "Let's go," I murmured, picking up both wine glasses in one hand and the bottle in the other. I could feel Missy's hand latch on the shirttail of my button down as she followed me.

I made the quick decision to take her into the living room and onto the sofa, rather than my bedroom. I considered it would be less threatening. I didn't want her to think full-blown sex was my immediate intention. No question, I wanted her, but I was more concerned with making her feel safe with me.

Missy sank down onto the couch as I refilled both glasses, handing one to her, and then taking a long pull on mine. I set it down and started to unbutton my shirt, keeping my eyes on her the entire time; I couldn't help but notice how she was looking at my naked chest as it was exposed, button-by-button.

Should I explain my action? The fabric didn't stretch, and it would be constricting, but I left it on, hanging open. I wanted to take off my belt and open my jeans for the same reason, but if I did that, my cock would spring free. I intended to pleasure her, not pressure her into sex; so, I stopped after I'd removed the belt and popped the button loose.

Missy sat as still and timid as a bird on top of the soft cushions. I reached down and plucked her glass from her hands setting it next to mine, along with the wine bottle, on the coffee table. I held out my hand, hoping she would take it. I wanted her to participate, to know this was all in her control.

She slid her fingers into mine, and I pulled on her hand a bit so she would rise, and then sat down and invited her to join me. "Come over here," I motioned with both hands for her to straddle me. She was a bit hesitant but then did as I asked. I took her hand and kissed the inside of her wrist before I placed it on my naked chest inside my open shirt. "Touch me, Missy."

Hesitantly, her fingers moved over my chest, threading through the spattering of soft hair there. My hands roamed her body, slowly, gauging her reaction to each and every touch. I dragged my hands down her arms, then up over her shoulders,

219

and I started to knead her back, up under her sweater. I bent my fingers and lightly scratched down her flesh with my nails.

"Uhhhh," she breathed, arching her back in pleasure.

It was the response I wanted, but her movement only served to push her body into my erection. "Oh, God," I groaned out, dropping my head to her shoulder and then moving to place a series of open mouth kisses along the column of her neck.

Of her own volition, Missy started to move against me, but I was mindful not to thrust up toward her to increase the pressure. My resolve was hanging by a thread.

My hands, still underneath her soft sweater, moved carefully around to the front, exploring the skin of her stomach and skimming the outside of her lace bra. My fingers curled around the fabric; my first instinct was to rip it away. My cock was in hell; her movements gave only a taste of the pressure I craved.

"Jensen," she breathed, her hands sliding into the back of my hair to gently tug at it. It was sexy as hell, and I couldn't stop my chin from tilting up in invitation. I kissed along her jaw, praying her head would turn just enough for our mouths to join in a passionate kiss.

"Mm, huh?" I mumbled. I reached up to thread one hand in her hair and pulled her face to mine. One hand closed around her denim-clad thigh, and for the first time, I met the downward movement of her hips with an upward push of my pelvis, as our mouths locked in a series of passionate kisses. It was pure, unadulterated bliss.

I hooked my arm around her hips and pulled her flush against my groin, increasing the pressure. We were both breathing hard, our hips moving together in slow undulation as our hands explored and we shared kiss after kiss; each one more passionate and more profound than the last.

"Missy," I groaned into her mouth. The pressure in my

body was building almost to the point of pain. "What do you need?"

Her hands stilled, and she buried her face in my neck, curling into my chest without answering.

I cupped her cheek, my hand tangling in her long blonde hair as turned my face to hers. Missy's delicious scent surrounded me. "What is it? Did I hurt you?"

She shook her head. The shroud of darkness over the living room kept her face in shadow, yet she wouldn't look at me. I stroked her hair down her back repeatedly.

"Sweetheart, what is it? Just say what you need to say."

"I've never had a man ask me what I needed." Her voice was quiet and trembling.

I paused, letting the gravity of her words sink in, and then I made a decision. There was no way I was going to make love to her on my sofa. I inhaled so hard it felt like my lungs would explode. I tightened my arms around her, and then, stood.

"No." She shook her head. "Jensen, I didn't mean for you to stop."

I was already walking across the house and into my bedroom, supporting her weight easily in my arms. "I'm not stopping." The door to the bedroom was open, and though there wasn't anyone else in the house, I pushed it shut with my heel. I wanted to be holed up with her, inside four walls, where it was just the two of us.

My room wasn't exactly neat; there were a few clothes and shoes scattered around, but at least the bed was made, and I set her down on it, bending to kiss her mouth in a soft, but lingering kiss. I pulled away and kicked off my shoes, finally peeling off my shirt and casting it aside. I unzipped my jeans and then sat beside Missy on the bed, lifting first one foot and then the other to remove her boots.

"Is it okay if I take off your sweater and jeans?" I asked,

not wanting to make even one move without her permission. I knew that the future of our relationship teetered on this moment. "We don't have to make love, but I want to give you pleasure." My voice was the only sound in the room, and it reverberated in the silence. "Trust me, babe." I gently pushed a lock of hair off of her face and behind her ear. "If I do anything you don't like, just tell me, and I'll stop. I promise, okay?"

She sucked in a long breath, but slowly nodded in agreement.

Without another word, I pushed the soft cashmere up and over her head, exposing a black lace bra that contrasted starkly with her creamy skin, and accented the swell of her breasts. My hands ran over her shoulders and down her arms. I bent to place an open mouth kiss on the curve between her shoulder and her neck, careful to keep my mouth light and sucking, punctuating each with a hard lave of my tongue. I wanted her to imagine what was coming. It worked because she let out a breathless sigh and went limp in my arms.

I used gentle pressure to push her back until she was laying on the bed, and as I loomed over her, I unzipped her jeans and pulled them down her supple thighs exposing the matching string bikini panties. Her body was perfect as she lay there exposed before me; her stomach flat, her breasts full, and the curve of her hips so seductive. When she saw me studying her beautiful form, she automatically covered her body with her hands trying to hide. I held her wrists to stop her movements, shaking my head. "No. You're absolutely gorgeous. I want to see every amazing inch of you."

I moved to lie on the bed and pulled her to me with gentle hands until we were lying facing each other and I could stroke her silken skin freely.

"I think you're beautiful, too," Missy murmured, closing her eyes. "So strong and virile."

My heart was pounding like a drum, and more blood surged into my dick making it throb. I knew I was falling head over heels in love with her, and maybe I was already there. There was nothing I wouldn't do to get her to relax and trust me.

"I don't think I've ever wanted a woman this much," I whispered, conscious of the head of my cock sticking out of my boxer briefs inside the opening of my jeans. I was fucking on fire, but my goal was to take care of this beautiful woman. "I'm going to go slow, but will you let me touch you?"

"Yes," she whispered. I felt her hand slide over the muscles of my arm and over my shoulder and electricity skittered over the surface of my skin, causing me to shudder. There was nothing I wanted more than to be in her arms, our bodies and mouths joined in glorious lovemaking.

"Just close your eyes and feel, babe," I coaxed, softly. "This is all about you."

"No, I want to see you," she whispered achingly. "You."

I threaded my fingers into her hair as I cupped the side of her head and lowered my mouth to hers. I kissed her deeply, as my hands worshiped, relishing every inch of her naked skin. I could feel her pebble-hard nipples tighten even more, as my palms cupped her lace-covered breasts. As my hands teased and worked lower, I buried my mouth in the curve of her neck. Her skin was intoxicating; her moans of pleasure were music to my ears. When she arched into me, her head fell to one side in pleasure. I didn't need another invitation to roll her onto her back. Hovering above her, I kissed and nibbled from her neck, using the heat of my breath to tantalize her breasts until my teeth grazed first one sensitive bud, then the other.

"Uhhh," she sighed and arched.

My hand slid down to the top of her delicate panties, over her concave tummy. I brushed the top of her pubic mound with the back of my knuckles, my eager fingers dying to delve inside her. I held back, increasing the heat in the kisses until her body was begging for release. She arched into my hand, her fingers tangled in my hair, and her tongue was hungry against mine.

"Oh, babe," I sighed against her lips; finally letting my fingers slide inside the waistband and down. Her body radiated unfulfilled desire as I parted the soft, slick flesh easily finding her clitoris. I concentrated on it, spread her wetness around, using it for lubrication, I alternated between circles and long strokes. She was so hot, and the initial nervousness that tensed her thighs relaxed and her knees dropped open.

Her breath soon came in soft panting breaths that let me know she was close. I slid my hand lower, pushing my middle finger to enter her just slightly. Her body tensed, and I stopped, thinking she didn't want any invasion into her body, but when I made a move to pull my hand from her panties, she grabbed my wrist.

"Don't stop. I'm sorry, I'll relax," Missy whispered, her voice drunk on arousal. "Kiss me," she demanded.

I returned my hand and did as she commanded, intent on bringing her an intense orgasm. I teased her sex with my hand, intermittently burying one finger deep inside her and then working on the little bundle of nerves. The kisses were magnificent, only adding to the magic of the moment. God, she was so fucking sexy. She let go of her fear and let me touch her, let me love her, and I was so hard I thought I'd burst. There was only one thing that would make it better.

When she was on the verge of tumbling over into orgasm, I moved between her legs and hooked my thumb under the side of her panties pulling them down and off. She helped me, her eyes trained on my face. I pushed her thighs apart and lowered my head to her moist heat.

"Jensen, you don't have to do that," she murmured.

"I want to," I said, placing my mouth where only moments

before my fingers had been. She moaned loudly; her fingers clutching almost painfully in my hair. I pulled her clit into my mouth and sucked softly, lightly flicking it with the tip of my tongue.

"Uh, uhhhh," she moaned, her head turned to one side, her hips pushing up against my mouth almost involuntarily. "Oh, my God. Mmmmmm."

I could have continued for hours, but she was so sensitive, I knew that she was ready to come. It had been barely thirty seconds since I'd gone down on her and, already, she was coming. Her body clenched and arched as she came in a shuddering climax. "Jen—sehhhhen," she breathed out my name.

I suckled lightly wanting to make it last, watching in awe as she came hard. Her hands were threaded in my hair pulling on it painfully. I placed a soft, sucking kiss on her inner thigh as she rode it out and then climbed up her body to hover over her, looking down into her face, amazed at her abandon. I was surprised at the speed and strength of her orgasm.

"Damn," I murmured. "That was fast. I was prepared to go for hours." I smiled softly.

Missy was like a limp rag doll, as she lay there spent. I hadn't even pulled down the comforter, I was so anxious to make love to her, but now she was shivering. I reached over the edge of the bed and pulled it around her like a burrito, rubbing the sides of her hips after I tucked her in.

Missy's eyes were serious as she stared into my eyes. "I don't think I could have taken it for hours. It was too intense."

I lay down next to her and gathered her to me; comforter and all. There was barely six inches separating us, our breath mingling. I was trying hard to ignore the protests of my hungry dick as it made me acutely aware of its unsatisfied state. We faced each other, and I curled one arm under my head on the pillow so I could look down at her, and I held her to me with the other.

"Did it feel good, though?" I grinned softly, knowing by her reaction that it had.

"Incredible." She nodded and her eyes glazed over. I couldn't tell if she was sad, embarrassed, or overwhelmed. "No one's ever done that for me before," she admitted.

I was taken aback, and I frowned. *What the fuck?*

"Are you serious?" I was incredulous. She was beautiful and perfect. How could her husband resist giving her pleasure?

Speechless, all she could do was nod.

"Why not?" I asked.

She cleared her throat. It was apparent the next words were hard for her to say. "Derrick said I was dirty down there."

That fucking piece of shit. How could he degrade such a beautiful, well-groomed woman? And was he the only man she'd ever been with? If so, no wonder she was so scared.

"No, you aren't," I insisted. "You're beautiful and sexy, and you smell amazing. Don't let that bastard make you feel anything less than the incredible woman you are. Is that why you didn't want me to do it?"

"Yes, but you're so unselfish; it's hard to believe you're real." A few tears dripped from her eyes, making her struggle to free a hand from the blankets to wipe them away.

I was stunned by her admission and also heartbroken. I was pissed at her slime-ball ex-husband, but so sad for her. What had she suffered at his hands? I brushed her hair back and leaned in to kiss her mouth, gently sucking her lower lip in between mine. "I'm going to make you forget anyone has ever touched you before me."

Her face crumpled, and she pulled me closer. "Oh, Jensen," she cried, holding on tight.

I held her against me for a long time. I didn't know how long we lay there in the dark, holding each other, but knew I wanted it to be forever.

"Hey." I nudged her chin with my thumb. "I have a surprise for you."

Her eyes snapped up, the moonlight shining in from the window made them glitter in the darkness of the room. "You do? What is it?"

"Well, three, actually."

Her lips lifted gently. "What are they?"

"Well, one, I am going to make you one mean sauvignon blanc float as soon as I can walk back out to the kitchen. Two, I'm producing for you and Jarvis this weekend."

Missy's face lit up in pleasure, and her arm tightened around me. "Really?"

I let out a short laugh. "Yes." I nodded.

The sadness had disappeared from her face, and it was a good thing because I was about to bare my soul.

"What's the last thing?" she asked eagerly.

I drew in a deep breath, filling my lungs to capacity, my eyes meeting hers. I hesitated, my fingers tracing her cheekbone.

"Jensen?"

"I'm falling in love with you."

Missy's brow creased as she fought with her emotions. Her hesitation gave way to waves of worry which compelled me to continue.

"Look, I know it's soon, and I'm sorry... but, when I look at you, my heart fucking explodes," I said, never meaning another thing so much in my life. More tears tumbled down her face, and I wiped them away with my thumb. "Say something."

"I love you, too."

HER *last chance*
BEGINS
in his arms.

Chapter 12

Missy

So much had happened in the days since my date with Jensen.

I was an emotional melting pot; excited about my new job, yet anxious about it, giddy and soaring over Jensen's attention, but worried he was too good to be true. Still, things were moving forward.

My mother had put her house on the market and would be moving to Atlanta soon. Jensen and I spent several evenings looking around for homes all over the city, often taking Remi and Dylan with us. Jensen was so happy, and Dylan gravitated toward him with an apparent wonder that both elated and terrified me.

I'd decided an apartment would be faster to find than a house and I put a deposit down on a nice, though modest, three-bedroom pretty much equidistant between the ESPN office, Chase and Teagan's, and Jensen's homes.

I was excited about the process and all of the time spent with Jensen was exciting, and Dylan was blossoming in our new life. I couldn't remember the last time I felt so alive. All it took for my heart to skip a beat was the briefest touch of Jensen's hand or an appreciative glance. The sexual tension between us was so thick I could physically feel it humming in the air when we were together. The goodnight kisses stolen when the kids weren't looking after Remi was back at home, or Dylan was sleeping, were so hungry they literally took my breath away.

Things were moving fast, and while Dylan would be a little sad to leave the obvious comfort of Chase and Teagan's luxurious home, my new place allowed us more privacy, yet the nearby location kept him in the school with Remi. Chase won that argument with Teagan. I was struggling with whether to leave him enrolled due to the high cost of tuition, but I hated to uproot my little boy again. Chase offered to pay for it, causally teasing that it was his soccer scholarship fund, but I didn't feel right taking his or Jensen's offer to help; they'd done so much for me already, and a big part of me wanted to make it on my own. Rent was lower than a mortgage, which was another solid reason for leasing. My heart yearned for Jensen. Though I hoped we would be together at the end of the lease, I reminded myself that it was too early to start thinking about that.

In a flash, the weekend was upon us, and for the first time in a long time, I felt confident and at ease with my decisions. In the few weeks that had passed since leaving Wyoming, my panic was easing little by little. I was finding it easier to push down my fear and stop looking over my shoulder waiting for something awful to happen.

When Jensen, the crew, and I flew off to Baltimore, I was still stuck in a state of dream-like awe and could barely contain my happiness because Jensen had taken on several days of extra work to be with me during my first assignment with ESPN. He knew how nervous I was, and he was making sure that I would be okay. It had been forever, well, *never*, that a man, other than my brother, had done something so unselfish to take care of me. I'd never felt so safe, or so loved. I couldn't deny he was putting his actions behind his words. I knew I could count on him unflinchingly and that was a wonderful feeling.

I floated through the first half of the weekend when we managed rare stolen moments alone. As the on-air time grew closer, I felt like I was having a nervous breakdown despite Jensen's reassurance that I'd be fine. Local news was peanuts compared to national correspondent.

Though the prospect of being on-air was exciting, it was scary at the same time. Knowing I'd have Jensen's voice in my ear giving me little quips and comments, helped build up my confidence and calmed me down somewhat. I found myself wishing he could be with me on every assignment going forward, even though he assured me that whatever producer was assigned would have my back. Jarvis was very sweet, and I felt confident that he'd be a huge help when Jensen wasn't around.

Until tonight, we hadn't been completely alone together since the magnificent night at his house when he made love to me, but yet, didn't. I felt my cheeks flush and the corners of my mouth lift in a secret smile at the thought. Even without actual sex, it was the closest I'd ever come to having someone make love to me. My mind and heart were overflowing with him.

My heart sank when Jensen walked me to my hotel room earlier in the evening and left me there after kissing me senseless at the door, whispering that he didn't want the rest of the crew feeding the rumor mill about us so soon.

His logic would have been spot on if it weren't for the long make-out session in the hall. His dimples deepened when I pointed out in a breathless whisper that any one of the crew could walk by at any moment and he should just come inside. His low groan went straight to my core. It was irresistible that he didn't want me to think he just wanted sex, but that was the farthest thing from my mind. It was already difficult to hide how we felt about each other, and we were both holding on to our professionalism for dear life.

Now as I lay on my bed alone, staring at the ceiling, I found myself aching for him and wishing I'd asked him to stay.

Who was I kidding?

I sighed and slammed my hand onto the mattress next to me, sucking in a deep breath. For sure it wasn't Jensen. My desire for him had to be written all over me when we were at dinner with the gang. It felt idiotic to deny it; especially when it felt so right. We'd barely spoken a word to anyone else during dinner, completely wrapped up in each other. It had to be screaming to the rest of the crew.

I felt heat seep into my face as the corners of my lips lifted in a contemplative smile. I sighed heavily and felt my chest rise and fall, trying to decide if I wanted to take a bath or turn on the TV to occupy my racing mind. It would be too late to call Dylan. My fingers ran over the material of the comforter on the hotel bed, and then I sat up, deciding the bath was the more attractive option.

I stood and walked over to my open suitcase and took out the T-shirt and plaid pajama pants I'd brought to wear to bed. I grimaced and then let out a little huff. Not exactly the outfit for the seduction scene worthy of Jensen. *I should have planned ahead better*, my mind scolded. *But, what the hell? I'd let him leave anyway.*

Derrick would have called me a whore if I'd voiced any desire of my own, but somehow, I felt that Jensen would welcome it. How different the two of them were. Derrick used his strength to punish; where Jensen was physically strong, his heart was stronger, and he was oh, so gentle. Derrick's touch made me cringe, but I couldn't wait to be close to Jensen. I ached to have his hands on my body.

As I padded into the bathroom and flipped on the light, I threw one of the white towels stacked on a shelf above the toilet onto the floor next to the tub with my pajamas, then peeled off my network sweatshirt and pushed my blue denim jeans down my legs and kicked them off. I turned on the water, adjusting the temperature, and adding one of the small bottles of shampoo sitting on the vanity in a lame effort to create a bubble bath. I rolled my eyes, making a mental note to bring my own with me next time.

"Nice try," I murmured to myself, just as my phone pinged from the bedroom.

My heart started racing as I ran to find it in my purse. Clad only in my bra and bikini panties, I shivered as I lifted my phone out of my purse praying the text was from Jensen. The air was cold, and my skin broke out in goosebumps; my nipples puckering against the chill. I smiled as I read his words on the screen.

WTH am I doing here when you're there? I won't be able to sleep.

My face broke out in an excited smile as my fingers quickly tapped out a reply.

Me, too. Are you crazy or something?

Crazy about you.

My heart started thumping inside my chest like a drum as he confirmed for the thousandth time that he was stunningly perfect.

Well...

Yes?

His response came back a split second later. I laughed as pleasure raced through me.

I suppose you could come back. I'm just getting into the bath, so can you give me a few minutes?

I'll see if I can rustle up some wine. Remember what I said. I just want to be in the same room with you. I don't expect anything to happen.

My breath hitched.

I know. Don't worry. I won't take advantage of you. Promise.

LOL. See you in a bit.

My heart was singing, and my insides began to melt. If I was frustrated, he had to be going out of his mind. Each night, when I closed my eyes to sleep, his handsome face and muscular form haunted my dreams and my waking moments were consumed with thoughts of him.

I wanted him, but I was concerned about the aftermath. If I gave into my heart and gave myself to him, would it change things between us? I drew in a shaky breath and decided that I'd have to take my chances. I trusted Jensen more than I'd ever trusted anyone.

Sounds great. See you, soon.

The next ten minutes flew by as I took a quick bath and reluctantly put on the less-than-sexy pajamas, ran a quick comb through my hair and applied a light coating of moisturizer to my freshly washed face. I stared at the sad reflection I made in the mirror.

"Oh, God." I groaned. "Could I be any less sexy?"

I was skinny, so the baggy shirt and flannel pants hid what small curves I had. I pulled the shirt tighter around my waist and thought about tying it in a knot, but that would make it seem like I was trying too hard. "Ugh!" I groaned and let the shapeless thing fall back into place. I pulled my hair up in a topknot and then put on just a little mascara. Resigned, I threw my hands up and let them fall to my sides again. "I guess this will have to do."

If the first ten minutes since Jensen texted flew by while I was getting ready, the next twenty dragged leaving me pacing the room and flipping through the limited channels on the television. Finally, his light rap on the door made me jump up. I almost ran to the door before stopping myself; forcing a deep breath and slower steps.

"Come on, Missy. Get a flipping grip," I whispered to myself, and then walked the short distance to the door and wrapped my hand around the doorknob before pulling it open.

A smile split my face when I saw him standing there with a bottle of wine and a dozen red roses wrapped in that grocery store cellophane.

"Hey—" I began, but Jensen interrupted me.

"Did you look through the peephole?" he demanded.

Instantly my face sobered, the happiness I'd felt only seconds before dissipating into thin air. "No, but I knew you were coming." I moved to the side and waved him into the room.

He shook his head and moved past me. "Always be cautious, Melissa." His words weren't harsh, but he used my full name and that said volumes. "Always."

I froze in place as the heavy door swung shut with a bang wondering what to do next.

My brow dropped into a frown. "Look, when you're my producer tomorrow, you can order me around, but not tonight. Not here in my room."

Jensen turned, his face softening as he walked over to hand me the flowers. "Look, I don't mean to be an asshole, but I worry about you."

I nodded, reaching out for the roses, only to walk past him to lay them on the short dresser that the TV sat on. My head dropped as I stood there, fingering the paper wrapping. "Thanks. Did you get these at Kroger?" My voice was soft; I was sure the disappointment I was feeling laced my words.

"No, Baltimore doesn't have Kroger. I got them at Safeway. I figured some of the crew would still be in the bar and since you said to wait a few minutes…" His words dropped off.

I wasn't looking at him, but I could feel his presence behind me. He was throwing off heat like the sun; I could feel his breath on the back of my neck and smell his delicious cologne.

After a moment's hesitation, Jensen's big palms settled on my shoulders and then ran down the length of my arms, and back up again. He bent his head to run the tip of his nose up the chord of my neck to just below my ear.

"Hey, don't be mad at me for being protective," his voice was low and seductive, the movement of his hands on my body, and the feel of his breath turned me to jelly. He was so close I could feel his lips move as they hovered over my skin. "I just— I can't help it."

As my previous disappointment faded at his admission, my head fell back to his shoulder, and my body leaned back against his. When his soft mouth opened and trailed slow, sucking kisses down my neck, I sighed in contentment. At my shoulder, his hand tugged on the sleeve of my shirt to pull the neckline aside giving him access to the flesh he was seeking.

"Jensen," I sighed out breathlessly. My heart filled with him and flames of desire instantly ran like lightning through my body. The long fingers of his right hand laced with mine as his mouth continued his onslaught of my senses and the front of his hard body pressed into my back and the curve of my butt. Clearly, he was as aroused as I was.

"Shhh," he murmured as his free arm slid around me, pulling me tighter against him. "I said I just wanted to be with you, so we should stop this before it goes too far. Do you wanna watch TV?" His nose brushed up my neck again as he sighed and stilled. He let out a deep breath that washed over my neck and shoulder. His hold loosened and he started to separate our bodies.

I didn't think it could ever go far enough with this man. My hungry nipples cried out for his touch, and I could feel my body opening. I squeezed the hand holding mine and slid the fingers of the other along his muscular forearm still lightly around my waist, stopping him from moving away from me.

I shook my head. "No. We both knew what would happen if you came to my room tonight. That's why you left earlier," I whispered in protest.

He paused, his forehead dropping to the back of my head and eased our bodies closer again. "Missy." The way he said my name felt like an ache that ran through us both.

My flesh was screaming for his hands to roam over it, yet still, he held me close to him without moving.

"I want you so much, but I want it to be special. It's not my intention to give you anything less than you deserve, and you deserve everything."

I felt as though I would spontaneously combust; turning in his arms and sliding mine up over his shoulders and around his neck, my fingers tangled in the soft hair at his nape. "Then," I stood up on tiptoe, so that I could reach his mouth with mine. "Give me everything. It doesn't matter where we are, Jensen. Only that we're together." I hoped, beyond hope, that my words correctly communicated what I was feeling. There weren't words enough to tell him how much he meant to me or how much I needed him to touch me, fill my body with his, and make me his forever.

"I don't want to rush you." The words were ripped from him, his face turning into the curve of my neck and his forehead pressing just above my ear. "We don't have to—"

I shook my head, ultra-aware of every breath that rushed over my skin, every place our bodies touched. "I don't feel rushed. It's like I've known you my entire life." My words, though softly spoken, were dripping with love and meaning. "It's never felt more right."

I could feel his muscles flex as his arms tightened around me and lifted me off the ground and his hungry mouth crushed down on mine in a series of passion-filled kisses. When his hands slid down my body, over my back, and down my butt cheeks and further still; down between my thighs to bring our bodies closer. My legs parted as he lifted me fully into his embrace, my legs wrapped around his waist until his erection was hard and throbbing; pulsing hot against me. Our kisses were on fire, but our bodies needed more. Something—anything to relieve the building pressure.

I was so wrapped up in our kisses, I wasn't sure how it happened, or how we ended up there, but Jensen was slowly lowering me to the bed, and then following me down, our mouths never separating from the luscious succession of kisses. My hands grabbed at his flesh, pulling him closer and parted my legs wider, anxious to feel his weight pushing me into the mattress, and then the glorious pressure of his hardness thrusting slowly and purposefully against my softness.

"Missy," Jensen moaned again. "Jesus, God. I feel the same way."

I gathered him closer, elated by his words, my heart thundering inside my chest. I wasn't sure if I was euphoric, on fire, in love, or full of sorrow because I hadn't met this man first. Tears filled my eyes, and my throat tightened painfully at the blessing of him in my life.

"Jensen," I said his name like an ache, causing him to pull back to look into my face, stopping the delicious trail of kisses down my neck, his big hand stroking the side of my hair over and over. I could see the desire in his smoldering eyes; his skin burned with excitement.

"What? Ask me anything, and I'll provide it." His eyes were intense and serious as they stared down at me. "Anything, Missy."

I knew he spoke the truth. I knew it as sure as the sun would rise in the morning. The intensity in his eyes made my mouth go dry, so I let my tongue snake out and moisten my lips before I answered.

"Make love to me. No one has ever made love to me, before."

His eyes darkened; his expression became pained as he looked down into my face. I wasn't sure what he was thinking or what he was going to do, but I was terrified I'd just said the wrong thing. Panic seized my lungs, and I reached up to touch his handsome face as words rushed out to fix it.

"Jensen," I said softly, but my voice cracked at the prospect I'd just ruined everything. "What's wrong? Are you angry with me?"

He closed his eyes, and his head fell forward a little as he shook it.

"No," he ground out as his eyes snapped open to meet mine again. "How could I be mad at you? You're innocent..." he breathed. Emotion pulsed between us like a heartbeat.

He rolled off of me and onto the bed beside me, his hand coming up to cover his eyes. I could see his jaw tense as he clenched his teeth. "I'm so fucking—!" he stopped abruptly, then, after a short pause, he spat the rest of the sentence. "Pissed! I mean..." Jensen stopped again, and hearing my sharp intake of breath, rolled onto his side toward me, propping his head up with one hand and taking one of mine in the other, gently rubbing his thumb back and forth over the top of my fingers. I knew what he was thinking.

When my hesitant gaze met his; the deep blue orbs were glazed with tears. "Please don't think of him right now. Not now."

He was struggling, and when he responded his voice had thickened. "You should be worshiped. You're so beautiful and gentle."

I swallowed hard, my hand lifting to stroke his cheek, meeting his eyes. My own eyes were full just before the first tear tumbled free. "So are you." The words hurt coming out, but I'd never meant anything more in my life. We lay there clutching onto each other; our foreheads pressed together while we both cried.

All I wanted was to love him. My fingers were hungry to touch him, my mouth starving for his. "Kiss me," I begged brokenly. Whatever this pain was, it was amazing, and I never wanted it to end. "Love me, Jensen."

His lips met mine gently, almost torturously slow, our lips brushing tentatively as if to reassure each other the kiss was real, but within seconds he was on top of me, and his tongue has pushed into the deepest recesses of my mouth to lave in a hungry tangle with mine. We explored each other's bodies with our hands, carefully peeling back layers of clothing, piece by delicious piece. Soon we were lying naked in each other's arms, heated flesh and heightened senses making our breathing heavy. It was the only sound in the room.

My body was on fire, melting into his. "Love me," I whispered again, achingly granting him permission to come inside me. He filled me with one smooth, but unhurried, movement allowing me to feel every inch of him as hard flesh met slick heat. The pleasure between us was profound in its magnitude.

"I do. So much." Jensen said between magnificent kisses and caresses ardent in their purpose. His movements slowed, and body and soul I protested, my hips arched up in rhythm with his, craving the release it so desperately needed; something I'd never experienced during sex. "God," he said. "I do, Missy... I want you to feel it."

The back of my eyes began to burn, even as the physical pressure began to build. I wanted him closer, deeper inside me; I wanted our kisses never to end.

Words stopped; our kisses punctuated by deep breathing, low moans, and sighs. My fingers curled into his hair, pulling his open mouth tighter against mine, hungrily sucking on his lower lip as one kiss ended, and another began. His nails raked a light teasing trail from the outside of my left breast, down my side and under my butt to pull me closer, coaxing out the rhythm he wanted. It was glorious. If I didn't know that I was in love with him before, the tender, yet passionate way he worshiped my flesh with a reverence no one had ever shown me before, confirmed it. Emotion overflowed, and a sob broke from me.

I wanted to tell him no one had ever touched me in the gentle, coaxing way he was ringing pleasure from me. I wanted him to know what he meant to my life, and how I'd suffer my past a hundred times if it meant I'd end up in his arms.

Jensen gently pulled his mouth from mine, and his body stilled, still embedded deep within mine. His hand pushed back the hair from the left side of my face as he stared into my eyes; his expression softly concerned.

"What is it? Did I hurt you?" His words were soft but laced with urgency. What am I doing wrong?"

I swallowed as two silent tears spilled from the corners of my eyes, rolling down the sides of my face and onto the pillow beneath my head. I shook my head. "Nothing. You're perfect. I just can't believe you're real. That being with you like this... is real. I never knew it could be like this."

A soft smile lifted the corners of his mouth, his eyes glowing with intense emotion as he bent to take my lips in a gentle, open-mouthed kiss. "I want to make you forget anyone else has ever touched you. From now on, it's only you and me."

I closed my eyes as his softly spoken vow reverberated over me. I gave myself over to him, allowing my heart to open, and my soul to trust like never before. He brought my body to the brink twice before finally letting me crash over in a hard, pulsing climax.

"Missy look at me," he demanded as wave after delicious wave of pleasure rushed through me. "Look at me," he whispered more softly.

My eyelids lifted languidly as my head raised trying to recapture his mouth with mine.

He thrust into me harder now, each one getting him closer to his own release, but still careful to press his pelvis into mine to ring the last shudders from me. "Uhhh," he groaned, "Ummmm." His voice was low and guttural as his muscles tensed and he finally allowed himself to come.

Jensen collapsed on top of me, his weight heavier as his breathing evened out. I wanted to wrap my body and my whole world around him. I used my inner muscle and clenched around his still hard cock, as I cradled his shoulders and head, kissing the side of his damp temple, and I wrapped my legs around his waist, not wanting to let him go.

A few minutes later when he lifted his head and stroked back my hair; his expression was serious. "I love you, Melissa. You're mine. Say you're mine."

Joy burst within me like fireworks, and I offered a trembling smile. "I'm yours."

The dimples in his handsome face appeared at both sides of his mouth, but his eyes never broke with mine. "Forever."

I bit my lip, even as my heart soared. "You drive a hard bargain, mister," I teased.

His expression sobered in a split second. "I want you; you and Dylan. It's all or nothing."

My heart stopped inside my chest. This was the moment I'd been waiting for my entire life.

"Well, let's see… I choose… *all.*"

I barely got the words out before his mouth swooped down and took mine in another series of passionate kisses.

And just like that, my future exploded, like fireworks, into a million brilliant possibilities.

HER *last chance* BEGINS *in his arms.*

Chapter 13

Missy

I stretched lazily in bed; my nakedness under the covers reminding me of the beautiful night spent in Jensen's arms. A slow, delighted smile spread across my face.

"Jensen?" I called, bolting upright into a sitting position. The blinds were drawn, and I couldn't tell if it was morning or the middle of the night. The room was silent and pitch black, but there was a lingering scent of shampoo hanging in the air, hinting that he had showered and was already gone.

For a brief moment, I was sad that he left without saying goodbye, but then I remembered what we were doing here in Baltimore; the game and the pregame interviews.

Instantly, I scooted over to the edge of the bed, fumbling around blindly on the nightstand for the switch to the lamp. When I turned it on, the room illuminated, and I squinted in the brightness. My short pajama pants had been unceremoniously dumped to cover the glaring red numbers of the digital clock. I laughed lightly. No doubt, Jensen had placed them there sometime during the night.

My phone pinged, and I moved away the offending garment to find it next to the clock. The time glared at me like some obnoxious cartoon bounding out to inform me how late I was.

Holy crap!

It was already 8:30! I dropped my phone and scrambled out of bed and into the bathroom to hop in the shower. What a way to start my new job.

Jensen said the "talent" didn't need to be at the stadium as early as the production crew, but I wanted to watch them set up and get a handle on the process, start to finish, and make notes. My only other experience on remote was the one trial weekend in L.A., and I had a lot left to learn. I shook my head, chastising myself as I quickly washed my hair and soaped, then rinsed my body.

"Awesome, Missy. Shit!"

Sleeping with my producer was bad enough. I wasn't going to let him lower his expectations or give me special treatment. I had to make sure he knew it. No. This wouldn't do at all.

I quickly dried off and used the blow dryer provided by the hotel on my hair but decided to forgo makeup. I cringed at my reflection. The last thing I wanted to do was see Jensen a la natural after our night of hot sex. I wanted to look my best for him, but right now, my appearance couldn't be helped. I inwardly groaned, wondering if I should take the navy-blue suit and chartreuse blouse with me, and change later, or just get dressed now.

Ultimately, I decided to stuff my high heels into the garment bag, throw on some jeans, the ESPN polo, and sneakers, and just get over there as quickly as possible.

I shoved my phone into the back pocket of my jeans, grabbed the keycard to the room, my press pass lanyard, and purse; then ran out of the room and to the lobby.

In the cab on the way to the stadium, my stomach grumbled, and for the first time, I remembered I hadn't eaten anything. "Awesome. Well, that's what I get," I mumbled.

"What was that, miss?" The cab driver asked.

"Oh, nothing," I said, reaching behind me and pulling out my phone after it pinged for the second time that morning. I was sure Jensen was wondering where I was. I read his earlier text, then the second.

Morning, Sunshine. Last night was perfect. <3

Are you up? Jarvis will bring you over to Bank Stadium with him. Can't wait to see you.

I could feel myself blushing. It was stupid. No one was looking, but still, I felt self-conscious. I needed the crew to see me as professional and in control of myself. I couldn't act like some giddy schoolgirl. Somehow, I'd have to put my evening with Jensen out of my mind.

I sucked in a breath, considering what to say. I didn't want him to think it didn't mean anything, but it was crucial for the future of my career at ESPN, that we not let the others know. At least not right away.

Hey. Last night was perfect. You were perfect. (Don't take this wrong), but I'm going to try to keep things on a professional level today.

I waited breathlessly for his reply, praying he wouldn't be hurt or angry.

No problem. I feel the same way. However, as you pointed out last night, we weren't fooling anyone.

I sighed, rolling my eyes at the irony of the words on my screen.

You're right, but still.] We don't need for our body language making it obvious to the others that we boned all night. Behave.

If I must. Sigh...

I giggled as I typed out my response. I wasn't sure we'd pull it off, but it would be fun trying.

You must. I'm on my way over now. I want to be there for everything, all day.

Okay. I'll text Jarvis and let him know you're already on your way. Just know, when I see you I want to kiss you. I won't. But I want to.

Me, too. XOXO

Just about that time, the cab pulled up to the press entrance on the south side of the stadium. I paid the driver and got out, dragging my suit bag with me, then lopping it over one arm.

"Thank you. Have a great day!" I beamed, waving, then turned hurriedly into the building, anxious to lay eyes on Jensen, but reminding myself to keep my smiles to a minimum. Maybe people would interpret my enthusiasm as first-day-on-the-job excitement. I'd just keep telling myself that.

Several local and national networks were covering the game with camera crews setting up at various points around the field, and around the locker rooms. The hallways were bustling with activity as I weaved my way through them in search of my crew.

Jensen had mentioned that the media booth was on the upper mezzanine level, on the South side of the stadium, and so I made my way in that general direction. Being so unfamiliar, it took me a few minutes, but finally, I found Liz running out of the booth in a hurry.

"Hey," I smiled brightly, stopping her with a hand on her arm. "Is this where I'm supposed to be?"

She glanced up and smiled but shook her head. "Hi! You're here early!" she exclaimed. Her face was flushed and covered in a light sheen. "The booth is already set up, but David forgot his headphones up here, and I have to get them down to the field." She held them up for me to see. David Bocker was our director and apparently, was somewhere other than the booth. "He'd forget his fucking head if it weren't attached," she muttered, irritated. "We're setting up for the pre-game interviews on the thirty."

Liz started to rush away, and I glanced behind me at the booth, unsure what to do next and then back at her, bewildered. "Liz! Before you go; what should I do?"

The woman paused in mid-step. "Oh," she looked at me. "Is your suit in that bag?"

I nodded. "I wasn't sure if should wear it all day. I didn't want to get it all sweaty if I had to haul equipment."

"Well, typically, the talent doesn't help set up."

"But I want to learn everything I can."

"Then, put it in the booth for now, and come with me. You wanna see everything, huh?" Liz's expression twisted wryly. "Hurry up. I'll wait! We're the third section over."

I was smiling as I turned and made my way through the door and into the glass booth that overlooked the field. The view was spectacular! I recognized one of the audio techs plugging in some of our microphones into the existing board in the booth.

"Hi, Jeremy!" I said breathlessly, my eyes searching for a spot to leave my garment bag.

"Hey, Missy!" He smiled, glancing up from his work.

"Where can I put this? Liz is waiting for me?"

He nodded toward the wall at the back of the booth, behind three rows of chairs. There was a row of doors that looked like closets, each one with a network name stenciled on the front of it. "Back there," he nodded at the door labeled ESPN. "You see it, right?"

"I do! Thanks!" I literally scrambled up the aisle and quickly hung the bag inside. "See you in a bit!"

"Okay, but if I don't, good luck today!"

I flashed him a quick smile. "Thanks!"

In seconds I found an impatient Liz waiting near the stairs outside the booth that would take us down through the stadium to field level.

"You know, you'll be sorry you're learning all of these things. If the director or the producer find out you can do more than smile in front of the camera, don't be surprised if they take advantage in the future," she threw over her shoulder as I followed her down the stairs. The stadium was big, and it towered above and around us when on the field.

"I don't mind. I'm just happy to have this job," I answered.

It wasn't the first time I'd been on a professional football field, but the massiveness of it was awe-inspiring. Soon, the doors would open, and fans would begin filling the seats, and the place would come alive.

"You say that now," she huffed under her breath as we walked up to the director, speaking to more of the crew on the sidelines. "Here, Dave," Liz said, handing over the headphones.

He took them without missing a beat in his conversation.

My eyes, hidden by my sunglasses, scanned for Jensen and finally located him a few yards away. He was speaking to a well-dressed man and woman. They both looked like they were some high-powered, Wall Street, big wigs.

I touched Liz on her arm, making her look away from the clipboard she was perusing. "Who is that with Jensen?"

250

I used one hand to hide the other one pointing in the direction I wanted her to look. She pulled down her sunglasses and glared. "Ugh," she moaned. "Agents. They're trying to get air-time for their players."

"We already have the list of interviews," I said under my breath, my eyes narrowing as I watched their interaction. The woman was blatantly flirting with Jensen; touching his arm and doing a little hair flip while laughing at something he said.

My eyes widened territorially, taking her in.

"Exactly. The players have to perform well in previous games to get interviews," Liz said. "Doesn't stop them from last-minute lobbying, though." She stopped, getting a closer look. "Good God, not Amy Hale." She rolled her eyes in disgust before shoving her sunglasses back into place. "She represents players from ten NFL teams." She huffed out her disapproval. "That bitch will stop at nothing to get new clients and then get her players in front of the camera. I bet her doc has her taking never-ending antibiotics. I've seen her coming on to Jensen before. Many times."

"Really?" I cleared my throat, doing my best to appear nonchalant, but I could almost feel the heat seeping up from my neck and into my face.

Jensen was casually dressed in jeans and the standard blue and orange ESPN jacket over a white button down, and I watched him while he spoke to the pair, drinking in his tall form, dark hair and handsome face. His expression was all business, but the woman was animated, flashing smiles and leaning in toward him.

Liz gave an over-exaggerated nod, pursing her lips. "Oh, yeah, definitely. The more he ignores her, the harder she tries. Just look at her; if she weren't so sickening, she'd be funny. Of course, no one would blame Jenson if he took what she so blatantly offers."

"She's certainly beautiful," I said, suddenly acutely aware of my lack of make-up and network attire. Unable to tear my eyes away from the woman, I mentally compared my dowdiness with her glamour. I was heartened to hear Jensen wasn't interested in Amy Hale; watching as he had turned his attention to the male agent and engaged him in a conversation, leaving the polished woman clearly chagrined; her face hardened, and her full red lips flattened into an annoyed line. It was clear she wasn't happy that Jensen had moved on.

Liz shrugged. "I guess, but Jensen is well aware that there's a booby-trap in her pussy just waiting to bite off the dick of anyone dumb enough to venture in," she dismissed dryly.

My mouth fell open, and my head snapped around to look at my new friend, stunned that she would say such a thing. She was grinning, tongue in cheek, and in less than two seconds, I burst out laughing with her.

"Nom, nom, chomp!" Liz continued outrageously, making me continue to giggle even harder. Her brilliant smile flashed as the trio glanced in our direction having heard us giggling. "Have a good show, hon!"

"Thanks!" I called as she walked away.

I was still grinning a few seconds later when I made my way over to Jensen's group, thankful for the sneakers on my feet. I bit my lip hoping to stop smiling.

The other woman's heels were sinking into the turf; she wobbled as she pulled first one, then the other foot, loose from the sod only to have them sink again as the second she replaced her weight on them. It was chilly, but not cold enough for the ground to be frozen. Surely, she knew what she was doing?

Idiot, I thought cattily.

The dimple in Jensen's left cheek appeared as I approached. He was definitely curious why Liz and I had been chortling. I sensed his first instinct was to slide his arm around my waist, but he stopped short. Still, a thrill shot through me: Jensen felt possessive.

"Here she is," he said warmly. "The new correspondent I've been telling you about."

"Hello," I murmured, nodding to the others, painfully aware that Amy was sizing me up and down. I extended my hand, first to the woman, and then the man. "I'm Melissa Ellington."

"It's a pleasure, Melissa," the man said. He was attractive, but not overly so, and polite. "I'm Steve Sheridan. I represent Mick Jade." He offered his hand, which I took.

Mick Jade was one of the names I remembered from the list. "Ah, yes. We're interviewing him, pre-game, I believe."

"You are," Steve beamed at me. "I just wanted to introduce myself so, when I call you throughout the season, we'll both have a face to put with a name."

"Good idea," I smiled at him. "Do you have other players, besides Mr. Jade?"

"Oh, yes, indeed," he responded.

"No doubt, it's too much for her to remember now, Steve," the woman interrupted sharply. "I'm Amy Hale. I hope you'll give my players the attention they deserve."

I could almost feel the hair at the back of my neck stand up. "Your reputation precedes you, Miss Hale." I smiled sweetly, and Jensen cast me a skeptical glance. "I assure you, I'll do my best, but as you say, I don't have them all committed to memory just yet."

After a bit more small-talk, Jensen excused us from the agents with the excuse of work. "Amy's reputation preceded her, huh?" The brow over his right eye rose and the corner of his mouth lifted in a grin as we walked back to our crew about fifty feet away.

"Oh, yes," I said, biting my lip. "Liz filled me in."

"She did, did she?" His tone was teasing.

I nodded but couldn't push down my smile, finally letting out a breathless laugh. "Yep. Nom, nom, chomp!"

Jensen's head fell back as he laughed hard, fully understanding the meaning behind Liz's comment. "Leave it to Liz. I couldn't have said it better, myself."

My eyes widened innocently as a secret smile still played around my lips. "What? Not a fan of the barracuda type?"

Jensen smiled briefly again, then sobered as our eyes locked. "Not at all. I prefer a much softer approach, as you well know. Last night was incredible," he said, making sure to keep his voice low. "I wish I could kiss you right now. I wish I could touch you, Missy." His words ran straight through me like an electric current; his blue eyes roamed over me like a physical caress. I knew that I had no reason to be jealous of Amy Hale or others like her. Jensen was an attractive man. *Too* attractive, and it was certain women other than me would think so.

I swallowed hard, not breaking our gaze. "I know. Me, too."

He ran both of his hands through his hair and turned to stand next to me, both of us facing into the field. "Right, so let's get through this damn day."

"Hey, this is my first assignment. I'm excited but scared to death."

"You'll be fine. I'll be right here. Right next to you."

His words held a deeper meaning, and we both knew it.

"What's next?" I shoved my hands into the pocket of my station jacket.

"We make sure everything is set up at the various two remote locations near each end-zone where you and Jarvis will each conduct the interviews of opposite team players during the pre-game and check with Jeremy and Michelle to make sure they're good to go."

He towered over me, and I had to look up into his face.

The sun was bright, despite the temperature, and we both had dark sunglasses on. "How much time will I have to get dressed?"

He looked at his watch before his hand briefly touched my sleeve. "You didn't have to come over yet. Talent doesn't have to be on set until the sound checks, and we've still got at least an hour before that."

Jensen took me through all of the procedures. In a flash, I was dressed in my Navy-blue suit, sitting in the make-up chair with a paper cape over my shoulders, as a young girl named Hannah applied foundation and contouring to my face. Jeremy fitted me with an earpiece, and microphone, then clipped the wireless power pack to the back waistband of my skirt. Jarvis was getting the same treatment in the next chair from other members of the crew.

Jarvis and I were hustled to opposite end-zones via golf carts, and I nervously went through my notes during the short drive. I was nervous, despite Jensen's reassurance and his presence behind me in the vehicle. When we arrived at our destination, he was out before me and gently removed my phone from my hand.

"Wait. I haven't finished preparing," I said and reached for the phone again. My notes were still up on the screen.

He helped me out and shook his head, still holding my hand. "You have a teleprompter. All of the questions and commentary will be on the feed. Remember, I'll be in your ear telling you what to say, and you only have three interviews. Relax. Jarvis will do most of the live commentary this time, and I'll tell you how to respond. Trust me."

Despite our agreement to keep things professional, Jensen's hand rubbed up and down one arm. I took a deep breath and looked up into his brilliant blue eyes. "I can't get used to you taking care of me. You won't be with me, after this."

He smiled gently. "Hey. Someone will be in your ear during

every game until you get comfortable. We aren't going to throw you to the wolves."

"Okay," I answered shakily.

"Five minutes," Liz called. "Get ready everyone. We're in the last flight of commercials before we go live."

"See? It's just you, me, Liz, and Eric, who is behind camera one."

I glanced to the camera, and sure enough, there stood the big teddy bear cameraman I sat next to on the plane to Los Angeles. I recognized the woman operating the second camera, too, but couldn't remember her name.

"I requested everyone you are familiar with at this end of the field. David is going to direct Jarvis, and Liz has you. You got this."

My heart swelled with emotion at his thoughtfulness. "You're amazing. Thank you."

"I've got you." Jensen winked then left me to get situated while he spoke to the Baltimore Coach, and quarterback, who were the first two of my three interviews.

Liz handed me the wireless microphone at the same time that Hannah retouched my hair. "Thirty seconds," she called and then motioned for the coach to come and stand next to me.

"Hello, Coach Harbaugh. I'm Melissa Ellington."

He nodded. "Nice to meet you."

"Good luck, today."

He only nodded because Liz started counting down.

"Ten, nine, eight, seven, six…" She put up one hand and continued the countdown with her fingers, then pointed at me when we went live.

"Hello, this is ESPN live, and I'm Melissa Ellington. I'm here in Baltimore on this beautiful and crisp day where the Ravens take on the Buffalo Bills. Standing next to me is the Raven's head coach, John Harbaugh. Welcome."

"Thank you, Melissa, it's good to be with you."

Everything became more natural as the day went on and the hours went by in a flash. The interviews alternated between the Ravens and the Bills, so Jensen had a few minutes to prepare me before each one of mine, and then during the actual game, he went up with me up in the booth. Jarvis did the bulk of the talking while we were live, and he was easy to follow. I knew that it wouldn't be long before I'd be able to hold my own. With Jensen and Jarvis' help, and with a bit more studying of the rules of the game, I'd be comfortable with my new job.

The entire crew, but especially Jensen, made sure that I wouldn't fumble on my first game. I always wanted to do well, but I found myself hoping to make Jensen proud of me.

I was tired at the end of the day, but I made sure to help pack up the equipment. Jeremy and the rest of the camera crew would drive the broadcast van carrying the equipment back, while the rest of us took a flight.

Boarding Southwest, passengers were able to sit wherever they wanted, and Michelle and Liz were so excited about my first completed assignment, they asked me to sit between them.

"Missy! Come sit with us!" Liz called just after I walked onto the plane. I looked up, finding she and Michelle seated about halfway back in the cabin.

"Missy!" Michelle motioned me toward the center seat on the left side of the Boeing 757. Jensen was behind me, and I wanted to be close to him, but we'd vowed to keep our relationship a secret.

"Go ahead," he murmured, just for me to hear.

I smiled at the two women and moved up the aisle toward them. "Okay! I'm coming!"

The rest of the ESPN crew moved in around me, and Jensen sat near the window across the aisle and three rows in front of me.

"How does it feel? Now you're an old pro!" Michelle said. "The interview footage was terrific. You gave me a ton of stuff to work with."

"Amazing," I sank into the seat and fastened my seat belt. "I hope my brother, Ben was watching."

"I'm sure he was. And, your little boy, too," Liz added.

I hadn't touched my phone all day and wondered if Ben or Dylan had called or texted. I was digging in my purse to find it when the flight attendants announced that electronic devices had to be turned off during the flight.

"Yes. I'm so flipping tired, but I'm anxious to hear what they thought."

"Well, I could tell you were nervous at first, but once you got into it, you did great!" Michelle put her hand in the air to signal the flight attendant just as I found my phone and pulled it out my purse.

Sure enough, there were quite a few messages from Ben, Dylan, Remi, Teagan and Chase; all of them congratulating, and in my son's case, asking me for another signed football. I realized that Teagan must have helped Remi and Dylan send theirs. I was anxious to see Dylan, hoping that Jensen and I would get back to pick up Dylan before Remi went to bed. I must have been smiling as I read them because Liz leaned and said, "You did everyone proud, today. Congratulations."

"I couldn't agree more," Michelle put in. "Let's order a few drinks once this bird gets off the ground."

"I'm so tired; I'm not sure I'll be able to stay awake if I have a drink." I was grateful for the friendship of the women by my side. It had been years since I'd had any real friends, and now I felt like I'd hit the jackpot.

I powered down the phone and the next thing I knew, we were wheels-up, and the flight attendants were passing out wine and cocktails to all of the crew. Jarvis was seated in the same row as Jensen; but on the aisle. He stood up, turned toward me and, with a knee on his seat, made a toast. "Congratulations to Missy on her first job, well-done. Welcome to the ESPN family!"

"Here, here!"

"Congratulations!"

"Welcome to the team!"

He lifted his glass as the other members of the crew cheered and added their congratulations. The passengers around us also raised their glasses jovially, and I nodded.

"Thank you, all. I love being part of such a wonderful bunch of people." I said sincerely.

My eyes flashed and caught Jensen's. He also stood for Jarvis' toast. When our eyes met, just before we drank, he mouthed "I'm proud of you." My heart skipped a beat at the emotion and desire I found behind those blue depths.

After more celebrating, we were landing in Atlanta before we knew it. Each of us was carrying or pulling our bags through the terminal and toward the outside. Somehow, Jensen maneuvered until he was walking beside me. "We may have a problem." His voice was quiet, and I could barely hear it over the cars and airplanes overhead.

"Like what?" I asked tiredly.

"Everyone will see that we're leaving, together. We didn't think about that."

I shrugged. "You know what? I don't even care. Liz and Michelle know that Teagan was watching Dylan this weekend, so…" My words dropped off, and I glanced up at him as we continued walking across the street and into the parking garage.

"Good, because I don't give a shit, either," he said wearily, huffing out a laugh.

Suddenly, I was acutely aware that he was catching another flight in less than twelve hours. Remorse hung over me, and I wanted to say something but decided to wait until we were alone inside his car.

Once we said goodbye to all of the others, who scattered to find their vehicles or were being picked up at the terminal, and our small carry-on luggage was stowed safely in the backseat, Jensen sat motionless for a couple of seconds after sliding into his car, before leaning forward to start the engine.

I reached out to cover his hand. "Hey, thank you for everything this weekend. I couldn't have done it without you." I wanted to touch him all day.

"You're welcome, babe." After the car was moving out of the garage toward the parking attendant, his hand reached over and threaded through mine. "I had an amazing time with you. I only wish you could come with me to Bristol, tomorrow."

I was so in tune with him that he'd just voiced what I'd been thinking. "I do, too."

He glanced my way with a lopsided smile. "Nah. Your son needs to see his mom."

"Yes, I missed him, but I'll miss you, too."

Jensen pulled my hand up to kiss the back of it right before we stopped to pay for the parking.

"Teagan texted and said it would be okay if I stayed at their house, tonight. Dylan is asleep, anyway, and I'm still not unpacked all the way. Besides, I don't want to keep you any longer than necessary. I feel bad that you worked through your weekend for me."

"Working?" Jensen grinned. "Is that what I was doing?"

I laughed softly. He had such a gentle, yet sexy way of seeping into every cell of my body, heart, and soul. "Mmmm," I agreed. "You need to get some sleep."

"Why don't we just skip going to pick up Dylan, and you come home with me?"

My heart sped up and heat spread through me. There wasn't anything I wanted more than to spend the night in

Jensen's arms.

"You're tired. We stayed up most of the night last night, and you've got more work tomorrow." I was lucky. I had the Mondays following Sunday games, off.

His hand squeezed mine, and his thumb rubbed back and forth across my knuckles. "Yes, I'm tired, but I'll sleep better with you."

"Jensen…" I began.

"What's the matter? Afraid you'll jump my bones?"

My soft laughter filled the car as I turned and looked at his profile as we drove in the dark night. He was smiling, but relaxed. He was beautiful cast in a glow thrown off the dashboard.

"Terrified, actually. But, in a good way."

"Yes, very good." He cast me an appreciative glance and pleasure within. "I can drop you at Teagan and Chase's before breakfast. Dylan won't even know you didn't come back tonight. What'd ya say?"

"I say, yes."

HER *last chance* BEGINS *in his arms.*

Chapter 14

Missy

"Mom!" Dylan called as he plowed down the stairs at Teagan and Chase's house at a breakneck pace. "Are you here?"

I was dressed casually in jeans and a plain navy-blue sweater that I'd had in my bag from the weekend, pouring a cup of coffee in the kitchen of the magnificent Forrester house. "In the kitchen, buddy!"

He rushed into the room still dressed in his P.J.s with his hair sticking up in a cowlick. "Did you bring me anything?" His bright eyes glowed in anticipation. I could see that if I let it, this was going to get out of hand. I couldn't bring him an autographed ball from every game. Where in the world would we store them in our small apartment?

I turned and leaned up against the counter. "What? No *hi, Mom, I missed you*?"

His head cocked as he looked at me wryly. "Hi, Mom. I missed you," my son acquiesced. "Did you bring me anything?"

He was excited, and I couldn't hide it any longer. I'd placed the football on one of the chairs to the table at the other end of the room which Teagan assured me had become his accustomed seat. I nodded in the general direction. "Go sit down. I made you some oatmeal with raisins."

"Aww, Mom." His face fell, thinking I didn't bring him anything.

Teagan was upstairs getting Remi ready for school, leaving me time alone with Dylan. "Hurry up. I don't want you late for school."

Shoulders slumped he shuffled to the table and pulled out the chair. "Awesome!" He looked at the signature scrawled in silver Sharpie. It was hard to read, even for adults, so he turned with questioning eyes.

"Lamar Jackson," I said simply, knowing he would be over the moon.

"Cool! Lamar Jackson! The kids at school won't believe it! Can I take it?"

I set my coffee cup down and walked over and removed it from his hands. "Sit. Eat."

Dylan pulled out the chair and scrambled onto it. "Well? Can I?"

I had already put milk and sugar on top of the hot cereal, and he picked up his spoon and started to eat. "What if you lose it? Your friends can come over once we get settled in our new apartment. You can show them your other ball and the jersey, too. But listen, honey, our apartment isn't that big, so I won't be able to get you a ball from every game. It might not be possible, in any case."

He seemed a tad disappointed. "I guess," he said. "Why can't we get a house?"

I sighed. "We will someday, but we're new to Atlanta, and once we get more settled, we'll look for one, okay?"

"Jensey has a house." He looked at me expectantly, shoveling in another mouthful of oatmeal. "He can keep my stuff safe for me if my room can't hold it all."

My eyebrows rose at his suggestion. "Well, I guess you can

ask him, but let's just wait and see how much your room holds, okay?"

"Okay." He reached for the small glass of orange juice I'd placed beside his bowl and drained it.

When he was finished eating, it took him no time to get dressed for school, but it took me longer to tame his hair into a respectable style. Finally, I gave up. It wasn't long before Teagan and I had the kids buckled into her backseat, and we were dropping them off at their school.

"Have a happy day," I called, as they unbuckled and slid out the back passenger-side door.

"Remi, Daddy is going to pick you and Dylan up after school."

"Okay, Mommy!" she answered and ran toward the door to the school behind Dylan. They disappeared inside the building, both surrounded by a group of their friends.

"What should we do, today, Missy?" Teagan asked as we pulled away from the curb.

I looked at her in surprise. "Well, I thought I'd just go to the apartment and start unpacking my stuff."

"Do you want some help?" she asked graciously. "We can get lunch delivered and make a day of it."

"Really? That would be so nice."

She nodded with a smile. "Why do you think I'm having Chase get the kids? He can keep them busy until around dinnertime."

"Wow, that would be a big help. Are you sure?"

"Of course!" Teagan was glowing with happiness. It was obvious all of her dreams had come true. She had an adoring husband, one beautiful child and another on the way.

"Are you going to find out the sex of your baby?" If it were me, I'd want to know.

"I want to, but Chase is old fashioned. He wants the

surprise because he missed Remi's birth." Despite her happiness, I could hear the regret in Teagan's voice. "I just don't have the heart to press him. I know he's dying to have a boy."

"I can see how much he loves Remi. If it's a girl, he'll love her to death," I said as we drove across town toward my new address.

"I hope he gets his wish because I'm hoping for a little version of Chase."

"Remi is so like him, though."

"Yes, she is, and he adores her, but Chase is really enjoying Dylan's interest in soccer. Remi kicks the ball around, but Dylan has a real desire to learn the sport, and that inspires Chase. I hope, if we have a son, he will love the game as much."

There was a Starbucks coming up on the left. "Do you want to get coffee before we get started? My treat," I said.

"Sure." Teagan turned into the parking lot of the coffee shop and into the drive-thru lane. It was busy at this time of the morning, and there were several cars in front of us.

"When does your mom move to Atlanta?"

"In just a couple of weeks."

She must have sensed my hesitation because she asked about it. "Don't you want her to move here, now?"

I inhaled. "I do. I need her to watch Dylan when I go out of town, and she's looking forward to spending time with him."

"But...?" The car inched forward in the line. "I sense a big *but.*"

I shrugged, embarrassed by my thoughts. I should be more grateful to my mother. After all, she was picking up and moving for me Dylan and me, but all I could think about was how her presence might intrude on my intimate time with Jensen. Teagan was easy to talk to, but sex with Jensen was something she had also shared, and I felt weird discussing my own experiences with her. "I don't know."

"Well, I do," she said matter-of-factly.

I fiddled with the handle to my purse that was sitting in my lap. "You do?" I felt coy and timid as if getting into this conversation would push me off a soaring cliff that there was no going back from.

Teagan laughed. "Hell, yes! You're afraid she'll cramp your style. Or rather, Jensen's style."

I blushed but nodded. I just knew my face had to be showing some hideous, horrified grimace.

She pulled up to the order board and looked it over before inquiring about my choice. "What would you like?"

"Just plain black coffee," I replied, glad for the pause in the conversation. My head was reeling.

She ordered my coffee and a green tea for herself before moving ahead in the line.

"Listen, you don't have to feel like you can't discuss private stuff with me," she picked up where we left off. "Honestly, I'm happy for you both."

"Don't take this wrong, but it is sort of uncomfortable discussing it with his ex-wife." I shifted nervously in my seat.

"Well, the good news is, that means Jensen finally made a move! But, really, you don't need to feel awkward; Jensen and I never did it."

Her tone was so relaxed as if the bomb she'd just dropped was a little feather, but my head snapped around. *Wait. What?*

I was dumbfounded. "But…" I began, but then stopped. "The whole time you were married, you never…?"

By now it was our turn to pay for the coffee at the second window, and she shook her head as she pulled up to it. I had taken my debit card out when we first pulled in and offered it to her. She waved it away and produced her own for the window attendant. Calmly handing me my coffee, she put her tea in the center console, unperturbed by my shock.

I sat in silence digesting what she had just told me. This was unbelievable.

"Yeah, we tried a couple of times when Remi was a baby, mostly because we both thought we should try to make our marriage work, but it just didn't feel right. I'd just had my heart broken, and ... he was Chase's best friend. Don't get me wrong, I loved Jensen, I still do, but as a best friend. I wouldn't have made it through Remi's illness or my break-up with Chase without his shoulder to lean on."

"Wow." I turned in my seat, clutching my untouched coffee in my right hand.

Teagan was beautiful, and Jensen was hot. *How could they not have sex in six years together?*

"We just kind of fell into a comfort zone and then when Remi got leukemia, we both focused on getting her better."

"I understand, but Jensen is..."

She nodded. "I know, right? He's so attractive, but my heart belonged to Chase and I was all messed up thinking he'd cheated. I didn't want to feel anything sexual because it reminded me that he'd been intimate with someone else. At least, I thought he had. I mean, no love songs, no romantic movies, no romance novels... I avoided everything that would make me think of Chase or how heartbroken I was."

What she said made sense in a way. I wanted to get rid of all memories of Derrick, too. "I understand."

"Once the pressure was off," Teagan continued unfettered, blowing out her breath, "we were both relieved. I felt guilty about it for a while, but Jensen was so understanding." She chuckled gently and took a sip of her tea. "He was probably just as relieved. I can't emphasize enough how wonderful he is. He's a catch."

I was still struggling to figure out what to say. A million questions were racing through my head. "Did you have some sort of understanding that he could see other women?"

"No." She shook her head. "I mean, he could have, and I wouldn't have minded, but I don't think that he ever did."

My eyes began to sting, and my throat felt thick, as emotions flooded my heart. Jensen was like no man I'd ever known.

"It isn't something I discuss with anyone, because I don't want anyone to judge Jensen as less of a man than he is. Chase knows, but he's the only one besides you. I didn't tell him right away, either."

"That must have been so hard."

"It was," Teagan agreed. "I felt so bad for so long, and it was worse when I found out the truth about that stupid phone call. Jensen sacrificed so much for Remi and me, and Chase… Ugh." She shook her head in dismay. "I thought he'd cheated when he didn't, but then, after I married his best friend, he was completely devastated. Guilt is an awful thing," she admitted with true sincerity. "Just awful."

"I don't know what to say," I said sincerely. I was still a little stunned.

Teagan pulled into the parking lot of my apartment complex and I pointed to the building that I lived in, so then she parked near the front.

She shut off the car and turned toward me with a serious expression on her face. "You don't have to say anything, Missy. It might be better if you don't even mention any of this to Jensen. I just wanted you to know the truth so you wouldn't feel awkward around me, and I didn't want you imagining Jensen and me the way I thought about Chase and his trainer. I don't want anything to mess things up between you. You both deserve this." She offered a gentle smile.

I was overwhelmed and a small sob broke from within me. I reached out my arms and hugged her close. "Thank you,

Teagan. Thank you, so much. You, Chase, Jensen and Remi... you're all so amazing."

Teagan's arms tightened around me, and her voice was teary when she spoke. "Birds of a feather, as they say. You are wonderful, too. You and Jensen deserve to be happy. I didn't want anything marring your chances at a relationship, least of all his marriage to me." Her voice cracked a bit, and it was apparent she was as full of emotion as I was.

When the hug ended, two tears were trailing down my cheeks which I quickly wiped away with my free hand.

Teagan's eyes were full of tears as well. She sniffed and unbuckled her seat belt. "Would you look at us? We're a pair of saps!" She flashed a smile and opened her car door.

I followed suit, and it wasn't a minute later that I was ushering her into the stark apartment. Everything was painted off-white, and the carpet was a greyish-beige. After the homey clutter of Ben's place and the elegance of Teagan and Chase's home, this was like a hospital room. There were white cupboards in the kitchen, and new linoleum with a light grey tile pattern on the floor of the entryway, laundry room, and kitchen. It was nice. I was sure that after I'd had time to decorate a bit, it would feel more like home.

"This is nice!" Teagan was encouraging. "There's a lot of space for Dylan to run around."

She was being gracious. The apartment was humble compared to her massive house. "It's okay. It'll work for a while. It's in a good location. Dylan loves his teacher."

"Did Jensen tell you that Remi had a bully pull her hair?"

I gasped as I removed my coat. "No!"

She nodded, a bit exasperated. "Yes. I say they're little kids, both Chase and Jensen have expressed a desire to transfer Remi to a different school. The tuition is even more ungodly. Ugh!"

"Oh, no," I said. "Dylan loves being in school with Remi.

Even if they squabble sometimes, deep down, they're friends."
I'd never be able to afford a more expensive school for Dylan, so
he'd have to stay put, even if Remi was moved. "Are you going to
do it?"

"I think it will pass. We've spoken to the parents of the
little boy, and they were amiable. They said they'd speak to him,
but we'll have to see how it goes."

I invited Teagan to remove her jacket and lay her purse on
the counter next to mine, and we both got busy unpacking. The
boxes were labeled, and I sorted them out, carrying them into
respective rooms, and making stacks once there. I refused to
allow Teagan to do any heavy lifting, so she contented herself
with sitting down, opening boxes, and pulling items out while I
put them away. She was sitting on Dylan's single bed and we were
unpacking his clothes, then hanging them up in the small closet
or folding them into the second-hand dresser Jensen and I had
purchased at a flea market, along with the bed frame, and a few
other pieces around the apartment.

I felt a little embarrassed by the humble belongings, and
she must have realized why I was so quiet. "This furniture is
great, Missy. With a few shelves and a toy box, this will be a
wonderful little boy's room. Jensen will outfit him with a bunch
of boy stuff. Wait and see." She smiled and handed me a stack of
folded T-shirts.

I turned and put them in the second drawer from the top.
"I'm sure you're right. He promised to take Dylan to a game this
week. He's so excited." My thoughts turned to Jensen and how
terrific he was with my son. "I hope things work out. I'm sure
Dylan would be as heartbroken as I would."

Teagan rolled he dark brown eyes. "I'm sure it will. Jensen
is happy. I haven't seen him smile this much in a long time."

My phone rang in the other room, so I jumped up to
answer it. "That might be him, now. I'll be right back."

I rushed into the kitchen and to my purse on the counter, pulling out the phone. I didn't recognize the number, but maybe Jensen was calling from a land-line at the offices in Bristol.

"Hello?" A smile laced my voice. A few seconds of silence followed, as a feeling of dread spread through me. "Hello?" I said again, this time more urgently.

"Well, well, well," a familiar voice sneered. "Looks like you're moving up in the world. I saw you on ESPN Sunday."

My heart fell to my stomach with a sickening thud. I sucked in a deep, startled breath. I expected Derrick to find me eventually, but I didn't think it would happen after my very first assignment. My instincts were to hang up, but that would only infuriate him, and incite him to show up in Atlanta. I couldn't have that.

I made my voice defiant, desperately trying to hide the utter terror I was feeling. "Good for you. What do you want, Derrick?"

"Is that any way to speak to me? I only called to wish you good luck at your new job." His voice took on that smooth, condescending tone that made me want to vomit.

Yeah, right, my mind screamed. One thing was certain; Derrick never wished anything positive for me. "Thank you."

"I want to see Dylan."

"Well, we don't want to see you," I snapped.

"You can't keep him from me forever."

"Watch me. In the years since our divorce, you haven't even tried to call him, so what the hell makes you so interested now?" Hate dripped from my words. No longer could I hide my real feelings from this bastard.

"Maybe I've changed."

"Maybe Hell has frozen over, too."

"Don't be nasty, Melissa. It doesn't become you. Give me a chance."

"Look, just stay away from us. Dylan is happy. Leave us alone!" I hung up the phone without waiting for a response. Only then did I realize how my heart was beating a thousand times a minute; so hard, I could literally hear the blood rushing in my ears, and I was shaking from head to toe.

I put a hand to my forehead and leaned against the counter to gather my composure before going back into the bedroom to Teagan.

What the fuck did Derrick want?

"Missy?" Teagan asked. She'd come into the kitchen, and her face was concerned. "I'm sorry, I couldn't help overhearing. Your voice was loud enough to carry down the hall. What happened?"

I walked the few feet into the living room and sank down onto the sofa, clasping my hands together to steady them. "My ex saw me on Sports Sunday." I shook my head, frustrated tears filling my eyes. "I was afraid this would happen, but I'd somehow managed to push it out of my mind."

"Oh, shit," Teagan murmured, sitting down beside me and covering my hands with one of her own. "What does he want?"

My eyes met hers. "He said he wants to see Dylan." Panic broke out inside me and I shook my head frantically. "He can't! Dylan will be scared to death!"

"I thought you had a restraining order against him," Teagan's voice was soothing.

"I did, in Wyoming. It doesn't cross jurisdictions."

"Well, we'll just get another one in Georgia. I'm not sure what the law is, but I bet because you travel for your job, we can get one that encompasses the entire country."

All sorts of awful thoughts were racing through my mind. "That might make it worse. Derrick is like a wounded animal. Confront him, and all hell breaks loose."

"But you can't just let him rule you; not after everything

he's put you through."

I brushed the tears from my face. "I don't know what to do."

"I can see you're afraid, honey. I'll look into the lawyer, and we will speak to Jensen and Chase."

At the mention of Jensen's name my head snapped up. "No! I don't want to dump this on Jensen. We're getting close and I don't want my bastard ex-husband ruining things. Please don't tell him. Or Chase. Teagan, please, promise me."

She sighed heavily. "I'm not used to keeping things from Chase, or Jensen, for that matter, but this is your business, so I won't mention it. Why don't you stay at the house tonight, just in case?"

Relief flooded through me at her suggestion. I had no way of knowing if Derrick was even in town, but I couldn't take the chance. I had to protect my son. "Thank you, Teagan. I can't tell you how grateful I am."

"No, problem. I can see how scared you are. Let's leave this for now and get back to my house. Do you think Derrick will go to the school?"

Panic seized my chest again. "I don't know. If he's in town, yes. In Dallas, he had the school in his pocket. They called him if Dylan was sick, or even if I picked him up early."

Teagan shook her head in disgust. "He sounds like one devious asshole."

"Worse; he's the devil," I murmured.

Teagan stood and put on her coat then handed mine to me. "Come on. Let's get out of here. Chase is picking up the kids, so what if Derrick confronts him? I think we should tell him."

I took the coat from her. "I just didn't want my relationship with Jensen overshadowed by Derrick's baggage." I slid my arms into the sleeves and reached for my purse.

"Have faith in him, Missy. Trust me, Jensen won't bail on

you."

I didn't think he would end things, but I was enjoying the rush of emotion between us, and the newness of us. I was afraid all of this garbage would take some of the bloom off of our magic. "I know he won't, but I don't want Derrick's harassment hanging over us."

She slid her arm around me after we walked out of the apartment and I locked the door behind us. "Then, he must be dealt with."

"Okay. Tell Chase, and I'll tell Jensen when he gets back from Bristol."

She smiled. Her friendship wrapped around me like a reassuring blanket. "Good. Let's have a movie night with the kiddos tonight, shall we? Nothing takes your mind off of your troubles like a Harry Potter marathon complete with a big blanket picnic! We can spend the afternoon making treats! I'll have Whole Foods deliver the ingredients."

I tried to smile. I needed to relax. Everything would be alright as long as I stayed rational. "Sounds good. Thank you, Teagan."

"What are friends, for?" she asked as we climbed into her car to start the drive back.

JENSEN

"Jensey!" Dylan called from his new bedroom. "Come play with me!" He was playing Sports Center on the PlayStation in his room. I'd just finished hooking it up to the small computer screen I'd brought over from my house. It was an older one that I didn't use anymore and would also work with cable TV. The little boy would be able to watch shows he liked, leaving the bigger TV in the living room for the adults.

"In a minute, D!" I called down the short hall toward his

room.

I'd seen Missy at the station earlier in the day but hadn't had an opportunity to talk to her, and she'd been introspective; which I thought was strange considering how we'd left things Monday morning.

She was still very quiet as she put away some of the kitchen utensils, pots, and pans out of the cardboard boxes stacked on one side of the kitchen. After the last night we'd spent together, I was expecting a little more enthusiasm. We'd ordered a pizza because the kitchen was a mess and were waiting for it to arrive.

"What's wrong?" I asked astutely. I leaned up against the counter's edge as I studied her. I wanted to hold and kiss her, but it felt like there was some invisible wall between us. I couldn't figure it out. Dylan seemed unperturbed, so whatever was bothering Melissa must not involve him.

Her eyes flashed up briefly before returning to her task. "I'm just tired. It's been a long day."

I wasn't buying her story, but I offered one single nod and folded my arms across my chest. "Did you get a chance to talk to David about how he thought Baltimore went?"

"Sure," she answered, without stopping unpacking the glasses and dishes we'd purchased at the local Walmart. "He said he thought it went well. Why? Didn't he tell you the same thing?"

"Yeah. He did."

We'd bought a bunch of second-hand stuff on one of the online sales apps, and she'd had a few things shipped from Wyoming, but she left her husband with literally the shirt on her back, so she had no household items. Maybe the lack of belongings was getting her down. I was already mentally cataloging what I could spare from the things at my home or when we could make time to shop for needed items.

I walked over to where she was standing and ran my hands down her arms, pulling her back against my body, savoring the closeness. "We'll get some more things for the apartment and before long, it will feel like home," I said, doing my best to comfort her.

I turned my head to kiss first, her temple, then her cheekbone. My body started reacting as she leaned back into me and arched her neck to give my exploring mouth access. My breath rushed out over her skin making her shiver. "I missed you." I let my mouth open over the skin at the base of her neck where her shoulder began. "I've been thinking about you day and night."

"Me, too," she whispered. I turned her in my arms, and hers slid up over my chest and around my neck as my mouth swooped down to capture hers in a soft, but hungry kiss.

"So... enlighten me. What's really bothering you," I demanded softly when the kiss ended.

Her forehead dropped to my shoulder, and she turned her face into my neck; saying nothing.

"Missy, you're scaring me."

The doorbell rang, and she startled unnaturally in my arms before she could answer.

"The pizza's here! The pizza's here!" Dylan came barreling out of his room and toward the door to the apartment.

"Dylan, wait!" Her voice had a frantic note to it that puzzled me. "Don't open the door!"

I released her, eyeing her skeptically. What could have her so upset? "I'll get it," I said, pulling out the wallet from my back pocket. "Be right back."

I watched as Dylan opened the door and a man I didn't recognize was standing there, but he wasn't holding a pizza box from Vincenzo's.

"No!" Dylan began to cry uncontrollably. "Go away!" he screamed. He turned, slamming into me in his rush to get away from the man at the door.

My hands closed over his shoulders then one moved up to cup his soft dark blond head. "Hey, buddy, it's okay." My eyes narrowed on the man. "What's this about? Who are you?" I asked the stranger.

"I just want to see my kid," the man answered, and realization dawned. My eyes narrowed. *This was Missy's ex-husband?*

"No!" Dylan said again, clamoring around until he was behind me and clinging to and peeking around my legs. "No! I don't want to see him, Jensey!"

"Go away, Derrick!" By now, Missy was walking up behind us. "You're not wanted here." Her words were shaky, and I could sense her fear.

"Take Dylan inside," I commanded softly.

"Shhh, baby. Come on." She pulled him away and lifted the crying little boy into her arms before disappearing into the apartment; down the hall into his room.

"Melissa has no right to keep me from my son," he commanded roughly. I could see the anger rising within him. His face was mottled, and the muscles of his neck and jaw flexed as his teeth clenched. "You sure as hell aren't going to stand in my way."

"Obviously, a judge in Wyoming didn't agree," I said in a low, but serious tone. Every cell in my body was poised to pounce. "Missy has every right."

The man backed up a step or two, and his demeanor softened. "Just let me talk to him. I mean no harm."

So, this was the mother fucker who hurt Missy and Dylan. I put an arm up until my hand wrapped around the door jam. I shook my head, a deadly calm overtaking me. He was shorter than me, but I could tell he was strong and worked with his hands. He was dressed in work clothes with Ellington Contracting embroidered over one pocket.

278

My blood ran cold that Missy still used this bastard's last name, but I'd pictured him differently; like some hot shot mob boss. Maybe he had been on a job site today, but his hair was slicked back with gel; I could still see he was a slimy bastard; as clear as day.

"That isn't going to happen." I put up a hand to hold him off. "Missy and Dylan have made it clear they want nothing to do with you, so you need to leave." My voice was fierce, making sure he got the point. "Now."

"Who the fuck are you, anyway?" he demanded, getting more and more agitated, using both hands to shove my chest angrily. It was a brief touch, but forceful and it hurt. "Are you fucking my wife?" His voice was loud, and the neighbors were probably getting an earful.

"Hey, asshole," I growled, incensed. "Touch me again, or either of them, and I swear to God, I'll lay you out. Don't let the pretty face, fool ya. Now, get the fuck out of here." I started to slam the door, but he used his body to block it; using his weight to keep it open. My muscles strained painfully against the force he applied.

"Not until I see my son!" He grunted.

Instinctively, I pulled back my right arm and landed a punch to his diaphragm causing Derrick to lose his breath. He grunted heavily and doubled over in pain.

"You've seen him. Stay away from them, or I won't be responsible for my actions. Be thankful you can still walk; you pathetic fuck."

This time, I was able to slam the door and throw the deadbolt into place. I inhaled deeply, running a hand through my hair as I walked back to find Missy and Dylan. If her ex didn't leave, we'd need to call the police.

Missy was sitting on his bed with Dylan cradled in her lap, rocking back and forth, trying to comfort him, and stroking his hair as he sobbed. "I don't want to see him! He's mean!"

"You don't have to see him, baby," she soothed, but her eyes were full of panic and tears.

I sat down beside them and put my arm around her, my hand cupping the back of her head. "When did he show up?" I asked softly.

"Jensey!" Dylan cried at the sound of my voice, looking up, then reaching for me. I pulled him onto my lap, and he wrapped his small arms around my neck, holding on for dear life. "You won't let him get me, will you?"

My free arm wound around the frightened child, while the other held his mother close. "No, buddy. He's not going to do anything bad to you, I promise. Well? When?"

"He called a couple of days ago," she answered softly.

"This is why you've been so quiet, isn't it? Why didn't you tell me?"

She nodded. "I didn't want to burden you."

Fuck that, I thought.

"I want to know everything." Emotions surged through me; anger at Derrick, and love and protectiveness for Missy and Dylan. "I want to know whenever or wherever he contacts you. Every time, Missy. Do you understand me?"

She nodded and wiped at a stray tear.

"You're not gonna let him take me, are you Jensey?"

"Never."

Not in a million fucking years, my mind screamed.

I stood, lifting Dylan in my arms. "Pack some things. You're coming home with me."

"Jensen," Missy stood and put a hand on my arm. "I won't let him run me out of my home. I don't want to give him any control over us."

I understood what she meant and what she needed, but there was no way on God's green earth that I was leaving her alone in this apartment with that creeper lurking about.

"Fine," I said tightly. "Then, I'm staying."

Dylan's arms squeezed my neck as he clung to me and I rubbed his little back with the flat of one hand.

"I'm staying," I said again.

HER *last chance*
BEGINS
in his arms.

Chapter 15

JENSEN

"Teagan mentioned he might be a problem," Chase said. I'd just begun to tell him about Derrick Ellington showing up at Missy's place earlier in the week.

"Really?" I was surprised that he knew.

"Yes. I picked the kids up from school on Monday, and Missy stayed the night. I wondered why, considering she had a new place. Teagan told me once we were alone in our room."

Anger began to rise up. It pissed me off that Teagan told Chase before Missy told me. Even when we spoke on the phone the night before, she said nothing. He could see by my expression what I was thinking. "So, this has been hanging over her head all week?"

"Chill out, man. Think about it. What could you have done from Bristol? It would have just messed with your head, and what good would that have done?"

He was right, but it still irritated me. "It doesn't matter. She should have told me that he called. I didn't find out until the fucker showed up on her doorstep."

"What the hell?" Chase asked incredulously, pushing the weight bar until his arms were locked in a bench press. I was spotting for him as I told him about the altercation at Missy's place. "You gotta be careful, man," he said through gritted teeth as he lifted the bar again. "He might be violent."

"I know. He has been in the past." It had been almost a week since the night when Derrick Ellington had stopped over at Missy's apartment. So far, he hadn't called her, and she was getting ready to head out with the crew on another assignment in a few days. "I don't want her to go to Philadelphia on Saturday, but I can't get her to agree to my going along. She doesn't want Bryan to know. The last thing she wants is for our boss to know she has a stalker."

"He can't fire her, can he?"

"It depends on how disruptive this dickhead gets. I mean, at face value, she'd have a discrimination case, but if this guy disrupts business, then Bryan would be justified."

Chase nodded. "Yeah."

We were at the gym where I had a membership while the women were at his house with the kids. The fortress-like security at Chase's place was the only reason I'd agreed to come out. Chase had weights and a couple of other machines at his house, but I wanted to talk to him without Missy around, so he'd agreed to go with me to get in a workout.

After his final set, Chase lifted the weight bar up, and I helped bring it up the last few inches until he replaced on the resting bar.

He sat up on the bench and grabbed a towel and his bottle of water from the floor next to the equipment. He wiped the sweat off of his brow and opened the water, about to take a long pull. "Is he stalking, or has she only seen him that one time?"

There was the rub. "Just once, but he's called a couple of times."

"Has Missy called the police?" Chase got up from the bench and wiped it down, making it ready for me to take my turn.

"Yes, but they told her that unless he tries to kill her, there was nothing they can do." I laid down and wrapped my gloved hands around the metal bar, getting ready to lift. I pushed the bar up and then lowered it to my chest with Chase's help. I started a series of bench presses, feeling my muscles strain more and more with each one. "Even if he threatens to kill her, they can do nothing until he tries. It's nuts. Unless that prick actually hurts her, they do nothing. It's driving me fucking crazy. I'm worried sick."

"I would be, too. If someone were sleazing around Teagan or Remi, I'd go fucking ballistic."

I pushed the bar up and down a few more times until the muscles in my arms began to shake and I had to grit my teeth. He was standing above me, his hands hovering beneath the bar as I lifted. "That's another thing. I'm worried about them, too. What if he comes around when they're all together?"

"Well, that shit isn't happening," he said, concern showing clearly in his expression.

Chase helped me put the bar back in place before I sat up, sweat running in drops down the side of my face and my entire torso. The bench press was the last exercise in our circuit. Both of us had pushed ourselves to the limit and were dripping with sweat. I stood up, and we started walking back to the locker room. "I know it's asking a lot because having Missy and Dylan staying there puts your family at risk, too, but—" I began.

Chase waved off my response. "It's the best place for them, but they can't be prisoners there, either. I can't picture either of the women agreeing to that, even if they didn't have work, school, or doctor's appointments on their schedules. We should probably hire security."

I huffed out my disgust. "You mean, like bodyguards?"

"Yes, that's exactly what I mean." Chase pushed open the door to the locker room, and I followed him inside.

"Missy won't even let me follow her around, let alone some muscle-head in a suit."

"You'll need to convince her. If she's hanging around with my pregnant wife and daughter, then she'll have to allow it. If this fucker is as bad as you say, she should welcome extra protection. If she still protests, then you can say it's for Teagan and Remi. The result will be the same."

I didn't think it would be that easy. If she didn't want Bryan and the crew to know about her issues, then the bodyguard would be too conspicuous. I also knew she'd regret the expense. "Maybe for Dylan…"

"What about another restraining order? I'll get my lawyer on it, right away. I just have to make a call. What do you know about this guy?"

"Chase, you don't need to pay for all of this," I said. I'd already been thinking about how I'd handle the expense by cashing in some of my 401K, but lawyers, security and private investigators were going to add up fast.

We were pulling off our shoes and sweaty clothes, leaving them in a pile by our duffels and heading to the showers. "I told you before, I have more money than I can ever spend, Jensen. What's it for if it's not to help a friend and keep my family safe?"

I sighed. It was a massive weight off of my shoulders but getting Missy to accept more financial help from Chase and Teagan would be a stretch. She was very proud, and she didn't like to let anyone know about the past abuse she and her son had suffered at her ex-husband's hands, let alone have someone else pay for her lawyers. "That's very generous, but it's not going to be that easy. I know she feels you and Teagan have already done too much."

"You're like my brother, dude. If I read you right, Missy and Dylan have a place in your future. So, by extension, they're family. End of discussion."

"Okay, but I'm going to chip in on the expense; I just got a promotion. We can speak to the women about it at the house, then." I should have known better than to argue with Chase, but it was a matter of pride that I do what I could to handle the situation myself. He didn't think helping me was charity, or make me less of a man, and I knew it.

There were a couple of teenage boys gawking at us as Chase turned on the water in the big tiled shower room. The two of them had hovered around while we were lifting, too, whispering to each other. At first, I wasn't sure if they recognized me from ESPN, or they were big soccer fans, but it became clear the more they hung around. Shit like this made me uncomfortable, but Chase took it in stride. If he noticed them at all, he didn't let on. I huffed out a laugh as I passed them on the way to the shower. "Stop staring, would ya? Yeah, he's Chase Forrester. You aren't delusional."

Hearing me, Chase smirked without speaking and turned his back to put his head under the spray.

"Do you think he'd give us an autograph?" one asked sheepishly.

"Yeah, maybe, but not while his junk is on display, got it? Wait for us outside the locker room door." I turned on my shower and adjusted the temperature, shaking my head as the two boys hurried away.

The larger of the two hauled off and slugged the other in the arm. "I told ya not to ask in there, dickhead!" he said, harshly in hushed tones as they moved out of the shower room. "You made us look stupid!"

"You're right, this stalker shit is creepy," Chase laughed out loud as he poured shampoo into his hand and lathered up his head.

I groaned. Like he didn't already know what it was like. "Unless supermodels are doing it, huh?" Chase was world-famous, and he had people coming up to him everywhere he went.

"Naw. That's just as creepy," he teased with a glint in his eye. "I'm a one-woman man, brother! After the shit we went through? No way."

I knew what my friend meant. He loved Teagan and didn't even look at other women, and for the first time in my life, I knew exactly how he felt. He'd known Teagan was the one from the first moment he'd laid eyes on her, and that was how I felt about Melissa. I'd only known her for a short time, but I felt centered and excited all at the same time whenever she was around. I'd never been happier, and it was looking like she felt the same way; until her bastard ex showed up. A resolve settled over me as I showered and dressed. I'd do whatever was needed to put Derrick Ellington in the past. I wasn't going to let anything stand in the way of our new relationship, and more, I was going to do whatever necessary to keep Missy and Dylan safe.

Missy

Teagan rubbed her lower back and her face contorted into a grimace. It was clear she was in pain as she stood at the stove making butter chicken. I felt guilty sitting on the chair watching. Dylan and I spent Monday night here, and last night at Jensen's. I felt anxious to get back to my apartment and finish getting settled, but it had only been 24 hours since Derrick had shown up at my door, and I wasn't convinced he'd left town. Until I was sure, I'd be in a constant state of fear. It would affect my work, and, my relationship with Jensen. As the weekend drew nearer and my next out-of-town assignment loomed, my uneasiness became more unbearable.

The kitchen smelled delicious; aromas of turmeric and cumin filled the air. I was amazed that Remi would eat something with such a complex flavor profile, but I had the peanut butter and jelly standing by for Dylan.

I slid off of the stool and moved toward the stove, where Teagan was stirring the piquant meat dish in the thick golden sauce. "Why don't you let me help? You're beat."

She smiled tiredly, her eyes telling me all I needed to know. "Being pregnant isn't the picnic I recall, but maybe I had too much other stuff going on, at the time, to really remember it."

I nodded at the barstool I'd just vacated on the other side of the kitchen island. "Get over there," I ordered good-naturedly. "I don't remember pregnancy being a party, either. Trust me. The good news is; you look great." I smiled broadly, knowing if Teagan felt anywhere close to what I felt when I was expecting, she felt like a beached whale with swollen ankles, and no amount of praise would make her feel differently. She did look amazing, though; the round baby bump the only tell.

She laughed softly, rubbing her swollen belly lovingly. "Can you please hand me that glass of water?" Teagan pointed to the crystal glass of iced water on the counter next to me. "I don't think I've peed in five minutes."

I did as she asked, chuckling, and then continued to stir the simmering chicken in the fragrant sauce. "I wonder what's taking the guys so long?"

Teagan's brows arched, and she rolled her eyes. "No doubt, they're plotting on how to save the world."

"In other words, how to deal with Derrick?"

She nodded, a somber expression settling on her face. "Don't judge them too harshly. They're close. They always ask each other's advice, and if one of them is in trouble, the other steps in to help. It's just the way they are. You'll see."

I made sure the chicken didn't burn and reduced the heat by half. Warmth spread through me. "I already do. The way you and Chase have helped Dylan and me; I know it's because of

Jensen."

"At first it was, sure. But now that we've gotten to know you, you've become like family all on your own."

"I can't stay here forever. I have to stand on my own two feet." I didn't want to intrude. Teagan was getting closer to her due date, and the last thing this family needed was un-related squatters intruding. I knew how special this time was for Teagan and Chase, considering he wasn't around for Remi's birth.

Teagan's shoulder lifted in a half shrug. "Sure, when you're not scared to death. This is a special circumstance."

"So? You and Chase need privacy right now. And, Remi. She's so excited about being a big sister."

Teagan made a short roll of her eyes. "She sure is, if I don't have a boy. She wants a sister, so badly."

"I can see where that would be fun, but she'll love the baby, no matter what."

The sound of the garage door whirring as it opened made Teagan jump up. "Speak of the devil! There they are now. I need to put on the rice!" She walked around to the pressure cooker sitting on the other side of the counter, with only the slightest waddle. "It's a good thing I have this contraption. It only takes ten minutes!"

Dylan and Remi were getting along better and had been playing video games upstairs in Remi's room. Jensen preceded Chase into the house; through the mud and laundry rooms into the kitchen. Both men came over to us. Chase leaned in to plant a brief kiss on Teagan's mouth, and Jensen came to stand next to me at the stove. "What are you cooking? It smells delicious." I felt the warmth of his hand move from the middle of my back down to my waist, and he kissed my temple as I concentrated on the pan in front of me. I wanted to kiss him full on the mouth, but something held me back.

"Yeah, I'm starving," Chase added.

"Hey," Jensen said softly, in my ear. "Are you okay?"

"Yes," I reassured him. My eyes met his as I nodded.

He was still standing close with his arm around me, and our hips were touching. His blue eyes were intent on drilling through any ruse. "Are you sure?"

I stopped and gave him a wry look. "Of course."

"Okay," he muttered and moved away.

Chase and Teagan were talking to each other in low tones, and he ran a hand down the back of her head before he moved to the cupboard and began taking out plates and silverware. "Should we just eat in here?" He asked his wife.

"Yes, if you don't mind," Teagan answered.

Chase nodded and started setting six places around the island countertop. It was clear this was routine because Jensen went to another cupboard and took out four crystal glasses and two plastic ones for the kids. "Milk for those two?" he asked.

"Yes." I nodded, turning the burner temperature to the off position, and put the clear glass lid on the pan. It would stay warm enough until the rice was finished cooking.

When the table was set, I went to the refrigerator and pulled out the salad Teagan had made earlier, along with a couple of dressing choices and placed them all on the table.

Chase was sitting next to Teagan and Jensen was leaning with both elbows on the end of the bar. Three sets of eyes were all staring at me intently.

Apparently, Chase and Jensen were cooking something up, and Chase had let Teagan in on it while when I wasn't paying attention. My eyes moved from one of them to another and then landed back on Jensen. "What is it?"

I cleared my throat. "Chase and I discussed the situation, and we both agree, that we should get the two of you, and the kids, some security." He was careful about his words, speaking slowly to gauge my reaction.

I looked across at Teagan who she put her hands up. "Hey, don't look at me. This is all them." She paused for a beat. "But I do think it's a good idea, Missy."

"I'm not taking any chances," Jensen agreed calmly. "We have no idea what his intentions are. Is he here on a job, or is he here just for you?"

I swallowed, considering my response. "I guess... I don't know. He never took jobs outside of Texas before. Maybe he's already gone back to Dallas," I added hopefully.

"We can't assume anything, so we need to get this in place, right away," Chase interjected.

I wiped my hands on a kitchen towel that Teagan had on the counter and then set it down again. Guilt descended like a heavy curtain over me, and my heart fell. "Maybe I should have stayed in Wyoming with Ben. Derrick didn't bother us." I sighed heavily. "I guess, after two years, I thought he'd leave us alone."

Jensen got up and walked over to me, taking my hand. "He didn't bother you because he knew Ben would beat the shit out of him if he tried anything. We've just got to convince him someone here will do the same thing."

"Or, two someone's," Chase added with a bright, over exaggerated, smile.

"Thank you for being so supportive, but I feel like a huge burden," I said wearily, putting a hand through my hair. "What exactly are you thinking?"

Chase shrugged. "Just one or two guys. Not a big deal." He was so casual about it, like adding security guards was an everyday occurrence.

I inhaled so hard that it felt like my lungs would burst. "It is a big deal. First, it will scare Dylan, and second, it's too expensive."

Jensen squeezed my hand. "I'm working out the money. Don't worry about it." He was so sincere my heart would have melted if the entire situation wasn't freaking me out. "Dylan will think it's cool. Sort of like his own secret service. You'll see." He was trying to sell it to me, and maybe he'd be able to convince Dylan it was an adventure and not because he was in danger, but I knew better.

"Even if you don't agree for extra guards for you and Dylan, I'm putting them in place for Teagan and Remi, either way." Chase moved around to deal with the pressure cooker when the buzzer went off. I flipped a switch and steam started to escape in a powerful stream from the top. "Did you want this in a bowl, or just dish it up at the stove, Babe?" he asked his wife.

"Just dish it up," Teagan answered, getting up from her chair and heading out of the kitchen. "I'll go get the kids."

Jensen's fingers were rubbing over the tops of both of my hands making me look up into his face. "I don't want this to be such a big deal. Derrick hasn't called—"

"Since Monday?" he asked, knowingly. "Why didn't you tell me it was Monday? It's been hanging over you all week?"

"It's not all week. It's only a couple of days. I didn't want you to freak out," I began. He opened his mouth to protest, but I shook my head. "No. You would, and you know it. I didn't want you rearranging work again. I don't want to give Bryan Walsh any concern about my ability to do my job. Jensen, this is so impor-tant. I need to get stronger and over my fear of Derrick. I *have* to." I hoped the emphasis on the word would make him under-stand that it wasn't just about my physical safety; it was for peace of mind. If I was ever going to be free of Derrick, I had to let go of the fear, too.

His head dropped until his forehead pressed against mine, his shoulders rising and falling as he sucked in his breath. His hands never let go of mine as he spoke softly. "I don't want anything to happen to you. I don't want you out of my sight."

My heart leapt at the intensity in Jensen's eyes. It was easy to see he meant every word. We were having a private conversation in the middle of the kitchen as Chase moved around us, getting the food ready and the children came racing down the stairs with Teagan following, but I barely noticed. "I'd rather you stay in Atlanta with Dylan. That would help me the most."

Jensen's eyes closed and I could almost hear his unspoken protest. "Okay. But we are getting the security guards."

"We don't even know if he's still around. What are ya gonna do? Send them with me on every assignment? Or, have them follow Dylan around at school every day? That's crazy."

"What the hell do you want me to do?" His voice was tight and full of anger, his head lifting until I could see his eyes flashing fire. "I can't sit here and do nothing!"

"Then, let me go to Philadelphia without worrying, and while I'm gone, you keep Dylan safe."

I could see it was hard for Jensen not to take charge of the situation and that the conversation was far from over. I had to convince him that the best way to handle Derrick was to give him as little power over us as possible and hope I could stay calm myself. I was scared of Derrick; old habits were hard to break, but I was sure that having him think he still had control of me would be the worst way to handle the situation.

"Hi, Chase! Jensey!" Dylan squealed as he came running into the room. "Are we going to a game tonight? Are we, huh?"

"Not tonight, buddy," he said regretfully, ruffling my son's head as he looked up at him. "I know I promised, but I couldn't get tickets tonight." I knew he was lying to my son. Chase and Jensen had planned on taking the kids to a Braves game tonight, but after their "Derrick" discussion, they'd must have decided to call it off. "But we can stay here with your mom and Teagan, and we'll all watch it together on the big screen."

"Awww!" he moaned. His disappointment was clear. "It's

not the same!"

"We can practice some soccer moves during the breaks," Chase added. "Is that better?"

"As long as it's out in the backyard!" Teagan said.

Dylan's face perked up, and he nodded his agreement. "Okay! What's to eat?"

"Teagan made something delicious. Butter chicken," I said, pulling out a stool. Jensen lifted first Dylan and then Remi up to sit at the table.

Dylan wrinkled his nose. "Butter chicken? What's that?"

"It's good; that's what!" Remi spouted happily.

"Dylan, I want you to at least try it," I ordered sternly.

"What's in it?" he asked in distaste.

"Dylan!" I said sharply. "Don't be disrespectful."

"It's chicken and rice, dumb dumb," Remi said indignantly. Her enthusiasm for the dish was patently obvious.

"Remi," Teagan warned, shaking her head. "We don't name-call."

"Yeah, but what's that yellow stuff?" Dylan seemed unperturbed by Remi's remark.

"It has a lot of yummy stuff in it. Just try it, honey. One bite, please." Chase had been dishing up our dinner at the stove and passing out plates, handing Teagan and myself smaller portions for the kids at the same time. I placed it in front of my son, as she put Remi's down in front of her. "Just one," I reprimanded again.

Dylan reluctantly picked up his fork and stabbed a piece of the chicken, sniffing it before putting it tentatively into his mouth.

"It's good, right?" Remi said, putting a forkful into her mouth.

Dylan nodded and continued to eat. "I guess it's good, but it doesn't look like butter."

FINDING TOMORROW

We all laughed as we sat down to the meal.

* * *

On Friday morning, I was feeling more at ease. Derrick hadn't made any other contact since Tuesday night, and Jensen had backed off of his insistence that bodyguards be assigned to protect us, though he was going to take Dylan for the weekend while I was in Philadelphia, just in case Derrick was lurking.

I called his office to see if he was in back in Dallas, but he wasn't available, and his secretary was not very forthcoming. It worried me a little, but I didn't tell Jensen. I just wanted Dylan to enjoy the weekend with him without worrying about Derrick showing up.

I parked in the parking lot outside the ESPN office building and got out of my car, locking the door behind me, and began to walk around toward the front entrance. It was then that I saw the Ellington Construction logo across the door of the big Dodge Ram truck parked across the street.

My heart skipped a beat and then started pounding like thunder, my steps faltered as I glanced around, looking for Derrick. I should have known he wouldn't give up so easily. I could only hope he was waiting for me outside and wouldn't make a scene inside the lobby. My hand fluttered to cover my heart because I found it hard to breathe. After a moment's pause, and with no sign of my ex-husband, I continued slowly into the building. A few of my associates nodded or murmured good morning greetings as I proceeded inside the glass-enclosed lobby.

Instantly, I scanned for evidence of Derrick, though I wouldn't have needed to. I was barely six feet inside the revolving door when he rose from his seat across from the reception desk. Once again, my steps faltered. Dressed in work clothes of jeans and chambray shirt with the business logo embroidered over the left pocket; he looked different than he had two years ago. He must have a job in Atlanta.

Shit! My mind railed. *What the hell would I do now?*

Derrick began to walk toward me, slowly raising both hands in front of him. "I just want to talk, Melissa," he said when he reached me.

I inhaled deeply. "This is my place of business, Derrick," I hissed.

"Then I suggest you not make a scene." He offered a smile, but it was for the benefit of the onlookers. His voice held a menacing tone that was all too familiar.

"I have meetings this morning," I protested, struggling to find a reason, any reason, to get rid of him. My first instinct was to find Jensen, but he was off today, and so wasn't in the building. "I don't have time to talk now."

"Make time," he said through clenched teeth. "I won't take that long, and I'll be out of your way."

I sighed and nodded toward the elevators. "Come up to my office, but I only have ten minutes." My first meeting was with Jarvis, but it wasn't for another hour, but I wanted him gone as soon as possible.

"Fine." Derrick nodded sharply, using his hand to indicate I should lead the way. I felt my skin crawling as he followed me into the elevators and all the way up to my floor. I felt my face burning with heat but prayed my associates didn't notice as we made our way through the cubicles to my office.

Derrick closed the door behind him, and I took off my coat and threw it down. "So talk, but make it fast." Every muscle inside my body was coiled as I gingerly lowered myself into my chair behind my desk, grateful for the barrier that it provided between us.

He took one of the two upholstered chairs opposite me.

"Look, I know you're going to cover the Eagles this weekend. I want to take Dylan. Get to know him again. I have a job in Atlanta that will keep me here a couple of months. I want to use that time to get back into his life."

"No." I shook my head adamantly. "You're not going to see Dylan under any circumstances." Derrick never knew my son. He just ordered him around and beat on him like a tyrant.

It was easy to see Derrick's anger rise. His neck seemed to swell before my eyes as color rose under the skin of his face, his expression was tight, and a muscle worked in his jaw. "I have a right to see him; he's my son, too."

"No. He's mine. I don't trust you, Derrick. He doesn't want to see you. He remembers how you treated him. Now, if that's all—"

His fist raised and slammed down on the edge of my desk, causing me to jump in my chair. "No! It's not all!" he said fiercely. "Who in the fuck do you think you are? You're just some whore I was stupid enough to marry, and I won't have you keeping me from my son!" He stood, looming over me. "I sure as hell won't let that other man raise him! I'll be damned if I'll let that happen!" he seethed. "Who is he, anyway?"

I was physically shaking, my body and mind reliving some of the times he'd beaten me in the past. His anger was a tangible thing. My eyes looked longingly at my office door. I routinely kept the blinds in the glass window between my office and the department closed, and I wished that I'd left it open. "Just a friend," I said, doing my best to calm him down. The last thing I wanted was for Derrick to target Jensen.

"You make friends fast, don't you? Don't think I don't know how broke you are, Melissa. I'll go to court, and I'll win."

"You didn't win in Wyoming, so what makes you think you'll win here?" I spat, fury giving me an unnatural bravado.

"Don't underestimate me, woman! I'll pay whoever I

need to pay to fuck with your career, to say things about you that you won't want made public. I'll ruin your reputation, and show you are not fit. You've robbed me of my son for long enough. You don't have a fucking restraining order here, and I will see him. Mark my words."

I stood, railing at him, and pointing a finger in his direction. "You don't have a son! You didn't give a shit about him for years! You never cared about him! He was just another thing to own!"

The door to my office suddenly opened; Jarvis put his head inside. "Everything okay, Missy?"

I smoothed down my skirt and then ran a hand through my hair as relief rushed through me. "Yes, Jarvis. We're finished here."

Jarvis must have been able to tell from my expression that something wasn't right, because, thankfully, he hovered in the doorway. "Good, because we have to be in the producer's office in five."

Derrick was still steaming mad, but he nodded and moved toward the door. "I'll go but remember what I said. I'll call you to make arrangements."

Jarvis moved aside to let Derrick leave before I could respond. I didn't know what to say anyway. I didn't know what to do, either.

HER *last chance* BEGINS *in his arms.*

Chapter 16

Missy

Jensen convinced me that I didn't need to worry about Dylan while I was away. He'd promised never to leave my son's side, and they were having a blast in Atlanta while I was sitting alone in my Philadelphia hotel room on Friday night.

Jarvis had gone to his room just after we'd gotten to the hotel, but the girls were pestering me with text after text requesting that I join them in the bar for a nightcap. Part of me wanted to hole up inside my room; the old part of me, but my new resolve to control my fear made me change my clothes and refresh my makeup. I would go down there and have some fun!

When my phone rang it was after ten, but I wasn't concerned anything was wrong. Jensen told me he was taking the kids to a baseball game and they would be home late.

Dylan's exuberance was palpable as his voice came excitedly through the phone. "We went to a Braves game, and Jensey and Chase took me into the locker room! I got a signed baseball from Sean Newcomb!"

"Wow! That sounds amazing, baby!"

"It was *so cool*, Mom! I got to meet the whole team and the coach!"

"Did Remi like it, too?"

"Nah, not too much. Miss Teagan wouldn't let her go into the locker room with us guys."

I smiled, loving how happy Dylan sounded, but I understood Teagan's reticence. All of the naked men walking around would explain her decision. I was a grown woman, and sports reporting was my job, and I was shy about it.

"Well, it sounds like you're having a fabulous time with Jensen and Chase!"

"I am! Chase has to go to Kansas City for practice tomorrow. I wish we could go watch, but Jensey said we can't this time."

I knew that nothing would enchant Dylan more than being on the field watching Chase and his teammates during practice. There was a game with Ecuador early in the season taking place in Orlando. Their baby should arrive by then, but I'd heard Chase and Teagan talking about it. Chase didn't want to go without his family, but it might be too soon for the baby to travel. He would have no choice but to go; he was the star forward on his team. Teagan told me about their wedding at Disney World, per Remi's expectations, and it sounded absolutely magical. I was sure the kids would want to go if given a chance. Dylan had never been to Disney, and he'd adore it, but he'd love seeing a live soccer game even more.

I shook my head, stopping my thoughts. I had no right to think of Dylan and myself as part of their family; as if we'd be automatically included in the future, but they'd all been so welcoming that it was difficult not to let my mind wander in that direction; especially when it came to Jensen. My heart was so full of him. He was literally like my knight in shining armor coming to my rescue when I needed it most, and equally important, becoming such an important role model for my son. It didn't hurt that he was strong and gorgeous, or that he stirred a physical and emotional response in me like I'd never known before.

"I'm sure he'll take you someday," I said, hoping against hope that our dreams of Jensen being part of our lives would come true.

"Yeah, that's what he said. He promised." I could picture my son smiling from ear-to-ear. He seemed content with Jensen's answer, trusting that he'd make good on his word. A far cry from what Dylan could have expected from Derrick.

"Is he there with you?"

"Yeah!" Dylan said with his mouth full; obviously eating something before he went to bed. "Wanna talk to him?"

"Yes, please. Be good, baby. I love you."

"Love ya, too, but could ya stop calling me that, Mom? It's not cool," he mumbled and then yelled into the room beyond the phone. "Jensey! Mom wants ya!"

I almost blushed. The innocent statement from my little man couldn't be truer.

"You want me, huh?" Jensen's smooth voice came across the line with a smile lacing his tone.

I smiled wide, my cheeks almost painful as I laughed softly. "Guilty, as charged," I admitted.

"Well don't worry, it's mutual," Jensen said. "Did our boy tell you what a great time we had? I have to get him some display cases for all of his sports paraphernalia."

"You spoil him," I replied, still blushing, my love for him growing deeper at his reference to Dylan as *ours*.

"He'll be okay. You should have seen him running around shaking hands with all of the players. It was classic."

"You've become so important to him. I think he'd trade me in if he could have you instead."

"That won't be necessary." His voice was sultry and made me physically tingle all over. "What are you up to?" he asked, his voice falling into a lower, more seductive timbre.

"Michelle and Liz want me to go down for a couple of drinks." I wished I could tell him that I'd rather spend the time talking to him on the phone and that he made my insides melt like butter.

"Are you going, then?"

"I am. For a little bit. We don't have to be at the stadium until tomorrow afternoon."

"I know," he answered. "Just be careful." I knew he meant that I should be on the lookout for Derrick.

"I am, I promise." I sank onto the edge of the mattress, wishing I hadn't told the girls I'd meet up. I'd much rather stay and talk to Jensen on the phone than be with anyone else in person. "Keeping track of me, huh?" I asked playfully.

He inhaled so deeply I could hear it over the phone line. "Exactly. No sign of the asshole at the ballpark. I was keeping my eye out."

"If he is lurking anywhere, it's around Dylan. I'm just glad he doesn't know where he is."

"I did some research today. He's working on the McIntire building downtown. It's a big project, so he'll be here for a while, unfortunately."

"He used to send a supervisor and a crew to any remote jobs. He gets bored easily." I wasn't sure if I was trying to reassure Jensen or myself that he wouldn't stay very long in Atlanta.

"Well, it isn't about the job this time; that's obvious. Don't worry. I got this."

"I know you do." At that very moment, a text came through on my phone.

"The girls are bugging me. I hate to run, but I think I should meet them."

"Sure, you go ahead. We're just having ice cream sundaes

and watching *Field of Dreams*."

"Hot fudge?" I asked playfully.

"Is there any other kind?"

I laughed happily into the phone before he continued. "Call me later if you want. I'll be up."

"Sounds good. I miss you."

"I miss you, too. Bye for now."

After I hung up the phone it wasn't Liz or Michelle's name that I saw on the screen of my phone as I'd assumed; it was Derrick's.

In an instant, I went from being happy and relaxed to anxious and freaked out. My heart started pounding harshly, feeling as if it would break free from my chest. My hand was shaking as I held on to the phone. I wanted to ignore it, but that wouldn't solve anything. It could make me even more vulnerable if I didn't know Derrick's location.

I opened his text.

Come downstairs. We need to talk.

Oh, shit! Was he in Philly or did he think I was at the apartment in Atlanta? Somehow, I had to find out, but I could barely type out my response.

In the parking lot?

I didn't have to wait long for his response.

No. The bar.

I dropped the phone on to the low pile of the carpet and put both hands over my face.

Fuck! He was here.

The hysteria I used to feel with Derrick was resurfacing.

My eyes began to blur, and the blood thundering at my temples made pain burst in my temples. Both hands clutched in my hair as I tried to calm myself down. Was I was having a panic attack?

My phone dinged from the floor again. Another text came in, and I scrambled down to pick it up.

Come down unless you want me to come up there.

I took a shaky breath. At least the girls, and hopefully part of the station crew, would be around and I'd find safety in numbers.

I'll be down shortly.

I stood and walked to the bathroom to check my appearance in the mirror. I wiped an errant tear away from beneath each eye and concentrated on even breathing. I touched up my mascara with trembling fingers, moved slowly into the other room and picked up my purse; sliding the phone inside. I couldn't let him see that he still had the power to make me crumble.

The elevator ride to the lobby was the shortest in history. I was still shaking on the inside, but the fake calm I'd learned to master in my years with Derrick had kicked in. Just before entering the bar, I texted Liz to tell her I'd be a little while and that I was meeting someone else in the bar first. I didn't wait for her to answer before I returned the phone to my purse and walked through the open doors of the hotel lounge.

My eyes scanned the perimeter for Derrick. He wasn't at the bar, though Liz, Jeremey, and Michelle were. They were all staring at me as I walked in and Liz lifted her phone. She'd gotten my text. I made brief eye contact with her, but then found Derrick sitting in a booth back in the far corner.

I made my way toward him as unwaveringly as possible. He didn't stand when I approached, but his narrow eyes burned into me as he waved a hand at the empty seat across from him.

I sat down and slid in. "What do you want?" I made sure to keep my voice even, and as unaffected as I could muster.

He had a drink in front of him, and from the amber color, it had to be some sort of whiskey or scotch. He always went for the hard stuff. Memories of him beating me in a drunken rage erupted like a horror film inside my head.

"I told you. I want my kid."

I met his eyes without flinching though I didn't respond.

He lifted his hand to call the waiter over and ordered me a glass of white wine. It was his habit when we were married. I didn't object, deciding to save my energy for the real fight.

"You followed me to Philadelphia to talk to me and convince me you've changed?" I spat in disgust. "This is you *not* stalking me?" I huffed angrily, shaking my head.

"I didn't follow you." He smiled in that condescending way that infuriated me. "I'm bidding a job," he said casually, digging into the bowl of cocktail nuts in front of him and removing a few. The way he chewed made me insane. My hatred for him had no bounds. I wished I could scratch his fucking eyes out of his smug, arrogant face.

"Sure, you did." I couldn't help crossing my arms over my chest, unsure if it was an unconscious way of protecting myself or trying to hide the trembling of my hands. "I'm not an idiot."

He popped some nuts into his mouth at the same time that he shrugged. "Believe me or not, I don't give a fuck, Melissa."

Well, at least that was honest. He never gave a damn about what I wanted, how I felt, how our son was affected. My animosity grew as I sat waiting for him to continue. I'd just let him say what he wanted to say and then get up and walk over to my friends.

"You're traveling every weekend, and so he can be with me. Where is he this weekend, anyway?"

I kept my mouth shut.

"If you don't let me see Dylan, I'll hurt you." Derrick's demeanor was calm, like a glassy lake in a mountain valley. He sat there calmly drinking from the glass and swirling what was left of the liquid around inside the glass, his eyes burning into me. He was such a ruthless bastard.

"I don't care," I said. And, I didn't as long as he didn't hurt Dylan.

"Really?" He continued to eat, unperturbed. "Do you care if I hurt Romeo?" His eyes locked with mine. "Ah…" He pointed at me, a sly smile sliding grotesquely over his lips.

"Sure, you will. That's why he beat the shit out of you the other night, right?" I couldn't keep the contempt out of my voice.

"I admit, he took me off guard, but he hardly beat the shit out of me. I have friends in low places, Melissa, so don't forget it. You won't pin anything on me, even if you tried."

"Stay away from us, Derrick, or I swear to God, I'll get another restraining order!"

"Oooooh," he said patronizingly. "I'm scared." He took another handful of nuts from the dish. "Look, Melissa, I just want to get to know my son, and you have no right to keep him from me." His face was still an angry red, but instantly, his expression changed. His demeanor changed on a dime. "I've changed."

"I can see that," I seethed. "Sociopaths don't change." It was a bold move that I knew it would piss him off, but I didn't care.

His face filled with hatred and he leaned forward menacingly, putting his elbows on the table.

"Look, you little whore, I won't have some pretty boy who

is fucking my wife raising my son! Jensen Jeffers, right? Yeah," he said, gauging me for any inkling of feelings. "I know who he is. I know he works with you." He tossed a few more nuts into his mouth and chewed, studying me. "I'll haul you to court for custody, and this time I'll win. I've got a hundred character-witnesses lined up to testify on my behalf," he warned. "Some were Dylan's teachers and doctors. Some of your old lovers who say you brought them into my house and screwed them with Dylan in the other room."

I gasped at the absurdity of it. He practically had me under lock and key the entire time we were married. "None of its true. We both know I was a virgin with you."

He laughed harshly, a sound I'd grown to despise. "Doesn't mean you didn't have affair after affair while we were married. I'm sure ESPN will love having two of their sportscaster's names in the national news for shacking up after they just met. I'm sure your boss will want a known whore working at ESPN."

"You'll never win."

"Won't I? I haven't violated the fucking restraining order once, and it's done now. Over. Yeah, I had a lawyer go to court in Wyoming, and because you didn't show up, I won. How does it feel, you little bitch?" He was furious, I could hear it in his voice, even though he didn't display anything physical for the other's in the bar to witness.

My eyes widened in shock. "I didn't know, because I wasn't notified!"

He shrugged casually, and his face turned mocking. "Well, see that's just it. That's not what our records show. We filed with the court, and let your lawyer know. Is it our fault he didn't notify you? How were we to know he'd be killed in a car accident right after we filed our motion?" Derrick sneered. "Yeah. I hear it was faulty brakes. It was a bloody, bloody mess." Terror ran through me at the picture he painted as he met my eyes. "I know what you're thinking, Melissa, but you'll never know, will you?"

I knew. He killed my lawyer. He'd orchestrated his death and made it look like an accident.

"Anyway, I got the result I wanted," he said casually, taking a swallow from his glass. "No show in court. Ta da!"

I shook my head, wanting to vomit. "You despicable bastard," I accused.

Derrick just laughed, taking pleasure in my misery. "Careful," he warned. "You haven't even let me talk to Dylan, and as I said, I have character witnesses galore. On both of us. I'm a saint, and you're unfit."

"Dylan hates you. Why do you want to see him now?" I asked, panic filling my soul.

"If he hates me, it's because you poisoned him against me. I won't let you give my son to someone else! I won't watch that asshole raise my son!"

I should have known it was all about control. Derrick couldn't care less about Dylan. He just couldn't stand being out of control of the situation, or of me. The truth was, I knew what my ex-husband was capable of. I knew he'd be able to buy people off. Worse, he could convince those who just met him that he was pure as the whitest snow, and their conviction was far more threatening than the truth.

Derrick could make anyone believe his lies, and come off as charming and charismatic, all the while having no empathy, understanding or remorse, ever. I'd come to understand just what he was years earlier. I had been a victim of his deception until he thought he owned me, and then it was like the flip of a switch. He turned into a monster.

"Dylan loves Jensen! Don't destroy this for him!"

Derrick's lip lifted in an ugly sneer. "He isn't his father. I am."

He must have taken my stunned silence for acquiescence

because he continued, unfettered, on with his rant. "This is what you're gonna do, Melissa; convince that fucker you're done with him, or he'll have an accident. Then, ease Dylan into the idea of seeing me gradually, and we can work out a reasonable visitation schedule for the time I'm in Atlanta. Tell him I've missed him or whatever you have to say; tell him that I want to be his dad again. If you do that, we'll work this out; I don't want to hurt Dylan, or you," his tone took on a commiserate, condescending tone.

I'd have to be mentally challenged to believe one fucking word that came out of this man's mouth. The back of my eyes burned with frustrated tears. "Yes, you want to hurt me. That's what you live for."

A sly sneer slid across his face; a face I once thought handsome was now revolting. "Maybe I do, but you better not give me a reason," he said, standing and throwing down a few small bills onto the tabletop. "Keep Dylan away from the daddy-wanna-be, or I promise I'll do something you and your lover-boy will both regret. I just want my son. Melissa. Maybe you can come back to Dallas, too, if you're really nice to me. Maybe I can forgive your whoring around. Who knows? I'll be in touch, sweetheart."

With that, he walked out of the bar, and for minutes, I just sat there shaking with the wine he'd ordered in front of me untouched. I couldn't breathe. I couldn't see. My skin was crawling, and I wanted to rip it off with my fingernails.

"Missy!" Liz's voice broke through my haze. "Who was that?"

I cleared my throat and glanced up at her as she stood by the booth; praying she wouldn't see the sheer terror in my eyes. My first impulse was to tell the truth, but then Derrick's presence in Philadelphia would get back to Jensen, and that would only make him worry. Instead, I took a deep breath and waved my right hand indicating she should take the seat Derrick had just vacated. I shook off my fear and gathered myself together, smiling as brightly as I could manage.

"Oh, just some agent trying to get me to interview one of his guys. He was an asshole."

"I guess you said no because he looked pissed," Liz observed sliding into the booth.

"Yes. My docket is full, and his player is second string." I shrugged. "I guess I'll have to get used to this type of thing, huh?" I responded as casually as I could, doing my best to cover.

Her lips pressed together, and she rolled her eyes. "I get it. At least he bought you a drink. What are you drinking?"

"White wine." I didn't want her to know I didn't choose it. "Want one?" I asked.

She shook her head and lifted the beer bottle she'd brought with her to her mouth with a smile. "Wine gives me a hangover," she laughed. "I'll stick with beer."

The evening continued with Michelle and the others from the ESPN crew joining us in the booth; even pushing another table closer to it and sliding up some chairs. It wasn't long before I was surrounded by others and was thankful for the safety it afforded; even if it was only symbolic. I spent the next two hours pretending to have a good time; all the while my mind was racing on how I was going to deal with Derrick's threats. I didn't want Jensen hurt, and I had to protect my son somehow. What was I going to do?

Lawyers were expensive, and a court battle would be long and tedious even if Derrick didn't stand a chance in hell of winning. He might lose in court, even with his *expert witnesses*, but he'd make life hell in the meantime; mine, Dylan's and Jensen's. Worse, there was a chance Derrick would become violent, and I needed to take him seriously. If he had my lawyer killed, he could order a hit on Jensen. It was more than a possibility that if Derrick didn't get what he wanted; he'd do something bad. I'd learned that lesson long ago, and it terrified me to the core.

JENSEN

Missy hadn't answered my calls since she'd been back, and it was driving me crazy. Things were getting weird.

She did a great job at the Philly game; coming into her own on the interviews and was learning to follow Jarvis' lead on the play-by-plays. I could see how receptive the players and coaches were to her, and I was damn proud. I'd watched the entire game on TV with the kids. Remi was used to seeing me on screen, and it wasn't a big deal for her, but Dylan was fascinated watching his mom. He ran around my living room as I repeatedly passed him the Nerf football we'd purchased earlier in the weekend, and copied some of the dance moves he'd seen on TV when he made it successfully into the "end zone" we'd designated at one end.

After she'd returned from Philadelphia, she stopped over to pick up Dylan and rushed out with him, saying she had to get home and do laundry. Sure, I had to jump on a plane a couple of hours later myself, but it would have been nice to have a conversation, at least. The funny thing was, there was a distinct difference in how she treated me. No hug when she came in, no kiss goodbye when she left, even though I tried both. I felt like an asshole standing there watching her leave as if we barely knew each other. Something must have happened.

I was sitting in one of the upholstered chairs opposite her desk, waiting. Waiting in my old office, now hers, for her to come in on Tuesday morning so I could confront her. I'd been climbing the walls the entire time that I was in Bristol for the past two days. Again, she wasn't answering my calls. One thing was for sure; I'd had enough, and I was sure as hell going to get to the bottom of it. I didn't give a rat's ass what she had going on this morning, even if her team meeting included Bryan Walsh, she wasn't leaving this office until I had some goddamned answers.

I sat there, staring straight ahead, tapping the tips of my tented fingers together, telling myself to remain calm and not lash out the minute she walked in, but it was going to be fucking hard. It felt like I'd been waiting for hours.

Cindy popped her head around the door after seeing me through the window in the office and wore a big smile on her face. "Hey, stranger! What brings you down here?" she asked brightly.

My head snapped around at her words, and I sat up straighter in my chair. "Waiting for Missy."

She huffed in amusement, still hovering in the doorway. "Obviously. Why?"

I gritted my teeth, annoyed. "Are you writing a book?" I asked, barely able to keep the snarl out of my voice.

Cindy was visibly taken aback. Her eyes widened, and she held up both hands, splaying them out in front of her. "Whoa. I'm not sure what's eating you, Jensen, but I don't appreciate your tone. Don't take your personal shit out on me!"

I stood up impatiently, facing her. "Who says it's personal? I don't appreciate waiting in here for Melissa for a goddamn hour, either!"

Cindy stepped back and folded her arms across her torso. "If you must know, she's talking to Jarvis about next week's interview assignments. You know... doing her *job*?" Cindy's eyebrows shot up in admonishment. "Is this about work?"

I felt embarrassed that I let someone I'd worked with for years see me in such an unprofessional light, let alone the awful way I'd snapped at her. I took a deep breath and then exhaled. "I'm sorry, Cindy, you're right. Something personal is bothering me, and I shouldn't be taking it out on my coworkers. I'm sorry. I thought I'd gotten in early enough to speak to her before her day started."

"I see." Her eyes scanned over my face appraisingly. Clearly, it was written all over me that this personal *thing* was between Missy and me.

"Well, I don't know how long she'll be busy, so why don't you leave her a note or something?"

"Since when are you her secretary?" I asked, my ill temper vivid in my tone. "You weren't ever mine when I had this job." I leaned up against the desk and crossed my arms. I wasn't going anywhere until I spoke to Missy. "So what gives?"

"Okay, be a stubborn asshole, if you want. I hope you have to wait in here all damn day." Cindy turned and stormed out of the office.

I glanced at my watch. I'd already been waiting for an hour.

"Fuck," I said aloud, running a hand through my hair. I'd spent a lot of time Googling her bastard ex-husband to see if there was any news about Ellington Construction doing a job in Atlanta. There was nothing to be found. Coming up empty-handed only made my frustration grow, and coupled with her deliberate avoidance of me, I was ready to self-combust.

My coffee was empty, and I considered going to refill it but saw Missy approaching through the glass wall of the office. She was coming down the hall toward her office, holding an open file folder and reading something inside. When she turned the corner into her office, she glanced up, and her steps faltered.

She was sexy as fuck in a tight black pencil skirt and flowing ivory blouse that clung to her breasts, the lace bra she had underneath, just visible. I could barely make out the scalloped outline of the cups under the opaque material, but I knew her lingerie style by now, and I knew what I'd find if I peeled her clothes away. Her hair was swept up in a messy bun, and she looked like we'd just made love. Her black stilettos reminded me, again, why I didn't want her covering a bunch of horny football players. Hell, I didn't even want her walking to the break room looking like this. I felt possessive. I felt cheated. I wanted to pull her hard against me, to kiss her within an inch of her life, press my hard length into her so she'd remember how it felt together. I wanted to, somehow, make her stop running from me and trust me. Instead, I let her have it.

"Would you mind telling me what *the fuck* is going on with you?" All of my intent not to lambast her flew out the window. "I've been worried sick! Did you even think of that?"

I could feel my heart pumping, feel the blood flowing; pulsing in the veins of my neck and wrists, and hear it rushing in my ears. I wasn't sure if I wanted to scream at her or pull her to me and kiss her senseless.

Missy swallowed and took another step into the office, pausing only to close the door behind her. "Uh... um..." she shook her head and closed her eyes briefly. It was evident she was taken by surprise. "Nothing. I've been busy, that's all."

"That's bullshit, and you know it." I pushed away from the desk as she walked around behind me, calmly taking her seat and placing the file on top of the smooth wooden surface.

"What do you want me to say?" She couldn't meet my eyes and instead shuffled some paper around on the top of her desk.

"I want you to tell me why you aren't returning my calls, or why it was so awkward on Sunday night? We were getting so close. Nothing's changed between last week and this one. Is your bastard ex on the scene?"

She cleared her throat and used one hand to rub the corner of one eye. She was uncomfortable; I could see I'd hit a nerve; even more so when she finally looked up at me.

One shoulder lifted in a half-shrug as she looked away again. "I've been thinking... All that security stuff sort of freaks me out. It's too much. I… I barely know you, and you're taking over my life. I don't want it. It's too soon."

"It's too soon," I repeated her words because the whole thing sounded so unbelievable to me. "You're just scared of him. I'm here now—"

"Why can't you just listen, Jensen?" she asked frantically. Her expression was strained, and she looked as if she would start to cry any minute.

"I'm listening to the bullshit you're trying to feed me, but I'm not stupid, Missy. You can't even look me in the fucking eye! I know what this is. It's because he came after you, right? What did that bastard do?" I was close to yelling now.

I could see her swallow hard as she struggled for words, her eyes imploring me to understand. "Nothing. I've decided to give him a chance."

Air rushed from my lungs in astonishment, and I fell back to lean on the door frame shaking my head in denial. "You *what?* I don't understand how you can do that after all the things you've told me about him, let alone— how it is between us!"

She stood up abruptly and ran around her desk to lock the door, so that we wouldn't be interrupted. "It's just something I *have to do.* Please try to understand." She lifted a hand and quickly brushed away a tear and squared her shoulders a little more before sitting down again. "Dylan deserves his father."

I could see her pain, but the thought of Dylan or Missy subjected to more of that psychopath killed me. I felt it physically, like a knife in my heart.

She wore her suffering like an invisible armor. I could see how nervous and uneasy she was by the way she was fidgeting. For the first time, she was uncomfortable in my presence.

I didn't know what to do or what to say. Was she breaking up with me? Was she just going to put her poor kid through the torture of seeing that cocksucker, or did she intend to go back to him, too? It took a moment to sink in, but I realized she wouldn't subject Dylan to him alone. She couldn't protect him if she weren't there, too.

"I'm here now. You don't have to do this. I told you —" I was calm, but desperate to change what was happening. "I'll take care of you. I'll take care of you both."

"You can't!" Panic filled her voice. She looked up at me, her light blue eyes flooding with tears. "It's over between us, Jensen!" The words ripped from her, but her face turned stoic.

The pain I felt turn into acrimony. Instantly, my walls came up. I was pissed. "So, all the time we spent together meant nothing?" I spat, letting anger replace my agony. "Nothing? Making love meant nothing; how much Dylan wants to be with me means nothing? How good it feels together means nothing?"

"Sure," she shifted in her chair, hedging. "It was nice. I'm grateful for all you've done—"

It was my turn to explode; my turn to interrupt her. It was a goddamned good thing she'd locked the door. "Nice? You're fucking grateful?" I shouted. "That's all you feel for me?" I asked, disbelieving, but seething.

Missy jumped at my outburst and brushed past me to close the blinds to the glass window that shown into the main office. I could smell the familiar scent of her perfume; feel the heat between us with just the briefest touch of her arm brushing against mine. Despite my fury, my cock twitched inside my pants.

"It meant something, but it's moving too fast. We should take a break."

I licked my lips and nodded, my jaw shooting out in consternation. I wasn't buying what she was trying to sell, but at least it seemed she wasn't going back to him, but I had to know for sure.

"You're going back to that bastard?" I asked tightly, feeling the muscle in my jaw start to twitch as I gnashed my teeth together.

"No!" she shook her head, insisting. "I'm not. I just think it's best for everyone if we take a break while this gets worked out."

"Uh huh. A break, right. So, you're not at all scared by your ex-husband, then? Not worried he'll beat you up or hurt your son. Not at all." I said it like a statement, rather than a question. I scowled and both hands planted on my hips. "Not at all."

"No," Missy said, but was unable to meet my eyes. She kept her hands busy by opening her laptop and signing on to company email. Her hands were trembling, though. Her cell phone rang from the purse she'd dropped on the floor next to her desk, and she jumped again, bringing both hands to her temples and closing her eyes. Her forehead creased and she flushed.

"How about if he rapes you again? Will that bother you at all? Because it sure as hell would bother me! Do you think I'm an idiot? I can see you're terrified. Why are you doing this?" I was mortified.

"Jensen, please," her voice broke on a sob. "*Please* don't do this! Just let it go!"

Instantly my anger faded and sighing heavily. I navigated my way through the small, crowded office to where she sat behind the desk and lifted her into my arms. She started to cry hard, clutching the front of my shirt. My arms wrapped around her and one hand cupped the back of her silky blonde head. She felt frail in my arms; thinner in just the few days since I'd seen her.

"Babe, you have to tell me what's going on," I insisted softly, turning my head so I could kiss her temple. "I assume he has a job here."

She nodded, crying harder and unable to answer me. My

arms tightened. "It'll be okay. I promise."

I held her for a few minutes, waiting for her crying to subside. I rubbed her back gently; brushing light kisses down the side of her face from her temple, over her cheekbone to the corner of her mouth.

"Why couldn't I have met you, first?" Tears still laced her soft voice.

My heart filled, expanded and threatened to explode. "It doesn't matter when you met me, I'm here now, and I'm not going anywhere."

The fingers clutching the front of my shirt relaxed and slid up my chest and around my neck, into the hair at my nape. Then, I used both hands to tilt her head back just enough so I could crush her mouth beneath mine. My eyes closed and my hands moved to cup her gorgeous face.

Missy whimpered. I couldn't tell if she was protesting or giving in to my love and lust; the same desire I knew she felt for me.

She stilled in my arms for a split second. Still, my mouth plundered hers until she let me in. Her lips opened at the same time her hands slid up my arms and chest until we were kissing like we were starving for one another. I turned her around and backed her up against her desk, bending to slide my hands down her perfect ass down her thighs. I pulled her skirt up, then easily lifted her onto its edge of the desk and pushed my way between her legs.

Missy moaned, and her hands fisted in my hair and pulled my mouth tighter against her. We were wild, hungry; our kisses growing more and more passionate.

She arched her body against mine, and I ground my hips into hers. "Christ," I breathed into her mouth. "I want you, Missy. You belong with me."

I didn't care if we'd both got fired. The need was bigger

than both of us.

She was pulling at my shoulders and arms as I leaned my weight into her. My swollen dick was throbbing, and I was dying for release. The time apart from her after such a passionate night was more than I could handle. Her lips were greedy, and mine were equally insatiable, pulling and sucking on her mouth. So delicious.

"Jensen," she breathed my name into my mouth almost like a plea. "Mmmmmm."

My hand reached under the hem of her dress, between her open legs until I found the damp silk beneath. I used my finger to pull them away from her center. She was warm and slick; ready. I pushed two fingers inside her, using my thumb to rub small circles on her clit. I loved the little sounds she made when I loved her. God, she was hot.

I dropped my head to her shoulder in defeat, knowing we couldn't stop. Her head fell back, and her lips parted as her body responded, clenching around my fingers and I pushed them first in, then out, of her.

Her hands fumbled with my belt buckle, and in seconds, my engorged cock was free. One arm snaked around her hips as the other guided my tip to her entrance, and I pushed into her with one hard thrust.

It felt amazing, as we moved together; each of us clinging, our hips heaving, our mouths feasting. I dragged my mouth down her neck, sucking and lightly biting. Missy wrapped around me, legs around my waist, arms around my shoulders and head.

I was panting hard, lost in her body, lost in this all-consuming love that was burning me from the inside out. I was helpless as I moved in and out of her, pushing us both mindlessly to our release. I could feel her muscles clench around me as she let go; feel my own orgasm build to the point of no return.

"Missy," I groaned out her name.

Her arms tightened, and one hand covered my mouth as I came hard.

I fell forward, one hand pressing down on the top of her desk to take my weight. I was breathing hard, still convulsing as the aftershocks shook through us both.

I sucked in a deep breath and gently disengaged from the woman who now owned me. I closed my pants then pulled Missy forward until her feet found the floor, and putting an arm around her to steady her, I used my free hand to pull the hem of her skirt back in place.

When her eyes opened, she stared at me with tear-filled eyes.

"See? You love, me," I said, gently brushing a loose tendril of hair back behind her ear. "So, enough of this nonsense about breaking up."

She swallowed and licked her lips. "Sex isn't love." She was doing her best to deny what was between us, but the tears in her eyes belied her emotions.

"You're right. But you know damn well, that was love. It's been love since the first time," I said softly.

Tears tumbled from her eyes, as her arms slid up around my neck. I pulled her tight against my chest, kissing the side of her face tenderly.

I could have held her all day, but I needed to find out what the hell happened in the past forty-eight hours that could cause this meltdown.

"So? What happened?" I prodded gently, still holding her close.

She pulled away a bit, looking up into my face. She was so beautiful; tear-stained face and running mascara, it didn't matter. I cupped her face and used both thumbs to brush the tears from her cheeks.

"He showed up in Philadelphia." Her face crumpled again, and I closed my eyes. Fury exploded inside me.

"Fuck me," I breathed out. "We have to call the police, Missy. You should have called them on the spot."

"He said he was bidding a job." She shook her head adamantly. "Even if he didn't intend to accept it, or he bid high to ensure he wouldn't get the job, it would explain his presence there. He's a snake. He thinks of everything." She closed her eyes, touching her forehead with the fingers of one hand. She frowned. "We can't talk about this here. You've got things to do, and so do I. I don't want anyone at the station to know about this, Jensen. I can't jeopardize this job."

I sighed again, the air making my lungs tight. She moved a few feet away and sat down at her desk, her fingers dropping from mine. I took the chair across from her once more.

I understood how much being independent had come to mean to her. This job was security and security that wasn't dependent on me, Derrick or any man. "I understand, but we have to deal with this prick," I said calmly, but sternly. "Tell me what he said. Everything."

She related the entire thing. He'd ambushed her in her hotel, threatened to hurt her, Dylan and me. I couldn't stand the trepidation in her voice. I couldn't stand that she was scared enough to sacrifice her relationship with me, willing to subject herself and her son to that fucker for even one single minute. "How could you agree to any of that?"

"I didn't agree!" she said with bitter sadness. "But I know what he's capable of, and at first, when I didn't answer your calls, I was trying to figure it out, but then—" she threw her hands up in defeat. "I decided you didn't deserve to be in the middle of all this. I didn't want you hurt."

"Chase and I—" I began.

"No! I can't endanger Chase! Teagan is about to have her baby, Jensen. They've already done so much. You all have, and I absolutely can't risk any of you."

There was no way in hell I was going to let her deal with this alone. I knew that people as inherently evil as Derrick Ellington do not change, and it would be over my dead body if he harmed one hair on either Missy's or Dylan's head.

"Well, I'm not letting you take chances with yourself or Dylan."

"I thought if I let him see Dylan, he'd realize how much work being a parent is and leave us alone."

"What the fuck?" I exploded. "I think that's denial! He's not going to give up until you're back in Dallas submitting to his abuse. I won't let you put Dylan through that. No fucking way in hell." I shook my head. "No way!"

She straightened her back in visible resolve. It was like she'd just given up any hope of resistance; not the strong, sassy woman I had come to know.

"Do you think I want to put him at risk? I know Derrick. I know how to handle his anger better than anyone. I don't know what else to do."

I rubbed a hand over my face and jaw. "Have you told me everything?"

"Yes. I have."

The way she said it; in that awkward, strained way made me doubt it was the truth. There had to be more to it, but for whatever reason, she didn't want to tell me.

"Well, we have to figure out a way to deal with this miserable son of a bitch." I was still unsatisfied with the outcome of this conversation.

"You and I can't see each other, regardless," Missy insisted. "It's for your own good."

"Fuck my own good," I said getting up to leave, opening

the door to her office. "I'll call you tonight."

"Think of Remi, Jensen. And Chase and Teagan. Don't underestimate Derrick. He is evil."

I stopped and looked back at her through the doorway. "I'm not underestimating him. Not at all. But I'll be damned if I'll leave you to deal with him alone, so answer my calls, and I'll tell Walsh I'm leaving early. I'll pick up the kids."

"Teagan said she would," she said.

"Nope, I'll let her know I'm picking them up. We'll all be over to their house because Chase is in KC, and I'm not leaving any of you alone. I'll have dinner delivered, so why don't you join us, and pack a bag. We're all having a sleepover."

She only nodded in affirmation, a look of relief finally settling on her beautiful features. "Thank you."

I nodded, leaving her office to head to my own, thinking the entire way. That motherfucker must have something over her, or he threatened her in some other way. In my heart, I knew Missy was as in love with me as I was with her. I was determined to find out what was really going on... and fast.

HER *last chance* BEGINS *in his arms.*

Chapter 17

Missy

I spent all day at work worrying. I was fidgeting with my phone, waiting for a call or text from Derrick; as if I was waiting for a bomb to drop. I wasn't answering Jensen's many attempts at contacting me because I didn't know what to say. I mean, what *could* I say? *I love you, you're the best thing that ever happened to me, but I can't be with you?* The thought alone made me die a little on the inside.

I struggled with how to break up with him and not lose it completely. Even though doing so was to protect him, I couldn't tell him I was miserable, or he'd never accept my decision to put the relationship on hold. I wasn't sure he would, anyway. He was smart, and he knew everything about Derrick, so how could I expect him to believe me? My thoughts were utter torture, and they were killing me. The last few sleepless nights were starting to take their toll.

Wednesday morning started off like shit when Jensen ambushed me in my office after my meeting with Jarvis, and it all went downhill from there. I tried to convince him that things were moving too fast and we needed to slow it down, but I should have known better. He knew me; really knew me, and it wasn't long before I'd melted into his arms and sobbed my heart out... and then wholly succumbed to my need and love; we had the hottest sex I'd ever experienced. I'd never be able to convince him we should take a break after that... but maybe I could convince him to keep it secret, for now.

I should be happy to have such a strong, sensitive man taking care of my little boy and me, but instead, I was terrified my ex-husband would hurt him in an underhanded and violent way and Jensen couldn't possibly be prepared. Derrick was viciously ruthless, and if I was honest, I was scared out of my mind for all of us.

After I'd gotten back to the hotel the other night in Philadelphia, I'd opened my laptop and Googled my attorney in Jackson Hole, tears rolling down my face due to what I found. The car accident was real, and it was bloody. He'd crashed through a railroad crossing at the bottom of a hill near his home, smashing his car into the side of a moving train, chopping it into pieces and sending it rolling for several hundred feet. His wife and young son also died in the crash. The picture in the local newspaper showed no skid marks, so Derrick was telling the truth. I wondered how he'd managed to tamper with the brakes on my attorney's SUV. It flashed through my mind like a scene from a Mafia movie. I'd felt sick and ended up puking into the wastebasket near the bed.

Finally, I looked up the court records to my case, and everything Derrick said was true. My restraining order had been overturned the day after my attorney was killed; noting no opposing counsel appearing. I wondered why he hadn't notified me about the court date, but at this point, it was moot.

I'd spent the entire night huddled in my bed, hugging my pillow and crying in desperation; wondering what I was going to do. What could I do? I had to protect Jensen and Dylan, and I had no idea how other than to give in to Derrick's demands.

Later that night when Jensen called, I was a coward and didn't answer my phone … I'd made it through the weekend assignment by the skin of my teeth, only because I wasn't taking Jensen's or Derrick's calls. It was the only way I could keep it together.

All the trepidation I felt in Philadelphia, was still there despite the morning with Jensen in my office. My beautiful new life was crumbling around me.

Now, it was 3:30 PM and I was still struggling and preoccupied; pretending to research the players and teams for my upcoming assignment when I was startled by my cell phone ringing. I picked it up; frantically fumbling with it, I almost dropped it. Part of me was afraid that it would show Dylan's name on the screen, but then I'd hear Derrick's voice when I answered. I felt sick to my stomach.

"Hey, Mom?" My son asked, and a wave of relief flooded over me. My entire body relaxed, alerting me for the first time how tense I'd been.

"Hi, babe!" I greeted brightly, hoping to sound normal as I gathered myself together.

"Mom! I asked ya not to call me that!" Dylan lamented.

"Oh, sorry."

He seemed satisfied by my apology, rushing on to the purpose of his call. "Can I go to Jessica's birthday party on Saturday? It's at PlayDaze! Remi and all the guys are going, and so *please*!"

My instinct told me I shouldn't allow it. I'd have to start talking to Dylan about seeing his father, and I was dreading his reaction. This party would be the excuse I needed to keep Dylan from Derrick, for at least one more weekend. I could leave him with Jensen or Teagan and Chase when I went out of town. It was the only way I knew he'd be safe and the only way I'd be able to do my job. Nothing said I had to tell Derrick where the party was, or who the child was they were celebrating.

"Who's the little girl?"

"She's in our class and her brother is into soccer n'stuff! I really wanna go! Please, Mom? I gotta tell Jessica today cuz her mom said so!"

I understood the urgency, but it put me on the spot. Birthday party venues required advance notice of the number of children in attendance at their events; I found that out when I had Dylan's 5th birthday party at *All Fun and Games* in Jackson Hole.

I sighed loudly. "Okay, honey. Can I call you honey?" I asked quickly, with a smile in my voice, realizing my mistake.

"Mom! Jeez! That's for babies!"

I couldn't win. "Oh, okay. I'll stop." I was sad that my little boy was growing up and he didn't want me calling him sweet names anymore. Hopefully, in a few years, he'd be okay with it again. Maybe I was just weepy because of the trauma from the previous weekend or the ocean of fear that I was drowning in, but my eyes flooded with tears; causing my surroundings to blur. "Please ask Jessica to tell you what time and which PlayDaze it will be at, okay?" I cleared the tightness from my throat.

"Yay! Thanks, mom! I gotta invitation! All that stuffs on it, already!"

"That'll be good, then! Make sure to bring it home." I tried to sound happy for him, but I was afraid to let him out of my sight. Maybe I could chaperone if it ended before I had to fly out. "Jensen is getting off early to pick you and Remi up. Not Teagan, okay?"

"That's awesome! I gotta go play with the guys!"

"Dylan!" I said, a little too sternly. "Make sure to stay with Remi, and both of you stay inside the school and wait for Jensen to come in and get you, okay?"

"Awww, Mom! Do I hafta? We were gonna play basketball on the playground," he bemoaned. "We started a game at recess, and my team is winning! Maybe Jensey could come'n play with us! Maybe he could call the plays like he does on TV!"

I couldn't help a little smile. When it was Jensen commenting, it was super cool, but when I did it, I was just his mom doing her job. I wasn't jealous. I was happy he loved Jensen so much, but it would only make the introduction of Derrick back into his life that much harder to bear. "Well, you can't today. Just stay inside."

"But, why?" he whined.

"Dylan, do as your told! I mean it," I said sternly.

"How come?" he persisted. My son had a mind of his own and was always needing answers.

"Because Jensen said he's coming into the school and he doesn't need to waste an hour sitting in the pick-up line, plus I don't want him looking all over the schoolyard for you," I lied. "Got it?" The last thing I wanted was to lie to Dylan, but even less so, to scare him.

"Okaaaay," he lamented.

"That's my boy. I'll see you at six."

I took a deep breath as I hung up the phone, setting it on top of my desk. I leaned back in my chair but had barely done so, and it began to ring again. I answered without thinking.

"Did you forget something?" I asked into the phone.

"You're hard to get a hold of. Are you ignoring my calls?" Derrick asked harshly. Any attempt at his fake facade was lacking. I could almost hear the snarl in his voice.

I gasped. "Actually, yes." I couldn't help my answer or the blatant hatred that dripped from my voice. I had more disdain for him after his threats than I'd ever had before; even when he was forcing himself on me, or during one of the beatings.

"Careful, Melissa. Remember what I said."

"How could I forget, you were so persuasive," I said sarcastically under my breath.

"Don't push me or I'll show you how persuasive I can be," he answered, making my blood run cold. His tone had softened, but he still sounded like the devil to me. He made my skin crawl with every syllable he uttered. "I'll pick up Dylan on Friday night at 6."

Anxiety had a stranglehold on my lungs, but I pushed out the words. "No, Derrick, I'm afraid that won't work."

"Make it work," he growled. "This isn't up for negotiation; your paltry little stall tactics won't work on me. I thought for sure you had learned one thing from me, and it's that I get my way."

I closed my eyes. The level of hatred I had for this bastard left me breathless. "I'm not stalling, Derrick. Dylan has a birthday party to attend on Saturday, and it's an all-day thing. He'd already been invited before you showed up in Philadelphia."

"I don't believe you. Why didn't you tell me, then?"

"Gosh, I don't know," I said, as sarcastically as I could manage. "Maybe because you stalked me and caught me off guard?"

"Don't be a bitch, Melissa."

I gnashed my teeth, and my jaw jutted out of its own accord. He was one to talk.

"All his friends are going, and he's very excited. Can't we work out something else? This whole thing will work better, and he'll be more receptive to you if you let him make a gentle transition."

I held my breath waiting for him to answer. Derrick was never gentle; I knew that first hand. Waiting was the worst part of dealing with Derrick. It always had been. I didn't know what to expect. Sometimes he exploded like a nuclear bomb and other times, was completely calm and reasonable. The not knowing was the killer, and I often wondered if it was a deliberate tactic designed to drive me insane.

"I can take him. Where is it?"

"Um… I can't remember right now." I hadn't seen the invitation yet, but it would implode the excuse that the party had been on Dylan's schedule for a while. Plus, there was no way in hell I was telling Derrick where my son would be. I scrambled for a response. "I'm still new to town, and I haven't gotten all of the pizza places and kid-friendly stuff down yet. I can let you know, but it starts early, so I can just take him."

"You leave town on Friday or Saturday, don't you?"

My mouth opened, then shut without saying a word. It was true. My work week was Wednesday through Sunday, and he knew it.

I finally found my words. "I'm leaving on Saturday evening this week," I said, honestly.

"Fine. Then I'll pick him up and keep him Saturday night and Sunday. Half a weekend is better than nothing. Who's been taking care of him?"

My right hand covered my mouth as panic took me. I was running out of excuses, and I cleared my throat. My mind was racing; I'd have to get a lawyer and at least try to keep Derrick from Dylan. Lawyers and court fillings took time; maybe a judge would put a hold on visitation while the case was in process.

"Answer me, Melissa!" Derrick demanded, shaking me out of my thoughts.

"A friend has been, but my mom is moving to Atlanta and will be here mid-week next week. She'll have him then."

"No, she won't. I'm his dad, and he'll be with me when you're gone. She can babysit if you have to work late, but I want first right of refusal if you can't be with him. I've already talked to my lawyer about it. He's putting it in the parenting plan he's drawing up."

I was verklempt. This was getting out of hand.

"He hasn't seen you for two years, and you want to hoist yourself on him all at once? This little father-act won't fool him, Derrick."

"Fuck you, Melissa. That friend you leave my son with better not be your pretty-boy. Did you end it with him yet? Lie to me, and I'll know." His voice was dangerously low.

"Not yet," I blurted. "I've been avoiding him since I've returned from Philadelphia. I'll talk to him, soon. And no, he isn't the friend I leave Dylan with."

"You'd better get rid of him, and soon. I don't need some backward prick coming between my son and me or screwing my wife. You're still mine, Melissa. I own you."

I wanted to scream that Jensen was the best thing to ever happen to Dylan and me, that Derrick was not only backward, he was utterly irrelevant to us, and I'd rather die than submit to him again. Instead, I held my tongue, clenching my fist so hard that my nails dug into my palm; the burning pain a sure sign of breaking the skin. "Let's just be nice about this, Derrick. I don't want anyone getting hurt."

"Smart girl. I'll call Dylan tonight. Make sure he's ready to talk to me."

Desolation set in again. Dylan would freak out if he knew in advance of the call and I wasn't about to ambush him. "Derrick, please let me speak to him a little more. He hasn't seen you in years, and he needs to get used to the idea. He's just a little boy. I promise…" I begged. "Just let me have a little time. It's only Wednesday."

There was a long pause on the line before he answered. "Okay, but nothing will stop me from seeing him on Saturday, Melissa, do you hear me? I'll call him on Friday night. Make sure you prepare him by then unless you want Romeo to have an accident."

My phone went dead in my hand. Derrick had hung up without waiting for my reply. I stood there, frozen for I don't know how long, struggling with how to deal with Derrick, how to tell my son, and how to convince Jensen we couldn't see each other anymore. I slammed it on my desk, lifted it and hit it against it again. I was breathing heavy, frustrated, angry and scared. *What the hell was I going to do?* I put a hand to my head.

Somehow, I had to convince Derrick that Jensen and I had stopped dating. I had to buy some time. I knew Jensen would fight me on it, but even if he agreed, Dylan was only six, and little kids weren't good at keeping their thoughts to themselves. Derrick would find out eventually. I must have forgotten to breathe because my body automatically sucked in a deep breath that startled me, and my hand came up to my throat.

I wouldn't put it past Derrick to have me followed. He'd know where and when I picked up Dylan. Worse, maybe he had someone watching my son. Trepidation caused me to shudder. My first instinct was to call Jensen, and that was just what I was going to do.

JENSEN

"Come on, kids!" I ushered Remi and Dylan in front of me and into the parking lot on the south side of the elementary school. I usually picked them up in front, but the situation called for a change of routine.

When I was a kid, kindergarten only went half-days, but I was thankful that their school had classes all day. It allowed me to duck out a little early from work in an emergency, without cutting a full day. This definitely qualified as an emergency.

Missy's frantic call not long after I left her office only intensified the urgency I felt. I wasn't sure how, but her bastard ex-husband needed to be dealt with; and fast.

When I picked them up, Remi and Dylan were excited,

chatting on and on about some birthday party that was happening on Saturday. I glanced around, checking out the parking lot and the cars parked across the street on the residential side. Nothing looked suspicious—no signs of any Ellington Construction vehicles or anything untoward.

"Hop up, you two." I lifted first Remi, then Dylan into the backseat and buckled them both in. I'd already purchased a second booster seat for the backseat of my vehicle.

After I had Remi settled, I moved around to the driver's side and opened the back door to check Dylan's seatbelt to make sure it was secure. He'd insisted on doing it himself, but it was better safe than sorry. "You got it, bud?" I winked at him and tugged on the belt, satisfied it was secure.

"Yup!" he exclaimed proudly.

I slid into the front seat, pulling my own belt across my lap and clicking it in. I glanced in the rearview mirror. "What's this I hear about a birthday party?"

"My friend Jessica is having a party on Saturday at PlayDaze," Remi explained.

"Yeah, and it's gonna be a blast! They got all sorts of games and stuff!" Dylan added. "Billy told me about it, cuz he goes there every weekend with his dad."

I put the car in reverse and backed out, then pulled out of the parking lot. "Hmmm," I said. "Did both of your moms okay it?" I knew Teagan probably had done so, but I didn't think Missy would, considering everything that was going on.

"Yeah," they said in unison.

My brow shot up. She'd been so scared when I spoke to her last, and I was surprised at Dylan's response.

"Jensey, can we get ice cream?" Remi asked.

"I want chocolate!" Dylan piped up.

"Okay, I guess we can if it's a small one. I don't want to get in trouble for spoiling your dinner. Dylan, did your mom say you could go? For sure?"

"Uh huh."

My eyes hidden behind my RayBans narrowed and my brow creased in a frown. Why would Missy agree when the situation was so precarious? Surely, she'd considered that Ellington might be lurking. I decided to talk to her about it later in the evening after the kids had gone to sleep and we were alone.

When we arrived at Chase and Teagan's estate, I entered the combination to the gate and pulled in and up to the house. The larger garage door was open, and Chase was saying goodbye to Teagan inside. He had a big game coming up and was spending the rest of this week and the weekend in Kansas City for practice. My friend was holding his wife, and they were kissing goodbye. They broke apart when they heard my SUV approach and Chase raised his hand to wave, then it settled on Teagan's swollen belly as he placed another kiss to her temple.

I parked behind Teagan's car so that Chase could back out around me, and then shut off the engine. Chase was already walking up to open the back, passenger door.

"Hey, kiddos!" he greeted happily. "I'm glad I got to see you before I left for Kansas City!!"

"Hi, Daddy!" Remi replied brightly. Chase reached in and freed Remi from her booster seat and then enfolded her in his arms.

"You be a good girl for Mommy and Jensey," he said, hugging her little body tight and kissing her cheek.

"I will!" Remi hugged him back and then pushed back to look into his face. "Dylan and I are going to Jessica's party on Saturday! It's gonna be a blast!"

Chase threw me a concerned glance over the top of the car. I had unbuckled Dylan and helped him out of the car. "You are, huh?"

"Yep! And Jessica's brother is a soccer player! I'm gonna ask him to play with me."

"Hmm. That's the first I've heard of this, but I'm not sure PlayDaze has a soccer field, buddy. You might ask him over to play when Chase is back from his trip," I amended, meeting my friend's gaze. I knew what he was thinking. He wondered why the kids were even being allowed to attend.

"Okay," Dylan sounded a bit disappointed.

"Hi, Mommy!" Chase had released Remi, and she had scampered into the garage to wrap her little arms as far around her mother as she could, pressing her ear to Teagan's stomach. "Please, be a girl, baby!"

Teagan's hand curved around Remi's silky head as she gazed down at her child and she smiled big in our direction. Chase was standing next to me, having walked around the car to talk to Dylan. He was grinning from ear-to-ear, as well. Obviously, he'd be happy with another little girl if his expression was anything to go on.

"Hey, D," Chase crouched down to get on Dylan's level and wrapped a hand around the little boy's upper arm. "We'll get a game together here with all of your friends in a couple of weeks or so, deal?" He ruffled his hair. "Run on in with Remi. I want to talk to Jensen. Love you guys!"

Dylan followed after Remi and Teagan, and after Teagan and Remi returned Chase's declaration of love, they disappeared into the house.

"What's this about a party?" he asked, his hands settling on his hips. He had put his duffel and his jacket in the back of his car but didn't seem to notice the briskness of the fall night air.

"Yeah, it took me by surprise, too. I'll talk to Teagan and Missy about it tonight. Dylan and Remi have become friends, and it's hard for Missy to tell him no when it's an event Remi is attending." I ran a hand through my hair. "It's great they're getting along, but it would be easier if they weren't such close friends."

Chase shook his head and sighed. "Well, that's not the case. I have two security guards on the perimeter of the house and grounds, already, and it looks like we need to get a couple more. Are you planning on staying here tonight?"

"If it's okay with you, yes."

"For sure. I've given your number to security in case there's anything suspicious going on outside. I don't want to scare the kids or the women, so I've told them to keep outside the gates."

"I think that's wise," I replied.

"I gotta fly but let me know what comes of the conversation about the party, and we can decide what to do from there."

"That dickhead is demanding that Missy stop seeing me and that he be allowed to spend some time with Dylan."

"What does Missy think?"

"She wants to do it!" I said shaking my head in consternation.

"That's crazy," Chase agreed.

"She thinks it's the best way to deal with Ellington, but I think there's something she isn't telling me."

Chase paused on his walk back to his car. "I hope you're wrong but find out what you can. I can have him investigated if you think it's needed."

I was grateful for Chase's gregarious nature, but I hated to see more money spent on Missy's asshole ex unless it was absolutely necessary. Twenty-four-seven security was going to be thousands a week, and it was anyone's guess how long we had to keep it up.

"I'd rather just beat the shit out of him, and be done

with it," I said. My statement was made tongue in cheek, but inside I was dead serious. I hated the mother fucker. "But yeah, thanks."

"Okay," Chase chuckled. "Talk to you later."

"Have a good flight," I said, landing a hand firmly on my best friend's shoulder. "Thanks."

"Don't sweat it." He looked me straight in the eye as he opened the door to his Audi A5. "It's all in the family. You get to tell the girls they'll have security following them around until further notice."

I huffed out a laugh. "Great, thanks. You take off and leave me with the dirty work."

He only laughed and got into the car and started it up.

After Chase left, I went into the house. Teagan looked tired, so I told her to take a break, and I'd handle dinner and taking care of the kids. She protested, but only for a couple of minutes. She was getting to the end of her pregnancy, and though she tried to hide it, I could tell she was exhausted.

I was tense waiting for Missy to arrive, wondering if she'd been followed. I peered out the window of the kitchen and then out the one in the front room to see if I could find the security detail Chase had enlisted, but nothing was visible. The street was too far away and hidden by the brick and wrought iron fence, but I trusted Chase. If he said they were there, they were there.

"Hey, Jensey," Dylan asked coming into the room and looking up at me. "Do you wanna play a game with us?"

My face softened as I looked down into his sweet face. Thank God, he looked like his mother and not that bastard. He'd become so important to me over the past few weeks. The little boy was so hungry for male influence, and I wanted to be that man. "Sure, I'd love to, but I have to figure out dinner and talk to your mom for a little bit. I will later, okay?"

"Aww!" he protested. "That's a long time from now."

Time must move slower for kids. I remember my mom leaving me at a friend's house, and his mom was mean to us. It felt like forever to me until she came back to get me, but in reality, it was only a couple of hours. I felt sick inside that Missy would subject this little angelic boy to Derrick Ellington for even one minute. Dylan's reaction to seeing him the other night was enough evidence for me to see that his father shouldn't be allowed anywhere near him. Bile rose up in my throat thinking of Derrick Ellington as Dylan's father… as Missy's husband. God… it made me ill.

"Well, we can find something for you to watch on Netflix or Amazon Prime. How about that?"

"As long as it's not some stupid girl movie," he lamented.

I smiled. "We have to find something Remi likes, too. Where is she?"

"Talking to her mom, I think. She likes to feel that baby in Teagan's stomach kick. She said it even did a somersault yesterday."

"It did, huh? It won't be long until it's born." I turned on the TV and flipped through the children and family choices, finally settling on Shark Tale. "How about this one? It's a cartoon about the ocean."

"As long as it has sharks!"

I grinned at him and turned it on. "It has a few of them! I'm going to find Remi. I'll be right back."

I headed up the stairs to the second level of the house and peered into Remi's room, but there was no sign of her. Chase and Teagan's bedroom was a couple of doors away, and I knocked softly. The door was ajar, and it slowly swung partway open. Remi and Teagan were sleeping in the middle of the king-sized bed, both lying on their sides, spooning with Remi wrapped in Teagan's arms. It was only a year ago that we thought we'd lose

Remi, and the sight filled my heart with tenderness and joy. I decided to let them be and go down to start dinner hoping I could convince Missy, then Teagan, that the birthday party was a bad idea.

I popped my head around the archway that led into the great room. Dylan was lying on his stomach in front of the big HDTV laughing at something one of the fish in the movie was saying, so I went back into the kitchen and started digging around in the freezer and cupboards trying to figure out what to cook for our evening meal.

I decided on burgers and box macaroni and cheese. It wasn't fancy, but I knew the kids would like it. I popped the frozen hamburger into the microwave on defrost and then looked for a pan to make the mac and cheese and rummaged through the pantry until I found a can of green beans.

My phone pinged as a text came in. It was from Missy asking me to open the front gate to the property so she could drive inside. I went to the house security panel by the backdoor to the garage and punched in the security code necessary. I then opened the side of the garage that Chase had just vacated and walked out motioning her to drive her car inside. There would be no visible trace that she and Dylan were on the property, and it would be safer for all of us, provided she wasn't followed.

I waited the minute or so it took her to pull in and then closed the door behind her.

"Is this okay?" she asked, getting out of the car. "Where's Chase's car?"

"He's on his way to KC," I explained. "He'll leave it at the airport."

"Oh, that's right." She looked as tired as Teagan. "Thank you," she said wearily.

I put my arm around her when she reached me, turning her to go into the house, and kissed her on the mouth. The kiss was firm, and desperate, tinged with a hint of the passion we'd experienced earlier that morning. "Are you okay?" She let herself lean on me, and I rubbed my hand up and down her arm as we walked into the house.

She didn't answer right away, and when we were further inside, I took her purse from her shoulder and helped her remove her coat.

"I'm okay. Stressed out, I guess."

All kinds of vile thoughts ran through my mind. "Did he do something? Threaten you?"

"Not since the call. I haven't heard from him again." She wrapped her arms around herself and then sat down on one of the stools at the kitchen island. Her blue eyes met mine, and she looked scared. "Where's Dylan?"

"Watching Shark Tale in the living room," I said dismissively. "He's fine." I wouldn't let her skirt the issue. "Did Ellington follow you?"

I could see her chest rise and fall as she inhaled deeply. "I don't think so, but I'm not sure. That's why I— I didn't go home to get a bag. I don't know how I can go to work tomorrow in the same suit." Her hand rubbed her temple.

"I'm sure Teagan has something you can borrow. You're scared, Missy. It's going to be okay."

The microwave beeped, and I took the package of now thawed meat out of it, setting it on a cutting board and bending to retrieve a skillet from one of the lower cupboards intent on forming the meat into patties and slapping them in the pan. "Do you want a drink?" I asked before I started cooking.

She nodded. "That would be nice."

I removed a bottle of white wine from the big stainless refrigerator and poured us both a glass.

She reached for it gratefully and took a sip. I went back to preparing the meal.

"What happens after Teagan has her baby, Jensen?"

Her question made me pause. "What do you mean?"

"I mean, you see Remi because you helped raise her. When you pick up Remi, will it be weird for Remi to leave her new brother or sister behind?"

I shrugged, my back still to her as I concentrated on what I was doing. I laid one patty and then another into the now smoking hot skillet. The air filled with the sounds of sizzling and a delicious aroma of garlic and other seasonings I'd mixed in. "I never thought about it, but I assume... I'll take them both. I can't picture that I'd think any differently of the new baby. Sure, Remi is special, but I'll be around this baby from birth, just like I was her."

"Do you think that's what Teagan and Chase want, too?"

I turned then and looked at her. She was leaning on her bent elbow with her hand holding her cheek. She was interested in my answer, but I couldn't help wondering if she was just trying to steer the conversation away from Derrick Ellington. "Sure," I shook my head. "I mean, they want what's best for their kids. I'm a big part of Remi's life, and Chase and Teagan are my dearest friends. I can't imagine we'd raise this baby any different than we have Remi. We're sort of a team, I guess."

"You're a family. I find it amazing after all you went through together."

"Yeah." The corner of my mouth tugged upward into a slight smile. "I think it just made us more solid than ever."

"I can see that." Her tone was sad, and though I had to watch the stove, I made sure to glance her way.

"Do you miss Ben?"

"Of course. He's been my rock since I left Derrick."

"Your mom will be here soon, too."

"I'm not sure I want to have her move right now. Not with everything going on."

I flipped the burgers and filled a saucepan with water, ignoring the instructions on the box. "I can see that. We have to get a restraining order on this prick, Missy. As soon as possible."

"I can't unless he hurts me, first." She looked and sounded so defeated. "It's so hopeless." Her voice cracked on the last word.

I turned and moved closer to her. "You don't have to be afraid of him. I'll be with you—"

She looked at me brokenly. "You can't be with Dylan and me, both, so I'd rather have you with him."

She was right, I couldn't be in two places at once, and I searched for the words to make her feel better. "Chase already has security in place."

Missy's eyes got big, and a look of utter terror flashed across her face. I was confused. She should be relieved, but instead, she shook her head wildly. "No! Derrick would go berserk if he knew that! Oh, my God." Her head fell into her hands, and her hair fell forward; hiding her face.

"You knew we were going to do that. I thought—" I began, taking the skillet with the finished hamburgers off the heat and leaving the pan of water sitting on the counter. The mac and cheese would have to wait. "That's what you wanted."

"That was before!" Her voice rose frantically.

I moved around the island and sat next to her. I reached for her wrists to gently pull her hands from her face so I could see her eyes. She was crying. "Before what, sweetheart?" I had to know exactly what we were dealing with.

Her eyes implored mine; tears rolling silently down her face. "Before I found out Derrick murdered my lawyer just to get rid of the restraining order in Wyoming."

"Holy fuck," I exclaimed incredulously, my mind racing. I needed to know the rest of the story, but I was stunned. I didn't ask her how she knew it or why she didn't tell me before; I believed her. She was visibly shaking, and everything inside me wanted retaliation. I hated seeing her so terrified.

"He threatened to hurt Dylan. He threatened to hurt you," her voice broke on a sob, and her hands curled into the front of my button down as she struggled to control her despair. I slid my arms around her and gathered her close, pressing my lips to her forehead. "And he told me to check my attorney's fate to prove he wasn't bluffing."

"It's gonna be okay, babe. I'll keep you both safe. I won't let anything hurt you again."

"What about you? You—you do—don't know him," she cried. "He's a lunatic! The-there's only one way to ma—manage him, Jensen."

As I held her, I could literally feel her grief and fear seep into me. She was desolate and anxious. Anger welled up, but ranting would not change the situation. My goal was to make her feel safe. "What can I do?"

Her arms slid around my shoulders, and she cried hard into my hollow of my throat. "We have to convince Derrick we don't see each other anymore, Jensen. Oh, God!" She was clutching at my flesh, gasping for breath as she cried her heart out. "I have to let him see my son. It's the only way he won't resort to violence."

My own breath rushed out of my lungs in a rush of protest. "I don't think that's the answer. That bastard hurt both of you when he thought he had you under his control, so giving him what he wants won't protect either of you," I tried to speak calmly, stroking my hand down Missy's back as I held her close. I turned and pressed my lips to her hair. She was fragile.

My own heart was pounding as emotions flooded through me, only amplified by the crying little boy I saw over his mother's shoulder. Dylan was standing silently between the formal dining room and kitchen and shaking his head no; chin trembling with tears rolling down his face. He'd obviously heard most of what was said.

I pulled back from Missy and nodded in Dylan's direction, regretful that he'd had to listen to his mother's sobbing pleas.

"I don't want that man to be my dad!" he screamed, his cries finally erupting into the room. "I don't want to talk to him! He hurts us!"

Both Missy and I scrambled away from the bar and moved toward the little boy, arms open and going down on our knees side-by-side. Missy enveloped him in her embrace, and I gathered them both in a tight hug. Tears formed in my own eyes as I listened to her comforting words, and Dylan's tearful protests.

"I want Jensey to be my dad, Mom!" Dylan cried harder and harder. "I want Jensey!"

Missy held him, stroking his hair over and over as he clung to her, tears running down her face. "It's gonna be okay, baby. I promise," she soothed, kissing the top of Dylan's head as I held them both close.

The sound of Missy's ringtone merged with the sound of his tears, and she stilled in my arms, pulling back to look into my face.

"It's him, isn't it? I asked, knowingly.

She nodded and started to extricate herself from my arms and her son's. "Can you hold him for a second?"

"Babe, don't," I commanded. "Ignore him."

Missy hurried to get her purse and remove her phone, shaking her head. "No. I'm just going to get it over with." She put it up to her ear. "Stop calling, Derrick! Dylan doesn't want anything to do with you. You aren't talking to him! You aren't seeing him! Just leave us the hell alone!" She hung up the phone; her eyes held a terrified expression, but her body sagged in relief.

"Now what?" I asked, still sitting on the floor cradling the crying little boy in my lap.

Missy sat down next to us and reached out to stroke the back of her son's head lovingly. "We wait, I guess. And try to keep the focus on me."

I felt like someone had just punched me in the gut. That was precisely how she'd dealt with that motherfucker for years; give in and take it. I'd never hated someone so much in my entire life! Protectiveness roared inside me. I wanted to take care of these two for the rest of my goddamned life.

"What?" I asked incredulously, shaking my head. "What are you thinking?"

"If he's focused on me; if I distract him, he'll turn it all on me. Then, maybe we can get the restraining order." A calmness overtook her; a determination to keep Derrick Ellington away from her son. Suddenly, I had the perfect picture of what her life used to be. She'd be the punching bag, take the beatings, submit to rape, just to keep Dylan safe.

I wanted to scream out my fury but knew that I couldn't say anything out loud while Dylan was within earshot, but my blood was boiling, burning me alive from the inside out. Even if that fucker made a move that would result in a restraining order, it wasn't likely to stop him. If Derrick Ellington was a murderer, a piece of paper wouldn't stand in his way.

"I want Jensey!" Dylan cried out in soft sobs into the front of my shirt, his little arms hugging my neck hard.

And then… my heart exploded like a nuclear bomb.

Chapter 18

JENSEN

After the phone call from Ellington, and Dylan's reaction to it, even Missy realized her plan of placating her ex-husband was impossible. I agreed to lay low and not to flaunt our relationship in case he was stalking her, but in my gut, I knew he had to be.

He left her alone for two years, so why now? I wondered. *What had changed? Surely, he hadn't had a sudden change of personality or conscience. Not from what I'd seen at her door.*

Late last night when Chase called, I told him everything Missy had shared about her attorney's suspected murder. He was as upset as I was and was flying back earlier than planned; late on Saturday afternoon; as soon as his last practice had wrapped up.

In the meantime, the security detail was magically doubled. Missy and Teagan would have two men with them at all times, and it was decided that both women would take their respective children to school separately and one of the security teams could stay with each of the kids. If Ellington made a move on Dylan, we didn't want Remi anywhere close.

Out of concern, I also hovered a safe distance outside the school watching to make sure both Dylan and Remi were safely inside the doors.

For two days, there had been no sign of Missy's ex-husband. God, I hated thinking of that monster touching her, hurting her... and hurting that innocent little boy. I was insane just thinking about it. If I had a chance, I'd love to take him into some back alley and beat him to within an inch of his life. Every emotion inside me was teeming with it.

While Teagan and Missy had consented to having security assigned, the private school refused to allow the men on their campus grounds; the headmaster insisted it would make the other children unnecessarily afraid. It was not an ideal situation, and I knew that if Ellington was going to make a move, it would most likely be during drop-off, pick-up or recess. All of us continued to sleep at the Forrester home as a precaution.

On Thursday afternoon, Missy and I met with the family attorney that Chase's legal team had recommended. She assured us we could file a custody motion to limit visitation, but there were no guarantees we would win, and it might be risky taking it to court. She said Missy's ex could win, and all we'd be doing was helping him by getting the matter in front of a judge when the other party hadn't filed a motion. With her help, we decided to wait for Derrick to start the process. She explained that fathers had rights, and we'd have to prove why he was unfit, and we only had a fifty-fifty shot.

Missy had been right about the restraining order; unless we could prove Derrick posed a tangible threat, the lawyer said that no judge would grant us a restraining order. However, she advised Missy to write a letter outlining Derrick's threats and past abuse and include what he'd told her about the murdered attorney in Jackson Hole, have it notarized and put in a safe deposit box. It would serve as proof in case something suspicious happened to her, Dylan, or anyone close to them.

It made me sick to think about it.

That was all we could do? Write a fucking letter and wait for that dirtbag to hurt one of them?

Missy had asked her mother, Jean, to put off coming to Atlanta for a while, explaining she deserved a vacation before moving. She'd gone to visit friends in Orlando without too much protest. The last thing we needed was more people to protect, but Missy couldn't tell her mother what was really going on. What was the sense in making her worry when there wasn't a damn thing she could do to help alleviate the situation? Having Jean with us might even make a terrible situation worse.

The past couple of days had dragged by because we were all on pins and needles. Missy hadn't answered any of Derrick Ellington's calls, but he'd called several times, and we were dreading the weekend. Both of us were stressed about Missy leaving town for her next assignment, though she was more concerned about leaving Dylan, and I was more worried about what could happen to her. If that sack of shit had followed her to Philadelphia, he might show up in Denver, too.

My first instinct was to go with her, but I was struggling with leaving Teagan and the kids alone in Atlanta with Chase gone, despite the security he had in place. Missy was adamant about me staying with Dylan, in any case.

Now, it was Saturday morning; the day of the dreaded birthday party. The kids had been talking about it non-stop and despite my appeals to forbid they go, both Teagan and Missy didn't want to disrupt the children's routine.

Waiting in the kitchen for everyone to come down for breakfast, I received an incoming Facetime call from Chase.

"What'd your investigator find out?" I didn't bother with pleasantries or greetings, and he wouldn't expect me to. His hair was plastered to head by sweat because, clearly, he was in the middle of a practice session or workout.

"That asshole's business is in huge trouble. He put all of his capital into a government road construction project, and at the last minute, it fell through due to appropriation issues at the state level. He purchased a bunch of equipment and supplies with a substantial loan using his payables as collateral. When the job fell through, the loan was called in. He had to sell the equipment for pennies on the dollar to recoup what he could. However, he still has a huge chunk of it to pay off; millions of dollars. It'll take him years to get square, but he's in default, and the bank will end up taking his business. He sold his house. He's in a world of hurt."

At least we had an answer about Derrick's timing, but I remembered my Google search. I shook my head. "He has the job here; McIntire project downtown. What about that? It has to be bringing in some money."

Chase shook his head. "Yes. It's on the report, but it's not enough to cover his losses on the highway thing, so he's more dangerous than we thought."

"I don't understand Ellington's thought process; Missy doesn't make enough for him to blackmail her over Dylan."

"Who knows what he's thinking, but people do awful shit when they're desperate."

I nodded in agreement. "Yes, I agree. Anything about Missy's lawyer?"

"The whole family were killed in the wreck, but the police report lists it as an accident. I think we're screwed on that front, man." Chase held the phone close, speaking in low tones.

I sighed. "Fucking deviant," I said under my breath, running my free hand through my hair.

"He needs money," Chase stated casually; as if it were nothing. "Maybe we can buy him off. I just got that big endorsement deal with Adidas."

I appreciated my friend's generosity, but I shook my head. "Even if we could come up with the money he needs, we'd be opening ourselves up to continued blackmail."

"I thought of that, too, but it may buy us some time. Have you had any signs of him lurking around? Security said there was nothing at the house or school to report."

"No, I haven't seen him anywhere, but he's called at least ten times in the past two days."

"Has he left any threatening messages?" Chase wanted to know. "That would help get a restraining order."

"No such luck. Obviously, he knows the drill. This bastard is smart, even if he is crazy."

Chase wiped his face on the sleeve of his shirt. "What about the birthday thing? Did you make a plan?"

"Yeah. I'm going with the kids. I've tried to dissuade the women from attending, altogether."

"Yes, I'd rather Teagan not go, for sure."

I understood Chase's apprehension. "It's a public place, but I'd hoped to take one security team with me and leave one with the girls."

"Sounds like a solid plan. I'll call Teagan and tell her that I agree with you."

I smiled. Neither one of those women were good at being told what to do. "Do you think she'll listen?"

He chuckled. "If I pout, she might, but she's worried about Remi and Dylan. She wants to be there."

The weight of the situation weighed heavily on me. "I'm sorry to have dragged you guys into this."

His face twisted wryly. "It isn't like you meant to get involved yourself."

"Maybe not, but I'm not sorry I met Missy, or that I have her and Dylan in my life."

Someone was yelling his name in the background, and he turned and looked over his shoulder. "Okay! I'll be right there!" he acknowledged, raising one of his arms into the air to signal he heard the summons. "I gotta go, buddy. I have a few more hours on the field; then I'm heading home."

"See you later."

"Be careful. I'll check in with security on my next break."

"Great. Can you ask the two coming with me not to dress like Men in Black? They don't blend."

He smiled again. "Yeah. Bye."

I ended the call just as Remi and Teagan appeared.

"We need our presents!" Remi squealed, running down the stairs. She wore a cute white top with the Little Mermaid printed on the front and a pair of matching teal pants. Her hair was pulled off of her anxious and exuberant face in a white scrunchie. Remi lit up with anxious anticipation. "Dylan!" she called up the stairs, where the subject of her hollering was getting ready with the help of his own mother. "We gotta hurry to Jessica's birthday!"

Teagan followed behind Remi a bit more slowly.

"Presents?" I asked, hoping I wouldn't be expected to stop at a store. The less time in public, the better.

"Don't worry," she said, rubbing her lower back with one hand. "I stopped yesterday and got a few things while the kids were in school. Remi and Dylan picked what they wanted to give Jessica, and I'll return the gifts they didn't choose. We still have to wrap them, though."

"Cool." No doubt, Remi picked a Barbie or some other such princess-y thing, but I wondered what Dylan chose. "Are you feeling okay, Teags?"

"Just a backache and I have to pee every ten minutes. I'm sure ready for this baby to be born."

"You only have a month left, right?"

"Ugh! Don't remind me." Teagan rolled her eyes. "I wish it was yesterday."

"Dylan!" Remi called again, running back to the foot of the stairs and yelling up. "Dyyyyyllllllaaaaaan!"

"Remi, hush!" Teagan scolded. "You have plenty of time. You have to have breakfast, and we have to wrap the gifts."

"The baby will be here before you know it." I squeezed Teagan's shoulder just as Missy was coming down the stairs with Dylan. My hand flew away from Teagan. I felt guilty about touching her, even though I knew there was no reason to be.

Missy's eyes landed on mine, but then quickly averted to Dylan scrambling across the room with Remi to climb up on stools where I had bowls of cereal waiting.

"Captain Crunch?" She asked, pursing her lips, as her brows rose. "Do you know how much sugar is in that stuff?"

I smiled, wryly. "Um… just enough to make it taste good?"

"Ugh," she groaned.

Teagan sat down on the stool next to Remi and Missy noticed how miserable she looked.

"Are you doing okay, Teagan?" she asked, alarmed.

"Oh, I'm just really tired today. My back has been hurting, and I didn't sleep well."

Missy's eyes met mine, before settling back on Teagan. "Could you be in labor?"

Teagan's eyes widened in a shocked expression. "Oh, God, no. I have an OBGYN appointment on Monday, so they'll check me, but I still have several weeks to go. It might be Braxton Hicks."

"Okay," Missy said, walking to Teagan and rubbing her arm while I poured milk on the kid's cereal and they dug in with gusto. "Maybe you should stay in and rest today."

"Yes. I can take the kids to Jessica's party."

"I'll go with them, too," Missy insisted, meeting my eyes. My mouth thinned. We'd agreed she'd stay in with Teagan.

Relief flooded Teagan's face. "Really? Are you sure? Chase asked me to stay home, but I don't know…"

"Absolutely," Missy agreed.

"I'll be there, too" I reassured. "Don't worry. Have you told Chase how you're feeling?" I knew Teagan, and she was one to keep stuff to herself if she thought it wasn't serious.

Teagan shook her head, leaning on the marble countertop where she was seated. "No. He'll be home tonight anyway, and I don't want to worry him."

I decided that I'd let the kids finish their breakfast, have Missy help the kids with wrapping the gifts and text my best friend about his wife. After hiding Remi's birth and illness from Chase for years, there was no way I'd hide anything from him now. "Well... I think you should call him, Teagan. He'd want to know. We learned that lesson, didn't we?"

"He'll be home. Even if I tell him, he can't get home any sooner. Why make him worry for nothing? He's already stressing that he isn't here for this party."

She had a point, but as soon as I could, I'd be texting my best friend. "Like I said, I'll be with these guys." I put a hand on both of their heads and gave them a little wobble. Dylan laughed, and Remi gave me a big grin, showing her missing front tooth.

"Will you play with me, Jensey?" Dylan asked. "Remi told me about the jungle gym and how fun the trampolines are!"

I grinned down at him and winked at Remi. "Of course! I'll play with both of my special kids."

Missy

I was sitting at one end of a low, kid-height picnic table with two of the other parents who were helping to chaperone the birthday party. Jessica's mother was putting out plates and drink cups for the two dozen or so children attending. The gifts were piled up on the adjacent table with the cake, and huge bunches of mylar balloons adorned both.

Jensen had disappeared with Remi, Dylan, Jessica, and a

few of the other kids. He was amazing. The kids were crawling all over him. I watched in awe as he climbed high up in the three-story play structure on the inside of the PlayDaze venue, with both Remi and Dylan clinging to his back and shoulders like monkey babies clinging to their mother. It made me smile. He was such an incredible man, and he made one hell of a father. A warm rush of love and lust filled me, and I almost felt my ovaries flutter. I'd love nothing more than to have his child someday.

There were trampolines, an arcade, a roller-skating rink, a huge ball pit for the babies, a snack bar, and the enormous jungle gym that took up most of the space inside the massive facility. There were also a few clowns entertaining children by making balloon animals and juggling.

My two security guys dressed more casually than I was used to, were nowhere to be seen. They'd disappeared into the throng of the crowd, and I could only assume one was following Remi and the other, Dylan.

Once again, I was thankful for Chase and Teagan's generosity. There was no way I could ever repay them for everything they'd done for Dylan and me, and without that added layer of peace of mind, I'd be a nervous wreck. And, Jensen was like a guardian angel sent down from heaven to watch over us.

Still, my eyes nervously scanned the venue, watching for any sign of Derrick. The place was bustling. The building was divided in several separate parts that made it impossible to see everything that was happening at once. There was more than one birthday party going on, and it was open to the public as well. Saturday was easily the busiest day of the week. I sighed, uneasily.

I hadn't had a chance to speak to Jensen about what Chase's investigator had uncovered. We hadn't had any time alone without the kids, and I knew Jensen wouldn't discuss it in front of them because he didn't want to frighten them.

The way Dylan had cried for Jensen to be his dad last Wednesday night made my heartbreak, and the tender look on Jensen's face made me melt. If only that were possible. I knew Jensen was serious about me and only time would tell where we'd end up, but it was my heart's highest wish that we'd be a family someday.

I loved him more in the moment when his arms wrapped around my sobbing son and me than I ever thought it was possible to love anyone. My heart was so full, and if it weren't for Derrick's threats hanging over us, I would have thought I was living a dream.

If only I weren't terrified and tied into knots. I knew how ruthless Derrick could be, and I didn't understand why he wanted Dylan now, after all this time, but worry petrified my soul; after finding out what happened to my attorney, I was desperate to stop my ex-husband.

My heart thudded inside my chest sickeningly. I felt nauseous, my stomach turning at the smells of popcorn and pizza permeating the air. I concentrated on breathing through my nose, struggling not to get up and run to the bathroom to vomit. I had to find some way to get him to hurt me so we could file charges. It was the only way to ensure he'd never get visitation with my perfect, innocent little Dylan.

I felt small, sitting there in the vast building as I glanced around. My eyes longed to find Jensen and the two kids so I could relax. He kept them both close, despite each of them wanting to run off with different groups of friends, and in spite of Tom and Mitch; Chase's security guys.

He was amazing with the kids. If only I'd met Jensen first. Dylan would be his, and we wouldn't be in this mess. My eyes flooded with tears and I dabbed at the corner of my eye with one finger, hoping no one would notice.

"This place is crazy!" Denay, one of the other mother's said, leaning in to speak loudly. In addition to a couple hundred screaming kids, there was pop music blasting over the speaker system. "It's so loud!" She stuck a finger in her ears.

I offered a weak smile. "Yeah!" I answered loudly. "I think I'll be deaf for days."

"Remind me never to have a party for Danni, here!" another of the mothers joined in.

"At least, not without earplugs! I wish I would have known! It's almost time to eat." Jessica's mom, Sara added. "Then we'll cut the cake, and Jess can open her gifts... if we survive that long." She laughed happily, glancing at the clock on the wall. Jessica was a pretty little blonde that was the spitting image of her mother. "Just ten more minutes."

The kids were told to meet back up at the table for Pizza, cake and ice cream. I couldn't wait for this party to end, and while ten minutes was a short amount of time, it dragged by.

Little by little, the kids started to filter to the table and take their seats, with Jessica at the head of the table. Soon, all of the kids were sitting down; except there were two empty seats. Dylan and Remi were not there.

I stood up, panic seizing my heart as my head snapped from side to side and I turned around in a circle; searching. I pulled my phone from the back pocket of my jeans and texted Jensen.

Where are you guys? The pizza is here.

I waited, my heart beating wildly, for his response. I waited for what felt like an eternity and still, he didn't respond. I left the table and hurried from one area to the next, getting more and more overwrought as I searched for them. I weaved around children and adults, becoming more and more frenzied. "Dylan! Remi!" I called over and over. People started looking at me, but I paid them no mind. "Dylan! Remi!" I screamed. "Jensen!"

A man playing with his little boy in the arcade stopped what he was doing and pointed to the front of the building. "Go up to the desk. Maybe they can help find them," he said sympathetically. "I'm sure they'll turn up. This place is friggin' huge."

I thanked him absently and ran to the entrance to speak to the attendant.

"I can't find my children!" My heart was beating at what felt like a thousand beats a minute. "Please help me!"

"Calm down, ma'am," the young attendant said. "What are their names and where would you like them to meet you? I'll page them."

"Dylan and Remi," I gulped out, tears starting to roll down my face. "They need to meet at the table for Jessica Walton's birthday party."

He bent to put his mouth near a mic and pressed a button. "Dylan and Remi, please join your mother at Jessica's birthday party!"

"Thank you," I breathed, pushing the hair off of my face. I felt claustrophobic, suffocated and sweaty.

"Go back to the table and wait a few minutes. If you don't find them, I'll get some staff members together to help find them. They're probably already at the table by now."

Staff members? I wanted to scream, but it wasn't this kid's fault that I was scared out of my head. He had no idea that my nut job ex-husband had made threats or what was really scaring me. I didn't just think they got lost; I thought they'd been abducted.

"Is there a back door to this place?"

"Sure, the employee entrance, but that is in the breakroom,

and customers aren't allowed in there. There are a couple of fire entrances, but those have been covered. The alarm sounds if they're opened."

"Okay." I turned around to retrace my steps back to the birthday party, and as I approached, I looked for any sign of my son or Remi. There was no sign of either of them.

Jensen ran toward me, flanked by the two security guards. "Oh, God," I cried seeing him without the kids, a sob breaking free. Jensen's frenzied expression said it all. My hands curled into the front of his shirt as his arms went around me. "Where are they?"

He swallowed hard; his expression was pained. "We climbed to the top, and they wanted to go down the biggest slide again. Two other kids were with us and got between Dylan, Remi and me. When I reached the bottom, they weren't there. I looked all over for them."

I felt faint, my knees started to buckle, and thankfully Jensen's arm slipped around me for support.

"We've been scouring this place, top to bottom," Tom said. "I'll keep looking."

"There is an employee entrance." I pointed toward it. "Look outside and in the break room or whatever they have," I said. It didn't sound like my voice. I felt as if I heard myself from underneath a mile of water. "How could you lose them?" I screamed at Jensen, pulling away just enough to pound on his chest with both fists. Over and over, I hit him. "How could you let them out of your sight? I trusted you!"

He grabbed both of my wrists but didn't try to stop me from beating on him as tears ran in rivers down his face.

"It was an accident! I didn't want to come to this goddamned party in the first place! Maybe next time you should listen to me!"

I stopped my assault and looked up into Jensen's face. His

skin flushed, and his brow furrowed; anguish was written all over him.

I realized he was right; we shouldn't have come here no matter how much the children protested. I closed my eyes and started to sob, tears squeezing out from between my closed lids. I went limp in Jensen's arms, sobbing my heart out and clutching at him like a lifeline. He caught my weight, pressing my head into his chest. "We'll find them, babe. We have to. I won't rest until we find them."

From somewhere far away, I heard Mitch on his walkie talkie. "We've got a situation. Send back-up to the PlayDaze on a hundred and thirty first. We have to lock this place down. Two small kids are missing."

Chapter 19

JENSEN

The next several hours passed in an anxiety-filled blur.

Security called nine-one-one immediately, and within minutes the birthday venue was swarming with local police officers and FBI agents; sirens screaming, and the parking lot was filled with flashing red lights and a SWAT team van.

The facility was placed on instant lockdown, and no one was allowed to come or go. An Amber Alert had been issued, and the police questioned Missy and me until we were ready to scream. The other children and adults attending the party went through questioning, as well. Thankfully we were able to find the two kids that went down the slide after Remi and Dylan.

Missy sat at one of the tables with her arms wrapped around herself, silently crying and dabbing at her eyes, while FBI agents and local law enforcement arranged to have Missy's phone tapped, and her apartment surveilled. I paced back and forth, feeling helpless; it was as if the world was ending. My little Remi and Dylan had to be terrified, and it was all my fault. Guilt threatened to suffocate me. I could barely look at Missy; fearful her face would be full of the loathing.

A gruff and weathered man identifying himself as Agent Webster, the field agent supervisor, walked over to ask more questions. He smelled like an ashtray, and his chin was marred by a deep and ragged scar. He looked like he'd cut a few years off of his life expectancy from doing this job. "We need to contact the other child's parents," he said, keeping his voice low.

I rubbed a hand down my face. How would I explain that I was one of her parents? How would I tell Teagan and Chase that I'd lost Remi along with Dylan? This would be rough. "I should do it. Remi's father is Chase Forrester, so—"

"The soccer player?" he interrupted. I could see the admiration flash over his face as I nodded in affirmation. "The press will go wild."

"Yes. I'd like to keep it quiet until I can tell Chase's wife. She's pregnant, and Chase is out of town until tonight. He's flying in from Kansas City around 5 PM, so he's probably on his way already." I knew it would kill Chase to tell him when he could do nothing until he got back to Atlanta.

"What airline? I can call and have them expedite him off the plane and have someone from my office pick up him up at the gate, but we need to get this out to the press a.s.a.p. so the public can help us recover those kids."

"I understand," I said wearily. "Don't you already have the Amber Alert?"

"Yes, sir. It's the first thing we do in cases of child abduction."

The situation was surreal, like something off of a TV crime series. This couldn't be happening in real life.

Missy was visibly trembling. I could see her shake from where I was standing twenty feet away, and I wanted to comfort her. As I started in her direction, Agent Webster fell in step beside me. I sat down and pulled her close against my side. I could see her try to push her emotions down, but a broken sob burst from Missy, and she buried her face in the curve of my neck and shoulder. I felt like hell. My heart ached, and I wanted to lose it myself, but instead, I steeled myself for the long hours and days to come.

"Those poor babies," Missy cried softly. "I have to call Teagan."

"I think we should get over there," I murmured in her ear. I wasn't sure how I'd get to Teagan before she heard it on the news or got the Amber Alert on her iPhone, but she couldn't hear about it without either Chase or me by her side. "Can I take Missy home?" I asked the FBI agent. "Maybe over to the Forrester house so we can be with Teagan, too? I don't think she should hear that her daughter is missing over the phone."

"I don't want to leave," Missy protested. "You go tell Teagan. I have to help find the children!"

"Ma'am," the older FBI supervisor interjected gently, bending down to speak to her. "It's too dangerous for civilians to get in the way of us doing our job. We've scoured this place top-to-bottom. The children aren't in the building. The best way to help is to be patient, and maybe call the suspect from a safe location so we can trace his phone. You can help us figure out what he's after. I know this is painful, but is he a pedophile?"

"No. But, he's abusive and controlling. He used to beat me. I did my best to protect Dylan, but I wasn't always successful."

"Ehh," Agent Webster was disgusted, wiping his lower lip against the back of his wrist. "I get so sick of these fucking slimeballs." He realized he'd cursed. "Oh, sorry."

"It's nothing I'm not thinking, trust me. His company is dead broke. He needs money," I added.

Missy looked up at me, questioning. "He does? How—?"

I nodded, still holding her close, but meeting her gaze. "Chase found out when he had Ellington investigated."

The man nodded. "Okay, that's probably the motive for taking the little girl, too. Do you know the PI agency? We need anything they've got."

I nodded and dug a card out of my wallet and handed it to him. "Perlington Investigations," I said the name of the firm.

"They're top-notch. The good news is, the suspect is most-likely still in the city, but either way, he'll probably be in touch with you. You just have to wait it out. I'll have a couple of agents escort you over to the Forrester home."

"Derrick told me he had my attorney killed in Jackson Hole," Missy admitted reluctantly.

The agent sighed, and his eyes widened at the gravity of her revelation. "When?"

"He told me in Philadelphia last weekend when I was at a game, but it happened a couple of months ago. My lawyer's name was Richard Anderson. His wife and son were also killed."

"I'll look into it. What was he doing in Pennsylvania?"

"He said he was bidding a construction job."

The agent looked pissed. "Did you call the authorities?"

She shook her head. "No, because I couldn't prove he wasn't there on a job and he wasn't threatening my son or my new... friends," she said shakily. "I didn't know if he was telling the truth about my attorney until I looked up the obituary and found a news article on a local network website. I guess the police report listed it as an accident. The car was hit by a train."

I ran a hand through my hair in agitation. "It's not as if the police could have done anything without proof of injury, anyway. We were told that even for a stupid restraining order, Ellington would have to physically hurt Missy or her son. Threats weren't enough."

Agent Webster's eyes narrowed, and he nodded. "Well, we're on it now."

"Not that I'm not grateful, but why is the FBI here? It's a local crime."

"The suspect is from out-of-state, so he might cross state lines, but in any case, the Feds get involved in all missing child cases."

I could have corrected the status of our relationship but left it alone, unwilling to expend the effort.

He took a statement from Missy about her encounter in Philadelphia while I watched another agent, a female wearing the same type of dark blue jacket with big yellow letters on the back, interview the two little boys I'd identified as those who had preceded me down the slide. She sat down with them and their parents at one of the tables in the corner. I hovered a few feet away, doing my best to listen and keep an eye on Missy as well.

"What are your names?" the woman asked the boys.

"Billy," one of them said.

"Davey," said the other.

"My name is Agent Tilly, and I'm going to need your help." The kids looked scared. The playing, the skating, all of it had come to a stop, and every customer and employee was made to sit at the tables or floor of the main room, while the facility was searched from top to bottom. Everyone was seated in one room and told to keep as quiet as possible. The agents were letting the families leave one-by-one after questioning. "Don't worry; you're not in any trouble. I'm a police officer, and we help people. I just need to ask you a couple of questions, okay?"

They stared at her face, their eyes wide. Both of their mothers were with them and told them it would be okay and that they should answer the questions.

"A little boy and girl are lost. They went down this slide right here." Agent Tilly pointed to the red plastic tube that came from three stories up. "They slid down in front of you, and I'm hoping you can help us find them."

It sounded like a ridiculous expectation. There were hundreds of kids here, all of them yelling and running around. It had been chaos at best. These boys had gone down that slide at least twenty or thirty times, and a hundred kids could have been in front of them at any given time during the party. Could we realistically expect them to remember anything?

The agent had Missy's phone and a photo she'd taken of the kids with me when we'd first arrived. "These two. Look at their picture?" She pointed at the screen on the phone. "Do you remember them?"

It was obvious they were scared as the woman questioned them. They were six years old and being questioned by the goddamned FBI because I wasn't watching my kids close enough. Guilt ate away at my gut. If anything happened to Remi... If anything happened to Dylan... I'd never forgive myself.

One of the little boys shook his head, but the other one nodded, and I perked up.

"Yeah. I saw!" he said excitedly. "They were talking to a clown."

Agent Tilly's eyes flew up to lock with mine, then back to the little boy. "Which clown? Do you remember what he looked like?"

"The one in the blue suit."

"What color was his hair? Was his face covered with make-up?"

"Pink," Davey, the other little boy piped in.

"Yeah, pink," said Billy. "He didn't have no makeup on. Just a big red nose."

The agent motioned to her colleague; a clean-cut young man who might have been an intern. "Go tell Morris to look on security tapes. Focus on the clowns and the area by the bottom of the slides and the entrances; even the fire exits. If they find anything, get the timestamp if you see the perp taking them out of the building. If we know what time he nabbed them, then we'll be able to calculate a perimeter for the search."

"I'm on it," he said, and then rushed away.

Fucking hell. It never occurred to me to worry about the clowns. I felt like an idiot.

I went to tell Missy what the boy had said after she was finished speaking with Agent Webster.

"Oh, my God," Missy groaned, putting a hand over her eyes. "How did Derrick know we'd be here?"

That was a good question. Our personal security hadn't noticed anyone following us. "I don't know. All I can figure is he followed us. But he didn't have makeup covering his face so he must have just gone into the employees-only room and stole the costume."

We listened in stoic silence while they told us that the best chance to recover the children would be within the first twenty-four hours, but we had no information on what Derrick was driving. Surely, he wasn't dumb enough to use his company truck. Several agents were on their phones and walkie-talkies, many of them speaking at once. In a haze, I heard one of them ordering an APB on Ellington and possible company vehicle, defining the description of Remi and Dylan, and a request for all of the hotel guest lists from throughout Atlanta, and an order to focus on all of the interstates leading out of state.

My heart was pounding. I felt sick inside as if my entire chest was a hollow shell, and my head was throbbing. *How in the fuck could I let this happen?*

"Mr. Jeffers, Ms. Ellington?" Two other agents appeared, one of them handed back Missy's phone to her. "My name is Agent Daniels, and this is Agent Webster. We've downloaded the information from your phone, but please keep it on in case the suspect tries to call. Do either of the kids have phones? If so, we can track them through the cell towers."

We both shook our heads.

"No," I said.

"They're just babies!" Missy blurted, tears starting in her

eyes again. "Who gives a six-year-old a phone?"

"You'd be surprised," the agent answered.

"Can you track Ellington's phone?"

"Already tried. It's either been turned off or the sim card removed. It's off the grid. If he uses it, we'll find it, though, don't worry," said the one called Webster. "Can you come with us, please? Webster told us to escort you back to the Forrester place. Can I have the keys to your vehicle? Someone else will bring it later. We have to search it, first."

"For what?" I was incredulous.

"Just procedure. We cover all of the bases."

"Okay," I said wearily, handing them over. "Come on, honey." I didn't know where our coats were, or if Missy had her purse. Within seconds, the officers were giving them to us, and swiftly escorting us outside and into the back of a waiting black SUV.

I was holding Missy's hand, but it was limp in mine. She was introspective but had stopped crying, zoning out. Her makeup was smeared, with black mascara tracks trailing down her face. I wanted to talk to her, to apologize and beg her forgiveness, but how could she forgive me, if I couldn't forgive myself?

"Should we call Ben?" I asked tentatively, beginning to rub my thumb over the top of her fingers. Should I call Chase's sister, brother and his parents? Should I call my parents or Missy's mom? Teagan's dad? Being a United States Senator, maybe he could do something to help. My mind was racing with any possibility of finding Remi and Dylan.

The weight on my chest was so heavy I found it difficult to breathe, and I struggled just to get air into my lungs. When she didn't answer, I called her name. Suddenly, her head snapped around to face me.

"What? Oh," her face crumpled, and tears started to roll

again. Missy put her free hand to her face as her pain spilled forth. "Yes. Ben. Dylan means the world to him." She pulled away from me and fumbled in her purse to retrieve her phone. Her shoulders started to shake as she wiped at her eyes with one hand and turned on her phone with the other.

"Ben?" she said into the phone a minute later. "Can you come to Atlanta? Derrick is in Atlanta, and he took Dylan and Remi." A sob broke forth. "Yes. He *took* them!"

I listened to her tearful conversation with her brother as she recounted the events of the past couple of weeks and of the day. I could hear Ben's deep voice, frantic on the other end saying he'd get a flight right away.

"Can't you drive any faster?" I asked the driver rudely. I looked at my phone and fiddled with it. I hadn't heard from Teagan, which was unexpected. Chase was on a plane, and his phone would be switched off, but she would have gotten the Amber Alert on her phone. My parents texted earlier, but nothing from Teagan. Something was wrong. I felt like I was about to explode. "Jesus Christ!"

"Sorry, sir. We're almost there."

My eyes burned and felt gritty from crying. I used the thumb and index finger of my left hand to rub them both at the same time. My heart was hammering like hell, and I sniffed at the remnants of tears. I might as well be dying, myself. I *would die* if we couldn't find the kids. Remi and Dylan were both mine. I wasn't either of their father, but they were mine just the same. I couldn't imagine loving them more than I did. I'd give my own life to get them back. I'd do whatever it took.

I closed my eyes and pinched the bridge of my nose and then looked at the woman who had become the center of my universe, terrified that she'd hate me after this. She was staring out the tinted windows as the sun was starting to set in the western sky. I vaguely registered the muted colors of pink and purple on the horizon.

"Missy," I murmured, rubbing her fingers again. "I'm so sorry." Words couldn't express the depth of my sorrow or regret. "I should have kept a closer eye on them."

"It's not your fault. We shouldn't have let them go to the party. They would have been upset, but at least they'd be safe right now."

"He would have just waited for another time. We wouldn't have been able to keep them from doing everything they wanted to do forever."

"You're right. He's ruthless. I hate him, so much." Her voice was thick and full of tears.

Something like fire exploded inside me, and I squeezed her hand. "We *will* find them. I will not let that motherfucker hurt my kids."

Her head turned toward me as she offered a weak smile. Her eyes flooded with tears and she swallowed, nodding. "I know."

She took out her phone again and rolled through her recent calls and touched on one of them. She lifted the phone to her ear. "Derrick, please don't hurt the kids. We'll give you anything you want. Just, please!" she cried. "Don't hurt them!"

Air rushed out of me as she hung up and then collapsed in a torrent of tears against me. I held her until we arrived at our destination, and I pushed the security code from the open window on the backseat of the driver's side of the SUV. Praying Teagan wouldn't see the flashing red lights coming from the dashboard of the vehicle. The first security team remained at the venue after we left, and second had been monitoring the situation from outside the Forrester estate and followed onto the grounds.

We parked in the driveway, and I helped Missy out of the vehicle. We all rushed up to the door. I had a key, and we quickly went inside. Agent Daniels stayed outside to confer with the Perlington team. Inside, Teagan wasn't anywhere to be found.

"Teagan?" I called. The house was dead silent. The TV wasn't on, the music had been turned off. "Teagan?" I yelled louder.

"Maybe she's upstairs," Missy offered weakly. Her eyes were red-rimmed and puffy.

"Maybe you should go up and look for her," Agent Webster added. "I'll stay down here with Ms. Ellington."

I didn't want to leave Missy in such a fragile state, but this was going to be just as devastating for Teagan as it had been for Missy. I had a very difficult conversation in front of me, and I was worried something was amiss with Teagan.

"Yeah, I'll be right back," I answered the agent but then turned toward Missy. "Why don't you get some water and sit down?" I said.

"Yes, if the perp wants money, he'll be in touch, ma'am," Webster added. "Sadly, we've seen a lot of these cases. Your ex-husband has no history of pedophilia, and we've received digital copies of the report from the investigators Mr. Forrester hired already. It looks like a clear motive for funds. We have to wait for him to contact you and we'll lock on to the signal."

Missy nodded, as Daniels entered the front door.

I moved quickly to the stairs and ran up, taking them two at a time. I looked in the hall bathroom first. It was empty. "Teagan?" I called again. I pushed open Remi's bedroom door and found no sign of her. Maybe she was sleeping. As I got closer to the master bedroom, I could hear her moaning in pain. I rushed in, banging open the door.

"Teagan?"

"Jenseeeeen," she groaned. She was in a fetal position on her bed still dressed in her pajamas from earlier, cradling her rounded baby bump with both hands. "Oh, God."

"For Christ's sake, Teagan! Are you in labor?"

Her hair was stuck to her furrowed forehead by a slight sheen of sweat as she nodded. "Yes," was all she said. Her eyes were swollen and red, traces of tears still on her face. *She knew.*

"Why didn't you call nine-one-one?"

She ignored my question. "I saw the Amber Alert!! You lost Remi and Dylan?"

Fuck. Could this get any worse?

My heart fell to the pit of my stomach for the second time today. I sat down on the edge of the bed, as Teagan convulsed in pain as another contraction overtook her. I rubbed her back. "Ellington took them from the venue. The FBI is on it." Did the shock of it cause her to go into premature labor?

"Ugggghhhh!" she moaned again. "I want Chase! He's got to be worried sick," she panted in pain. "My battery died, and I couldn't call!" she cried frantically. "Oh, my God. Remi!"

I stood up and took out my phone, dialing nine-one-one.

"Chase won't know until he lands, but the police are picking him up. I'll have them meet us at the hospital."

"What about Remi and Dylan, Jensen?" she asked accusingly, her voice strained. "How am I supposed to have this baby when my daughter has been stolen by some lunatic?"

"You don't have any choice, right now, Teagan." I cupped her silky head with my free hand.

"Hello, what is your emergency?" a woman asked from my phone.

"I need an ambulance at 10857 Jefferson Terrace, in the Presidential Estate Development, Atlanta. A woman is in labor."

"How old is she, sir?"

"She's twenty-seven. It's Teagan Forrester."

"How far apart are the contractions?" she asked.

I didn't know the answer. "How far apart are your contractions coming, Teags?"

She grimaced, jerking on the bed. "Maybe five or six minutes. I don't know," she panted.

"She said five minutes, but it could be closer. I just arrived and found her doubled over."

"How long has she been in labor?" she asked.

"A couple of hours, I think." Why couldn't that woman just send the goddamned ambulance?

"The paramedics are on their way. Is it a gated community?"

"Yes," I answered quickly. "I'll open the gate, and the one at the edge of the property."

"Yes, sir, stay on the phone until the paramedics arrive."

"Okay," I told the emergency dispatcher. "Teagan, I'll be right back."

I left the room and hurried down the stairs, past Missy and the FBI agents. Missy was sitting down on one of the dining room chairs, and they were standing nearby, talking to her.

"Is Teagan alright?" Missy's tear-stained face was concerned.

"She's in labor. I'm opening the gates for the ambulance," I said frantically in passing.

"Oh, my God," Missy said sadly, standing up and running toward the stairs. "

"She'll be fine, but we need to get her to the hospital," I answered loudly from the laundry room as I pushed in the gate code.

In less than a minute, we were both sitting on the bed next to Teagan as she writhed with labor, and the FBI agents were in the living room using their phones to communicate with their fellow agents and field office.

"I'm so sorry, Teagan," Missy cried, reaching out for her hand. Teagan took it, clutching tight. "I love Remi."

Both of the women had tears running down their faces.

"It's not your fault." She closed her eyes tight and grimaced, clutching her round stomach as another pain hit her. "Mmmmm… Uhhh… I love Dylan, too. Ugh," she moaned again, suddenly curling around her stomach as another pain seized her. "We have to—Uhhhhhh," she groaned again, her face straining from her pain. —find them."

All I could do was stand there and watch these two amazing women. I closed my eyes against the burning behind them. I wanted to cry, too, but being on the phone with the dispatcher, I couldn't tell Missy or Teagan what I wanted to say; that if it took my last breath, I'd get them back unharmed.

Within minutes, the sirens sounded in the driveway, and I could hear the FBI agents directing the paramedics upstairs.

"I'm going to hang up now, sir," said the woman on the phone.

"Okay, thank you." I ran out of the room to show the medical team which was Teagan and Chase's bedroom. "She's in here," I said.

I backed out of the room with Missy, holding her hand in the hall as we waited for them to get Teagan on the gurney, get her hooked up to fetal monitors, and take her blood pressure. We could hear them offering her soothing words. "We have a good healthy heartbeat. How far along are you."

"Just thirty-six weeks. I'm early," I heard Teagan's voice answer weakly.

"I'm sure you'll be fine, ma'am," one of the men said.

"Jesus," I moaned; leaning tiredly up against the wall.

Missy wiped away an errant tear. "What about Dylan and Remi," she asked, her face crumpling.

"Chase will be with Teagan, and I'll be with you. We'll find the kids. I won't rest until I find them, Missy."

She nodded and leaned into me, placing her head in the curve of my neck. "I hope so."

"Do you trust me? I know I failed you today," I admitted. "I'll make it up to you, I promise."

"I told you, it's not your fault. Derrick would have kept at me, and Dylan until he got his way. I'm so sorry about Remi—"

I put up a hand to stop her. "If Ellington wants money, we'll give it to him even if I have to put a second mortgage on my house. Chase will be all in on the cash, too. I know it's hard, but we can't waste energy panicking. We have to use all of our resources to find Dylan and Remi, and losing control of emotions, won't help. We have to keep our wits about us." I tried to keep my voice calm and glanced at my watch. It was five-thirty, and my friends' plane would have landed by now. "We need to let the FBI agents know to take Chase to the right hospital."

I nodded toward the stairs, and Missy understood. She didn't let go of my hand as we walked downstairs and I spoke to the agents, but they'd already made the call when the paramedics arrived.

At that very moment, my phone rang. Chase's name flashed on the screen, and I answered as quickly as I could.

"I can't reach Teagan, and Remi and Dylan have been abducted by Missy's ex-husband?" he sounded frantic. "Does my wife know what happened today?"

I took a deep breath. "She does. You can't reach her because they're taking her to the hospital. You're having a baby, brother."

"Holy hell, it's too early! Christ! This is too much. Which hospital?" I felt sorry for him.

"I assume Emory. The agents will inform your driver, but from experience and what the paramedic just told Teagan, if it's past thirty-six weeks, the baby will be fine, Chase."

"Can you meet me there?" Chase asked, his voice sounded frenzied. He had to be freaking out. "I want to be with Teagan, but what about Remi and Dylan? Right now, I want to kill that bastard! She'll probably want me to go after the kids."

"I'm there with you. I've never wanted to rip someone limb from limb before, but I do today. We think he wants cash. It's the only logical explanation. He hasn't tried to see his son in all this time, but we haven't heard from him yet. We don't know for sure."

The paramedics were wheeling Teagan down the stairs on the gurney. She had on a blood pressure cuff, and an IV line was inserted into her arm. "Is that Chase?" she asked tearfully, reaching out her hand for my phone, but one of the men carting Teagan out on the gurney shook his head.

"No time," he said.

I nodded and took her hand. "He'll meet you there. Are you taking her to Emory?" I asked the first paramedic. He nodded, maneuvering the gurney past us, through the house and out the door.

"Emory, Chase. ER entrance."

"Okay. Thanks for being there for Teagan." His voice thickened, and he cleared his throat. "Again."

The unspoken hung over my conversation with Chase. Sure, I was here with Teagan, but Remi was taken while in my care. "Chase, we'll get Remi and Dylan back."

The ambulance in the driveway turned on its flashing lights and sirens as it left the property.

"Let's talk at the hospital. If he wants money, I'll drain my bank account to get my daughter back. And Dylan," he added. I knew my friend, and he rarely cried, but I could tell he was right now. "How could someone do this to two little kids? I mean... what the fuck? I can't imagine how scared they must be."

I nodded solemnly, even though my friend couldn't see. "He's desperate. You said so, yourself. The FBI has Perlington's data already. They're working it."

"Okay. Good, but if anything happens to—"

"It won't, Chase. Okay? I won't let it. You know how much I love Remi… and I love Dylan, too."

Missy's phone pinged. She had it in her pocket and quickly pulled it out. "It's not a number I know," she said, her eyes locking with mine.

"We think he's calling in, now, Chase."

"Okay, go!" he said and disconnected the call.

Agent Daniels rushed over to take down the number from Missy's screen and then left the room, while the other stayed beside us. "Turn up the volume, then answer it and keep him on the line as long as possible."

Missy nodded and did as requested. "Hello?"

"You just had to defy me, didn't you?" Derrick seethed. "Now see what you've done?"

"Derrick! Where are Dylan and Remi?" she screamed into her phone.

"Safe enough." His words were clear as day in the dead silence of the big house. "For now," he threatened.

"What do you want? I don't believe you want Dylan, Derrick. If so, you wouldn't steal him!" She kept her voice relatively calm. "You wouldn't have waited so long."

Missy didn't point out the obvious that now he'd be a convicted felon and seeing his son was off the table.

"You kept him from me! You should have let me see him, Melissa!" Ellington sneered.

"You need help, Derrick. You really do. You hurt me. You hurt Dylan. You're sick! Just bring the kids back, and we'll get you the help you ne—."

"Don't patronize me; you stupid little bitch!" he snapped. "You took my son, and now you think you can put me in some nut house for doing the same? He's mine, too!"

The FBI agent made a rolling motion with one hand,

silently telling her to keep the call going. "You took Remi, too!"

"That was an accident! The little brat didn't leave Dylan's side all day! I didn't have a choice! Now that I have her, I want something from her famous dad. Forrester has loads of money, he won't miss a few million."

Here it was, I thought. *As if that wasn't his motive all along.*

"We have to talk to Chase and see about the money, Derrick. You kidnapping their daughter put his wife into early labor. We need time to get the money together. The banks aren't open on the weekend, but we will. Please... may I speak to Dylan?"

"If you're lying as a stall tactic, I swear, Melissa, I'll know! Don't push me!" Ellington's voice sounded crazed.

"Nuh-no!" Missy struggled, obviously terrified. "It's true, Derrick. In a few minutes, you can call Emory hospital and ask if Teagan Forrester is a patient! I promise! She's having her baby, tonight."

It was all I could do not to rip the phone from her hand and threaten the cocksucker within an inch of his sorry life.

"Fine. I'll call back in a few hours."

"Can I speak to Dylan? Please!"

"No," he said. "No, Melissa, you *can't*. How does it feel?"

Then the call went dead, and we both looked expectantly at the FBI agents, hoping they got a bead on the cell phone.

"Did you get his location?" I asked.

The older one nodded. "A south Atlanta Walmart. The evidence from the surveillance cameras inside the store will help the case, but we don't know what he's driving so even if we send squad cars to the location, we may not find him. He probably stashed the kids somewhere else. In a hotel nearby, maybe. Let's hope local police get there fast enough."

"Can't you get a lead on the phone? I know it's not his, but the towers have to pick it up..."

He shook his head sadly. "I've seen this a hundred times. Criminals buy those prepaid phones and then dump it in the trash somewhere, and that's what shows up on our tracking. He'll probably use a different one the next time he contacts you."

"Motherfucker," I exploded, making Missy startle at my outburst. "Isn't there anything you can do?"

Missy sank down on the chair she'd occupied earlier as I paced around the room.

The agent nodded. "We have to set a trap for him—a swap. The problem is, he's only willing to give up the girl. We need them both."

A low wail came from Missy as she buried her head in her folded arms on the dining table. "I hate him! I absolutely hate him more than I've ever hated anyone!" she cried.

"Do you think he'll hurt them, ma'am?"

"Hell, yes, he will. He's like a ticking time bomb. Any little thing sets him off."

I pulled out the chair next to her and rubbed her back to try and ease some of her tension. "Maybe if we offer more money or say we won't press charges?" I suggested.

"This is a felony. You don't have that option to drop charges; it's up to the district attorney's office if they want to prosecute. Unless this dick is planning on disappearing, he knows he's in a lot of trouble," the agent answered. "He's probably planning to skip the country with the kid and the cash. We have to get him in custody at the drop, or our job gets a whole lot harder. It's the best chance we have. We'll surveil the airport and the interstates, but again, we don't know what he's driving."

"Babe, we need to get to the hospital so I can talk to Chase," I said gently, sliding my arm around her hips and pulling her close as best I could from where I was sitting on the chair near hers. "The sooner we go, the sooner we can catch this bastard."

She nodded and put a hand on my arm. "Thank you."

I swallowed at the rapidly forming lump in my throat. "No need to thank me. I love you. And... I love those kids."

Chapter 20

JENSEN

When we got to the ER, a nurse said that Teagan had been admitted and was in full-blown labor. A nurse directed us to the waiting area on the maternity floor.

I texted Chase a couple of times, but he only responded once asking for an update. I relayed that Ellington was willing to trade Remi for a payout. The only thing we could do was wait for that sicko to contact us again, so we decided Chase should stay with Teagan and help her have their baby. He deserved to be there this time, but how could he fully enjoy it knowing how scared Remi had to be?

Remi and Dylan.

They were all I could think about as Missy and I waited in the maternity waiting room. Agent Daniels and Agent Webster were with us just in case Missy's mad-man ex called back. The PI teams were dismissed.

As my mind reeled, Missy was curled up on my lap on one of the couches. Her earlier tears left her exhausted and finally caused her to fall asleep.

The hours ticked by with agonizing slowness as my I worked through all the ways I wanted to kill Dylan's father, how scared the little ones had to be, and how I could get them both back safe and sound.

What kind of man traumatized little kids? The kind that could kill an attorney and his family to get rid of a fucking restraining order, I realized. *Fucking bastard.*

My thoughts were killing me. I couldn't stand the thought of what he'd done to Missy or Dylan, or what he might be doing to those two little ones now. I swore under my breath as my rage grew. Ellington had to pay for every piece of the pain he caused.

"I want Jensey!" I could still hear Dylan's sobbing cries ringing inside my head and feel them fill my heart. I was worried about my little Remi, too. The poor little thing. She'd already been through so much in her short life, and she didn't deserve this. I wanted him, too. I wanted to marry Missy and adopt that little boy. A burn started deep inside my heart, as determination and resolve overwhelmed me.

Holding Missy in my arms, I was grateful that she still loved me and didn't blame me for the kidnapping. It didn't matter, though; I blamed myself enough for both of us. I was outwardly calm but railing on the inside.

I wanted a life with Missy and Dylan more than anything. Missy, Dylan, Remi... Chase and Teagan and the new baby... and hopefully, more kids for me with Missy. This was the beautiful future I imagined; all four of us raising our kids together, relying on and helping each other as the kids grew up. Then this asshole shows up to ruin everything. I was sick to my very soul.

I leaned back and shifted in the small, uncomfortable sofa. The room was full of grandparents and friends of other families, and I wondered if I should have called Chase's parents to let them know that Teagan was having the baby. I would have had to tell them Remi was missing, too. The thought left me bereft. Had they heard the Amber Alert? Had Jean heard about it? What a fucking nightmare.

I shot off a short text to my friend.

Hey, did you tell your folks? Should I call them?

Five minutes later he responded.

I called them when I first arrived at the hospital. They knew about Remi, but not the baby. I asked them to stay put until we knew more.

It made sense, I thought, as I put my phone back in the pocket of my pants. I knew I should call my family, too. They were further away and weren't big television watchers, at least not the news stations, so they probably didn't know yet. It wouldn't be long until some of their friends asked about it, and then I'd have them to deal with, too. It was all so overwhelming.

The waiting room doors burst open and Missy's brother, Ben, rushed in; glancing around until he found us. His eyes landed on his sleeping sister. He looked unkempt and rumpled, and he had no luggage. Obviously, he'd gone to the airport straight from his fire station in Jackson Hole.

"Hey," he said, folding his tall body into the chair across from me. "Why the hell are you at the hospital? Has Dylan been hurt? Is Missy okay?" he asked urgently, his eyes scanning her from top to bottom. "I'm freaking the hell out! My flight was the longest in history."

"We're all going a little crazy. Missy was just exhausted from crying. This bullshit made my best friend's wife go into premature labor. Dylan and Remi are still with that deranged prick." I couldn't think of words awful enough to describe Derrick Ellington. "We don't know where they are."

"That cocksucker needs to die," Ben said under his breath. "No question." The fingers of his right hand folded into a fist, and his left closed around it. "Do you think he'll hurt the kids?"

"Define hurt," I said bleakly. "He's basically demanding a ransom for Remi, but he believes he will be able to keep Dylan with him."

"Like hell. I'll kill him first. He's got a history of beating that little boy, so we need to find that bastard," Ben said, seething. "And fast."

"Agreed. It's all I can do to sit here and wait for the damn phone to ring." I nodded to the agents sitting across the room. "We think he'll wait until morning, so Chase has an opportunity to get his hands on some heavy cash."

Ben looked disgusted. "You're not actually thinking of paying that greedy fucker off, are you? Let's just go beat the shit out of him."

I agreed with Ben. "My thoughts exactly, but we need to know where Dylan and Remi are first. He may bring Remi to the drop, but probably not Dylan," I said stoically. "I've been running every scenario I can think of over and over in my head, trying to figure out how to get them both back, unharmed, so I don't think we should wait."

"It doesn't sound like it," Ben agreed. "So, what do we do?"

"I don't know, but I don't want to only find them; I want Ellington out of both of their lives for good. I know that's what Missy wants, too."

"She has since her divorce, but he wouldn't leave her alone. That's why she moved in with me. He knew I'd beat the hell out of him if he came anywhere near either of them."

Missy had said Ben was well networked with the law enforcement agencies in Wyoming, and he might get away with assault there... but he wouldn't here.

"Did you call your mom? With everything going on, I don't know if Missy did?"

Ben shook his head. "Not yet. I was hoping they'd be

found before I even got here, but all of you are high profile, so I'm sure it's all over the national news."

As if on cue, Ben's phone rang, and he answered. "Hey, Mom. Yeah. Calm down. I know. Missy is okay. She's asleep. Yes, I'm in Georgia, with her." He got up and walked to the other side of the room for some privacy from onlookers.

Agent Daniels was talking on his phone a few feet away, and when he finished, both agents moved toward us. The others in the waiting room all looked on with blatant curiosity. If the story of the kids' abduction hit national news, it had to be all over the local stations, too, but I hadn't been paying attention to what was on the TVs around the waiting room. Both of the agents had removed their jackets with FBI emblazoned across the backs to stop the whispering and speculation of the other patient's families, but it hadn't stopped it all.

"Can you wake her up?" Agent Webster asked, nodding at Missy.

"Sure. Hey, sweetheart," I shook Missy a little, causing her to stir. My leg on the side where I'd been holding her weight had fallen asleep and came to life when I moved. My flesh shot through with pins and needles. I wiggled my foot to try to fend off the terrible sensation.

"Hmmm?" she said nodding awake. Her eyes fluttered open.

"The FBI wants to speak to us."

"Oh," she glanced around the room and saw her brother for the first time, and her eyes widened as she instantly jumped off my lap. He stood to take her in his arms.

"Ben," she breathed. "Oh, Ben. I'm so glad you're here."

"Where else would I be? I gotta help find my little man." He held her close. "It will be okay. Let's listen to the agents now, okay Sis?"

Missy nodded and took a seat next to me when Ben

released her. I reached for her hand and gave it a gentle squeeze, hoping to offer a little comfort.

"So, I just spoke with my field office, and the special agent in charge has asked that when the perpetrator calls again, you try to arrange a ransom drop. We'll set up a perimeter and close in, and hopefully take him into custody."

"Have you considered he wouldn't bring Dylan to the ransom exchange?" Ben asked.

He was affirmative. "Yes. We'll have to put a tracking device in the money, in case."

"This is Missy's brother, Ben," I explained.

"Have they investigated the murder in Jackson Hole?" Missy brought up the awful subject because if it could be proven, it was the sure way to keep Ellington away from her and Dylan for life.

"What?" Ben asked, in surprise. "What murder?"

"My attorney died, in a supposed accident, the day before a court date to remove the restraining order," Missy explained quickly. "Derrick won the judgment because we were a no-show, and he admitted it to me last weekend."

Ben leaned back in his chair, his chest rising as he sucked air into his lungs. His jaw jutted out in disgust, as he shook his head. Abhorrence was dripping off of him.

"We're looking into it, but right now it appears to be an accident," Agent Webster explained.

"It's too convenient to be an accident," I insisted.

"The agents in Jackson Hole are looking for evidence to connect him to it, but we aren't sure if we can get enough to make a charge stick. The car was completely demolished in a train accident, and the pieces have been taken to a local junkyard. We're doing our best to find out what we can, but so far, we haven't found any witnesses."

"When Derrick was gloating about it, he mentioned faulty

brakes!" Missy told him. "Can you look for that?"

Ben got up suddenly, pulled out his phone and walked away down the adjacent hallway.

"I'll let them know. Thanks."

"Also, if we catch him—" Missy began.

"*When* we catch that bastard," I said adamantly.

"Yeah, *when*," Ben agreed, returning and shoving his phone into the back pocket of his jeans.

She glanced our way, then back at the agent. "Is there any way to make him sign over his parental rights?"

"I'm no judge, but it seems logical that if we get him on a kidnapping charge, the judge will automatically terminate them."

She took in a shuttering breath. "I just don't want to deal with him anymore."

"But if we can get him on the murder charge, that would be even better. The kidnapping is pretty open-and-shut if we can catch him, but a murder conviction would put him away for much longer. Not to worry you ma'am, but if he'd stoop to this, would termination of his rights really stop him?"

"No, it wouldn't. We have to put him in jail," I said. "For as long as possible."

"Throw away the key," Ben added. "Maybe some big dude on the inside will make him his bitch," he added hopefully.

Missy's phone rang again, but from a different number this time.

"This is most likely the suspect." Agent Daniels quickly placed a recording device on her phone this time. "It's okay to answer it, ma'am." He nodded. "Remember, just like before; keep him on the call as long as you can."

Missy nodded and answered after one more ring. "Hello?"

The FBI had a device on her phone to record the call, but Ben and I both leaned closer so I could hear Ellington's demands. The waiting room was not conducive to cranking up her phone volume, so thankfully, they were recording it in addition to trying to locate his phone from the cell towers.

"Has the kid been born yet? Do you have the money?" Derrick asked. He seemed agitated.

"We're still waiting, Derrick. Can I call you on this phone when we hear any news? Or, we can make a time to meet on Monday. I'm sure Chase will get the money, but the banks will be closed tomorrow."

The agent gave Missy a thumbs up. I closed my eyes in horror. There were more than thirty hours until the banks opened, and all I could think about were those poor kids. However, we couldn't arrange a time before Monday and appear legit.

"I want three million dollars; cash in small, unmarked bills," Ellington demanded.

"That's a lot of money, Derrick."

"If Forrester wants to see his darlin' little angel again, he'll get it. I know he's good for it."

"Oh, Derrick," Missy said, forlornness lacing her words. "Why are you doing this? Just bring the kids back, and we won't press charges. You can't think you'll get away with this. What about your business?"

"Shut up Melissa. If you cared so much about me, you wouldn't have left me in the first place! Just tell him he'd better get the money!"

It was all I could do not to grab the phone from Missy's hands and scream into it. I was seething. Ellington's voice was so cold. He had no emotion for Remi or even his own son.

"I will, but Derrick, please; can we pay more to get Dylan back, too? Please don't take my son from me!" she pleaded, tears filling her eyes and tumbling down her face. "He needs me! He barely knows you anymore. Please…" she cried. "Don't take my baby away from me!"

"You took him away from me! You're crying now, but this is your fault." Ellington's voice changed tenor. "If you want him, you'll have to come with us. I told you, I want you back, baby."

I could see how revolted Missy was by her expression. She closed her eyes in disgust, steeling herself and wiping at her tears. "Okay, Derrick." Her words took on a smoother tone, but I could tell they tore from her. She had her role down cold. "Whatever you want."

"Get rid of the cops! Do you think I don't know they're swarming all over you? Don't make me hurt one of these little bastards."

"You wouldn't!"

"That lousy piece of shit!" Ben said softly, shaking his head, his fists clenching.

"We'll see," Ellington answered menacingly. "I've got one kid I don't want!"

Fuck, I thought, standing up running my hand down my face.

Missy saw the horror on my face, and it echoed on her own. "Okay, Derrick! I'll ask the FBI and police to back off, and we won't press charges! Just give me some time to get the money."

"If you're screwing with me, Melissa, so help me God, you'll be sorry."

"I—I'm not, Derrick. I just want to keep Dylan safe. Please don't hurt him, or Remi. They're just little kids. They're innocent. You're mad at me, not them."

"You're right. They won't stop their infernal sniveling. I can't wait to get this over with, so hurry Forrester up!"

"As I said, Monday is the soonest it's feasible unless you want a wire transfer? You'd have to give us your account number, but then authorities might trace it or freeze the account, so let's just meet Monday," she tried again. "What time?"

Ellington paused. I was proud of Missy for thinking on her feet. She was right, and we needed a face-to-face exchange to catch him and get both kids back.

"Okay. I'll be in touch," he said.

Missy's shoulder's slumped as her phone went dead. "Sorry," she said, defeated. "I wish he would have let me talk to Dylan."

"He'll call again, ma'am," Agent Webster said. "I'll have my office send more agents out as soon as we peg the suspect's location."

"I say we start combing the city." I rose to my feet, ready to take action. "You could tell us where that despicable bastard is when you know."

Ben stood up beside me. "I'm in. Let's go."

Agent Daniels put both of his hands up to stop us. "Wait. You can't just roam around looking for criminals. Under no circumstances can we give you the location. It's dangerous, and it's our job."

"Those are our kids out there!" I said sternly. "I'm going nuts! It's been almost twelve hours since they disappeared!"

"We can't just sit here, man!" Ben stated. "I'm a fireman, so I'm no stranger to dangerous situations. Those kids are six years old! Imagine how terrified they are!"

Both of us were adamant, and together, we were both in the faces of the FBI agents. No doubt Chase would want to go along if he could, but he had to be there for Teagan at this moment. My heart hurt for my friends. They didn't even know what was going on... not really. I pulled my phone out and glanced at the screen, but I had nothing new from Chase.

"I'm going to check with the nursing staff about Teagan's progress before we get the hell out of here."

"Sir—" Agent Webster said. "You can't—"

Missy stood and came closer, standing between Ben and

me and the agents. "Jensen, please be careful. I'm so scared for the children, but maybe they're right," she said, indicating the agents. "I couldn't bear it if something to happen to you and Ben."

"Are you kidding? That asshole may have hurt them to keep them quiet; they might be hungry or thirsty, tied up or tortured! They could be locked up alone somewhere! You told me what he's done already! Do you think by some miracle, this will be any different?" I asked adamantly.

Heat began to sweep up across my chest, up my neck, and into my face. Ben's face showed his fury as well, and his hands landed on his hips in a determined stance.

"I'll be damned if I'll sit here while those little kids are out there somewhere scared out of their minds and may be suffering. There's no fucking way I'm waiting for him to do something worse, Missy!" Ben insisted.

The truth was… we didn't know what Ellington had already done. Missy's face took on a resigned expression, and she nodded. "Okay, I'll wait here for Chase to let him and Teagan know what's happening with the search."

The two FBI agents huddled in a discussion a few feet away, and I glanced to them and then back to Ben and Missy.

"I'll send him a text, as well. Hold on a second." I left them and walked to the reception desk in the waiting room. "Excuse me, can you please give us an update on Teagan Forrester?" I asked. "Has her baby been born?"

"Are you family?" she asked. I paused only briefly before replying. If I wasn't family, I didn't know who I was. "Yeah. I'm her brother-in-law," I lied.

She smiled and looked at something on her screen. "Okay. It looks like she just delivered about twenty minutes ago. It's a boy. She'll be in her room on fourth floor maternity soon, and the baby is going to NICU."

"Is something wrong with the baby?" I prayed he was okay. We didn't need any more bad news today.

"I'm sure Mrs. Forester is doing fine if it's been noted she'll move to maternity within the hour. Sometimes the NICU is just a precaution, but I'm not privy to the details, sir. You'll have to speak to one of the parents."

"The baby was a month premature. Can't you tell me something to ease my mind?"

"Sorry," she said, shaking her head. "Why don't you have a seat and then you can go up and see the new mommy in her room in a few minutes?"

I was worried, but I went back to tell Missy and Ben what I'd learned. "Remi won't be happy. She wanted a sister, but she has a baby brother."

"Are they both doing alright?" Missy asked anxiously, concern furrowing her brow. "What did the nurse say?"

"She isn't a nurse. She couldn't tell me the condition of the baby, but Teagan is fine."

I'd barely got the words out when the double doors opened, and Chase came through pulling a blue surgical gown off of his arms, and plastic gloves off of his hands. His hair was covered with a blue cap, as well. He pushed it off his head in one swift motion, then wadded all of it up together and shoved it in the trash can in the waiting room.

"Are they both okay?" I wanted to know.

"Yeah. They're moving Teagan to her room and our son into the NICU."

"Is something wrong with him?" Missy was close to me and reached out a hand and placed it on Chase's arm. "Is he okay?"

"He's healthy; just a little too pink. He's early, so they say he has jaundice and needs to be under some blue lights for a couple of days. He's perfect," It all rushed out of my friend in a flurry, but his fatherly pride showed even though he was worried about Remi and Dylan. I knew he wished he could pause to enjoy the birth of his son, but his main focus had to be on Remi now that the baby was here safely. "What's going on with the kids?" His eyes scanned over Ben and the FBI agents, then back to me. "Have they been found, yet?"

"No." It took about a minute to share what we knew from the FBI and local police, Ellington's latest demand, and Ben and my determination to search the city.

He turned on one of the FBI agents. "What the hell have you all been doing all night? When are you going to start looking?" I understood Chase's frustration. I felt it, too, but I knew yelling at the officers would not help find Remi and Dylan.

"We're already working on it, Mr. Forrester. It's our advice that the three of you wait until the banks open, so Ellington will be under the illusion you have gotten the cash he wants. Even if it's fake, we can arrange a drop. He says he isn't interested in keeping your little girl. You can't do anything until then, so why not go be with your wife and baby?"

Chase was wound as tight as Ben and me. We were all ready to let our emotions fly, but Chase did.

"My daughter is missing! My wife is crying when she should be happy right now! Christ! You want us to pretend everything is fine?"

I put a hand on my friend's shoulder, expecting him to turn around and slug me. He jumped at my touch and wheeled around. "Chase, let's go out looking for them." I patted his shoulder again, trying to calm him down. "Ben and I can't sit here, either." My friend nodded, placated. "We're going nuts."

"Where are you going to look?" Agent Daniels asked, indignantly. "This city is huge. You can't drive around endlessly without knowing what to look for, or even where to start."

All three of us held our ground, unwilling to acquiesce and

do nothing. I threw Daniels a frustrated look. He knew where the second cell signal came from, so he could tell us if he wanted to. Obviously, he'd never experienced the sheer terror of a child in danger. "What would you do if it were your kid?"

I inhaled and nodded. "He probably has the kids in a motel for the night. One that takes cash," Daniels offered, finally caving into our steadfastness. "The second phone call was one of those throwaway phones again. We already have a team honing-in on the location."

"So?" I looked at him expectantly.

"If you know, you *have* to tell us," Chase said, more calmly. "*Please.*"

Agent Daniels let out a resigned huff. "Midtown, Atlanta."

"The dive hotels in mid-Atlanta, it is, then." Ben's resolve showed as he calmly slid on his coat. "That's where we start."

"That's close by," Chase said.

Adrenalin started to race through my body. Ben shifted from one foot to another and Chase ran both hands through his hair, then laced his fingers together on the top of his head.

Agent Daniels looked at his partner. "Webster, you stay here with Ms. Ellington and Mrs. Forrester. I'm going with these men."

"Shouldn't you call for back-up?"

"For what? I will if we find something. Let's go, gentleman," he said, to us, using his arm to indicate we should follow. "But if we do locate the suspect, we don't make a move. We watch and wait for the rest of my team to arrive, and even then, the three of you stay put. The suspect might be armed, and we err on the side of safety. Got it?"

I glanced between Chase and Ben, meeting their eyes knowingly. I knew that there was no way in hell we'd be capable of sitting by if we found out where Ellington was holding the kids.

"Yeah," Chase nodded.

"Right," Ben agreed.

"For sure. Now can we get the hell out of here?" I asked.

Missy

After the men left with the FBI agent, I went to the bathroom to splash some cold water on my face, and then found Teagan's room on the maternity floor. I wondered if Teagan's dad or Chase's siblings and parents were notified. Everything had happened so fast, and the law enforcement officers who surrounding us all day made it impossible for Jensen to get a free minute. He appeared reluctant to call about the baby because he'd be forced to break the news about the kidnapping.

When I knocked lightly on the door, her voice, though weak and tired, bid me entrance.

"Hey," I peeked inside and found her small form huddled on the bed.

She looked exhausted, and her brow was creased with worry as I entered.

"Did they find Remi and Dylan?" she asked, her face crumpling. "I left my phone at the house so Chase can't text. The battery was dead, anyway." She wiped away an errant tear. "I'm trying not to cry, but I'm so scared, Missy."

I moved into the room and sat on the edge of the bed next to the woman who had become my closest friend. I reached out and squeezed her hand. "Me, too," I agreed. "But I have my phone, and Jensen will keep us informed. He, Chase, and my brother, Ben, went out looking for them with one of the federal agents."

"But, how?" she asked, surprised.

"Derrick called again, and his signal was traced via the cellular towers. It's one of those dummy phones, but I guess the

FBI can still locate it." I wanted to give Teagan some hope, even if I was feeling fragile myself. It was the least I could do, considering all she'd done for Dylan and me; considering her child was in a precarious position along with mine; and all because of me. I didn't tell her that if Derrick pitched it in the trash, the search would be a wild goose chase like the one earlier in the day had been. "Those three men are the only people on earth that make me feel safe. I have to believe they won't stop until they find the kids."

Teagan's face crumpled in profound sorrow. I'd cried a thousand tears over the past twelve hours, but she'd been giving birth and probably had yet to deal with her emotions over the kidnapping. "I do, too. I've never met Ben, but I feel he's a good man."

"The best," I agreed. "The three of them are very alike. Did you call your dad or Chase's family? Should I do that?"

"We've asked them not to come right now. They heard about Remi and Dylan on the news. Chase said he called them back when they were cleaning me up, and that my baby was sent to NICU. With the police, FBI, and most likely the press, we felt it best for them to wait until we get Remi and Dylan back," her voice cracked on a sob.

"I bet you wish you never met me," I said. My vision blurred and my voice caught on the last word.

Teagan shook her head. "Oh, Missy, don't think that. Of course, I'm glad. I love you, and you're so good for Jensen. I love Dylan. And Remi," her voice broke again, and she put her wrist to her mouth. "Oh, God!"

"We have to have faith, Teagan," I said the words, but my own was shaking. I was so scared.

"I'm trying," Teagan answered, sadly. "We shouldn't have let them go to that birthday party."

I lifted one shoulder in a defeated shrug. "I said the same

thing, but Derrick wouldn't have stopped until he found another opportunity."

"How could your ex do that to his own child?"

I blinked to clear my vision. "He's a sociopath who only thinks of himself. He lives for control, and he doesn't care who he hurts in the process. I don't know if he ever wanted Dylan, in the first place. He was just another way to hurt me. I think he just wants to punish me. I wish I'd never met him."

"If you didn't, you wouldn't have your son. You can't be sorry about having Dylan."

Teagan was right, but once again, I wished more than anything, that Jensen were his father. "I don't. Not for a minute."

"When Remi was sick, I thought God hated me and that He was punishing me for not telling Chase about her. I cried because I couldn't take away her suffering, and I couldn't take back what I'd done to Chase or Jensen... but I'm so glad I had her. We all thank God for her every day."

I smiled through my tears. "I know you do, and believe me, I see how much Jensen adores her. As do I. She's a blessing, and so is your new baby!" I tried to turn the conversation to a happier one despite my heavy heart. There was nothing either of us could do to get Remi and Dylan back. We had to put our faith in God, the authorities, and our men.

Teagan smiled sadly. "He's so perfect. He looks just like Remi did when she was born. It's hard to be happy when we're so scared about Remi and Dylan. Chase cried."

"Of course, he did. I can't imagine the tumultuous mix of emotions you two are going through." Another rush of guilt and grief came over me. It was all I could do not to burst into tears all over again. "A baby is a precious miracle. He's okay, then?"

Teagan nodded, reaching for a Kleenex to wipe at her nose and eyes, then pulling another from the box and handed it to me. "Yes. He has a little touch of jaundice. His liver doesn't process properly yet, but a little suntan action under ultraviolet light and he should be fine in a few days." She smiled sadly. "The nurses said they'd take me to see him in a few minutes. You can come with me."

"I can't wait to see him. What's his name?"

"We aren't sure yet, but I want something that sounds similar to Chase, and I'd like Remi to help choose. Is that silly?"

"No." I swallowed at the growing lump of pain in my throat. I could see the love Teagan felt for Chase and Remi shine out from within. I was sure I'd feel the exact same way, if I were lucky enough to ever have a baby with Jensen. "I think it's perfect."

Chapter 21

JENSEN

Once we got outside the hospital, Agent Daniels got on his com inside his vehicle, and we all piled in. He spoke with his commander and then called dispatch for an update on the case.

A list was compiled of all single men, or those with children, who checked into area motels. The parking lots of the motels were patrolled and searched for rentals or stolen vehicles. One vehicle description matched as one stolen, but the plates on it did not coincide with the registration.

A woman from FBI dispatch was talking. "A stolen vehicle has been identified in the parking lot of the Motel 6 at 311 Courtland, Atlanta. Agents have confirmed the description of a male in room 26 matches the suspect in the Atlanta child abduction, though no children had been seen. Agent Webster is already en route to the location and requests back-up. Proceed with caution."

"Bingo," Daniels said, starting the engine. "Here we go."

"That's about a half mile from here," I said, disbelieving Missy's psycho ex would hide out so close. Everything in me wanted to race over there and storm his room.

I was in the front seat. Chase and Ben were both in the back, though they were hunched forward as they listened on with interest.

"What happens now?" Ben asked impatiently.

"I make a call, then we can figure out our best course of action," the agent returned.

We all listened intently as the FBI agent conversed with who I assumed was Agent Webster. It had been several hours since I'd spoken with him at the PlayDaze, but it was apparent they were all working overtime, and I was grateful for their dedication.

"Webster tells me you have Mr. Jeffers and Mr. Forrester with you."

"Yes, sir. Ms. Ellington's brother, Ben Brady, also."

"That's a break in protocol, Daniels." Webster sounded irritated.

"Yes, sir. They were going to look for the perp on their own. I felt this was my only course of action to control the situation."

"We'll discuss it later. Right now, we have to figure out how we're going to get those kids out of that motel room unharmed."

"What's the plan, sir?"

Chase, Ben, and I sat silently taking it all in. All three of us were still as stone, but if expressions were anything to go by, Chase and Ben were wound as tight as I was.

"We can wait until morning and hope he emerges from the room for some reason, or we figure out a way to get in there tonight without a shit storm and someone getting hurt. I don't want to wait until the banks open Monday because those kids are suffering. We know where he is, and he more than likely has the kids with him. I think we take a chance of losing him if we let him move again," Webster's voice came through the radio.

Daniels drove the short distance to the motel, but by the time we arrived, three unmarked vehicles were already blocking off the parking lot entrance, but none of them had their lights flashing. By now, it was 2 AM, and there wasn't much movement on the streets. Only one or two of the rooms had lights on inside, but the curtains were drawn, leaving only a sliver of illumination peeking through.

"Can we coax him outside to take him down?" Agent Daniels inquired. "Are we sure it's the suspect in the identified room?"

"We don't have any witnesses that saw him with any kids," Agent Webster's voice filled the silent vehicle. He must also be proceeding to the scene. "Tilly said the desk attendant identified Ellington from a screenshot she took from his company website."

I clenched my teeth, and the muscle in my jaw flexed. Every instinct I had propelled me to rush the hotel room. I met Chase and Ben's eyes as we waited, and I was sure they were thinking the same thing.

"He wants money," Chase reasoned. "Can we use that angle to approach him?"

Agent Webster was able to hear Chase's question from the open com. "Maybe, but we'd have to be able to contact him, and we have no way to do so. He ditched the phone he used to make the second call. We don't want to let him know we've got him surrounded. He might do something desperate, and our main concern is getting those kids out safely."

"I think we all agree, that's all of our first priority," I added.

"But, who in the hell wants to put those kids through another day of being terrified?" Ben interjected.

"Right," Chase agreed. "Can't we do it tonight? I can't sit here knowing my scared little girl is only yards away."

"They could be injured, hungry or dehydrated," Ben put in angrily. "I think we should break the fucking door in."

"And beat that son of a bitch until he can't walk," I added.

"He'll never believe we just happened to know where he is and in possession of the three million dollars he's asked for. If we storm the room, we risk someone getting hurt," Agent Daniels said.

"It's an inside room, so the only way in or out is through the front door or the window next to it," Webster said over the com. "Never-the-less, I have agents positioned on all sides of the building in case he makes a run for it.

"Who cares if that bastard questions how we found him?" I huffed, furious. They had FBI agents out the ass surrounding this place, in the parking lot, overhead… so what the hell were they waiting for? "Let's just go in there and get Remi and Dylan."

"Yes," Chase agreed. "Let us go." He used his hand to indicate himself, Ben and me. "I'll knock on the door and tell him I have his money and all I want is my daughter back. I can make him believe I'm alone and he can keep his son with him."

"The FBI can hang back. Be there, but wait just until he opens the door," I coaxed the FBI agents, desperate to do anything I needed to so they would move, now. "Then, move in."

"It's too dangerous." Agent Daniels shook his head. "I can't risk civilians."

"We're aware of the risk," Ben was adamant. "We'll be responsible for ourselves, right, guys?"

"Yes!" Chase and I insisted simultaneously.

"Your conviction is admirable, but what about those children in there?" Webster asked angrily over the com. "Do you accept responsibility if anything bad happens to them?"

"I'm a firefighter; I take risks like this daily. If I can take a forest fire head-on, I can take on this little fucker."

I sucked in a deep breath. Chase was equally frustrated,

throwing himself back into his seat. "What the hell are we supposed to do, Agent Webster?" he wanted to know. "Sit here all night? As Ben already pointed out, we don't know if he's fed them, beat them, or given them anything to drink. Dehydration can kill them!"

I decided to take a different tack and changed my tone. "Look, we're all just desperate to get Remi and Dylan back. What if they were your kids who had been snatched by this nut job?" I implored. "Their entire world has been turned upside down. Can you imagine how traumatizing that must be?"

"I think we know about the trauma. We do this for a goddamned living," Daniels added, his tone getting pissy. "Child abductions are all that we do. Day in and day out, we deal with these dirty fuckers over and over again."

"Yeah? What's your track record?" Chase demanded.

"The odds of retrieval are better when it's a friend or family member. Children are less likely to perish."

"Well, as comforting as that is, this guy is crazy," Ben's tone and sarcasm elevated, his words dripping with animosity. "He's hurt my sister and my nephew many times already! And what about my sister's lawyer? Apparently, Ellington admitted to having him killed!"

"Wait, what?" Chase asked urgently. "That's it!" He opened his door and got out of the SUV and Ben joined him.

"Wait!" Agent Daniels demanded, opening his door and hopping out. "Stop!"

As I followed Chase and Ben, exiting from the passenger side, the door of one of the other vehicles blocking the driveway opened, and Webster got out in a hurry. He'd been listening over the walkie talkie, and he rushed over with one of his hands held out; silently indicating to the agents in the other cars they should hold in place.

"Okay, hold on, now. You gentlemen need to slow your

roll. If we're going to do this, we have to do it right." He made another motion, and four FBI agents crouched down and silently moved in two wide arcs through the parking lot to take tactical positions, on either side of the door to room 26. They were dressed in dark clothes and carrying weapons, and they plastered themselves tightly against the building making certain they couldn't be seen from the room's window. Webster put his walkie talkie to his mouth. "Is the bird close?"

"Yes sir," a man said in response. "We're ready. If the suspect runs, we'll follow with the spotlight."

The place was crawling with agents, but the parking lot was deadly silent. The only sounds were those of traffic from the nearby interstate and the sudden soft whir of helicopter blades high above us.

"Okay," Webster said in a whisper. "This is against my better judgment, but it might be our best chance. Daniels go with them but hang back to the left. The three of you create an arc around the door to the room, so he can't see much beyond the three of you, especially you, Mr. Forrester. Get him outside the room if you can. We want to make the arrest as quickly and quietly as we can and keep the commotion to a minimum. We can't fire weapons because we can't risk hitting the kids or civilians in adjoining rooms with stray bullets. Give me a few minutes, and I'll get a sniper in place."

I sighed, sucking so much air into my lungs that I thought they would explode.

Ben was leaning back against the black SUV with his arms crossed, and Chase was pacing back and forth. When his boss indicated it was a go, Agent Daniels nodded and pulled a Glock from the holster inside of his jacket and cocked it just when an armed Agent Webster reappeared, walking in from the perimeter of the parking lot.

Daniels glanced over his shoulder apparently seeing what

he needed to see. "Webster is ready for us to move," he said, calmly. He motioned with his gun for us to go toward the building. "We're right behind you. Be careful. We don't can't know if he's working alone, so keep on high alert."

"Holy shit," I said quietly as we hunched down and then hurried stealthily through the parking lot and toward the room. There were more agents huddled behind some of the cars of the motel patrons closer to the building with guns drawn but hidden out of sight of Ellington's hotel room. My blood was pumping like a raging river, my heart pounding the adrenaline through my veins. I glanced at Chase and Ben. We hadn't considered he might have paid thugs with him.

"I'll knock first," Chase said. "He demanded the money directly from me, so it will be more realistic if I make the offer."

"Right, and when he emerges, I'll jump out between you both and grab him," Ben offered. "The two of you go in and get the kids out."

I wanted the whole thing over, but it was playing out in slow motion, like a scene from a crime drama. All I wanted was to hold Remi and Dylan in my arms and let them know that they were safe.

"He's completely off his rocker if he expects to get away with this," Ben said with bravado. "I can't wait to get my hands on that fucking moron."

"Be careful," Daniels warned him. "Don't get involved in an assault that we'll have to charge you with."

"What if his face just happens to fall into my fist? Multiple times," Ben said stoically, a seriousness to his expression. The corner of Daniel's mouth lifted in amusement, but he didn't say a word.

The four agents dressed in black tactical gear were waiting in their positions against the wall on either side of the hotel room door. They looked more like a SWAT team, or military unit than FBI agents.

Chase and I stood shoulder to shoulder in front of the door, with Ben on his haunches behind us. Webster and Daniels were crouched just off to either side behind two parked cars. There was a goddamned militia poised to take down, what we hoped, was only one man.

Chase and I shared a knowing look, and we both tried to calm down. His hand crept forward so that the bent knuckle of his right index finger could knock softly, and I covered the peephole with my thumb.

Seconds ticked by and the curtain on the window moved. Ellington was looking to see who was knocking.

"Derrick, it's Chase Forrester and Jensen Jeffers. We have some of the money you requested. We brought as much as we could get our hands on, now, but we will get more from the bank on Monday."

"We just want the kids, Ellington," I said firmly. "We just want our kids, back safely."

The door cracked. The deadbolt released, but the chain was still in place. "You're not getting Dylan, only the girl," his eerie voice rasped out. "Missy knows that. Get the rest of the money; then we'll talk."

Dawn had not yet started to break and thankfully, we were still under a veil of darkness.

"Open the door, so we can talk, Ellington. This is just a negotiation. I'm sure you don't want to hurt those little ones. Maybe we can get the police to back off."

"Do you think I'm an idiot? Show me the cash, asshole!"

Chase glanced at me from the corner of his eye. He didn't have any more money than he normally carried, and I only had a couple of hundred on me. We both knew what we had to do. It was unspoken between us.

"Not until I see Remi!" Chase proclaimed, louder now.

"Daddy!" Remi cried from inside the room! "Jensey! Help us!" Her voice was weak and scratchy as if she'd been crying hard for a long time.

"Shut up, you stupid brat!" Ellington screamed, and there was a loud clatter and the sound of shrill screaming from both of the children from inside the room.

"Remi, you and Dylan get into the bathroom, right now!" I called out, furious, but grateful to hear her voice.

"Jensey! We can't!" I heard Dylan's voice coming from inside the room for the first time as we both bolted into action.

"Let's move," Ben said softly from behind us. "We have to go before he gets the deadbolt back in place."

"On the count of three," I said under my breath. Chase and I were poised to use one foot each to bash in the door, hoping our combined strength would move the locked door. "One, two, three!" The force of our combined effort caused the loud crack of splintering wood as the door gave way from its frame and sent an unexpecting Ellington reeling backward: the heavy door crashing down on top of him and into the room.

Ben flew between us, bolting over the fallen door that was lying on top of Derrick Ellington. He threw all his muscular weight into action, bouncing up and down a little more than he had to. The man beneath it groaned in pain, clearly pinned to the floor by the door, and the force Ben was applying. "How do you like it, you twisted fuck?"

What ensued next was chaos. Agents flooded in, and the room was suddenly illuminated by floodlights.

"FBI!" was shouted as Chase and I rushed inside and over the door into the shabby room searching in unison for the little ones. The bathroom was too close to the door for the children to get to when I'd commanded, and we found them both huddled together on the floor cowering and crying behind the second bed against the far wall. Dylan was holding his left arm with his right.

My heart broke. They were dirty and disheveled, but I was so relieved to find them alive.

"We've got you," I said, as I bent to retrieve Dylan and enfold him into my arms. He cried out in pain, and I slowed my movements. "You're okay now, buddy." I breathed into his hair. He smelled sweaty and felt clammy, but I could think of only one other time I'd been this grateful or relieved; when Remi's leukemia was cured.

Chase was already holding Remi and stroking her hair as her little arms wrapped tight around his neck. "You're safe, baby girl. We're here now."

"Derrick Ellington, you're under arrest. You have the right to remain silent..." We heard from the other side of the room as the FBI agents descended into the room. Ben got up and lifted the door allowing Derrick Ellington to be handcuffed and pulled to his feet.

Both Chase and I sat on the edge of the bed cradling our children, Chase reaching out to pat Dylan's back, while I cradled the back of Remi's soft head. Her long hair was a matted mess.

We were both tearing up, sitting there, holding them close until the two of them started to squirm.

"Are they okay?" Ben asked, towering by the foot of the bed.

"Uncle Ben?" Dylan's head lifted. "You came all this way to rescue me?" He asked incredulously.

"You bet I did, buddy! You and this little lady," he said tenderly, pointing at Remi. "Are you guys alright?"

Dylan shook his head, and Ben sat on the bed next to us, the mattress sinking to accommodate all of our weight. He ran his hands over Dylan's arms and legs gently, then his ribs. Dylan let out a sharp cry.

Sirens ensued, and the parking lot filled with flashing

lights.

"Remi, are you okay, sweetheart?" I asked gently. I wanted to hold her, but Chase was kissing her head and hugging her tight.

"Yeah. That mean man yanked my arm and hit my face! Dylan tried to stop him, but then he got shoved hard into the wall."

I was full of rage, and my eyes ricocheted from Ben's to Chase's. So that was what happened to Dylan's arm. I could see they shared my hatred for this man. The FBI agents were reading Ellington rights.

"Dylan, we're going to get you to the hospital and fixed up as good as new."

"It hurts so bad!" he cried and cried. I felt helpless. All I could do was hold him until the ambulances arrived.

Ben was the only one of us not holding on to a child. "I got this," he said, rising, "for all of us. For the kids." He walked unceremoniously over to the man now in handcuffs. In one smooth motion pulled back his arm and delivered a sucker punch to Ellington's stomach.

Ellington doubled over, grunting as the air rushed from his lungs. He fell, first to his knees and then hard onto the floor. The agents who had been holding onto both of his elbows let go, letting him crash to the floor.

"We are going to nail your ass to the wall, Ellington," Ben said viciously, leaning down to speak to the man he'd just put on the ground. "My nephew has a dislocated shoulder, you son of a bitch! Touch him or any kid again, and I swear as well as I'm breathing, I will put you down like the dog you are. I swear to fucking God!"

Chase and I looked on, pleasantly stunned, as Ben walked over to Agent Daniels and put his hands together ready to be cuffed.

"Shit, I wish I could have done that," Chase admitted.

"Me, too," I agreed.

The agent looked at Ben blankly, glancing down at his offered wrists and then scrubbed down his weary face with one open hand. "What are you doing?"

"Don't you want to arrest me for assault?" Ben asked calmly.

Two of the officers wearing black, holstered their weapons and lifted the still suffering bastard to his feet again, and started to remove him from the room. "Yeah, he assaulted me!" Ellington moaned. "Arrest him."

After he was taken out of the room, Ben still stood there, towering over the shorter man, calmly waiting to be arrested.

"Did you see anything?" Daniel's asked Webster.

The older man shook his head. "Nope. Did you?" He looked at Chase and me.

"See what?" Chase asked, still comforting Remi. "It's okay, baby," he said, kissing her hair.

"The only thing I saw was you guys taking out the trash," I added, my lips lifting in a half grin. Dylan was still whimpering on my lap, and I held him gently, careful not to bump or touch his injured shoulder.

"I knew you'd come, Jensey."

I sighed into his hair, so grateful he was okay. His shoulder and the bruise on Remi's cheek would heal. It could have been so much worse.

Paramedics came in and lifted both of the children from our arms, laying each of them on separate gurneys, and quickly examining them. Chase, Ben, and I stood close by watching. Their small little bodies looked even smaller as they lay there, surrounded by paramedics and police.

"They both are dehydrated and need IV fluids, but since the hospital is only half a mile from here, we won't start a line now."

I went down on my haunches to place a soft kiss on Remi's forehead while the paramedics examined her. She has a nasty purple bruise on her cheek and under her left eye, which was swollen. No punishment Derrick Ellington could suffer, or no amount of prison time would ever be justice enough for what he'd done. I could only hope that he'd get what he deserved.

Chase gave me some space to talk to Remi, and I could hear him promising Dylan he'd take him to the game against Ecuador in Orlando that was coming up in a few weeks.

"Your dad is going to ride with you in the ambulance, sweetheart, so I can ride with Dylan. Is that okay?" I brushed her injured cheek with gentle fingertips. Remi was so precious to me. Chase needed to tell her about her new baby brother and might do so on the short ride to the hospital. She nodded and tried to smile. "You know how much I love you, right?"

"Love you, too," she said. She nodded again. "You know, I was Dylan's damsel, Jensey. Even more than Tommy's," she said.

I smiled broadly, remembering the story she told me a couple of months before about Tommy rescuing her on the playground. Apparently, Tommy was out as her 'boyfriend'. "You are, huh?"

Remi nodded. "Yeah, and even though he didn't have any shiny armor, he was my knight."

I wanted to laugh out loud, but the paramedics were lifting the gurney.

"We were scared, but he told me you and Daddy would come save us from that bad man."

I pictured the scene in my head. Dylan had to have been scared to death, yet he was brave for Remi. Love, unlike any other, filled my heart for both of these perfect little people. "I'll see you at the hospital, baby," I said. "Your mommy is there, waiting, too."

We followed the gurneys out of the motel room, and I watched Chase climb in behind Remi as I waited for them to load Dylan into his ambulance.

"Jensey!" Dylan called weakly.

"I'm here, buddy." I put a hand on his leg; conscious not to touch him anywhere near his shoulder. His injured arm had been placed in a sling to hold the joint still until it could be set back into its socket at the hospital.

I settled in next to him for the short ride to the hospital. He was clearly suffering, and I wondered if he'd been given anything for it. "What will they do to my shoulder?" he asked.

"Well, they'll give you some medicine to make you sleep, and then you'll wake up, and your arm will be fixed," the woman paramedic said. Her name, Shelly, was embroidered on her uniform jacket.

"Will I be well so I can watch Chase play Ecuador?"

I couldn't help but smile, shaking my head. Soccer was all he could think about, even as hurt as he was. "Let's just concentrate on healing, okay?"

"But, will I?" he asked urgently.

"Well, when is that?" Shelly inquired.

"Three weeks from now," I answered.

"Yeah, can I? Chase said I could go on the field with him and sit on the bench with the team!" His eyes filled with tears. "I can't miss it!"

"Wow!" Shelly said, smiling. "You'll have to be good and do everything the doctors tell you, so you heal up. You might still have a sling, though."

"Awww!" he said.

"Just take it easy, little man," I advised. "Going with a sling is better than not going."

"I want us all to go. Can we?"

"Who's all of us?"

"You, mom and me, Remi, Chase, Teagan, and Uncle Ben. My whoooole family!"

A fresh rush of love came over me for this little guy. I wanted to give him and his mom everything they'd never had. "I think we can work it out." I yearned to tell him that Teagan had a new baby boy, but I wanted to make sure Chase had told Remi first. I didn't want to ruin that special moment for them.

We were pulling into the hospital ER entrance, waiting for them to unload Remi from the other ambulance which had arrived in before of us.

"Can mom and me live with you now, Jensey? I don't want my other dad to get me again."

My heart swelled to the point of bursting. "He isn't going to hurt you anymore, Dylan. We're going to make sure of it, okay?"

"I don't want to see him anymore. He's a bad man."

"A very bad man, but a lot of good men love you, Dylan." I didn't want the little boy to feel bad because his real father was so awful. "Chase, Ben and me. You've got all of us."

Dylan's blue eyes met mine, imploring. "Jensey, do you think you could be my real dad?" Incredulity made me speechless. "Cuz… well… I just feel that way, okay?"

Shelly's head turned to glance my direction. She smiled softly, both of her hands crossing over her heart. "Awww," she mouthed silently.

I nodded; my eyes clouding over with emotion. I blinked, wishing I could hug him tight. "I'd love nothing more than to call you my son… son." My throat was very tight, restricting my words and as I tried to clear it before I continued, blinking rapidly to stop myself from tearing up at the same time. "Ugghghghg. We have to ask your mom, though."

Dylan smiled the brightest smile I think I'd ever seen. I

found myself wishing, more than anything, that I'd be able to adopt Dylan someday.

"Cool! Can I have your last name, too?"

I swallowed hard, dabbing at the tear in the corner of my eye as manly as I could manage. "I think Dylan Jeffers has a certain ring to it. I'll do whatever I can to make that happen, okay?"

"Cool!" he said again, his exuberance was contagious. "Does that mean I get to call Chase, Uncle Chase?" His eyes flashed with excitement.

I laughed out loud, nodding my head in the affirmative. "I think he'd be down with that. I absolutely do."

The ambulance doors opened, and another paramedic appeared to start pulling Dylan's gurney out.

Shelly put her hand on my arm to stop me for a moment. Her eyes filled with tears. "He's absolutely precious. He obviously adores you. It's plain as the nose on your face. You are one lucky guy."

Chills ran over my entire body as her words sank in. "I know. I feel like the luckiest man on earth today."

She gave me a wink, and then I hopped out of the ambulance to follow my son into the ER entrance.

Chapter 22

Missy

We were both so relieved.

Teagan and I had melted into a puddle of hysterical tears when Ben texted that they had the kids and that Chase and Jensen were riding to the hospital with the children and so couldn't let us know themselves.

Dylan and Remi were both given IV fluids in the ER. My son was given IV pain meds before the procedure to put his shoulder back into place, and thankfully, it hadn't worn off. We'd just gotten home, and Jensen had placed his sleeping form into his bed in our new apartment.

It didn't feel like home, having spent most of my time in Atlanta staying with Jensen, or Chase and Teagan.

Dylan would be very sore for a while, but he'd fully heal in time. He wasn't happy that he had to wear the sling for a few weeks, but Chase had placated him by agreeing to arrange for the entire family to fly to Orlando for his soccer game with Ecuador and spend some time at Disney World.

I was grateful that Derrick hadn't hurt him even more than he had. It was horrible to think of the terrible pain my son had gone through when he was thrown against the motel room wall. The hatred I had for Derrick before only burned deeper inside me, now.

I cried through a laugh when Remi told me how Dylan stepped in front of her, screaming at Derrick to stop him from hitting her again. It was hard for me to listen to the description of the scene because it played out in slow motion inside my mind. Teagan and I shared a proud motherly moment when Remi told us that Dylan was going to be her prince forever and ever after.

"What about Tommy?" I'd asked.

She'd lifted her little shoulder in a half-shrug. "Well, he's gonna need to understand, I guess. He's still my friend, but Dylan saved me bigger than him."

"I guess that's that, then," Teagan said, hugging her little daughter close. "Dylan is really special."

"Yep!" Remi agreed.

I couldn't stop smiling after that. It was so incredible, and I was happy that Dylan had Remi. She really helped him settle into the new school and make the transition from Jackson Hole easier, even if they'd argued a little at first.

Now, Chase was with Teagan and their new baby at the hospital, while Remi was staying with Chase's family at their home. His parents, brother, and sister had all rushed to Atlanta when they'd heard about Remi and Dylan's kidnapping. They wanted to see with their own eyes that the kids were safe and to meet the new edition to the Forrester line, little Mace. After meeting the entire clan, I had a better understanding of why Chase and Teagan needed such a huge house.

Ben was flying back to Jackson Hole in a couple of days, but not until our mother arrived tomorrow. She was cutting her "vacation" short and was adamant about spending time with Ben before he left Atlanta. Her main concern was my son, of course, but she hadn't seen my brother in more than a year, so naturally, that was important to her.

Ben was sleeping on the couch, and I was laying up against Jensen in my bed, snuggled under the covers, with my head on his chest. It was the middle of the afternoon, but we'd all been up all night and were exhausted. This was my happy and safe place; close to Jensen.

"Thank you," I said into the silent and dimly lit room. I was tracing figure eights on Jensen's bare chest, and my leg hooked over his. One of his strong hands was holding my thigh, and the other held my head; his fingers playing in my hair.

Jensen turned his head toward mine and brushed a soft kiss on my forehead, his lips lingering. "For what?"

"For rescuing Dylan. For just… being here for me. Always. It means a lot to me."

His breath rushed warmly over my skin as he spoke. "No need to thank me," he said sleepily. "I love you."

My fingers stopped their teasing motion, and I slid my arm around his defined abs. I gave him a squeeze. "I love you, too. So much, Jensen."

"I'd be making love to you right now if I weren't so dead tired."

"And, if Ben wasn't in the other room," I murmured, feeling sad that we couldn't, but also sad that he had to leave in a few hours.

"That, too." Jensen agreed.

When Remi and Dylan had come into the hospital in the middle of the night, we'd focused on them. Jensen didn't have much time to tell me what happened when the children were found, though he did explain how the three of them accompanied Agent Daniels and how they caught Derrick. I guess Ben had given him quite the smack down in the middle of the flashing lights; in front of several FBI agents and local law enforcement officers. Jensen and Chase were laughing when they related the story of how my brother had fully expected to be arrested for the assault but didn't give a damn. Leave it to Ben.

"Maybe in Orlando," I said regretfully. It was Sunday and Jensen would be flying to Bristol to do his Sunday and Monday night NFL shows.

"What's wrong?" He shifted in the bed, turning to face me and pulling me into his arms. He kept my leg over his body, now resting over his hip. It was a provocative position, and something deep within me stirred. His eyes opened, and he stroked my hair back.

"I'm sad you have to leave soon, that's all."

He bent to place a series of soft, deliciously tempting kisses on my mouth. It wasn't long before we were breathing hard and his hips were thrusting involuntarily into mine, his hand on my thigh, slid higher to my bottom, pulling my hips closer to his. "Mmmm...." he moaned. "Do you think we can be quiet? I want you so much, baby."

"It feels like forever since you touched me..." I breathed out against his mouth, the tip of my tongue sneaking out to lick his top lip.

"Four days," he breathed in between kisses, and then his mouth opened more forcefully over mine. I gave him full access to its warm recesses.

I could feel him harden, his dick involuntarily bobbing against me, and pressing into my leg. We weren't naked in case Dylan called out and needed one of us, but in that instant, I was regretting it. Jensen had on sweats, and I was wearing a pair of short pajamas. Jensen pushed my top up to wrap one warm hand over the fullness of my breast, lightly kneading, his index finger and thumb gently tugging on my nipple. Instantly, I felt my body open as desire shot through me. I let out a wanton sigh and bit my lip.

He rolled me underneath him in one swift move and

buried his mouth in the curve of my neck at the same time as he pushed his hips into the cradle of mine. "What do you think? Can you be quiet?"

"Me?" I said softly, laughing.

"Sure. You know how you get." Jensen chuckled softly, still torturing me with pleasure as his mouth continued with soft licks and gentle sucking on the sensitive skin of my neck. He pulled the neckline of my shirt aside to gain access to my shoulder, slowly grinding and rubbing his lower body with mine. I could feel myself start to bloom, opening like a flower. His body pressing into me creating the delicious friction we both craved, despite both layers of clothing between us.

"How do I get?" I couldn't help but ask.

His mouth swooped and took mine in a deeply passionate kiss. My body arched and my I pulled my knees up higher, seeking more of the incredible pressure as he sank down further, closer into me. The combination of his movements against me and his softly sucking mouth had me melting.

"All soft and warm," he whispered against my neck. "So irresistible."

"I'm glad I warrant your attention," I panted, praying to God he wasn't going to prolong the torture. I was starving for his touch; to have his body inside mine, his mouth on my skin, teasing, tasting. The thought alone fueled my response.

"Mmmmmm...." A soft moan escaped his mouth as it closed around the peak of one tender breast and his hand snaked between us to massage the place where I wanted him the most.

"Clothes are overrated," he whispered. He continued to thrust against me, rubbing his rock-hard length against the crease of my hip and thigh while his fingers worked their magic on my uber sensitive flesh. "But I can still make you come, at least."

My hands slid down his muscular back to his firm buns and my fingers grasped around his tight ass through his sweats.

My body was humming, my hips rising to meet the rhythm of his fingers, but my mind protested. "Jensen..." I whimpered.

"God, I love hearing my name on that sweet mouth." His tone was guttural, and his breathing was getting harder. "Sweet Jesus," he groaned. His forehead had dropped to my shoulder, but I wanted his mouth on mine again.

One heel dug into his solid calves, and the other slid higher as we moved. I surged against him as we clung together, thrusting and building the pleasure between us. I closed my eyes against the combination of pleasure and pain. I loved him so much. He was so beautiful; body and soul. I couldn't stop looking into his gorgeous face. He filled my entire being; I wished I could absorb him into me. I reached my hand to feel the soft scruff populating his unshaven jawline. He was so incredible that I had no words to describe him.

"Let me touch you," I begged. His weight was heavy upon me, but there was enough space created by his hand and wrist between us for my hand to join his, slipping inside his tented sweats. My fingers closed around the shaft of his rock-hard penis begging for release. I moved my hand up and down, my thumb moving over the head. The soft material was already damp as precum pooled.

"Missy, stop," he pleaded. "I'll come, and we'll have a mess."

"It's okay. I want you to," I panted, close to the edge myself. "Huh, huh, huh... uhhhh." I couldn't breathe, but I wanted him to kiss me. "Kiss me."

He granted my wish, and as we kissed over and over, both of us pleasuring the other as silently as we both could manage. My orgasm began to build slowly and finally crashed over, my body surging with wave upon wave of ecstasy. My fingers threaded through his hair as I convulsed around him, my insides shuttering as the shocks of pleasure moved through me.

Jensen rolled off of me and put his hand inside his sweats to keep the mess to a minimum, but I regretted he didn't let me finish him to the end of his orgasm. He moaned, burying his face in the pillow and side of my neck and his body convulsed with the power of his own climax. I reached up to tangle my fingers in the silky hair at the back of his head.

"Shit," he sighed heavily when he finished.

"Are you okay?" I was so full of love for this man that I could barely speak. I closed my eyes, my arms tightening around his muscular back, my fingers stroking his skin lovingly.

"Other than a handful of jizz, I'm great," he said, his voice was slightly amused.

"You didn't have to do that. Catch it, I mean."

He huffed in amusement and climbed out of bed, going into the ensuite bathroom to clean himself up. "No worries," he said flipping on the light. I'd pulled the black-out shades, and the room that had been dark was suddenly flooded with a beam of light.

"Mommy?" Dylan called from the other room. His voice sounded frightened.

I jumped out of bed as simultaneously Jensen's head popped out from around the corner of the doorjamb; his expression filled with concern.

"I'll go," I said, throwing on my robe over my skimpy pajamas. I'd have to change them, too, after I made sure my little boy was okay.

"Tell him to remember that promise I made to him… I'll make it happen, but he needs to keep it a secret, just between us."

"What promise?" I asked, curious.

"It's between us," he said wryly. "Dylan and me."

My brow wrinkled quizzically. "Really?"

"Yep," Jensen dismissed, coming out of the bathroom

and crawling back into my bed.

"Mommy! Mommy!"

"Go," Jensen commanded gently.

Dylan had been calling me Mom pretty much all the time, so it was clear that he was traumatized from the events of the last day and a half. I ran from the room and Ben, who had been sleeping on the sofa, met me in the hall and flipped on the light. "Is he okay?"

I put a flat hand on my brother's chest. "He'll be fine in time. You go back to bed."

"Are you sure?"

"Yes. I'll let him know you'll be here to play with him when he's rested."

"Okay. Tell him I'll read him a book," Ben said. "Or we can watch the Avengers, again."

"Okay," I said absently, already on my way to my son's room. The hall light illuminated the room enough for me to see Dylan sitting up in bed, the white sling stark against the darkened room. "Hey, honey," I said, moving to the side of the bed and kneeling down. "What's wrong?" I reached for the lamp by his bedside and switched it on. "Did you have a bad dream?"

There were tears on his face as he nodded. I brushed his hair back and wiped at his tears with my fingers. I wanted to gather him close against me, but I didn't want to hurt him. "Yeah. That man..." he looked at me with sad eyes. "Do I have to call him Dad?"

My heart dropped to my stomach, but I shook my head. "No, honey." I didn't know if I should ask him for the details of the dream because I didn't want him to relive it.

"He was so mean. He hurt Remi and me," he cried, almost sobbing and my heart broke into a million pieces.

Gently, I moved up next to Dylan on the side of the bed, sitting down, but trying not to jostle him. I put an arm around him, careful not to touch his injury. He leaned onto me, and I turned my face to kiss his forehead. "I know, baby, but the police put him in jail, and he won't be able to hurt you anymore. Or Remi."

He was sitting, hunched against the pillows but his chin lifted, and he met my eyes. "Or you, either?"

"Nope," I said keeping a happy tone in my voice. "So, you don't have to worry or have any more bad dreams, okay?"

Dylan nodded and put a little hand to his injured shoulder, but the fear eased from his eyes. "How long until I'm better? Uncle Chase said we're going to see his next game."

"Uncle Chase?" I asked, my brows rising.

"Yep," he said proudly. "He said Uncle Ben can come, too, you know? So he's not jealous or anything."

"I know! You have a lot to look forward to! I'm sure Uncle Ben would love to come if he can get away from work, sweetheart. He said he'd read to you or watch that superhero movie you love when you're feeling up to it."

"The Avengers!" Dylan perked up. "That one?"

"That's right," I agreed, stroking his hair with one hand. I was sitting up against the headboard of the twin bed with my son, who was curled into me, on his good side. "And Jensen asked me to tell you he'd keep the promise he made, but it's a secret. Just between you and Jensen."

"I know," Dylan said, not surprised. His response had me more curious than ever. "A promise is a promise."

I smiled, but my eyebrows shot upward again. I was in heaven that he trusted Jensen so much. "What is it?" Curiosity got the better of me.

"I can't tell, Mom!" Dylan said incredulously. "It's a secret."

I sighed through a smile. "Jensen, Ben, and Chase were so anxious to find you and Remi. They all love you so much."

"I know," he said, equally nonplussed. "We figured Jensey and Chase would come, but then Uncle Ben was there, too! That was awesome!"

I huffed out a small laugh. "I know! See how special you are?"

"Yup! Can we go see Remi's new brother?"

"Maybe we can later, honey. After you sleep a bit more, have some dinner, and feel better. Maybe tomorrow would be better."

Chase wheeled Teagan down to the ER, and after Remi had been examined, the three of them had come in to see Dylan following the procedure to reset his shoulder. Her injury wasn't as severe, and they had all waited for Dylan to wake up from his sedation.

"Wasn't it cool how we got to pick Mace's name? Even though Remi was sad the baby wasn't a sister."

"Yes," I leaned down to kiss the top his head, remembering. "I was happy she shared that with you."

The ER only allowed two visitors at a time, but Remi had been a patient minutes earlier, so they allowed the exception. She sat on Teagan's lap in the wheelchair while Chase and Jensen had gone out to the waiting room.

Remi pouted a little after she found out the baby was a boy but cheered up when Teagan reminded her that she could help name him. Dylan had asked if he could help, too, and Remi and Teagan had readily agreed.

"Mommy wants it to sound like Daddy's name, okay babe?" Teagan coaxed.

"Like Chase?" Remi asked.

"Okay, but it can't be Ace cuz that's what he's called by his fans," Dylan had piped up.

"That's a good point, Dylan." Teagan smiled at me, then winked. Happiness shrouded the room; such a stark difference from the terror we felt only two hours earlier.

"So, how do we choose?" he asked.

"We can go through the alphabet." Remi was matter-of-fact. "We just put different letters in the front!"

"Well, that's very smart, Remi!" I said.

"That sounds like a plan, but we still have to pass it by Daddy, okay?" Teagan put in.

Both of the kids nodded in unison then proceeded to begin spouting off names left and right.

"Bace?" Dylan began, but they both wrinkled their noses.

"We gotta skip C cuz that's my daddy's name already. Dace?"

Teagan shook her head. "Let's skip e," she put in. "That won't rhyme well."

"Face!" Dylan's enthusiasm made him forget the sling on his arm. During his procedure, the medical staff had injected a local anesthetic to give a few hours of pain relief, and I was grateful.

Remi and Dylan both burst out giggling.

"No," Remi said. "Gace?"

"Hace!"

They both shook their heads in unison. Teagan made a mock motion of wiping the sweat off of her head as we both enjoyed our children's enthusiasm for the task. "Whew!"

"Jace!" Remi said, but then she frowned. "That's my stupid cousin's name."

"Remi," Teagan reprimanded.

"Well, he's mean!"

"I'll talk to Aunt Kat about that, okay?"

It seemed to appease her, and she and Dylan continued through the alphabet until they arrived at M.

"How about Mace?" Dylan asked

"I think that sounds good," Remi agreed.

"Yeah!" Dylan agreed. "That's a good name!"

Teagan nodded, and I agreed. "I agree! It sounds sweet," I said.

"Sweet?" Dylan protested. "It sounds cool!"

Chase loved the name the children had chosen, and it was just one more confirmation that Teagan and Chase, Remi and Jensen, had made Dylan and I a real part of their family.

"Baby Mace will be fun. He's so cute. Wait until you meet him," I said.

Dylan waited a beat before asking; "Will he be Jensey's little boy, too?"

I inhaled and considered my answer carefully. "Well.... Jensey, Chase, Teagan, and Remi are family, so I think he'll treat Mace the same as he treats Remi."

"Oh." He sounded disappointed. "Okay."

"Babe, what's wrong?" I kissed his head again. "Jensey loves you. Doesn't he make you feel like you're just like Remi?"

"Yeah," he said, his expression still sad. I hoped my next sentence would cheer him up.

"Well, I think you're special to Jensey because of your secret, right?"

"He didn't tell you, did he?"

"Only that two of you had a secret."

"Did he tell you what it was?" he asked accusingly, his brow furrowing deeply.

I shook my head. "Then it wouldn't be a secret," I soothed.

"He made me a promise," Dylan divulged with a smile. It seemed he was so excited about it, he couldn't keep it inside.

"He did?" My son nodded. "Well, I know he loves you, sweet pea."

"Really?"

"Yes."

Instantly, Dylan's face broke out into a big smile. "Really?" he asked again.

"Definitely!" I assured him. "I don't know what the secret is, or what the promise was, but you said Jensey always keeps his promises, right?" My son nodded. "So, this one will be no different!" I bent to whisper. "But, can you give me a hint?"

Dylan grinned, bigger now. "No way!"

I ruffled his hair. "Are you hungry?"

Before Dylan could answer, Jensen knocked on the door jam. Dressed in business casual, he was ready for his plane ride to work. My heart fell a little that he had to leave and would be gone for the next two days.

"Hey, buddy. I have to go to work, but I'll see you first thing on Tuesday morning."

"Awwww!" my son lamented. "Do ya hafta go to work today?"

"Yeah, I have to. Your mom missed work this weekend, so someone has to make the donuts," Jensen joked. "Besides, you've got Uncle Ben to keep you busy, and your grandma will be here soon, too!"

"I know." Disappointment was written all over my son.

As Jensen came into the room, I got up from the bed so he could take my place next to Dylan. "Listen, I'm going to fix you something to eat," I said moving to the doorway of the room. It was like the two of them didn't hear a word I said so I lingered to watch the interaction between them.

The light from the lamp put a golden glow on both of them, and I was in awe at the admiration and hero-worship I saw on my son's young face.

"You won't be back at school on Tuesday, and I don't have to work, so we'll go out for a while, okay? We'll get lunch and make an afternoon of it." Jensen nudged Dylan's chin. "Spend the day."

"Just you and me?" Dylan asked hopefully.

"For sure." I watched the man I love nod, and then glance over his shoulder to find me hovering. He bent to whisper something in Dylan's ear. Apparently, it was what he wanted to hear.

"Yeah! Awesome!"

JENSEN

"This one?" I asked. Dylan was sitting on my lap, and we were looking at a tray of engagement rings.

I'd narrowed it down to three styles, and then I let Dylan make the final choice. We'd gone out to lunch and then to an arcade at one of the local malls. We'd had a great time eating and playing the racing games, and anything else we could find that Dylan could manage with one hand, at the arcade. He was anxious to get to the real reason for our outing.

Even though Missy and I had only known each other for a few months, there was no doubt in my mind that I wanted to marry her and raise the little guy sitting on my lap. Last Sunday, just before I'd left for the airport, I'd told him I needed his help to pick out the engagement ring for his mom so that I could be his real dad.

Dylan beamed from ear-to-ear, and Missy had looked on, perplexed. Dylan had gone from sad to excited in the matter of mere seconds. I knew our secret was driving his mother crazy, but that would make the surprise all the better in the end.

Derrick Ellington was being held without bail under federal kidnapping charges while Ben's law enforcement connection investigated the murder of Missy's lawyer up in Jackson Hole. The district attorney assured us that the kidnapping was an open and shut case and that it would be easy to have Ellington's parental rights severed. I couldn't wait for that day because it would be the day that I'd start the legal proceedings to adopt Dylan.

Chase and Teagan's new baby was adorable, and I knew that Remi would cherish him despite her earlier rants that she didn't want a brother. He looked just like her, and my friend was puffed up like a peacock.

Teagan was released from the hospital before her son due to the baby being premature, but he would be out soon. We were planning a family dinner in a week because Mace would be home by then. Remi and Dylan were clamoring to meet Mace, but the hospital restricted children from visiting the NICU. Jean had arrived, and Ben had flown back to Jackson Hole. Chase's mother was still in Atlanta to help Teagan when the baby came home, and to help care for Remi. Teagan adored her mother-in-law, and the feeling was mutual.

"Yup! I think mom would love that one!" He picked up the ring he'd just pointed to and held it out for my inspection.

The salesman told us that the cushion cut diamond was one of the more unique styles. It was a rounded square and was certified colorless and flawless. It was about three-quarters of a carat, but I decided that Missy would rather have a more perfect stone than a larger, less pristine diamond. Especially if Dylan helped pick it out. The end result was a beautiful ring, and Dylan and I devised a plan on exactly how we wanted to give it to her, too.

"Wrap it up." I smiled, handing it to the man behind the counter.

"Excellent choice, gentlemen." He leaned down to Dylan, who was perched on a tall stool peering down into the jewelry case. "I'm sure your mom is going to love it."

When we had the ring boxed and bagged, and were walking out of the mall, Dylan slid his little hand in mine. I felt a rush of love for him as my fingers closed around his smaller ones. He'd had such a shitty time, and I made it my personal objective to make sure his life was much better going forward.

"I love you, Jensey."

Dylan's little voice saying those words as he looked up at me with his sweet round face, really choked me up. "I love you, too."

"Will Remi be mad if I call you dad and she doesn't?" he asked seriously.

I shook my head. "No, I don't think so. Chase is her dad. She's always called me Jensey."

Dylan considered this as we walked through the mall, out of the double doors, and into the parking lot. My SUV was parked a few rows away and a bit back from the building. "But I call you Jensey, too."

"Yes, but when your mom and I get married, I'll be your dad."

"My real dad?"

"Yep," I assured him. "We'll go in front of a nice judge, and he or she will have us sign some papers and ask me if I promise to take care of you and love you forever, and of course, I will, and that will be that."

Dylan considered my answer for a minute or two as we walked. "Well, when can I call you Dad, though?"

I bent to pick him up, positioning him on my hip as I walked. I held my keys and the ring bag in the other hand, positioning the little boy on my hip and holding him there with one arm. His good arm slipped around my neck. "Any time you want. I've thought of you as my little boy for a long time now."

"Sometimes you just know stuff," Dylan said as we approached the car.

"That's right," I said, my eyes starting to burn, but a smile playing on my lips.

"Let's just hurry and ask your mom, so it doesn't have to be a secret for very long."

"You wanna tell everybody?" he asked, beaming.

I nodded. "Yep. Everybody in the whole world!"

I pushed the remote key to my car, and it honked indicating it was unlocked as we arrived at it. I pulled the back door open and settled Dylan into the booster seat I'd gotten for him shortly after I'd met his mom. I could speak as I buckled him in.

As I slid into the driver's seat and started the engine to head back to my house where Missy was meeting us later, Dylan kept chattering. "Can we ask her tonight, Dad?" he asked.

My heart filled with happiness. This was the first time anyone had ever called me Dad, and it couldn't have meant more coming from anyone else. I still loved Remi with all my heart, but I realized that I loved Dylan just as much. Both of them had been through hell, and they were still such special, amazing kids. I felt very fortunate.

"What about our plan?" I asked. We planned to fly to one of the games Missy was commentating on and ask her live on the jumbotron when she didn't know we were there. I still had to set it up, but it would be easy to work out with whatever teams were playing the day we decided on. "It's a good plan."

He shrugged with his good shoulder. "I don't wanna wait that long. Is that okay?"

"Sure," I answered a bit hesitantly. I thought I had the perfect idea to make it something Missy would never forget, but I understood Dylan's desire to do it more quickly. Waiting was going to be agony for me, too.

"Can we ask her tonight after dinner?" I glanced in the rearview mirror, and he was yawning. He needed a nap while I got ready for dinner and did the cooking. Missy was working until six.

"Well, sure, but then I think we should have something better than spaghetti, don't you?"

"I love psghetti. We can have meatballs. That makes it better."

I chuckled. Life was so simple when you were six.

"Okay. I'll make meatballs." I didn't know exactly how to

do it, but I hoped I could find instructions or a recipe on Google or YouTube.

"Can we make those yummy peanut butter crispy treats, too?"

I silently inventoried the ingredients I had on hand to see if I needed to stop at the store on the way home. Butter, marshmallows, peanut butter and crisp rice cereal. I had all of it. "Yeah, we can make them if you want to."

"Then we can dig a hole in Mom's and put the ring in it, okay?"

I smiled so hard the dimples in my cheeks started to ache. "Sounds like we have a new plan."

* * *

It was almost six-thirty, and Missy would be here any minute. Dylan was sitting at the small kitchen table next to me as I carved a groove into the top of the dessert we'd made together before his nap.

I didn't want to cut them into bars yet because they'd dry out, but I couldn't very well make a ditch in one to accommodate the ring with Missy looking on. I'd managed to find hundreds of recipes for meatballs and found the one marked easy with the most reviews and the most stars. I'd tasted one, and they were a tad rubbery for my taste, but Dylan gave them his stamp of approval.

"Do you think your mom will say yes?" I grunted as I dug the point of the knife into the sticky treats again after trying to insert the ring shank and finding it wasn't quite wide enough to hold it.

"Oh, yeah," he said casually. "She loves ya, a lot."

"She does, huh?" I laughed out loud, eyeing him. I was certain she did, but this might be too fast for her after the horrible marriage she'd had before.

He nodded, reaching for the glass of water I'd gotten for him when he woke up.

The front door started to open. Missy had a key, but I'd left it open for her. Dylan and I both scrambled to hide the evidence. He jumped off of his chair, and I shoved the pan of dessert into the microwave. He snatched the ring box from the table, and I slipped the ring into the front pocket of my jeans.

Missy looked beautiful in her business suit; her hair was swept up into a loose knot and tendrils framed her beautiful face. She looked more gorgeous than she had in a while; the stress of her ex-husband neutralized and her face had taken on her former serene glow.

"What's all this? My two men making me dinner? Wow!" she beamed at Dylan, and I walked over, slipped my arm around her waist and planted a kiss soundly on her luscious mouth.

"Yeah. We're having psghetti, garlic bread, and meatballs!" Dylan exclaimed. His cheeks were rosy, and I could tell he was bursting at the seams to tell her what was up.

She turned to put her purse down in the other room, and I put a finger to my mouth silently asking Dylan to keep our big secret.

"No salad?" she asked skeptically looking at the table and the stove.

I pulled a large bowl of microgreens with tomatoes out of the refrigerator and plopped them on the set table. It was one of those bagged salads, but what the hell? It was green. "What do you have to say about that?" I challenged.

"Awww! Do I hafta eat it?" Dylan bemoaned.

"Yes," Missy affirmed. "You can't live on meat and carbs."

"How come? That's the stuff that tastes good."

I rolled my eyes. We both laughed as Missy reached for

the glass of red wine that I'd just poured for her. "He's right, you know," I agreed.

"Great. Just what I need; two against one." She cocked her head and widened her eyes, silently warning me not to encourage Dylan's abhorrence of vegetables.

Dylan grinned and plopped back down in his chair, looking up at me expectantly. "Let's eat now, kay?"

Missy's eyes met mine. I scooted Dylan's chair closer to the table and then moved to hold the one to Dylan's right out for her. She sat down at the table, and I seated myself across from her with Dylan between us.

The truth was, I was nervous. More nervous than I'd realized.

"Did you Facetime Remi today, Dylan? Did she tell you what you've missed at school?"

The dinner conversation ensued as normal, we decided that after his follow-up doctor's appointment and if the doctor cleared it, he wanted to return to school as soon as possible. She asked about our day, we related about our time at the arcade.

Missy told me about her upcoming game in St. Louis, and Dylan went on and on about Chase's game in Orlando next month.

Missy cut his food into manageable bites, which he ate very fast, even for a six-year-old who wanted to get to dessert.

"For goodness sake, Dylan!" Missy scolded as he shoved the last few bites into his mouth. "What's gotten into you?"

"I want dessert!" he said, with his mouth full. "I even ate the green stuff."

I tried to hold back a laugh but didn't quite manage.

"Well, you're not going to have dessert if you act like a little piggy," she admonished.

I took a sip from my wine glass just observing, then refilled both hers and mine with the deep burgundy wine. "Aw, come on, Mom. Lighten up a little!" I said, then took a long swallow, my eyes locking with hers. She was sexy as hell, and her come hither expression excited me for what I knew would come later in the evening. "We had a good day today. He's just happy."

"Happy?" she asked incredulously. "He's going to throw up if he's not careful."

Once again, I grinned. "Dylan helped make the dessert."

"Oh? What is it?"

"It's a surprise. Can we get it now?" Dylan looked at me expectantly.

I smiled and nodded. Instantly the little boy got up from his chair and scurried into the kitchen.

"Dylan be careful! If you fall, you could hurt your shoulder!" Missy called.

I placed a calming hand on Missy's shoulder after I rose from my chair, then gave it a slight squeeze. "Relax. He's fine."

"Do you need any help?"

"Yes, I need help. But not with the dessert," I winked at her. "Later."

She smiled like the sun, and I bent to give her a deep, lingering kiss before I heard the microwave door slam hard from the kitchen.

"I better get in there while I still have a kitchen. We'll be right back." I touched the silky skin of her chin with my thumb, before leaving to follow him.

When I got into the other room, Dylan had pulled one of the kitchen chairs over in front of the stove and climbed on top of it. How he'd managed to do it with one arm in a sling, I had no idea, but he was determined.

"Hey, wait a second." I lifted the glass pan down, and we soon had the crispy treats cut and placed on individual plates.

I retrieved the ring from my pocket and placed it in the groove I'd made before. It sat perfectly perched as if in a ring box. Dylan beamed.

"Can I take it to Mom? Can I ask her?" Dylan was wired, nearly bouncing out of his skin. "Can I? Please?"

It wasn't the most conventional of proposals, but I couldn't deny him. "Sure," I said, keeping the tenor of my voice low so Missy wouldn't overhear. "Do you think you can do it without dropping it? You only have one hand right now, buddy."

"Yes. I can do it! I won't drop it; I promise!" Excitement radiated out of him, and his beaming smile said it all.

"Okay, but let me set yours and mine down first, and then I can kneel down beside you before you ask her, okay? It's important to kneel on one knee."

"Okay!" He threw his unconfined arm around me and hugged my neck tight.

I held him close and kissed the top of his head. "Let's do this." I held out a hand, and he slapped it as hard as he could.

He nodded enthusiastically, his blue eyes shining. "Let's do this!" He repeated.

I inhaled deeply to settle myself, and then took the two plates without the ring and walked in before Dylan.

Missy was waiting; watching me curiously as I sat first one, then the other plate down on the table. I was acutely aware of the little boy standing behind me so that Missy couldn't see him or the plate he was balancing on one hand. "Whatever happened to ladies first?"

"Well, there are times for that, but this isn't one of them." I smiled, taking in the curve of her face, her soft smile, and sparkling eyes. This was the last time I'd ever propose to anyone, and I wanted to commit every second of it to memory.

I stepped aside, and Dylan stood there; balancing her plate on one hand. "Put the plate on the table, Dylan," I said softly, then knelt before his mother.

Missy's eyes widened and her eyes filled with tears.

"Mom..." Dylan said as soon as the plate was safely on the dining room table, the ring sparkling in the center of the crispy treat. He looked at how I was kneeling, then he copied me, but used the opposite knee, catching his mistake and quickly correcting it. He wobbled a bit, and I steadied him with one hand on his back.

When he was kneeling, too, he blurted; "Mom, can Jensey be my dad?"

Both of Missy's hands flew to her cheeks as tears spilled over. I couldn't believe the words I just heard. Not; "Will you marry Jensey?" but "Can Jensey be my dad?" Nothing had ever sounded so beautiful to me. I held my hand out; waiting for Missy to place her left hand in mine.

I reached for the ring and waited.

Her eyes closed, and she cried as if her life depended on it.

"What the matter? Aren't you happy?" Dylan was perplexed.

She nodded, opening her eyes finally. "Very happy!"

'Well?" Dylan demanded. "Why are you crying, then? Jeez, Mom. We planned this out and everything. Can Jensey be my dad, or not?" He waited with wide eyes.

She laughed through her tears, as I smiled up into her beautiful face, my own eyes starting to blur.

"I love you, so much. I love your son. Will you both be mine?" I could hear the tremor in my voice as I said the words.

"Yes!" she said, and I slipped the sparkling diamond on her finger. "Oh, my God! Yes!"

Missy slipped off of her chair and down to the floor to take her place beside Dylan and me. I enfolded both of them in a tight embrace.

"I'm so happy," Missy cried. "I love you both, so, so much."

I wanted to kiss her hard, but I was still holding Dylan between us, and I was conscious of his injured arm. He solved the problem.

"Is it okay if I go Facetime Remi? Mom?" he looked back at us. "Dad? I wanna tell her!"

I flashed a smile, and Missy melted into more tears.

"And so… it begins," I said. "Yes! Go Facetime Remi!"

As our son ran down the hall to find his iPad, and I kissed his mother breathless.

Epilogue

Missy

The crowd went wild!

Remi and Dylan were standing in their seats jumping up and down and shouting. Teagan and I were seated with the little ones between us. Jensen was to my left and Ben to his. He'd flown to Orlando for the weekend, and to all of our delight, so did Chase's parents and both of his siblings, Kat and Kevin, with their families. The location of the game was the perfect excuse to take a week-long family vacation at Disney World.

Teagan had the baby strapped to the front of her body in one of those baby carriers and sweet, adorable Mace, was blissfully asleep against his mother's chest despite the endless crowd yelling and the visceral chanting for Chase at high decibels all around us. He was precious. Little cherub cheeks and a full head of soft dark hair, and Chase's green eyes.

"Ace! Ace! Ace! Ace!" We all happily joined in the chant that echoed the entire stadium. "Ace! Ace! Ace!"

Chase was passed the ball, and he took it a few yards down the field only to kick it back to one of his teammates as they worked it masterfully down the field. The score was tied; 2-2, and the mood was tense. It had been an amazing game, but now, all eyes were glued to the field which was teaming with the yellow uniforms from the Ecuadorian team that contrasted starkly with the striking red, white and blue of the USMNT. It was like eleven American flags were running up and down the field, with twenty or so more on the sidelines, but everyone was watching one man. The stands of Orlando City Stadium was filled to the brim with red, white and blue, and our group fit right in.

We all watched, speechless, as the clock wound down to mere seconds. The ball passed to Chase one last time. The entire game was riding on these final seconds. I'd never been to a more exciting sporting event. The ball flew through the air toward Chase, who launched himself up to back-kick the ball right into the goal. He landed hard on his back, but then rolled over and onto his feet, raising both fists into the air. Within seconds his teammates converged on him and hoisted him into the air, to the delight of the crowd. Everyone was shouting.

Remi and Dylan screamed at the top of their lungs and clapping like crazy, their little faces flushed with exuberance. We were all so happy.

"Yeah!" Ben yelled. "That was frickin' amazing! Ahhhmaaazing!"

"Oh, my God!" I said, leaning into Jensen. "I think I might like soccer more than the NFL," I yelled, so he could hear me. The pace was certainly faster, that was for sure.

Teagan was holding both arms up and clapping over her head unconsciously rocking her baby at the same time. I couldn't help but envy her. I wanted my own little one, and it turned out, I wouldn't have that long to wait. I glanced down at my beautiful engagement ring as it glittered in the sun, sending rainbows of light coming off the brilliant diamond and shooting them off in all directions.

I'd gone on the pill right after I'd started having feelings for Jensen, but not before we made love for the first time. That was too long ago to be when we'd conceived, but I knew no form of birth control is one hundred percent effective.

I'd puked my guts out in the trash can under my desk three times last week, and instantly, I knew. I went to my OBGYN this past Monday, and she confirmed what I already knew. The ultrasound showed a healthy fetus only about three weeks gestation. It looked like a bean on the screen of the machine. I was lucky I had morning sickness early, so the continued use of the pills wouldn't harm the baby's development.

I was excited, longing to tell Jensen my news, but I'd hoped for the perfect moment. I'd shared with Teagan who was ecstatic, going on and on how we'd have two sets of kids of similar age who could play together, grow up together and how nothing could be more perfect! She assured me that Jensen would be over the moon and told me how she'd dropped the bomb about her pregnancy to Chase at the altar, and I didn't think I could wait that long to tell him. Jensen and I hadn't even set a date because we'd only been engaged a few weeks, though we weren't planning to make it an overly long engagement.

Jensen put his house on the market, and we were going to purchase a larger one, closer to Chase and Teagan, together. My mom was going to take over the lease on my apartment. Somehow, it was all working out.

The game ended with Chase's killer aerial shot leaving the score 3-2, USMNT.

As the fans started to clear the stands, Remi turned to Teagan. "Mommy, I have to go to the bathroom."

"Okay, sweetie," Teagan answered, right before Mace started fussing.

"I'll take her," I offered.

"Really? That would be so great. Thank you!"

"Sure. Dylan stay with Dad and Uncle Ben." My eyes met

Jensen's, and he smirked. I was still getting used to referring to him as 'Dad' but doing so felt right. My son, on the other hand, didn't have any issues making the transition.

I held my hand out to Remi, and she took it. We maneuvered down a few flights of stairs and into the stadium, weaving through the massive horde of people rushing around to leave. There was a very long line of women waiting at each of the ladies' bathrooms, so we got in line to wait our turn.

"Missy, should I call you Aunty Missy now? Since Dylan calls my Dad Uncle Chase?" she pouted her lips as she thought it over.

"I don't know. What do you want to call me?"

She shrugged. "I don't know. I love you, though."

A delighted smile lifted the corners of my mouth. "I love you, too, sweetheart," I touched her chin with my index finger as she gazed up at me. She was so precious, decked out in a red, white and blue sundress and white flip flops, her hair in curls down her back and her green eyes sparkling. It was warmer in Orlando than it was in Atlanta. There was no trace of the nasty bruise Derrick had left on her cheek.

He'd been arraigned and locked up without bail and was awaiting his trial. Thank God, the District Attorney's office told us that there was enough evidence since he'd been caught red-handed, so there was no way he'd get out of a lengthy jail sentence. They were still investigating the murder of my lawyer in Jackson Hole, but the kidnapping alone was enough for the judge to terminate Derrick's parental rights, but that wouldn't happen until the verdict in the jury trial came back guilty.

I knew that both Jensen and Dylan wanted the adoption desperately, and I had faith that it was going to happen. We already had an attorney drawing up the paperwork.

"Are you excited about going to Disney World this weekend?"

Remi nodded, with a smile. "Yes! My favorite is The Magic Kingdom cuz that's where all the princesses live, but Dylan wants to go to the jungle one." She wrinkled her nose. "I just want to stay with the princesses."

"Animal Kingdom," I corrected. "I bet that one is fun, too! I hear there is a safari and a bunch of other fun things to do. We get to see all of them."

Today was Thursday, and we weren't going home until the following Wednesday. The plan was to spend one day at every park, and then one day at one of the water parks, though admittedly, Magic Kingdom might be the most kid-friendly. Though, now that all of the smells made me want to vomit, I didn't know how much I'd enjoy myself or if I'd be able to hide being pregnant from Jensen. I wanted to tell him, but only at the most perfect moment. He'd given me so many perfect moments since I'd met him, I just wanted to create one for him.

"Mommy can't go on rides with me because of my brother," Remi said sadly.

Knowing that some of the rides would make me sick, I offered an alternative. "How about we trade off? I can stay with the baby sometimes, honey. Your mommy, daddy, Jensen or I will be with you and Dylan on every ride, okay?"

"What about Uncle Ben, Grandma Jean or my other grandma and grampa?"

I nodded.

Remi and Ben had hit it off, just about as well as Dylan and Ben. Ben had a knack for kids. "Ben, too," I agreed. "Though, I'm not sure how many rides the grandparents will go on." My mother was with us at Teagan's insistence. She had only just moved to Atlanta, and Teagan thought it wrong to go on a family vacation and leave one member of the family behind. I was amazed. One by one, my family had been intermingled beautifully with the Forrester and the Jeffers families. I'd never had a large family because my mother was an only child, as well. I had no cousins, aunts or uncles, and having an extended family was a wonderful thing.

"Do you and Jensey wanna get married at the castle, like Mommy and Daddy did? It was so pretty, and I got to wear a princess dress!"

The bathroom line was decreasing slowly, and we moved closer and closer to our destination. "Wow. That sounds amazing, but I'm not sure if we'd have the time to arrange it while we're here."

"Mommy and Daddy could help," she insisted. "My mom is good at planning stuff."

"Don't you think your mom and dad will want to be the only couple in the family to get married at the castle? It's sort of special to them."

Remi shook her head. "I think they'd want to share," she said simply as if to think any other way would be absurd. "Especially with you and Jensey." There was a pearl of wisdom to her words; knowing what I knew of them.

Truth be told, it would be surreal and timely, considering my current condition plus, Ben was here, and he could only get so much time off of work each year. There was no way I would get married without him. Since my dad had deserted us, Ben was the only one I'd want to give me away. I certainly didn't want to usurp Teagan's memory of her wedding. Besides, Jensen and I hadn't even talked about a date yet.

"We'll see, sweetheart," I said, trying to placate her.

"You'd make such a pretty princess, and it could be at my castle, too!"

The other's in the line in front of, and behind, us couldn't help overhearing and were smiling from ear-to-ear at the precocious little girl's exuberant attempt to arrange my wedding.

"Seems she has a knack for wedding planning," a kind-faced, older woman with greying hair said. "And, so pretty!"

"She's quite something, that's for sure!" I looked down at Remi, now hugging my legs and beaming up at me. I cupped her beautiful little face in my hands remembering another bathroom trip that we took together the very weekend that Jensen and Remi flew to meet Dylan and me in Omaha. "She's an extraordinary little girl. I simply adore her."

JENSEN

Was I really standing here, in the same place we were standing a little less than one year earlier when my best friends were married? Except this time, I was the groom, and Chase was my best man.

I didn't care that the wedding had even fewer guests than Chase and Teagan's. It didn't matter that hardly any of our ESPN colleagues were with us, because Chase's family, Jean, and Ben were all here. Jarvis flew down on short notice and was standing on the other side of Chase. My parents were seated in the front row.

When Remi had climbed up on my lap at the end of dinner Thursday evening, right after Chase's game, and suggested that Missy and I get married at her castle, I was dumbfounded. I admit, at first, I didn't think it was a good idea. I thought Missy would want to plan out a more elaborate affair, but after Remi had barely said the words, I glanced over at Missy. She smiled and nodded slightly. Clearly, she and Remi had been plotting. It was hard to believe that it had been just three short days ago.

"We have just about everyone here that matters," she answered my unspoken question. "It depends on if your parents can get here."

Everyone at both tables had suddenly stopped eating dessert; all conversations coming to a halt while they waited with bated breath to hear my response.

"Do you think we can pull it off so quickly?" I asked out loud, certain that we wouldn't be able to. "Surely the venue is already booked."

"I checked already," Teagan popped in with a sly smile. "Before dinner, when we all went to our rooms to change," she explained. "Sunday night is open. I had a feeling about it."

I looked down at the little girl on my lap. "What have you been up to? Conniving?"

She giggled happily. "Well, Missy's a princess, and I think she should get married to my Jensey at my castle, wearing a very pretty dress."

My eyebrows rose, and a grin spread out on my face just before my gaze flew up to briefly meet Missy's bright blue eyes. She was trying to hold back a smile, but her eyes were dancing with mischief.

Chase was holding the baby, so that Teagan could finish her food. "If you don't want to do it, we understand, but I'm happy to cover the cost of the venue."

"Oh, Chase, that's too much," Missy put in. "If we do—"

"Shush," he commanded teasingly, gently jostling his little son gently as Mace suckled greedily on a bottle.

"Hey, I just got a raise, you know," I objected.

"That's fair, but Teagan and I went ahead and put a deposit down to hold it when Teagan called to see if it was available. It has to be fate, right?" He smiled, glancing between Missy and me.

When Missy's hand closed around my bicep, and she put her forehead down to touch my shoulder, I was flabbergasted. Then, she looked up into my eyes; her love shone so brightly that it just felt right.

"What do you think?" she asked. "It would be kinda wonderful."

"Yeah! Then you can be my real dad right, right now!" Dylan added enthusiastically, sitting in the chair to my left.

"I think…" I sputtered, still blown away, but still, I slid an arm around my son and pulled him to my side. Everyone was watching me for my response. "Okay," I was incredulous. "I'll have to call my parents."

The entire table had burst out in hoorays and guffaws, and Dylan picked up my phone and handed it to me.

And poof. It had all materialized in a matter of days.

My parents were surprised but happy to fly down

impromptu the next morning and had immediately taken to Dylan. He and Remi had dragged them around the Magic Kingdom for two straight days, and now, here we were, having our wedding in the same fairytale-like setting that Chase and Teagan had celebrated their marriage; with everyone who mattered to us in the world here with us.

Because the party was so few people, everyone there was wearing beautiful dresses and black tuxedos. The music was played by two men, one on a single acoustic guitar, and the other on a keyboard, and a woman on a single violin. The trio was playing a variety of wedding instrumentals before the ceremony. Missy let me choose the song she'd walk down to, and I hadn't told her what it was.

But once it started, it shot through my soul. Calum Scott's, *You are the Reason,* sung as a duet between the woman and one of the men. It was a beautiful version of the song and spoke of getting over the past and looking to the future. It was perfect for us, the ideal way to tell Missy how much she meant to me, and how committed I was. Forever.

"Once again, Mandi, Mellie, and Jaylan, Chase's nieces, came down the aisle dressed to the nines in glittery dresses with rings of flowers in their hair. This time they all wore the same style dress in a salmon pink color. Though Dylan, decked out in his little black tux walked down with Remi, who of course, wore a tiara on her head above cascading curls, and her dressed matched those of the other little girls. My heart felt like it would claw right out of my chest. They were both so sweet and beautiful; pride threatened to overwhelm me. Chase's hand came down on my shoulder in silent communication as we both stared at the perfect picture they made.

I cupped both of their heads with my hands when they arrived at my side. Remi stood between Chase and me, and Dylan stood on my left.

Teagan came next. She was beautiful as ever, glowing in a fitted pale coral dress, that sparkled ever so slightly in the moonlight. She had small ivory and coral roses holding back one side of her long hair. Her bouquet was made up of all ivory and light coral roses.

I glanced at my best friend, and he couldn't take his eyes off of his wife. I hoped that the adoration I felt for Missy would be as visible to her as Chase's was for Teagan. Teagan stopped at the other side of the altar.

Then it happened.

I looked up and saw Missy, standing with Ben awaiting their short walk to me. Her dress, mostly ivory lace over a light coral lining, was the perfect foil for her peachy completion. Her hair was swept up in a crown of curls with a delicate wreath of ivory roses, scattered with tiny coral ones, rested above the sheer veil cascading down her back; the edges trimmed with the matching lace of her dress.

All of it sparkled gently in the candlelit night. My heart stopped, and my breath caught in my throat. My bride was breathtaking. I doubted she could look more spectacular if she'd had a year to order her dress.

"She's sure pretty, huh, Dad," Dylan said looking up at me and holding tight to my left hand. I couldn't help but smile and glance down for a split second. The others in the group smiled and laughed softly.

"She sure is." I agreed. "Very beautiful, son." I touched his cheek with my index finger.

I could see the love that Ben had for his younger sister; it radiated from him; evident in the hand he placed over the one she tucked into the crook of his bent arm. And, he was proud. Jean was crying big tears, as was my mother, and Chase's.

Ben handed her over to me after kissing her cheek. He placed her hand in mine. "Take care of them."

"Always," I promised, taking her hand. She gave her bouquet to Teagan, and Dylan stood between us as we said our vows through tears and emotion, nearly choking us.

The rings were simple, but to me were the most precious things on earth. I reached up to wipe her tears away when the minister said I could kiss my bride. Our lips met and clung together, for first one, then another, lingering kiss.

"You look perfect. Breathtaking." My fingers traced Missy's high cheekbones and then the line of her jaw. I wanted to worship this woman until my dying day.

"I love you, Jensen. Forever," she said, still crying.

My world was made. I had everything any man could ever want.

The recessional music began, then Missy reached over to retrieve her bouquet from Teagan, and Teagan winked at her.

"Now?" Missy asked, her eyes sparkling with happiness.

Teagan nodded with a happy and gracious smile. "Yes! It's tradition, apparently."

"What?" I asked curiously, lifting my bride's hand to kiss the top of it. "What's tradition?"

"I'm going to have a baby, Jensen."

My mouth fell open as I looked from Missy's smiling face out at Teagan's equally exuberant one, then back again. "What?"

Missy nodded. "It's true."

I faced the rest of those in attendance, stunned but exhilarated. Missy's mom was crying, and mine had both of her hands over her heart. "We're gonna have a baby!" I shouted amid a burst of exclamations from our family and friends.

I couldn't believe it, but in that very moment, I knew that I was the happiest man on earth. I lifted Missy into my arms and twirled her around.

When I sent her down to begin walking up the aisle, I put a hand at the back of my new wife's waist. Remi and Dylan were just in front of us, walking together, holding hands, and having their own conversation.

"Maybe I'm gonna have a brother, now, too!" Dylan exclaimed.

"Yeah, I guess mine's not so bad," Remi agreed. "Except'n when he pukes." She made a face and stuck out her tongue.

"That's gross!" Dylan agreed. "Since Jensey is my dad now, will I be your brother, too?" he asked. His face took on a pout as they stopped in front of us, completely oblivious that their pause made us all stop or that everyone in our small group was listening to their words with rapt attention.

Remi turned and put her hands on her hips. She faced Dylan, a small frown gracing her face as her head shook so hard that her beautiful curls swooshed back and forth across her little back.

"Are you crazy? I'm your damsel, silly."

The End

BE A DAMSEL
Sometimes

If you enjoyed this book,
PLEASE HELP OTHER READERS FIND ME BY
LEAVING A REVIEW!
Amazon • BookBub • Goodreads • iBooks • Barnes&Noble •
Kobo.

Readers are the reason I write! • Your Reviews are GOLD.

GET YOUR DAMSEL T-Shirt on TEESPRING:
https://teespring.com/the-trading-yesterday-
damsel#pid=266&cid=6135&sid=front

If you're a victim of domestic abuse, you are not alone.

THE NATIONAL DOMESTIC ABUSE HOTLINE

1-800-799-7233 • 1-800-787-3224 (TTY)

Call for help 24/7.

If you enjoyed TRADING YESTERDAY & FINDING TOMORROW

Ben & Marin's story is coming in July 2019!

EMBRACING
Today

Remi & Dylan's story is coming October 2019

FOREVER
& Always

Sign up for Kahlen's NEW RELEASE ALERTS!

https://landing.mailerlite.com/webforms/landing/i7w8k4

UPCOMING TITLES

Embracing Today (A Trading Yesterday Novel)
Forever & Always (A Trading Yesterday Novel)
#SexyMF (#SexyDuet 1)
#SexyAF (#SexyDuet 2)
Smut University
LICK (An After Dark Novel)
Hold Me After Dark
Covered in Raine
Beck and Call Girl
You and You Alone
Unfinished Business
Hostile Takeover
Boxers & Briefs
So Damn Beautiful
Stripped
Freeze Frame
Composure
Marriage Material
Written On My Soul
The Other Half of the Sky
City Girl's Cowboy (Full Novel)

AVAILABLE NOW IN FRENCH

The Remembrance Trilogy & Prequel
The After Dark Series

AVAILABLE NOW IN SPANISH

The Remembrance Trilogy & Prequel

ALL TITLES COMING SOON IN ITALIAN

from Hope Edizioni

CONNECT WITH KAHLEN

FACEBOOK
Facebook.com/kahlen.aymes.author/

GOODREADS
Goodreads.com/author/show/5768062.Kahlen_Aymes?
from_search=true

TWITTER
Twitter.com/Kahlen_Aymes

PINTEREST
Pinterest.com/kahlenaymes/

INSTAGRAM
Instagram.com/kahlen.aymes/

YOUTUBE
Youtube.com/user/KahlenAymesAuthor

BOOKS+MAIN
bookandmainbites.com/users/15876

JOIN KAHLEN'S READER GROUP
KAHLEN'S BOOK BABES
Facebook.com/groups/kahlensbookbabes/

OFFICIAL WEBSITE
KahlenAymes.com

Merchandise • Signed Copies • Julia's recipes • Missing Scenes
Appearances & Events • Kahlen's Blog •Series Playlists

FOR NEWS, FREEBIE ALERTS, EVENTS, & GIVEAWAYS PLEASE SIGN UP FOR MY NEWSLETTER

https://landing.mailerlite.com/webforms/landing/b4f0v4

RIGHTS MANAGEMENT
Represented by Sarah Hershman
Hershman Rights Management
P.O. Box 216
Guilford, CT 06437

Email: sarah@hershmanrightsmanagement.com

CPSIA information can be obtained
at www.ICGtesting.com
Printed in the USA
BVHW030225170719
553672BV00001B/78/P

9 780999 671313